Once Upon a Kiss. . .

JENNIFER LEWIS
MICHELLE CELMER
OLIVIA GATES

MILLS &
BOON

First Published in Great Britain 2016
By Mills & Boon, an imprint of HarperCollins*Publishers*
1 London Bridge Street, London, SE1 9GF

ONCE UPON A KISS . . . © 2016 Harlequin Books S. A.

The Cinderella Act, *Princess In The Making* and *Temporarily His Princess*
were first published in Great Britain by Harlequin (UK) Limited.

The Cinderella Act © 2012 Jennifer Lewis
Princess In The Making © 2012 Michelle Celmer
Temporarily His Princess © 2013 Olivia Gates

ISBN: 978-0-263-92069-7

05-0616

Our policy is to use papers that are natural, renewable and recyclable products and made from wood grown in sustainable forests.The logging and manufacturing processes conform to the legal environmental regulations of the country of origin.

Printed and bound in Spain
by CPI, Barcelona

THE CINDERELLA ACT

BY
JENNIFER LEWIS

Jennifer Lewis has been dreaming up stories for as long as she can remember and is thrilled to be able to share them with readers. She has lived on both sides of the Atlantic and worked in media and the arts before she grew bold enough to put pen to paper. She would love to hear from readers at jen@jenlewis.com. Visit her website at www.jenlewis.com.

For Jordan

One

"Are you sure this is safe?"

Annie tried to keep her eyes off Sinclair Drummond's enticing backside as he climbed the rickety wooden stairs to the attic.

"No." He flashed her a grin that made her knees wobble. "Especially with the curse hanging over our heads."

"I guess I'll take my chances." As his employee, Annie Sullivan could hardly refuse. She stepped onto the first rung of the hand-hewn stairs that were barely more than a ladder. They led up into the ceiling of the old barn, which was attached to the house so Drummond ancestors didn't have to face bitter winds howling in from Long Island Sound while tending to their animals. Now all it contained was an impressive collection of spiderwebs and brittle horse tack. The steps creaked alarmingly. "Have you ever been up here?" She hadn't, which was strange in itself.

Sinclair reached the top and pushed open a trap door. "Sure. When I was a kid. I used to hide up here when my parents argued."

Annie frowned. She couldn't imagine his quiet, dignified mother raising her voice, but she'd never met his father. He'd died in some kind of accident years ago.

"I doubt anyone's been up here since." He disappeared into the dark hole, and she climbed the stairs behind him with a growing sense of anticipation. A light snapped on, filling the opening with bright light. "I'm glad that still works. I didn't fancy searching by candlelight." Rain drummed on the shake roof overhead. His voice sounded far away, and she hurried to catch up to him. Her head cleared the entrance and she saw a row of uncovered bulbs dangling from the center beam of the windowless attic. Boxes and crates were piled along the sides, among disused tables, chairs and other, less identifiable pieces of furniture. The far wall was almost hidden behind a stack of big leather trunks bearing steamer labels. Despite the size of the room, very little of the wood floor was visible.

"So this is what three hundred years' worth of pack rats leave behind them. Where do we start?" Her fingers tingled with anticipation at rifling through the Drummond family's possessions. Which was funny, since that's what she did every day in her job. Of course dusting and polishing silver wasn't nearly as exciting as opening an old steamer trunk filled with mothballs and mystery.

Sinclair lifted the lid of a chest, which appeared to be filled with folded quilts. "Hell if I know. I suppose we just start plowing through and hope for the best." He'd rolled up his sleeves, and she watched his muscular forearm reach boldly into the fabric. "The cup fragment is made of metal, apparently. Possibly silver, but more likely pewter. It doesn't have any inherent value."

His shirt strained against his strong back as he reached deeper. Annie's heart rate quickened. Why did her boss have to be so gorgeous? It wasn't fair. She'd worked for him for six years and he'd only grown more handsome with age. He was thirty-two and his thick, dark hair didn't bear a single strand of gray, despite his two expensive divorces.

"And it's supposed to be cursed?" Annie suppressed a shiver as she glanced around. Her Irish ancestors would be crossing themselves.

"It's the family that's cursed, not the cup." Sinclair lifted his head and shot her a disarming glance. "Three hundred years of misery, which can apparently be lifted if the three parts of this ancient cup are put back together." He snorted. "I think it's a load of rubbish, but my mom is really excited about it. She's sure it will change all our lives."

"I was glad to hear she's doing better. Did they ever find out what made her so sick?"

"A rare tropical disease, apparently, similar to cholera. She's lucky to be alive. She's still quite weak so I've told her she should come out here for some rest."

"Absolutely, I'd be happy to take care of her."

"I'm hoping she'll come nose around up here herself. Then you won't have to do all the work."

Annie's heart sank a little. So she couldn't look forward to a summer in the attic watching Sinclair's broad hands reaching into mysterious boxes. She'd worked here for six years, yet on some level they were almost strangers. She loved being alone with him when there were no guests to entertain and she got a glimpse of a more relaxed Sinclair. The search for the cup seemed like a great opportunity to get to know him better. Instead, she'd be up here sweating under the rafters by herself. Still, the history all around her was intriguing. She walked over to a tall woven basket and lifted the lid. Coiled rope filled the inside, and as she pulled at it, she could imagine the hands that wound this rope in an era before machines. Everything around them must tell a story. "Why does she think the family is cursed? You all seem very successful."

Her own family would probably kill for a fraction of the abundance the Drummonds enjoyed.

"The Drummonds have done all right for themselves over the years. An old family legend has my mom convinced, however, that we're all cursed, which is why she got so sick." He lifted out a pile of clothes and she blinked at the powerful muscles in his thighs, visible through his pressed khakis, as he leaned to touch the bottom of the trunk. She startled as he suddenly looked up. "And why none of us can stay married for long." His blue-gray eyes shone with a wry mix of humor and remorse. "She's on a quest to unearth the three pieces of the cup and put them back together. She's sure it will turn things around for the Drummonds." He shoved the clothes back in the trunk and slammed the lid. "Of course I don't believe in the curse but I'd do anything to help her recover, and this has her really excited so I promised to help."

"That's sweet of you."

"Not really." He shoved a hand through his hair as he surveyed the piles of debris left over from former lives. "If it keeps her occupied she won't start nagging me to marry again."

Annie had watched grimly as he'd courted and dated his calculating and phony second wife. She wasn't sure she could stand to go through that again. "I suppose she's desperate for grandchildren."

"Yes, though you have to wonder why. Is it really necessary to carry the curse through to another generation?" His crooked smile made her smile, too. Of course his mother wanted grandchildren to spoil and fuss over. Though she wasn't likely to ever get any, if Sinclair's taste in women was anything to go by. She'd never met his first wife, but Diana Lakeland wasn't the type to risk her figure on a pregnancy. She'd married Sinclair for the wealth and prestige that made him one of New York's most eligible bachelors, then grown tired of him when he didn't want to jet around the world attending parties every night.

If only he could see he was wasted on those spoiled princesses. She couldn't tell him that, though. It was part of her job to be friendly, even intimate. But she also had to know where to draw the line between professional and personal, and never cross it.

She moved away from the basket of rope—more than enough to hang yourself with—and lifted a small wooden box from a high shelf. She opened the lid and found a cache of what looked like hairpins. Expensive ones, carved from tortoiseshell and bone. She wondered what Drummond damsel had tucked them into her tresses. "This does feel like looking for a needle in a haystack. Though it's an interesting haystack. Who did the cup belong to?"

"The Drummonds come from the Scottish Highlands. Gaylord Drummond was a gambler and drinker, who lost the family estate in a wager in 1712. His three sons, left penniless and landless, set out for America to seek their fortune. The brothers went their separate ways after their ship docked, and apparently they split up a metal chalice of some sort, each of them taking a piece. They intended to reunite the cup once they'd all made their fortunes. One of them settled here on Long Island, and built a farm where we sit today."

"I suppose that explains why you have such a large piece of prime waterfront real estate." The original farmhouse had been expanded over the years into a magnificent shingle-style "cottage" with bold gables and wide verandas. The old potato fields had been transformed into pristine lawn and lush orchards of apple, pear and peach trees. Once a sleepy village, Dog Harbor was now surrounded by the suburban sprawl of New York City. One ancestor had sold a field to a post-war developer to build tract housing. Sinclair's father had bought it back at great expense—houses and all—and turned it back into an emerald sward of grass. The cool water of the Long Island Sound lapped against a neat pebble beach about three hundred feet from the house.

Sinclair laughed. "Yes. The old homestead has matured into an excellent investment."

"What I don't understand is…how do you break up a cup?" It seemed hard enough to find a whole cup in this mess, let alone a piece of one.

"My mother says it was specially constructed to be taken apart and then put back together. She suspects it's an old communion chalice that was constructed like that so it could be hidden, maybe from Viking invaders or Protestant reformers, depending on how old it really is.

The story of the cup has passed down from generation to generation, though no one knows what happened to the pieces. My mom says she's tracked down the descendants of the three brothers, and contacted each of them about her quest."

"I think it's exciting. And a nice opportunity to reunite the family."

Sinclair shrugged. "I've never heard much good about the other Drummonds. We're all surly sorts who keep to ourselves." He raised a dark brow.

"You're not surly." She immediately regretted her pointless comment. The last thing she needed was for him to know she was smitten with him. "Well, not all the time, anyway." Now she was blushing. She hurried to a darker corner of the attic and pulled at a drawer. "Where do the others live?"

"One brother became a privateer raiding the East Coast and the Caribbean."

"A pirate?"

Sinclair nodded. "So the legend goes. His ancestors are still down there—or one of them, anyway—living on an island off the Florida coast. Since Jack Drummond's a professional treasure hunter I hardly think he'll help us find the cup."

"He might be interested in the family angle."

"I doubt it. The third Drummond brother got rich up in Canada, then went back to Scotland and bought back the family estate. His descendant lives there now. My mother hasn't been able to even get James Drummond to reply to her emails. She's tireless, however, so I'm sure she'll get through to him eventually, once she has her strength back." He lifted a box down from the top of an old armoire. "There aren't a lot of Drummond descendants out there. They don't seem to have had many children and a lot have died young over the years. Makes you wonder if the curse is real."

Was Sinclair cursed? If anything, he seemed to live a charmed life, dividing his time between his Manhattan penthouse and his other fabulous houses. She saw him for only a few weekends of each year, and maybe a couple of weeks in the summer. Just enough time to gaze dreamily at him but not enough to know his secrets. Did he have secrets? Passions and longings?

She tried to shake the thought from her mind. His inner life was none of her business.

"Some of this stuff really shouldn't be moldering away up here." Annie lifted a porcelain serving platter from its perch underneath another coil of rope. "I bet you could take this on *Antiques Roadshow*."

Sinclair chuckled. "And have them tell you someone bought it at Woolworth's in the 1950s." He stood over a big wood trunk, larger and obviously older than the steamer trunks piled high in several places. The inside appeared to be filled with folded clothing.

"Wow, look at that lace." Annie moved beside him, trying to ignore his rich masculine scent. She reached into the trunk and fondled the snowy cotton. "It doesn't look like it's ever been worn." She lifted the garment, which unfolded in a single soft movement, revealing itself as a delicate nightgown or petticoat. "Who did this belong to?"

"I have no idea. I confess to only ever rifling through the boxes with firearms and other guy stuff in them." Again his mischievous grin made her heart quicken. "I never touched the girlie stuff."

"Would you look at that." Setting the petticoat aside,

she peered into the large wooden chest to examine a richly worked bodice of green satin with red-and-gold edging. The needlework was exquisite and the material shone as if it had been woven yesterday. "I've never seen anything like it."

Sinclair pulled the garment from the trunk and held it up. Low-cut at the neck and with a tiny waist, the dress was an extravagant ball gown.

"It's stunning. And that blue one underneath it looks spectacular." She reached in and fondled a striking peacock-blue silk garment with tiny pearl bead accents. "These should be in a museum." It seemed a crime to leave them unseen in the dusty attic even a minute longer. "Let's bring them down into the house and hang them properly."

"If you like." Sinclair looked skeptical. Of course he probably only cared about finding the cup. "Sure, let's do it."

Had her face betrayed her disappointment so readily? His sudden change of heart touched her. She smiled. "Great! I'll carry as many as I can."

Sinclair strode down the narrow, rickety stairs without a moment's hesitation, despite his arms being filled with clothes. Annie teetered behind him, the heavy garments weighing her down and making her worry about missing her footing. "We can put them in the big wardrobes in the yellow bedroom. They're empty since your mom gave away those old fur coats."

She followed Sinclair back into the house and they laid the garments on the wide double bed. "I can't believe how beautiful this gray silk dress is. How on earth did they weave the silver and blue into the fabric?"

"Probably took someone years. Things were done

differently back then. Each item was a handmade work of art."

"I suppose ordinary people never even touched anything like this." She fingered the delicate fabric with its intricate ribbon detailing. "Unless they were helping madam fasten her corset, of course." That's what she would have been doing back then. Hey, she was still more or less doing it now, in a time when most women her age sat in plastic cubicles talking on the phone all day. She let her fingers roam inside the deep pleats at the waist and sighed. "What a stunning dress. I've never seen anything like it."

"Why don't you try it on?" Sinclair's deep voice surprised her. She'd almost forgotten he was there.

"Me? I couldn't possibly. They're museum pieces, and my waist isn't nearly that small."

"I disagree. About your waist, that is." His eyes settled on her waistband for a moment, making her stomach clench. Had her boss ever glanced at her waist before? She didn't think so.

Her heart pounded with excitement at the prospect of trying a dress on. Of course she could always wait until she was all alone in the house. But then someone would notice it had been worn, and she'd look foolish. What if this was her only chance? "Well…" She plucked gently at the peacock-blue evening gown. "I still don't think they'll fit, but…"

"That settles it. I'll discreetly turn away until you need help with the fastenings." He strolled to a tall arched window on the far side of the room.

Annie's heart quickened. She had an odd sense that a line between them was about to be crossed. Sinclair wanted her to try on the dresses. What did that mean?

Nothing, silly. He thinks it would be fun for you and he's humoring you. Don't get carried away. Really. This was foolish. She'd end up ripping a seam. "I'm sure they're supposed to be worn with all sorts of elaborate corsetry and I don't think—"

"Do you want to go back up and hunt for the cup?" He lifted a dark brow.

She hesitated, her fingertips still pressed against the rich fabric. A tiny smile tugged at her lips. "Maybe just one dress."

Sinclair nodded, a smile in his eyes, and turned away.

How sweet of him to let her try on a family heirloom. But which one? Without hesitation, she chose the rich peacock-blue. She held it against herself for a moment—the length was about right—and though the waist was narrow, it wasn't quite as tiny as she'd first thought. Maybe it would fit, after all.

She resisted the urge to turn and check on Sinclair as she unbuttoned her Oxford shirt. She knew him too well to imagine even for a second that he'd be sneaking a peek. He had women falling all over him wherever he went, and barely seemed to notice them.

She lowered her khakis and stepped into the crisp blue fabric. It was creased from being folded and smelled slightly of camphor, but otherwise looked fresh as if it were sewn yesterday. The tiny pearl beads tickled her arms as she pushed them into the short, puffed sleeves. The low-cut neck revealed a broad expanse of her white Cross Your Heart bra, so she quickly undid the bra and slipped it off through a sleeve. She had done up nearly half the tiny, fabric-covered buttons by the time Sinclair asked if she needed help.

"Just a few hundred more buttons." She smiled, already feeling like a princess in the luxurious gown. It fell to the floor and gathered there slightly, suggesting she should wear heels.

"Wow." Sinclair had turned and stood, staring at her. "Annie, you look spectacular." His eyes widened slightly as he surveyed her, slowly, from head to toe. "Like a different person." He crossed the room and fastened the last few buttons. "As I suspected, it fits."

"Odd, isn't it?" She fought the urge to giggle like a little girl playing dress-up. It didn't help that Sinclair's fingers were so near her skin that she felt giddy. "But why would we think people had different bodies two hundred years ago? They weren't so different from us."

"No, they weren't." Sinclair's voice was lower than usual. Done with the buttons, he moved in front of her again. His gaze rose over her neck and cheek, and she self-consciously tucked away a loose curl that had escaped her bun.

He frowned slightly. "You look pretty with your hair up."

"I always wear my hair up." She reached self-consciously for her bun.

"Do you? I don't know why I didn't notice it before." His gaze heated her skin.

"It's the dress."

"Maybe it is. You hide under your clothes and conceal the fact that you have a beautiful figure."

Her breasts swelled inside the fitted bodice. The cut of the dress acted as a bra, lifting things front and center. "Funny, I'm not sure I've ever had cleavage before." She tried to laugh, to hide her shock at her own bold statement, but the sound withered under Sinclair's stern regard.

"It suits you," he said gruffly. "You should dress up more often."

"I don't really get the chance." She glanced across the room where she could see a partial reflection in the mirror on the large wardrobe. She looked imposing in the long dress, and the dramatic blue brought out red-gold highlights in her hair. Sinclair's tall form blocked one half of the view, his broad shoulders concealing the cleavage he admired. From this angle they almost looked like a couple, the distance between them fore-shortened as if they were pressed together.

Like that could ever happen.

She attempted another carefree laugh, and again it vanished in the air, which suddenly felt hot and oppressive. Sinclair's frown deepened, and she shivered under his fierce stare. Words failed her as their gazes locked for a second, two seconds, three…

Sinclair's lips met hers with sudden force as his arms gathered her close. She melted, her mouth welcoming his and kissing him back with six years of unspent passion.

His kiss was intoxicating as strong liquor. Annie's legs wobbled and she clung to him as their tongues wound together. Her nipples thickened against the luxurious silk.

His scent was subtle, masculine and inviting. She'd never been this close to him before. His skin looked smooth, but now she could feel the roughness of his cheek as he nuzzled her. His fingers wound into her hair, loosing her bun, and a rough groan escaped his mouth.

A coil of lust unwound inside her. His desire, his need, was palpable. She could sense it vibrating in his thick muscles and heating his tanned skin. His breath grew hot on her cheek, further stirring the passion unfolding in her belly.

What are we doing?

The thought seemed very far away, as if someone else was thinking it. Her fingers climbed into his thick, dark hair. It was silky to the touch. She could feel his hands sinking lower, to cup her buttocks, and she arched against him as he squeezed her. His breath came hard and heavy, giving their kisses an air of fevered desperation.

I'm kissing Sinclair. The thought flashed in her brain like a power surge. But instead of setting off alarms of warning, it sent ripples of excitement dancing to her fingers and toes. How many nights had she lain awake imagining this moment?

His kisses were rougher and harder than she'd imagined, fueled by desire more powerful than she'd dared to dream of. His hands fisted into the delicate fabric of her dress, feeling for her body beneath. He pulled her closer and his thick erection jutted against her. She gasped at the sensation, such a bold sign of his desire—for her.

His name fell from her lips in a rasped whisper. She pulled his shirt loose from his pants and reached for the warm skin of his back. His muscles, thick and roping, moved beneath her hands. She'd seen him without a shirt more than once, but never imagined the feel of all that strength under her fingers.

He plucked at the buttons along the back of her dress that they'd only just fastened. Her skin tingled at the prospect of being bared by his hands.

Are you really going to let him undress you? Her entire body answered, *yes.* Sinclair must have been hiding feelings for her the same way she'd been hiding them for him. Which was odd. She'd had no idea.

She giggled as he slid a hand inside the back of her dress. She'd already removed her bra and his fingers felt risqué and sensual against the bare skin of her back. More so as he lowered the dress and bared her breasts to his appreciative gaze. A lock of dark hair hung uncharacteristically in his eyes as he carefully pushed the dress past her waist. It seemed a shame to take it off after only a few minutes, but apparently it had already worked some kind of magic.

She stepped from the dress while unbuttoning Sinclair's shirt. She parted it and sighed when she saw his chest. Taut muscle with a slender trail of dark hair disappearing below his belt buckle.

Her nipples had stiffened to tight peaks, which bumped against his chest as she fumbled with the belt. The leather was stiff and Sinclair distracted her by nibbling on her ear. She could feel his fingers dipping below the waistband of her panties—if only she'd worn more sensual ones! She blushed at the thought of him seeing her oh-so-practical cotton granny briefs.

But Sinclair didn't seem to notice. His breath came hot and hard against her neck, in between ravishing kisses that stole her breath. His erection interfered with her efforts to unfasten his pants. When she finally got the zipper down she could see him straining against his boxers.

Her own breathing was labored and unsteady. Heat licked at her insides and she longed to press her naked body against his. With effort, they both pushed his khakis down past his strong thighs and he stepped out of them. They stood facing each other, a few scant inches between them. His body was perfectly toned, his stomach flat and hard behind his fierce arousal.

Annie swallowed. Were they going to make love right now? All signs pointed in that direction. Sinclair's eyes were closed, and his hands roamed over her body. Her skin stirred and sizzled under his touch. She felt the curve of his strong cheekbones and kissed him gently on the lips. How could such an ordinary day take such a wonderful and extraordinary turn? Maybe it was something to do with the mysterious cup.

Or was it the curse?

A dark shard of doubt cooled her skin like a sudden draft from a window. This man was her boss. On the other hand, the train had left the station. They stood naked in the fourth guest bedroom, the crumpled remains of their clothes at their feet. It was already too late to turn back and pretend that nothing had happened.

And she wanted nothing more than to take this surprising intimacy even further. She wondered if she should tell him she was already protected by the IUD she wore to ease her painful periods? She didn't want to spoil the delicious moment, so instead she kissed him again on the mouth.

"Annie," he groaned. "Oh, Annie." She almost exploded at the sound of her name on his lips. He wanted her as much as she wanted him. Her body ached to mesh with his and soon they were on the bed, him entering her with exquisite tenderness, while feathering kisses over her lips and groaning with unconcealed pleasure.

Annie wasn't a virgin. She wasn't all that far from being one, but she had some idea what sex was all about. Still, she'd never experienced anything like the intense sensations that rocked her body. Sinclair's fingertips pressed into her flesh as his mouth claimed her, licking and biting her with abandon until she gasped and squealed with pleasure.

She'd never imagined Sinclair having such an uninhibited side. He always seemed so straitlaced and conservative.

Sinclair moved with deft prowess, skilled at taking her to new heights of pleasure, and keeping her there until she was ready to burst into flames, then shifting position for an entirely new approach to ultimate sexual bliss. To see—and feel—him breathless with excitement and driven by obvious hunger for her, almost drove her insane with pleasure.

"Oh, Annie." Again he murmured her name, licking her lips and burying himself so deep she thought they'd become one.

"Oh, Sin." She'd imagined calling him that, fantasized about it being her pet name for him like he was some duke from one of her favorite novels. To hear the affectionate abbreviation on her lips, for it to sound so natural in the air, almost made her laugh with pleasure.

Sin. Surely that's what this was. But it felt so good it couldn't be entirely wrong. Sinclair claimed her mouth with a powerful kiss and her body burst into a convulsion of pleasure that left her shivering and gripping him.

Goodness. She'd never experienced that before. It must be the famous orgasm magazines loved to rave about. Sinclair released a deep, shuddering groan and fell against her, gasping for breath. Then, without a pause, he rolled them both over until she was on top and held her there, his arms fast around her and his eyelids shut tight.

"Damn," he said at last. "Damn."

Two

Sinclair wrapped his arms tightly around his lovely companion. Her strawberry-blond hair fell across his face. Her pretty, pale blue eyes looked at him shyly behind long lashes. He kissed her mouth again, her lips so soft and wet.

The sense of relief was extraordinary. Apparently going through his second divorce could set a man way off balance. He couldn't even remember the last time he'd felt this relaxed and at peace. He leaned forward and nuzzled her soft skin, with its pretty freckles. "You're a miracle," he whispered in her ear. Her cheek plumped against his as her lips formed a smile. The blissful weight of her body on his pushed him against the soft mattress, trapping him in the aftermath of such sweet pleasure.

He let out a long, deep sigh. Sometimes life could be so complicated, and you just needed to get back to basics. He let his fingers play in the silky red-gold hair waving softly about her cheeks.

"That was unexpected." Her voice sounded like music.

"Yes." His brain was too fogged for conversation. "And wonderful."

"It was. Though I hope my pot roast is okay. I totally lost track of the time."

Pot roast? Sinclair managed to find his wrist somewhere underneath her soft back and pulled it reluctantly out. "It's nearly five."

Sinclair's muscles were tensing up all over. Five in the afternoon. Pot roast overcooking somewhere. Present-day reality crept, unwelcome, into his mind. This delicious sylph in his arms was not a pre-Raphaelite fantasy maiden come out of the mists to entertain him.

She was his longtime housekeeper, Annie Sullivan.

"What's the matter?" Her soft voice filled with concern.

His stomach tightened as he lifted his arms from her. Had he really kissed her on the lips and pulled her into bed with him? His mind swam. He must have been in a psychosis of lust. His friends had warned him that going without sex for too long could do crazy things to a man's brain.

And now he was naked, sweaty and breathless, weighed down by the unexpectedly curvaceous body of the woman who polished his silver.

His head crashed against the pillow. In a way this was very stereotypical. Just the kind of thing his un-savory ancestors probably did with their staff. An-other damning proof that he was no better than all the lying, cheating, philandering Drummonds who came before him.

Annie had noticed his change of mood. She, too, had stiffened and now pulled away, moving off him and to the side, with the snowy matelassé coverlet wrapped around her. Sinclair tugged the sheet up over his exposed flesh.

It was his fault, of course. "I'm so sorry."

Annie's cheeks were stained with red. She tucked her tresses behind tiny pink ears. He burned with shame that he'd taken such a good woman to bed without, seemingly, a moment's hesitation.

"Honestly, I'm not sure what came over me." Still reeling, he sat up and held his head for a moment. Was he in the grip of madness? Perhaps the same tropical malady that kept his mother in a delirium for nearly a week?

Contraception. The grim thought stabbed at his already pounding brain. "I don't suppose you're…on the pill." The unromantic utterance hung in the air like a poisonous cloud.

"Not the pill, but something similar. I won't get pregnant." Her silvery voice had shriveled to a tinkle. She climbed from the bed, back to him, still holding the coverlet about her naked body.

And what a body. He had no idea Annie was hiding such lush and inviting curves below her staid Oxford shirts and loose khakis. Desire snuck through him again, hot and unwelcome, and he pulled the sheet higher over his chest.

Annie had already tugged her rumpled shirt and khakis back on, and buttoned them with urgent fingers. He averted his eyes, cursing the demon of lust that had led him so badly astray. He'd better start exercising more regularly, and taking cold showers, to make sure nothing like this happened again. It was bad enough to be unprofessional in his own house, but what next, would he sleep with his administrative assistant, or the office receptionist?

A hushed curse escaped his lips, and Annie flinched. He startled, now aware that he'd added insult to injury. "I was cursing myself. I don't know what came over me."

"Me, neither," she muttered, tucking her shirt in. She picked up the blue dress from the floor, avoiding his gaze. "I'll hang this in the closet." Her voice was flat, devoid of emotion. Her lush body once again hidden under her practical attire.

Sinclair drew in a slow breath. He had to get out of here and back to Manhattan—stat. Annie left the room and closed the door behind her. He climbed out of bed and pulled his clothes back on, still in a daze of confusion. As he reached for his shoes, he saw her ponytail holder where it lay on the floor. It must have fallen out of her hair, releasing her locks as they...

He shook his head. How could this happen? He prided himself on maintaining control in all aspects of his life. He glanced at the pile of dresses where they lay on a wooden armchair, the lush fabrics lifeless, so different from how that dress had looked draped over her sweet hourglass figure.

He hurled himself from the bed with another curse. Clearly he was in the grip of temporary insanity. He'd better bury himself in work and make sure neither his brain nor his body had time and energy enough for such foolishness.

He dragged his clothes on and exited the room. The hallway was silent, the wood floor shining in mid-morning sun. Annie had tactfully disappeared, something she had a proven talent for doing. He also knew she would conveniently reappear if you happened to need her. She had almost magical qualities as a house-keeper.

Now he wished to hell that he didn't know about all the other qualities she possessed. He'd much rather not have felt the velvet texture of her skin under his finger-tips. He'd rest a lot easier not knowing that her breath tasted like honeysuckle, or that her eyes turned that par-ticular shade of sea-foam blue when she was aroused.

Rarely did he pack anything when he came here for the weekend. He had a closet full of casual wear that he pulled from. All he needed was his wallet and keys, which he found in their usual place on his study desk. Pocketing them with relief he strode for the side door, where his car stood ready to drive him back—at high speed—to normalcy.

The screech of tires on gravel confirmed what Annie had hoped for and feared. Sinclair was gone. She leaned against her bedpost for a moment, letting the odd mix of emotions flow through her. Her body still hummed and throbbed with the sensations he'd unleashed only a few minutes earlier. She could still feel the urgent im-pression of his fingers on her skin as he drove her to unknown heights of pleasure.

She closed her eyes and squeezed them tight. Why? And why now? Everything had been going so smoothly. She'd set up a savings account and a budget and was socking money away at an impressive rate, with the goal of buying her own forever home. Her own mini-Drummond mansion, where she could build her own self-contained world. She'd even found a fun sideline making crocheted cuffs and scarves to sell on the internet, with a view to being fully self-employed one day. Maybe she'd even own her own shop. All of this was largely possible because she was alone here 95 percent of the time, while the illustrious Drummonds lit up Manhattan or visited their homes in warmer or more fashionable places. This job was a dream for someone who simply wanted peace and quiet in return for some dusting and polishing. The fact that it paid well and came with a full slate of benefits was almost ridiculous.

And now she'd ruined everything.

She peered out the window toward the driveway, to see if she'd imagined the car leaving. No, the expanse of gravel was gray and empty, the old oaks standing guard on either side. Sinclair had sped back to his other life, and no doubt to all the women who awaited him there.

Drawing a breath down into her lungs, Annie stepped out into the hallway. Her own bedroom was on the ground floor, near the kitchen, away from the family suites. The house was empty and quiet as usual, but somehow the peaceful atmosphere had been whipped into a frenzy of regret. She headed along the downstairs corridor, where everything looked oddly normal, to the fourth spare bedroom—the one they hardly ever used—where they'd...

She pushed on the door gingerly, afraid of what she might find behind the polished oak. Her heart sank at the sight of the rumpled bed, one pillow flung carelessly aside and the sheet pushed to the end of the mattress. Her eye was drawn to the stack of rich Victorian dresses piled on the stark wood chair. The closet stood open where she'd hung the dress he'd buttoned onto her, then peeled off her. It looked so innocent draped there over the hanger. She could hardly blame a dress for what she'd done.

Two decorative embroidered pillows, scattered in the heat of their passion, lay on the floor. Where had the passion come from? She'd harbored fantasies about Sinclair almost since she first met him. Who wouldn't? He was tall, dark, handsome and filthy rich, for a start, but he was also such a perfect gentleman, so quietly charming and old-fashioned. A chivalrous knight in twentieth-century garb. Always polite and thoughtful to her, as well as his wealthy guests. It was impossible not to dream about him.

She picked the pillows up and automatically plumped them, then put them on the dresser. She could hardly put them back on this chaotic bed. She'd have to strip the sheets and wash them. She couldn't resist sniffing the pillowcase before she removed it. Faint traces of Sinclair's warm, masculine scent still clung to the white cotton. Her eyes slid closed as she let herself drift back for a second to the blissful moments when he'd held her in his arms.

Idiot! He probably thought she was a "fast woman." Which, apparently, she was. They'd gone from playing dress-up to the bed in less than five minutes. It didn't get much faster than that.

She shook her head and yanked the pillow from its case. Would she ever be able to look him in the face again?

Annie was hugely relieved when Sinclair didn't arrive the next weekend. She followed his instructions and continued sorting through all the old stuff in the attic. After a couple of days she'd found so many intriguing items that she decided to start an inventory. There was no sign of the cup fragment yet, but she found all sorts of other things that would probably make jaws drop on *Antiques Roadshow,* and it would be a shame for them to rot away for another three hundred years because no one knew they were up there.

The inventory also kept track of how much stuff she'd looked at, when it seemed like she'd barely made a dent in the piles of belongings stacked against each wall. She didn't want Sinclair to think she was slacking off now that she'd slept with the boss.

The memories made her cringe. He hadn't called, but then why would he? He'd already apologized for what he no doubt regarded as a disgusting lapse of judgment. What more was there to say?

Her heart could think of more things, but she told it to keep quiet. Sinclair Drummond could never have real feelings for her. In addition to inheriting money and estates, he'd started his own hedge fund business and made millions, which she'd read about in *Fortune* and *Money* magazines. As many articles as she'd read, Annie still didn't even fully understand what a hedge fund was. Sinclair had a degree from Princeton University, and she had a high school equivalency diploma. He'd been married twice, and she hadn't even had a serious relationship. They had literally nothing in common, except that they both slept under the roof of this house—her far more often than him.

Another week went by with no sign of Sinclair. Then the weekend loomed again. Friday evenings always made her jumpy. That's when the weekend guests would show up. Usually there was warning, but not always. She kept the house in a state of gleaming readiness, basics in the fridge, fresh sheets on the beds and fresh beach towels at the ready, just in case.

In the past she'd waited anxiously near a window, hoping that Sinclair would show up, preferably without some gym-toned investment banker girlfriend in tow. Today she chewed a nail. What if he did turn up with a woman? Could she greet him with her usual smile and offer to take their bags, as if she hadn't felt his hot breath on her neck and his hands on her bare backside?

When a car pulled in, her blood pressure soared. She immediately recognized the sound of Sinclair's engine. Fighting an urge to go hide in the pantry, she hurried to the window. *Please let him not have a woman with him.* Spare her that at least, until she'd had more time to forget the feel of his lips against hers.

She cringed when an elegantly coiffed blonde alighted from the passenger seat. *Thanks, Sinclair.* Maybe he wanted to let her know, in no uncertain terms, that there was no possible future between them. Not that his hasty and apologetic departure two weeks ago had left any doubts on that score. Should she greet them at the door?

She wanted to run out the back door and head for the train.

You're a professional. You can do this. She patted her hair and straightened the front of her clean pink-and-white-striped Oxford shirt. If he could pretend nothing had happened, so could she. Sooner or later they'd talk about it, and maybe they'd laugh.

Or maybe they'd never mention it. It would just be one of those wild, crazy things that happened.

Except that they usually happened to people other than her.

She pulled open the front door. "Good evening." Bracing herself against the supercilious presence of his newest lady, she nodded and smiled.

"Hello, Annie." His rich voice stabbed her somewhere deep and painful. "You remember my mother, of course."

Annie's gaze snapped to the elegant blonde. "Mrs. Drummond, how lovely to see you!" Thin as a rail and tanned to a deep nut-brown at all times of year, Sinclair's mother gave the appearance of being much younger than her fifty-odd years. She spent most of her time traveling on exotic art tours, and Annie hadn't seen her for nearly eleven months. Now, in her neurotic state, she'd transformed her into an imaginary rival.

"Annie, darling, I do hope I won't be a burden." Her big, pale gray eyes looked slightly glassy, and her tan wasn't quite as oaken as usual. "But the doctor says I'm out of the jaws of death and ready for some sea air."

"Fantastic." She hurried around to the trunk where Sinclair was retrieving their weekend bags. Then the rear passenger door of the car opened. She almost jumped. A tall, slender woman with dark hair climbed out, mumbling into a cell phone.

Annie's heart sank. Just when she thought she'd dodged that bullet, here was the new girlfriend.

She reached for one of the expensive bags, but Sinclair muttered, "I've got them," took them both and strode for the door. She quietly closed the trunk, painfully aware of how he'd avoided meeting her eyes.

"Mrs. Drummond, why don't you come in and have a cup of tea. If you're allowed to drink tea, that is."

She glanced back at the willowy young woman attempting to close the car door while juggling three large bags and her cell phone. It was probably in her job description to seize her bags with a smile, but she didn't have it in her.

"Annie, dear, this is Vicki." Mrs. Drummond indicated the girl, who looked up from her phone call long enough for a crisp smile.

Great. Vicki looked like exactly the kind of girl Sinclair didn't need. Arrogant, cold and demanding. Shame, that seemed to be the kind of girl he liked.

Maybe he deserved them.

"Hello, Vicki. Let me take that." Apparently she did have it in her, she thought, as she reached for the big silver bag with the D&G logo. Vicki, engrossed in her call, handed it over without a glance. Her sister always told her that she shouldn't be waiting on these people hand and foot like an eighteenth-century parlor maid.

With a suppressed sigh, and of course, a polite smile, she led the way into the house, glad she'd kept it polished and ready as usual. Sinclair had disappeared, probably up to his room. With a heavy heart she climbed the stairs with Vicki's bag in her hand. Vicki followed, laughing gaily into her phone. A glance into Mrs. Drummond's usual suite confirmed that Sinclair had already dropped his mom's bag on the bed. His room was the next one over, and she hesitated for a moment, wondering if Vicki's bag was supposed to go in there, too.

"You don't think I'm going to sleep with Sin!" Vicki's voice pealed down the hallway.

Annie wheeled around. Vicki strolled along the hallway laughing. "God, no. I don't think I even slept with him when we were teens, but it's so long ago I can't remember."

"Vicki can go in the blue suite," said Mrs. Drummond.

"Perfect. Suits my mood." Vicki stopped and rested a bag on her hip for a moment, giving Annie time to take in her skinny gray parachute pants and skimpy white tank top, with a strange silver symbol dangling from a chain between her high breasts.

Annie blinked. "Of course." So Vicki wasn't Sinclair's new girlfriend. Apparently she was someone from his past.

"Vicki's an old and dear friend of the family. I'm surprised you haven't met her before, Annie."

"It's been a long time since I've had the pleasure of a visit to the Drummond manse," said Vicki, hoisting her snakeskin clutch higher under her arm. "Funny how the years have slipped past. I'm thrilled to be here with you all."

Annie caught what might have been the barest possible hint of sarcasm in her voice, and her back immediately stiffened. Was Vicki here to take advantage of their hospitality, then make fun of them? She certainly didn't look like Sinclair's usual friends, with their carefully coiffed blond hair and cashmere twinsets.

"And we're thrilled to have you here, darling." Mrs. Drummond walked up to Vicki, placed a hand on either side of her head, and gave her an effusive kiss on the cheek. Vicki's eyes closed for a second, and her forehead wrinkled with a pained expression. Annie stood staring. She'd never seen such a display of emotion from Mrs. Drummond. "It'll be like old times."

"God, I hope not." Vicki shook herself. "I do hate traveling backwards. But it is good to be among old friends." She looked ahead down the hall. "Which is the blue one? I'm dying for a shower."

Annie jolted from her semifrozen state. "Sorry, it's this way. I'll bring fresh towels. Do you need some shampoo and conditioner?"

"I've got everything I need except the running water." Vicki's gaze lingered on Annie a teeny bit longer than was conventional. Annie's stomach clenched. She got a very odd—and not good—feeling about Vicki. Who was she, and why was she here?

For dinner, Annie prepared one of Katherine Drummond's favorite meals, seared salmon with blackberry sauce, accompanied by tiny new potatoes and crisp green beans from the local farmers market.

"How lovely! Obviously Sinclair remembered to tell you we were coming. I'm never sure if he will." Katherine shot a doting glance at her son.

Annie smiled, and avoided looking at Sinclair as she served them. Experience had taught her to be prepared for almost anything. And she did get real satisfaction from doing her job well. The room glowed with fresh beeswax candles handmade by a local artisan, and the windows sparkled, letting in the warm apricot light from the evening sun. If anything about the house was the least bit unwelcoming or unpleasant, it wasn't from lack of effort on her part.

She leaned over Sinclair to top up his white wine. His dark hair touched his collar, in need of a haircut.

Her breath caught in her throat as she remembered its silky thickness under her fingers.

An odd sensation made her look up, and meet Vicki's curious violet gaze. She turned away quickly and topped off Katherine's glass, then Vicki's. Had Vicki noticed her looking at Sinclair?

"It doesn't seem entirely fair for Annie to be running around topping things off when she made this lovely meal." Vicki's silvery voice rang in the air. Annie winced.

"She's right, of course," chimed in Katherine. "Annie, dear. Do bring a plate and join us. We're just family tonight, after all." She reached across the table and took Vicki's hand.

Vicki's eyebrows lifted slightly, but she held Katherine's hand and smiled. "You're so sweet."

Annie hesitated, humiliation and mangled pride churning inside her. She'd been enjoying this meal as the server, but sitting down at the table with them opened all kinds of uncomfortable doors. How would she know when to get up and bring the next course? Should she join them for a glass of wine, or stick to water so as not to burn the chocolate soufflés? "I already ate, thank you." The lie burned her tongue.

"Do join us anyway, won't you?" Katherine indicated the empty chair next to Sinclair. "I'm dying to hear how your investigations in the attic are going."

Annie pulled out the chair, which scraped loudly on the floor, and eased herself into it, as far away from Sinclair as possible. He hadn't looked up from his salmon. Had he even glanced at her once all evening?

Better that he didn't. She couldn't bear the thought of him looking at her with disgust and disbelief at his lapse of judgment. "I've gone through quite a few of the old boxes and trunks. I've made an inventory. Shall I get it?" She itched to get up. At least her notes would give her something to do with her fingers.

"No need for that right now. I'm guessing you haven't found the cup piece yet."

Annie shook her head. "I'm looking at every item I pick up to see if it could possibly be part of a cup, but so far nothing even comes close. I don't suppose there's a description of it?"

Kathleen sipped her wine. "Only that it's silver. It isn't jewel-encrusted. In fact we suspect it's not silver at all but pewter or some base metal. Odd, really, that something so precious to them would be so valueless."

Vicki leaned back in her chair. "It demonstrates an awareness of human nature. If it had real value, someone might have melted it down or pried the gems off to make earrings. By making it valueless to anyone but the family, they ensured its survival. Was it contemporary to when the brothers sailed from Scotland?"

"We don't know." Katherine took a bite of her green beans. She ate very slowly and cautiously, as if she wasn't sure whether the food was poisonous or not. Probably an effect of her illness, but it didn't help Annie's already frayed nerves. "The cup could be much older than three hundred years if it was passed down through the Drummond family before they came to America. No one knows where the legend about it first came from. When I first married Steven, Sinclair's father…" she looked at Annie "…his mother was still alive and loved to tell stories of the family history. She often wondered aloud whether it was time for us to put some serious effort into finding the cup." She raised a brow.

"Her own marriage wasn't a happy one, and all of her sons—including my own husband—were rather wild."

She looked thoughtfully at Sinclair for a moment. He appeared to be engrossed in cutting a potato. "Since then I've often wondered if finding the cup would somehow shift the course of fate and make life easier for all members of the family." She leaned conspiratorially toward Vicki. "The legend says it will restore the fates and fortunes of the Drummond menfolk, and I think as women we all know that makes life easier for us, too."

Annie felt a nasty jolt of realization. Katherine Drummond had brought Vicki here in the hope that she really would become a member of the family—as Sinclair's next wife.

A cold stone settled in her empty stomach.

"There are all kinds of interesting things up in the attic," she said quickly, anxious to pull herself out of a self-involved funk. "So far I've found everything from an old hunting horn to a huge pearl brooch. That's what made me decide to make a list. It would be a shame for so many special things to stay buried."

"Sometimes keeping things buried keeps them safe," replied Katherine with a slightly raised brow. "Especially in the age of eBay. Though I imagine Vicki might disagree."

Vicki laughed. "I believe in matching objects with their ideal owner."

"Vicki's an antique dealer," explained Katherine.

"Though some people have other words for it." Vicki lifted a slim, dark brow. "After all, value is in the eye of the beholder."

"I thought that was beauty." Sinclair said what were

possibly his first words of the whole dinner. A hush fell over the table.

"Aren't they really the same thing?" Vicki picked up her wineglass and sipped, gaze fixed on Sinclair.

Annie swallowed. Vicki oozed confidence, both intellectual and sexual. Of course Sinclair would be interested in her. She, on the other hand… "Let me clear the dishes." She rose and removed two of the serving platters.

"Value and beauty often have no relationship at all." She heard Sinclair's voice behind her as she exited for the kitchen. "Some of my most profitable investments have been in things that no one wants to look at: uranium, bauxite, natural gas."

"So you most value things that are plain and dull." Annie cringed as if Vicki's comment was directed at his interest in her. Not that he had any obvious interest in her. As far as she could tell, he hadn't looked at her at all since their perfunctory greeting.

"I most value things that are useful."

"What are we going to do with this son of yours?"

Annie scooped leftover potatoes into a plastic container to save for her own dinner.

"Well, Lord knows I've tried to loosen him up over the years, to no avail." His mother's voice carried from the dining room. "I think this legendary cup may be our only chance." The women's laughter hurt her ears. She was so clearly not a part of this tight-knit group.

And she'd better go retrieve the rest of the plates. She entered the dining room quietly. Conversation had shifted to some upcoming party. For a split second she felt like Cinderella, destined to help everyone get ready for the ball, knowing she'd never get to go.

She picked up the untouched plate of bread rolls, and couldn't resist sneaking the briefest glance at Sinclair as she lifted it off the table. When she looked up, their eyes met.

His cool, dark gaze sent a chill through her, at war with the swift, hot wave of attraction. Then he looked away. "I'm going sailing tomorrow." He spoke in his mother's direction. "I'll be gone all day."

"All the more time for Vicki and myself to make ourselves at home in the attic."

Annie's hands trembled, clattering the two plates she carried. Was she being ousted from the task of looking for the cup? She realized with a pang of disappointment that she'd come to feel quite proprietary about the attic and its trove of discarded treasures.

Which was silly. None of them were hers and they never would be. That blue dress hung in the closet a few yards away from where she stood, in the spare bedroom. For a few brief moments it had felt like hers, like she was meant to wear it. In retrospect it had been wearing her, and had turned her—briefly—into another person. Maybe it was better that she stay away from all this odd old stuff with mysterious powers.

She carried the plates into the kitchen, scraped them and put them in the dishwasher. Her ears were pricked for the sound of Sinclair's voice, but all she heard was the chatter of the two women.

He doesn't care about you. It was a momentary lapse of judgment. An act of madness.

"Annie." His voice right behind her made her jump. She wheeled around and saw him standing, larger than life, in the kitchen. "We need to talk."

She gulped. "Yes."

"Tomorrow." His eyes narrowed. Stress had carved a line between his brows. "When we can be alone."

She nodded, heart pounding. Sinclair turned and strode from the room, his powerful shoulders hunched slightly inside his starched shirt.

He'd been so taciturn tonight, barely joining the conversation. Was he thinking about her? She rinsed the cutlery and put it into the dishwasher. For a while she thought he'd simply pretend nothing had happened. He made no contact with her after they'd made love and two weeks had gone by. She'd almost started to believe she imagined the whole, crazy thing.

But now he wanted to be alone with her. Wanted to talk to her. Her blood pumped harder. Worst-case scenario, he wanted to fire her. Best-case scenario?

She chewed her lip.

"Annie, darling, could you bring more Chablis?"

She wiped her hands on a towel and headed for the wine cellar.

Three

Sinclair usually preferred to help himself to some toast and coffee, but Annie never knew what guests might want, so she hovered in the kitchen ready to make an omelet or oatmeal. She wondered if Sinclair would come down first and they would have their talk before the others awoke.

To her dismay, Vicki was the first down the stairs, yawning, her sleek black hair knotted into a casual but elegant twist and her taut body showcased in skimpy capris and a cutoff T-shirt. "Morning, Annie. Is this where you ask me if I want breakfast?"

"You're way ahead of me. What can I get you?" Annoying guests weren't unusual. She managed a cheerful smile.

"Do you have any grapefruit?"

"I made a fruit salad of cantaloupe, grapes, honeydew and pineapple, but no grapefruit, I'm afraid. Would you like me to get you some?" Probably she was on some crackpot diet eating twenty-seven grapefruits a day and nothing else. She had that kind of body.

"God, no. Your fruit salad sounds fab. I'd kill for some scrambled eggs and bacon to go with it, if that's a possibility. Any sign of Sinclair?"

Annie blinked. "Not so far."

"Probably snuck out early to avoid us." Vicki shot her a conspiratorial smile. "Not much of a people person, is he?"

Annie glanced up the stairs. Had Sinclair really left the house already? He did sometimes slip away right at dawn. She wasn't sure where he went but he often came back wet, so possibly the beach. He didn't do that when guests were staying, though.

She didn't answer Vicki's question. He seemed very good with people from what she could see. He wouldn't have a successful investment company if he wasn't a people person. "Do you like your bacon well-done?"

"That would be perfect." Vicki wandered into the dining room and picked up the *New York Times*.

Annie headed for the kitchen. People like Vicki gave orders effortlessly. She'd been brought up that way. It was her own job to make sure those orders were carried out without a moment's hesitation, even if she had to run out and wrestle down a pig to make the bacon.

Happily she was well prepared and kept the freshest local bacon on hand. Three rashers were sizzling on the stove and the eggs bubbling in a pan when the kitchen door swung open. Annie nearly jumped out of her skin, expecting to see Sinclair's imposing form and stern gaze.

A smile settled across Vicki's shapely mouth. "Goodness, you are jumpy. Expecting someone else?"

"No." Annie answered too fast. She whisked the bacon and eggs onto a plate, hoping her red face would be attributed to the heat from the stove.

Vicki lounged in the doorway, watching her. "Sinclair is a dark horse."

Annie burned to disagree, or at least ask why she would say such a thing, but her gut told her that would be playing into some plan of Vicki's. "Will you take it in the dining room?"

"I'll take it from you right here." She thrust out her hands and took the fork and knife from Annie. "And thank you very much for making this. It looks yummy." She flashed another oh-so-charming smile.

Annie let out a hard breath when the door closed behind Vicki. What did she mean by that comment? Did she suspect something between herself and Sinclair? Sweat had broken out on her forehead and she pushed a few strands of hair off it. Surely she hadn't given anything away?

Katherine came down around 10:00 a.m. and ate a few bites of her custom-made muesli. "Has my son already abandoned us?"

"I'm not sure. I haven't seen him all morning." Annie refilled her juice. How had Sinclair managed to slip away? She'd been up since before first light. He must be very determined to avoid her. That didn't bode well for their planned talk.

"I'm dying to head up to the attic, though I have to take it slow. The doctor says I'm not allowed to stand up for more than thirty minutes at a time." She shook her head, and her elegant blond bob swung. "I don't know how you're supposed to do anything when you have to sit down every thirty minutes, but he is the top man in his field and I promised Sinclair I'd follow his instructions slavishly."

"How are you feeling?"

"Weak." She laughed a little. "I poop out easily. I'm supposed to eat all kinds of super foods to boost my energy but I don't have any appetite, either. I might try acupuncture. A friend of mine swears by it."

Annie ventured into the conversation. "My sister tried it to give up smoking and it didn't work. I blame my sister, though, not the acupuncturist. I think she was more determined to prove him wrong than she was to quit."

Katherine's warm smile lit up the room. "I'm determined to get well. I have far too much to live for. I haven't even met my first grandchild yet."

Juice sloshed in the jug as Annie's hand jerked. Sinclair was Katherine Drummond's only child so obviously her fondest dreams lay in his next marriage. A prospect that made Annie's muscles limp with dismay. "That is something to look forward to."

"What about you, Annie? Is there anyone in your life?" A blond brow lifted.

Annie froze. Did she also suspect something between her and Sinclair?

"You seem to live here so quietly and I worry that we've cut you off from civilization. Maybe you should try one of those online dating services."

Annie's heart sank a little when she realized it hadn't even crossed Katherine's mind that she and Sinclair might be involved. "I'm quite happy. One day my prince will come." She smiled and hoped it looked convincing.

"These days it doesn't pay to wait around for princes to show up. Better to go out and find one yourself before all the good ones get snatched up."

Sinclair's been snatched up twice, but he's still available. She did not voice her thoughts. And really, was a man who'd been divorced twice such a good prospect? She suppressed a sigh. "I don't have time for dating. I'm planning to take an evening course at the local college."

"Really?" Katherine's eyes widened.

Annie regretted her words. The plan was still half-formed in her mind and now her employer would probably worry about her slacking off in her duties. Why had she said it? Was she so afraid of seeming like a pathetic spinster who'd be polishing silver for the rest of her life?

"Nothing very demanding. I was thinking of learning a little about business." She shrugged her shoulders apologetically. Probably better not to tell Katherine about her dream of opening a shop one day.

"I think that's wonderful, Annie. If there's anything at all I can do to help, a reference to get you into the program, or something like that. I'm sure Sinclair will be thrilled."

She doubted Sinclair would feel such strong emotion on the topic. Though he might be happy to hear she was trying to broaden her employment prospects. He'd hardly want her hanging around in his house for years after they'd had that…accident.

That's what it felt like. A sudden car wreck. Or maybe just a fender bender. Either way it had left her bruised and dented and unsure of her previously planned route.

"Thanks, can I get you some more toast?"

"No, thanks. I'd like to head up to the attic, if you're ready."

They spent the day rifling through the boxes and crates of old possessions. The space grew hotter as the day went on. Vicki was surprisingly quiet, examining objects with a studious eye, as if making mental notes about them. They found several pieces of eighteenth-century scrimshaw and a carefully packed box with two old Chinese vases, but most of the stuff was obviously worthless—boxes of celluloid shirt collars and scrofulous-looking moleskin hats. By late afternoon they were winding down their search. "I think it's time for a glass of iced tea," Katherine said, getting up from the folding chair Annie had brought up for her.

"You go ahead, I'll be down in a minute." Vicki's nose was deep in a black trunk.

"Something interesting in there?" Katherine fanned herself with a slim hand.

"Not sure yet. I'll let you know if I find anything good."

"Let's go down, Annie." Annie cast a backward glance at Vicki. It went against all her instincts to leave her here among the family treasures. "If you'll just give me a hand down the stairs."

With no choice but to help Katherine, Annie headed back into the house and spent the next hour making scones and spreading cream and jam on them, while listening for every slight hint that Sinclair's car might be pulling back into the driveway.

Katherine was nodding off in a shaded armchair, and Vicki engrossed in texting on her phone, when she heard the purr of that familiar engine. Her heart immediately kicked into overdrive. She hurried into the kitchen so she didn't have to watch him kiss Vicki warmly on the cheek. If he wanted to see her, he knew where to find her. She cursed herself for checking her reflection in the polished side of a stainless-steel pot and smoothing her hair back into its bun.

Heavy footfalls on the wood stairs sounded his ascent to his bedroom. She heaved a sigh of relief mingled with disappointment. Obviously he wasn't burning with a desire to see her. She could easily go up there on the pretext of bringing fresh towels or collecting his laundry. In fact, on a normal weekend, she'd probably do just that.

But nothing would ever be normal again.

Softer footfalls on the stairs suggested Vicki heading up, too. Maybe she was going to throw her arms around Sinclair and beg him to tell her all about his sailing adventures.

Annie cursed herself for caring. Sinclair was never hers to be possessive about, not for a single instant. If she didn't want to feel this way, she should never have let him kiss her. If only she could turn the clock back to that moment of madness when his lips hovered just in front of hers.

"He is one of the most insightful portraitists working today, but if you're sure…" Vicki's voice carried along the upstairs hallway later that afternoon. "Katherine, Sin doesn't want to come with us. We're on our own."

"I keep telling him he should pay more attention to art, for its investment potential as well as its beauty, but he won't listen. What time does it open?"

Annie listened to them plan their stroll through the village to the art opening and mentally calculated how long she'd be alone with Sinclair. Certainly long enough to talk. Probably long enough to get into a lot of trouble, too, but she had no intention of doing that again.

She prepped for dinner while the women primped themselves. Katherine was immaculate as usual, her golden hair cupping her cheekbones, dressed in a sleek pantsuit with a bold jade necklace. Vicki looked like she'd just climbed out of bed looking like a goddess, an effect that must take considerable effort. A diaphanous dress clung to her slender form, revealing long, graceful legs that ended in pointy ankle boots.

Annie resisted the urge to look down at herself. She was not in competition with these women. She was not even on the same playing field as them, and no one expected her to be. But then, why did her usual "uniform" of preppy classics feel dowdy and frumpier than ever?

She hid in the kitchen after the door closed behind them. If Sinclair wanted to talk to her he could come find her. And he did.

"I didn't hear you," she stammered, when she saw him standing, tall and serious, in the narrow doorway. The old colonial kitchen had been remodeled with the most extravagant chefs' appliances, but that didn't change the low ceiling and old-fashioned proportions that made Sinclair look like a giant, standing next to the hand-carved spice racks.

His hair was wet, slicked back but with a long tendril falling over his forehead. He wore a pale gray polo shirt and well-worn khakis, and she noticed with a start that his feet were bare. How could he manage to look so elegant and breathtakingly handsome in such casual clothing?

"Listen, Annie…"

Like she had any choice?

"About the other day." He frowned. "I don't know how to explain—"

"Me either," she cut in. "It was very unexpected."

He looked relieved. Somehow that hurt. Still, at least he wasn't trying to act as if nothing happened.

"I think we should both forget that it ever happened."

His mocking echo of her thoughts cut her to the quick. "Of course." The words flew from her mouth, a desperate attempt to save face.

He could have left right then, the pact between them safely sealed, but he didn't. He stood in the doorway, blocking her view of the hallway and—now that she thought of it—her only escape route. "You're a nice girl, Annie."

Oh no, here it came. The "don't be too hurt that I'm not at all interested in you, some other schlub will be" speech. If only she could run from the room and spare herself his pity.

"You're nice, too." She cringed. It sounded like something a preschooler would come up with. No wonder he had no enduring interest in her—she sounded like someone who had the intellect of a turnip.

"Not really." He rubbed at his chest with a tense hand, and she could remember the thick, taut muscle hidden beneath his gray shirt. She'd rested her cheek on his chest and sighed with sheer pleasure. Now his dark eyes looked pained.

He was probably thinking of his ex-wives. The last one had said all kinds of nasty things about him in the press after she realized she hadn't been married long enough to get alimony. "I know you didn't want to... do that." She couldn't even say it. What had they done? It wasn't "making love" or "sleeping together." Having sex. Pretty simple, really, but she still couldn't voice the words. "I know you didn't plan it and that you regret it." She swallowed. What had possibly been the most perfectly blissful hour of her life was an embarrassing footnote in his.

"Exactly."

His words sank through her like a stone. Why could she not shake the pathetic hope that all those kisses and so much passion had meant something to him? It seemed so strange that his breathless moans could be nothing more than a gut physical reaction.

"I don't know what came over me, either." *Except for the fact that I've adored you from afar for far too long.* "But I'll make sure not to try one of those dresses on again." She managed a shaky smile.

One side of Sinclair's mouth lifted, revealing a devastating dimple. "You looked breathtaking in that dress, Annie."

The sound of her name coming from his mouth, right after the compliment, made her heart jump.

"Oh, I think it was the dress that looked breathtaking. They're all so beautifully made. I haven't looked at them since I hung them in the closet but they don't seem to have ever been worn."

"Except that one, now."

"And that wasn't worn for long." She let out a breath. Being in such close quarters with Sinclair played havoc with her sanity. She could smell the familiar scent of that old-fashioned soap he used. She had a close-up view of the lines at the corners of his eyes, which showed how often he smiled, despite all rumors to the contrary. "Maybe there's a reason those clothes ended up in a trunk in the attic and were never worn."

"A curse?" He lifted a dark brow. Humor danced in his eyes. She could tell he didn't believe a word of the superstitions that so excited his mom.

"A spell, perhaps." She played along. "To turn even a sensible woman into a wanton."

"That was a very effective spell." His eyes darkened and held her gaze for a moment until her breath was coming in tiny gasps. "Not that you were a wanton, of course, but…"

"I think we both know what you meant." She shoved a lock off her forehead. She was sweating. If only he knew that the slightest touch from him might accidentally turn her into a wanton at a moment's notice.

Had she imagined it, or did he just sneak a glance at her body? Her breasts tingled slightly under her yellow shirt, and her thighs trembled beneath her khakis. She could almost swear his dark gaze had swept over them and right back up to her face.

But she had no proof and right now that seemed like idle fantasy. Or maybe he was wondering what the heck came over him to find himself in a compromising position with such a frump. He was hardly the type to risk legal trouble with an employee for a quick roll in the hay. The whole incident was truly bizarre.

And totally unforgettable.

Great. Now she just had to spend the rest of her life comparing other men to Sinclair Drummond.

He walked across the kitchen and took a glass from one of the cabinets. She should have asked him if he wanted something, but it was too late now. His biceps flexed, tightening the cuff of his polo shirt as he reached to close the cabinet. She watched the muscles of his back extend and contract beneath the soft fabric, which pulled slightly from the top of his khakis. Just enough for her to remember sliding her fingers into his waistband and...

She turned and headed for the dishwasher. This line of thought was not at all productive. "Can I get you some iced tea?"

"No, thanks, Annie. I'll help myself to some water." He pushed the glass into the dispenser on the front of the fridge.

She'd have to find another job. This was way too awkward. How was she supposed to wait hand and foot on a man while remembering how his body felt pressed against hers?

There was no way she'd find a job that paid as well as this one, where she'd get to live—free of charge—in a beautiful house near the beach and be her own boss 95 percent of the time. She didn't have a college degree. She hadn't even finished high school properly. This job had allowed her to pile up savings in the bank, and she was about to fulfill her dream of going to college right nearby. If she left she'd probably eat into her savings subsidizing her "Would you like fries with that?" job.

Sinclair's Adam's apple moved as he drained his glass of water. How awkward that they were in the same room, not talking at all. Then again, that wouldn't have been at all strange until two weeks ago. Sinclair wasn't the chatty type, and neither was she. They were both the kind of people who enjoyed listening to the sounds of a spring evening, or just letting thoughts glide through their heads.

Or at least she presumed that's what he was doing. Maybe it was all in her imagination. She was so different than the rest of her family, who seemed hell-bent on filling every moment with talk, music or the sound of the television. Maybe other people were quiet for different reasons.

"My mom wants to stay here for the rest of the summer." A tiny line appeared between his brows as he said it. "And I do think it's the best thing for her. The fresh air will do her good, and she can rest with you to take care of things."

"That's great." Her heart was sinking. Much as she liked Katherine Drummond, all she wanted right now was to be alone to lick her wounds. The prospect of having to be "on" all the time seemed unbearable. And maybe this was Sinclair's way of saying, *Don't quit until the summer's over. My ailing mom needs you.*

"Vicki will be here to keep her company, so you won't have to feel obliged to entertain her."

Annie flinched, accidentally knocking against a canister of sugar. Could this get any worse? Sinclair obviously knew this was all unwelcome news. He shoved his hand through his hair again, ruffling it. "And Mom's convinced me to work from here for the next couple of weeks at least. She thinks I'm working too hard." His dark gaze held hers for a second.

"Great." The word sounded empty and insincere.

"You and I are both sensible adults." His dark eyes fixed on hers. Was he trying to convince her? "I'm sure we can move beyond what happened."

"Of course." She didn't want him to know how much

that afternoon had meant to her. He must never know. It was hard to look at him. Even the world-weary aspect of his face only added to his charm, his gaze hooded and guarded. She wasn't sure he wanted any woman, least of all her. "I'll be the soul of discretion."

The furrow in his brow deepened for a second. "I knew I could count on you, Annie." The sound of her own name sent a jolt of pain to her heart. Hearing it on his lips made her yearn for when he'd breathed it in passion. It seemed so…intimate. She could never say *Sinclair* so boldly and often.

But that was the problem, wasn't it? They were from completely different social strata. In the twenty-first century that shouldn't matter, but it did. She might have been able to climb to a different level herself if she'd managed to go to college and start a successful career, like his. She could have been an executive by now, rubbing shoulders with him in a New York City boardroom.

But that wasn't how things had worked out. She was destined to rub shoulders with him while wielding a sponge in his kitchen.

She wished he would leave. This was so awkward. He kept…looking at her. But it was his kitchen and she was his employee. He could stand there and look pityingly on her all day if he wanted. And now she couldn't even start combing the classifieds. She could hardly leave his mother in the lurch while she was still so weak.

"I'm heading out for a walk." Still he hovered in the kitchen, his large, masculine presence filling the room.

"Okay." As if her opinion mattered.

He hesitated again, brow furrowed, and pierced her soul one more time with that intense brown gaze before he turned and left.

She sank against the countertop as the sound of his footsteps echoed down the hallway. How was she going to survive this summer? The worst part was that she kept feeling something that he wasn't saying. Something odd and unsettling in the way he looked at her. Like some of the madness still lingered inside him the way it did inside her.

But that hardly mattered if he intended for them to forget that magical afternoon ever happened. She'd just have to get through it one day at a time. Starting with tonight's dinner.

Four

Sinclair stayed in his room as long as possible, reading research one of his staff had compiled on a gold-mining company in Uruguay. He'd much rather be at work than "relaxing" here with his mom organizing things for him to do every minute of the day. Today's festivities included a croquet party she'd arranged, and he was expected to put in an appearance and actually wield a mallet. If she hadn't come so close to death... He let out a long breath, then closed his laptop and swung his feet off the bed.

"Sinclair, is that you?" His mom's voice came from the corridor. Had she been listening outside, waiting for him to betray signs of life? He shook his head and ran his fingers through his hair. She'd probably arranged for eight to ten attractive single women, dressed in designer croquet attire, to battle each other to win his heart.

Couldn't any of them tell he didn't have a heart to win?

"I'll be down in a minute."

"Good, dear, because everyone's here."

A glance out the window confirmed that "everyone" was at least fifteen of Dog Harbor's most well-heeled citizens. They milled about clutching drinks, stiletto heels sinking into the smooth lawn. He yawned. His mother's social occasions made even the most brutal business negotiations seem like a cakewalk.

And Annie would be there. Not playing croquet, or batting her eyelashes, but serving the iced tea and salmon squares. He searched for her among the small crowd but didn't see her. The resulting wave of disappointment shocked him away from the window and toward the door, tucking in his shirt and smoothing his hair on the way. Maybe all these people would at least take his mind off Annie for a while.

Either that or he was losing it for good. Lust. That's what it was. The curse of mankind, or at least the male half of the species. Abstinence didn't really work for men, they just ended up doing something crazier and more stupid than if they'd been in a normal relationship.

Shame he wasn't capable of a normal relationship. Two failed marriages didn't leave too much doubt about that.

He descended the stairs and went out to the garden. Voices called out, "Sinclair, how lovely to see you! It's been such a long time." Scented kisses covered his cheeks and he was forced to make fluff conversation about how his business was doing. Happily, neither of his ex-wives was there, but several of their close friends were. No doubt his mother considered them potential future wives. She was nothing if not determined.

"Would you like a glass of white wine?" Annie's soft voice made him whip around.

"Iced tea would be fine, thanks." The words sounded so inadequate, so laughable, after what had happened between them. A pang of regret stabbed him as she moved silently away to get his drink. He'd made things so awkward with a lovely woman who deserved to be treated with respect, not stripped naked by a man who couldn't control his basest urges.

"You're up first, Sinclair." His mother, beaming and looking happier and healthier than he'd seen her in ages, thrust a mallet into his hand. She loved parties and was never happier than when entertaining. Of course she wasn't a true Drummond. She'd married into the family, or she might have shared the taste for solitude that so annoyed her in his father and himself. None of the other Drummonds she'd tried to contact about the cup had bothered to respond. He wouldn't have either if she wasn't his own mother.

Annie returned with his drink. "Oh, you're playing now. Maybe I'd better hold on to it for you." Her lashes were a dark gold color that turned darker at the root near her pale blue eyes. Her hand hovered, waiting to see if he'd take the drink. His groin tightened and heated as a memory flashed over him—of the lush, curvy body hidden beneath her loose-fitting clothes.

"I'll take it now." He grabbed the glass rather roughly, afraid he'd somehow betray the fever of arousal that suddenly gripped him. All he needed was her lingering somewhere nearby, drink in hand, while he attempted to tap a wooden ball around the lawn.

"We haven't seen you out here in ages, Sinclair. If your family hadn't owned the place since biblical times I'd worry you were going to sell." A sleek brunette he recognized from the yacht club held her drink up near her ear as a smile hovered around her glossy lips.

"Couldn't do that. The ancestors would rise up and haunt me."

"We're doing teams." His mother rushed over. "Sinclair, why don't you team up with Lally." She gestured toward the brunette, who murmured that she'd love to.

Sinclair's heart sank. Why couldn't people leave him alone? Now Lally would be offended if he didn't flirt with her vigorously enough, and again when he failed to ask her out. Or, if he did ask her out from a sense of duty, she'd be upset when he didn't want to sleep with her. Maybe he should sleep with her right here and get it over with.

His flesh recoiled from the possibility. "Sure. Why don't you start?" He handed his partner the mallet, and she handed him her drink to hold. It looked like Annie's famous Long Island iced tea, a shot of every white liquor plus a splash of Coke for color. It tasted deceptively sweet and was utterly lethal. He contemplated downing it in one gulp.

"Oh, no, we're short a hand." His mom rushed around, stabbing in the air with her finger as she counted the assembled guests. "Philip canceled at the last minute with a toothache."

Lucky Philip. No doubt he'd found something better to do than be clawed over by single girls with ticking biological clocks.

"How's your hedge fund doing in this market?" The brunette, Lally, attempted to look interested. He launched into his standard dinner-party-conversation reply, leaving the rest of his mind free to wonder what about her made his mom see her as third-wife material. She was pretty, mid-twenties, slim as a kebab prong. All things his mom found essential. Personally he preferred a woman with some curves to hold on to, but apparently that wasn't fashionable anymore. Her teeth looked like Chiclets, or maybe that was an effect of her ultrawide smile and overglossed lips.

"Wow, that's so cool. It must be wonderful to be good with numbers."

His mom flapped toward him. "Darling, have you seen Annie? We need her to make up the last team."

Sinclair stiffened. "She can't have gone far." She was probably hiding in the pantry, trying to avoid getting roped into this charade. Since when did anyone over ten play croquet, anyway? "She's probably busy."

"Nonsense. I had everything catered and people can help themselves to drinks. I'll go find her."

Sinclair swallowed and returned his attention to Lally, who'd moved so close he was in danger of being suffocated by her expensive scent. He resisted the urge to recoil. "What do you do?" This was usually a good question to keep someone talking for a while.

She threw her head back slightly. "It's rather a revolutionary idea, actually." She looked about, as if worried someone might overhear and steal it, but with a big smile like she was hoping they would. "I host Botox parties. You know, where people come and have their cares smoothed away."

Genuine horror provoked Sinclair's curiosity. "You mean where people come and have a neurotoxin injected into their face?"

She laughed. "It's absolutely harmless in small doses, otherwise I'd be dead, wouldn't I?"

Sinclair blinked. "You've used Botox? You can't be a day over twenty-five."

She winked conspiratorially. "Twenty-nine, but don't tell a soul. I'm living proof that the product works." He couldn't resist staring at her forehead, which was smooth as the backside of his titanium laptop. "Still think it's crazy?"

"Absolutely." He had a violent urge to get as far away from Lally as possible, but politeness demanded that he survive this round of croquet first.

"You should invest. I'm going to be taking the company public some time next year. Of course, my main goal is to get bought out by a…" She rambled on, but his attention shifted to the sudden appearance of Annie. His mom had hooked her arm around Annie's and pulled her onto the lawn. Annie looked rather startled and, he noted with alarm, teary-eyed. Was she okay? Her nose was red as if she'd been crying.

"You don't need to know the rules. Just follow along. Your team will go last so you'll have plenty of time to figure it out, and Dwight will be happy to explain anything you miss, won't you, Dwight?" The tall, sandy-haired male with whom Sinclair had shared a long-ago sailing holiday agreed effusively. Jealousy kicked Sinclair in the gut.

"Are you okay?" He couldn't help asking her.

Annie looked up with a start. "Sure, I'm fine." She spoke quickly, her voice rather high. "It's allergies. They're terrible at this time of year."

He frowned. He didn't remember her having allergies, but no doubt that was just one of the many things he didn't know about her.

"Sinclair, we're up first." The feel of soft fingers on his back made him flinch. Lally tugged him up to the start. "You should watch so you see where the ball goes." Her vigorous tap sent the ball flying through the first hoop and raised a smatter of applause from the gathered crowd. Lally turned to him beaming, which, he noticed, had no effect on any other part of her face than her mouth. He handed her drink back to her, partly to ease the temptation of knocking it back to dull the pain of being there.

He snuck a glance over her shoulder at Annie. Her eyes had dried and she was engaged in conversation with Dwight about something very entertaining, at least judging from the way she kept laughing. His muscles tightened. What could Dwight be saying that was so funny? He didn't remember him being such a wit. He strained to hear their conversation, but couldn't make out a word of it over a nearby damsel bleating about her new vacation villa in Saint Lucia.

Annie's nose had a light sprinkling of freckles, and a sweet way of wrinkling as she talked. She didn't throw her chin and limbs around to punctuate her conversation the way the ambitious Lally was currently doing. He managed to nod in pretend interest to her conversational foray about yachting in the Caribbean. But all the while he was sneaking glances at Annie. He was glad her usual attire hid her hourglass figure, with its high, full breasts and slim waist. He could still feel the curve of her shapely backside against his hand.

"What did I do with my drink?" he asked, cutting Lally short.

"I don't know. Where's that girl who was passing them out?" She looked behind her. "Oh, there she is. Sinclair needs a drink!"

Sinclair stiffened as Annie looked his way. Her eyebrow lifted slightly. "Of course. Wine, or something stronger?"

He fought the urge to laugh. She could see right through him. "No, no. I'm fine."

"But you just said—" Lally's smooth face almost blocked his view of Annie.

"I said, I'm fine. If I need something I'll get it myself." His curt response rather startled both women. He attempted to lighten up. "I can't believe you're worrying about drinks during this cutthroat game of croquet. Your attention should be fixed entirely on the fate of our balls."

Dwight guffawed. "Easy for you to say, Sin. Some of us are still holding our balls." He winked at Annie, and again Sinclair felt a hot flash of unfamiliar emotion.

"Don't be so crude, Dwight." Vicki materialized beside him. "You'll shock Sinclair. He's a man of old-fashioned tastes and sensibilities."

She was right, of course. Though he couldn't understand why his mother had invited Vicki for what was apparently going to be an extended stay. He hadn't seen her more than in passing for years, and his mom could hardly think Vicki was going to be his next wife. Then again, his mom could get strange ideas.

"My son is a gentleman of the old style." His mom materialized next to him. Was this some kind of staged sketch where everyone knew their lines except him? "I think we all have a lot to learn from him."

He snuck another glance at Annie. She was looking

down at her croquet mallet like she wished she was anywhere but here. The feeling was mutual. The only safe course of action was to wrap this hellish game up as soon as possible. "My turn, I believe." Having a strategic nature, he'd been taking mental notes while his opponents tapped their balls ineffectually around the course. He sliced his through the hoop at an angle, taking out two other balls on the way, then drove it hard through the next two hoops without blinking. He would have happily launched it all the way to the home post but that wouldn't be sporting, so he pretended to miss and set his ball up to knock his opponents' flying.

"I am glad I'm on your team, Sinclair." Lally's unlined face glowed. "You're quite ruthless."

If only he was ruthless enough to tell his mom to leave him in peace and stop trying to enhance his social life. She probably wouldn't leave him alone until he married again, now she'd got the future of the Drummond dynasty on her mind. On the one hand, he actually liked the idea of having children. They'd be a lot more fun to play croquet with than this crowd. The marriage part, on the other hand, he wasn't up for at all. Women changed once you put that ring on their finger.

"Hey, Sinclair, do you remember me?" A svelte redhead in a green dress sauntered over, mallet in one hand and drink in the other.

"Of course, Mindy."

"I hear Diana's in Greece for the summer."

Why did people think he'd want to know what his ex-wife was doing? "I imagine that will be good for the Greek economy."

Mindy laughed. "You're such a card, Sinclair. And not at all bitter! I love that in a man."

"I'm glad to see everyone getting along so well." His mom walked among them, wreathed in smiles and carrying a tray of pastries. "Such a lovely way to spend a summer afternoon."

"Let me pass those around." Annie leaped forward and tried to wrest the pastries from his mom's hand.

"I wouldn't dream of it." His mom waved her away. "You're a member of our party now and have a far more important role to play."

Annie glanced nervously at him. As their eyes met, a jolt of raw and unsettling energy flashed between them. He looked away sharply. Why Annie? Why did he have to share steamy, hungry and unfettered sex in the arms of the one woman he'd previously enjoyed an utterly uncomplicated relationship with?

Obviously the gossips were right and he was simply impossible.

Emotionally exhausted from the effort of not looking at Sinclair, while attempting to make polite small talk and to participate in a game she'd never played before, Annie washed and rinsed the serving platters when all she wanted was to crawl into her bed and sob. Earlier, in an uncharacteristic Cinderella moment, she'd become teary-eyed while plating the caterer's canapés and watching all those beautiful women pulling into the driveway, dressed to impress and woo him. She'd been discovered mid-sniffle by Katherine. Now she was going to have to stage a pretense of using antihistamine drops and sneezing over flowers for the rest of the summer.

"What's going on between you and Sinclair?"

She almost had a heart attack when she realized

Vicki was standing behind her. Had she been muttering to herself? Did she say something about Sinclair?

"Nothing."

"Goodness, no need to bite my head off." Vicki reached for a slightly shriveled cheese puff from a nearby plate that had not yet been cleared. "I can see I've hit a nerve."

"I don't know what you're talking about," she lied.

"Hmm. The color rushing to your cheeks contradicts your words. Don't tell me you don't find him attractive, because I wouldn't believe you. I think he's gorgeous." She ate the cheese puff and reached for another. "Handsome and rich. What more could a woman want?"

"Are you asking me a question, or just thinking aloud?" Letting Vicki think she was a mousy pushover didn't feel like a good idea.

Vicki laughed, tossing back her silky black mane. "Thinking aloud, I suppose. Do you think I'd look good in a wedding picture next to him?" She lifted a slender brow. It was hard to tell if she was joking or not.

The image of her haughty, delicate features next to Sinclair's sent a fist of hurt to Annie's heart. "You'd make a very attractive couple," she said truthfully.

"Shame that isn't enough, really, is it?" Vicki moved closer and pulled a piece of celery from another platter. Annie wished she could physically shove her out of the kitchen. "Life would be so much easier if you only had to look good together."

"I suspect Sinclair would agree." She knew he'd been devastated by the failure of his second marriage. Partly from snippets of conversations she'd overheard, but also by a dramatic shift in his demeanor after his wife left him.

"What happened between him and Diana?"

"I really don't know."

"Come on, you're in the same house."

"Diana didn't like Dog Harbor. Too dull. They hardly ever came after they got married." Though he'd come here a lot afterward, probably to lick his wounds in peace. "I don't know what they got up to elsewhere."

"Rather like watching only one story thread on a soap opera." Vicki leaned one hip against the kitchen counter and crossed her arms. She wore a dress of crinkly white parachute fabric that revealed a lot of slender, barely tanned leg. "I bet you wish you could TiVo the rest of the episodes sometimes."

"I have plenty of other things to keep me busy." Annie scrubbed at a stubborn grease spot. "What they did was none of my business."

"I'm not so sure." Vicki regarded her silently for a moment. "I'd think that since it's your job to keep Sinclair happy, what he's up to is your business."

Annie threw down her sponge. "My job is to keep the house clean and make sure there's milk in the fridge when he shows up." Her voice rose, along with frustration and humiliation at being forced to endure Vicki's inquisition. If they were on neutral territory she could tell her to get lost, or simply walk away. But here, Vicki was a guest of her employer, so she couldn't.

"Now, now, don't burst a blood vessel." Vicki's eyes were brightening, if anything. "I suspect there's a lot more to you behind that placid smile." She studied Annie's face for a moment, as Annie's blood pressure rose. "I've seen Sinclair looking at you, too."

"Why wouldn't he? I'm his employee." This was almost unbearable. She was lying with one side of her brain, while the other madly considered Vicki's bold statements. Was Sinclair really looking at her differently? And how would Vicki know? She hadn't seen him for years. Probably she was just trying to wind her up. "It's hard to wash these dishes with you distracting me."

"So leave them. They're not going anywhere."

"I can't. I have to get dinner ready soon and they'll be in the way."

Vicki tilted her head to the side. "It can't be easy slaving away in the kitchen while everyone else reclines on the patio and sips champagne. I think it would drive me half-mad."

"It's my job. We all have one."

"Do we?"

"Sinclair works very hard at his business."

Vicki's eyebrow shot up again. "You are loyal. And I'm sure you're right. In fact, sometimes I wonder if he'd ever do anything else unless someone forced him into it."

"Is it wrong to enjoy your work?"

"I think it's ideal." Vicki frowned.

"Do you work at an auction house?" Annie couldn't resist asking. She'd been wondering if Vicki had a real job.

"Between you, me and this wilted stalk of celery, I'm between gigs right now." She took a bite of the celery.

"I suppose you're independently wealthy." She rinsed the dish and put it in the rack.

"Something like that." Vicki shot her a fake smile. "Gotta dash. It's been interesting chatting with you."

Annie felt herself relaxing as Vicki moved toward the

door with her characteristic floaty walk. "And I still think there's something going on between you and Sinclair."

The next morning Katherine asked Annie to help her search the attic. Mercifully, Sinclair was out playing golf with a business prospect, but unfortunately Vicki was there, her violet eyes seeming to peer below the surface of every human interaction.

"This set of hunting knives is probably worth something." Vicki held one of the tarnished blades up to the light. She jotted something in a little notebook. "I could find a home for it if you like."

Annie frowned. She'd noticed Vicki taking an interest in many of the items. She'd filled quite a few pages with notes.

"That's probably a good idea. What would we do with them anyway?"

"They're just moldering away up here."

"They are part of the Drummond family history." Annie felt called upon to suggest that Sinclair might want them someday. Of course it wasn't her place to say that explicitly.

"True." Katherine looked thoughtfully at an odd contraption of leather and woven rope. "Though perhaps the Drummonds need to shed some of this unhelpful baggage in order to make room for wonderful new things. That's what my friend Claire says. She's mad about feng shui."

"I couldn't agree more." Vicki made another note in her book. "Sometimes an object will sit in one place for a hundred years, doing nothing but collect dust, when in another person's hands it could enjoy full and active use."

Annie tried to picture some of these objects taking on new lives. Did anyone really have a use for old celluloid shirt collars? Then again, future generations might one day enjoy seeing the crazy things their ancestors wore. "I think Sinclair's children might have fun going through these things one day."

Katherine looked up as if shot. She paused a moment, then nodded. "You're absolutely right, of course, Annie. We'll put everything back where we found it."

Annie couldn't resist a glance at Vicki, who glared at her for a split second, then assumed a forced smile.

She enjoyed a brief flash of pride at defending Sinclair's inheritance. "Did you hear back from the other branches of the family?" She knew Katherine had sent them both letters.

"Not a word. I phoned about a week after sending the letters. I left a message with some elderly Scottish person at the family estate in the Highlands, but no one has called back. For the Florida branch, I left a message on some robotic voice mail system so I don't even know if anyone heard it. Exasperating, really. It would be pointless finding one part of the cup if we can't convince them to produce the others."

"Do they even know about the cup?" Annie sorted through some mismatched plates.

"They do now, if they got my letters. I know there's bad blood between the branches of the family, but it's time to put that behind us. Sinclair's father is gone, and so are most of the Drummonds of his generation. Which is proof enough that the family needs to change its luck. The ones in charge now are all Sinclair's age, or close, and have no reason to feel enmity toward each other. Young people these days don't carry centuries-old grudges for no reason."

"Or do they?" Vicki asked enigmatically.

"Sinclair doesn't." Katherine shook out a brocaded jacket. "Of course, the flipside is that he shows no interest whatsoever in the family or its history." She sighed and let the jacket fall in her lap. "Including the pressing need to produce the next generation."

Annie cringed. If she wasn't on birth control she might have had the next generation of Drummonds growing inside her right now. They certainly hadn't stopped to chat about contraception in their rush to tear each other's clothes off.

"There's still plenty of time." Vicki looked up from making notes on a set of spoons. "He's young."

"I know, but I'm not. I want to enjoy my grandchildren while I'm healthy and energetic enough to have fun with them."

Annie wanted to laugh. Katherine Drummond barely looked forty-five. Though that was probably due to the art of a number of fine surgeons and dermatologists. She was probably somewhere in her late fifties. Hardly old, however you looked at it.

"Sinclair will find the right woman eventually." Vicki peered into a small wooden chest.

"Will he? I'm not so sure. He found the first two by himself and I think it's time I took over. He needs women who aren't so driven by personal ambition. Sinclair doesn't want to set the world on fire or fly around in private jets every weekend. He needs someone quiet and simple."

Annie's soul nodded in agreement. Maybe she really was perfect for Sinclair, and they'd all realize it if she only waited patiently.

Vicki laughed. "I'm not sure many women want to be described that way. I know I wouldn't."

"I don't mean simple-minded, just someone without complex ulterior motives. Sinclair is a simple man, brilliant—"

"And gorgeous…."

"But simple." Katherine and Vicki said it together, then laughed. Annie had a feeling Sinclair would hate being discussed in this trivializing fashion. Didn't they care if he loved the woman?

"So I take it this means I'm not supposed to sink my own claws into him." Vicki lifted a cloudy etched-glass trophy and peered at it. Or pretended to.

Katherine shrugged. "For all I know, you're the breath of fresh air he needs. At least you've always been a straight shooter and everyone knows where they stand with you."

"Some would say that's my least attractive feature."

"Only if you don't want to hear the truth." Katherine smiled.

Annie's mind raced. Had Vicki been telling the truth about how Sinclair looked at her? Maybe he really was still attracted to her. Or perhaps even had deeper feelings.

Heat rushed inside her and she walked to the far end of the attic to bury herself in shadows. If these women had any idea what was going through her mind—and who knew what powers of perception Vicki possessed beyond those she boasted—they'd be scandalized. As it was, they talked about Sinclair's love life right in front of her as if she didn't exist. It obviously didn't cross

Katherine's mind that her beloved son might have had an affair, no matter how brief, with the woman who served the *brie en croute* and refilled her wineglass.

She let out a quiet sigh.

"He didn't seem to like Lally much, did he?"

"Not at all. I think that shows excellent taste on his part."

"She's from a very good family," said Katherine with conviction.

"Is that important?"

"I think so. Don't you?"

"Not in the least. I've always secretly dreamed of marrying one of the dastardly Drummonds, despite the family's dubious reputation."

"Oh, Vicki. You and Sinclair would make a striking couple."

"So I was telling Annie." Vicki shot a glance at her, where she hid in the shadows. "She completely agreed."

Katherine clapped her hands together and laughed. "Well, then, maybe things are moving in the right direction."

Vicki glanced at Annie again, as if seeking her gaze, but Annie kept herself busy rummaging through a tall chest of drawers. Was Vicki deliberately trying to torment her? Maybe she took pleasure in the fact that she could have Sinclair if she wanted to, and Annie couldn't.

Whoever said life was supposed to be fair? Her grandmother's ominous words rang in her ears. If she wanted to keep her sanity, she needed to forget that wild afternoon of lovemaking ever happened.

If only it were that easy.

Five

Her heart pounded with trepidation as she approached Sinclair. He'd been gone for much of the past week, out sailing, fishing or playing tennis. She might suspect he was trying to avoid someone, if she didn't already know that was true.

But she couldn't hold her tongue any longer.

I'm crazy about you.

No, she wasn't going to say that, though the thought almost drove a manic laugh to her lips. She drew in a deep breath as she opened the door to the sitting room. "Sinclair?"

He was reading alone, in front of the big, carved fireplace. No fire burned, since it was downright hot and the house, being ancient, had no air-conditioning. He looked up from his newspaper. "Hello, Annie."

Her insides melted. Why did he always greet her by name? Did he know that it half killed her to hear her name—boring as it was—fall from his mouth in that deep, warm tone? It would be so much better if he just uttered a curt "What?"

"Um." She pushed a lock of hair behind her ears. Then glanced behind her. She didn't want anyone to overhear what she was about to say. "It's about Vicki. Do you mind if I close the door?"

He frowned slightly, and curiosity appeared in his eyes. "This sounds mysterious." He glanced at the door. She took that as an invitation and quickly shut it.

"She's been up in the attic with your mom and me, looking through all the old stuff." She paused, wondering how to say this next part.

"I know. That's why she's here, ostensibly." He leaned toward her slightly, and she felt the increased closeness almost like a hug. Which was ridiculous, since she was still several feet away.

"It probably isn't my place to say anything, but I couldn't keep quiet because I know the house and everything in it is important to you."

He regarded her with no expression. Probably thought she was nuts. Maybe it would be better if she didn't say anything. In some ways it was none of her business. On the other hand she was the housekeeper, which, taken literally, could mean she was responsible for keeping the house from being looted. "Vicki's been taking detailed notes on a lot of the items in the attic, and I've seen her researching them on her laptop."

"She's an antique dealer."

"I know. I've also seen her looking at auctions on eBay. I think she might be planning to sell some of the items."

"Perhaps my mom has asked her to. There's way too much junk up there."

She shook her head. "I heard her bring the idea up, and your mom said we should put everything back where we found it, to save it for your children." She didn't mention her own part in helping Katherine to that decision.

"Typical." He shook his head. "Why does everyone have to have children? Would it be such a tragedy if this branch of the Drummonds died out with me? Put it all on eBay. That's what I say." A wry smile played about his lips. "But I do appreciate you worrying about the fate of our old junk. It's very thoughtful."

Was he making fun of her? He certainly didn't seem to care whether Vicki took everything home in her suitcase. Maybe he really didn't want children and everything in the house would end up at an auctioneer one day. "You should have children."

She gasped when she heard her own words on the air. Sinclair sat up slightly in his chair, startled. "I can see you feel strongly about it. May I ask why?" Humor glittered in the depths of his eyes.

She wished she could melt into the Persian carpet. *Because you'd be a great father. Strict, but kind. Because children would bring out the child buried inside you.* "I don't know. It would be a waste, that's all. And your mom would be very disappointed."

"She'll survive. I don't live my life to please other people."

"Don't you want children?" Why did she keep digging herself further into this hole? Sheer burning curiosity drove her to ask.

"I used to, once." He looked up at the window. Then

his brow furrowed. "But I don't intend to be a single father and apparently there isn't a woman alive who can put up with me."

"That's not true." Her heart squeezed. Did he really feel so totally unlovable? "You just haven't met the right person yet." The light played in his dark hair and across his bold cheekbones. If only she could tell him that he had met the right person and she was standing here in front of him.

But he'd told her to forget their magical afternoon ever happened. He wasn't interested in her. He'd lost control for a short while, and now that his sanity was back he wanted nothing from her. Well, other than freshly laundered sheets and homemade dinners.

His brow had furrowed slightly and an odd expression played across his sensual mouth. "Maybe you're right." He looked away sharply. "I don't know."

Tension thickened in the air. Her fault. She'd come in here and started this far-too-personal conversation after accusing one of his old friends of fraud. She'd be lucky if they didn't fire her. "I'd better go make dinner."

"Yes, you'd better." That glint of amusement twinkled in his eyes again. "Before you make any more rash and unsettling statements."

Something hovered between them. Unspoken words. Feelings that weren't supposed to be felt. At least she felt them. Maybe he just wished she'd leave him in peace.

She turned and hurried for the door before she could make things worse.

During dinner, conversation turned to an upcoming dance to be held by a music mogul celebrating his twentieth wedding anniversary.

"We ran into his wife, Jess, at the nursery today." Katherine almost shone with excitement. "She was looking at floral arrangements for the centerpieces. Apparently everyone up this end of Long Island is invited, and when I told her Vicki was staying she insisted that she come with Sinclair. Oh, it will be sensational. I wish I was feeling strong enough to come. I remember the party they gave to celebrate their son's graduation— an entire Russian ballet company performed and there were a hundred black swans swimming on that big lake behind their conservatory. Vicki will need something *fabulous* to wear."

Annie disappeared back into the kitchen, carrying the dishes from the main course of swordfish steaks with spinach sautéed in sesame oil. She did feel a little like Cinderella right now. Everyone would be going to the ball, and it wouldn't even cross their minds that she might be sad about not being invited.

She returned with freshly made peach pie and a jug of thick cream.

"We'll have to go into the city. A trip to Madison Avenue is definitely in order." Katherine looked like she was ready to leap out of her chair and hail a cab right now.

"I'm not so sure." Vicki looked oddly hesitant. "I probably have something I can wear."

"But darling, this is the perfect occasion for a big splurge. I saw this amazing purple dress at Fendi when I was in visiting my doctor. It would look so striking with your complexion."

"Oh, I don't know. Sinclair, are you going to buy yourself a shiny new dinner jacket?"

"God, no." Katherine spoke for him. "He'd wear antiques from his father's closet if I let him. I'll make sure he looks presentable." She flashed him an indulgent smile, which he ignored.

"You've given me an idea." Vicki paused, cream jug in her hand. "Well, maybe it's crazy."

"What?" Katherine leaned forward.

"Those dresses you found up in the attic, before I arrived. Maybe I could wear one of those."

Annie froze in the doorway where she stood with a tray of brandy snaps. Her heart crumpled at the thought of Vicki swanning through the house wearing that peacock-blue dress that had totally deprived Sinclair of his sanity.

"What a marvelous idea. If they don't fit we could always get one altered. But you're so slim you could wear anything and look good. They're all hanging in the spare bedroom downstairs, for reasons beyond my comprehension. There's a blue one in there that's stunning. It looks like Thai silk, with a glorious shimmer."

Annie glanced at Sinclair, who picked up his wineglass and took a gulp of the white wine.

She slunk back into the kitchen. This must be some kind of lesson in humility. Now she'd have to see Vicki wearing the dress to a party the way its maker must have intended. Her donning it, even for a few minutes, was a foolish mistake that continued to have humiliating repercussions.

"Let's go look at them now, before dessert." Katherine rose from her chair. "It'll be fun. Annie, do come with us. You can help us move them somewhere more sensible."

She wanted to make some excuse about needing to decant the ice cream but her brain wasn't fast enough.

"Okay." She followed mutely as they walked down the hallway to the spare bedroom with its big walnut wardrobe.

"What a lovely shade of lavender." Katherine pulled a hanger from the rack. A pale, almost snowy, lavender dress billowed on the hanger. The wrinkles from years of packing seemed to have fallen out of it, leaving it ready to wear. Delicate black beading around the neckline and sleeves added a touch of drama. "Who were these made for, I wonder? The quality is so exquisite."

Sinclair stood in the doorway, almost filling the frame. His dark blue polo shirt stretched across his broad chest as he leaned against the doorjamb. He looked indulgently at his mother. "Probably someone who died before she had a chance to wear them. It was a different world back then. People died almost overnight from things that barely warrant a doctor's visit today."

Annie was touched by how much he obviously cared about his mom. He'd all but abandoned his work and thrown himself into keeping her happy and entertained since her illness began. If she didn't already admire Sinclair, she would now.

"You're so right. Still, it might be interesting to find out. I wonder if she was a Drummond by birth, or someone who married into the family." She pulled out a gray-green dress with a dramatic dark red trim. "It was obviously someone rather fashionable."

"I've done some research, actually." Vicki moved forward. "The trunk the dresses were stored in had the maker's name on it, from Lyme, Connecticut."

Annie snuck a glance at Sinclair while everyone listened to Vicki. His eyes looked slightly shadowed, tired—or haunted. How she'd love to get him to relax for a while. He never seemed to be able to relax when there were other people in the house. He was quite a different person on the rare weekends he came out here by himself.

When it was just him and her.

Though of course he didn't think of it like that. He probably thought of it as being there alone, since she served a similar function as the anonymous mailman, or the gardener who pruned the bushes and trimmed the lawn.

"Ran away with the groom! You're joking." Katherine's shriek dragged Annie back to the present. "I didn't think anyone did that outside of mournful ballads. I bet she lived to regret it."

"Well." Vicki rearranged her artfully casual bun. "The man she was supposed to marry, Temperance Drummond, tried to have the groom arrested for theft."

"Of his fiancée?" Sinclair raised a brow.

"Of his horse and cart. The groom was part of her personal staff from Connecticut, but he absconded with the master's soon-to-be lady in the Drummonds' carriage."

"Did they find her?" Katherine looked fascinated.

"Nope. At least there's no record of it that I could find. They disappeared into thin air in 1863 and were never seen again. Or at least not around here." She turned to Sinclair with a raised brow. "What do you think happened to them? Did they travel out west, join a wagon train and get rich in the gold rush in California?"

"Who knows? Maybe they did." Sinclair looked thoughtful. "Though I doubt it."

"What about you, Annie? Do you think they enjoyed decades of happy marriage?"

She shrugged. Vicki's attention was always uncomfortable. She was too much of a loose cannon.

"Do you think people from different social circles can live happily ever after?"

Annie shrank. Worse yet, her gaze darted involuntarily toward Sinclair, and met his. A jolt of energy shocked her. She groped for a response in the hope that no one would see how flustered she was. "I don't see why not. If they have the right things in common."

"I'm not so sure." Sinclair's mother fingered the black trim on the lavender dress. "I think one tends to have more shared interests with someone from one's own circles. Sinclair's father has been gone a long time and I've never had the slightest interest in dating the gardener." She laughed as if the very idea was comical. Which it was. The gardener was a taut and muscular woman of about twenty-five. "Though I do admire her abs when she wears those cutoff tops."

They all laughed. Annie was glad that the moment of tension had been defused. "They're lovely dresses. It's a shame she didn't take them with her."

"I know. Odd, really. They were part of her trousseau. It was all up there in the attic, packed for her honeymoon. They were going to be married three days later. I found the whole story online in the transcribed memoir of the old biddy who lived next door." Vicki turned to Sinclair. "You should read it. She has a lot to say about your ancestors. Temperance married five times and his wives kept disappearing."

Katherine shuddered slightly. "The curse. Or whatever it is. The Drummonds can never find happiness. But we're going to change all that, so Sinclair can find happiness." She beamed a smile at him.

Sinclair grimaced, now resting his elbows above his head on either side of the door frame, which provided an eye-popping view of his powerful muscles against the sleeves of his shirt. Annie dragged her tormented gaze in the other direction.

"I'll make sure he finds happiness at the dance, at least." Vicki fingered another dress, a frothy pink taffeta with seed pearls encrusting the bodice. "I won't try these on now, though. Another time. I'm pretty sure at least one will fit fine with no alteration."

"Let's go have coffee," said Sinclair gruffly.

Annie was glad to get away from the spectacle of Vicki handling the dresses. She shouldn't think of them as *her* dresses, because they weren't, but she'd felt proprietary about them ever since she'd tried that one on and been so entranced by it. It was even less encouraging to learn they'd belonged to some long-ago woman whose life had gone off the rails. How likely was a woman to find happiness by running away in a stolen carriage?

She'd never find out. She wasn't nearly daring enough for that kind of high-risk endeavor. That's why she'd be watching other people's exploits over the rim of her teacup rather than living on the edge.

"You're going to that party, Annie." Vicki's whisper sliced into her ear as the taller woman slid past her in the hallway.

"What?" Annie froze. But Vicki had already disappeared into the living room with Katherine and was talking about something else.

Six

"But I can't." Annie faced Katherine and Vicki over the pile of fresh peas she'd been shelling for Katherine's dinner. It was 5:00 p.m. and Vicki should have been getting dressed for the dance.

"Let me guess, you have nothing to wear." Vicki crossed her arms over her chest.

"Not just that. I'm not invited, and I don't…" She hesitated, not really wanting to say it out loud.

"Don't belong there?" asked Katherine, with perfect accuracy. "Nonsense. It's a party, and it's huge. Over five hundred people. Sinclair can't go alone because it's a couples theme and they have all these silly activities planned."

Annie's eyes widened. Romantic activities? Was Sinclair's mom actually trying to set her up with him?

"Of course you and Sinclair won't do anything romantic." She laughed at such an outlandish idea. Well, that answered one question. "But I'm sure you'll have a good time. I know he'll refuse to go if he isn't required to escort anyone, and why shouldn't Cinderella go to the ball for a change?" She laughed again, obviously delighted with the idea Vicki had planted in her mind. She turned to Vicki. "Do you need more aspirin, dear?"

"Probably. Maybe I should just take the whole bottle." Vicki had been complaining of a headache since mid-afternoon. "Then again, when I get these headaches no medicine even helps. I'm out of business for the rest of the day."

"Poor thing. Why don't you go lie down?"

"Oh, no," Vicki said quickly, then held her head. "Helping make Annie gorgeous will take my mind off the pain." She flashed a smile at Annie that made an entirely different kind of pain shoot through her. Why was Vicki trying so hard to humiliate her?

"I really don't think it's a good idea." Annie wished she could put her foot down. Surely attending a big, fancy party couldn't possibly be described as part of a housekeeper's duties. "I'm sure Sinclair would rather go alone."

She knew that part was true. He wanted to pretend he'd never kissed her. Never made crazy, unexpected love to her and breathed hot moans in her ear. Bitter disappointment trickled through her—again.

"Nonsense. And you'll enjoy it, Annie. It'll be the party of the summer. They're probably spending two million on it. Think of it as an experience, rather like an adventure vacation. Now, we need to find you a dress. I think I have a loose-fitting Zang Toi that's a bit big for me..."

"We won't need that." Vicki put a proprietary arm

around Annie, who shrank from her. "She can wear one of the dresses from the abandoned trousseau."

Katherine looked doubtfully at Annie's waist, which she instinctively sucked in. "I'm not sure those will fit."

"I suspect Annie's a lot trimmer than her usual attire would have us believe. Let's go have a look." Vicki marched purposefully down the corridor, with Katherine in hot pursuit, leaving Annie no choice but to slouch after them.

She couldn't even begin to imagine the look she'd see on Sinclair's face when they paraded her in front of him wearing one of the dresses that had already caused so much trouble. He'd be appalled. He'd probably think it was her idea. Some crude scheme to ensnare him.

Maybe he'd point-blank refuse to go.

"I think the silvery gray one will look lovely against her complexion."

Did silvery gray look good against beetroot? Annie avoided looking in the large mirror on the front of the wardrobe. Vicki held up the long dress with its low-cut princess neckline and huge skirt.

"Of course, they would have worn it with a crinoline and loads of extra petticoats, but we'll spare you that. Especially since we don't have any. We'll wait outside while you put it on."

Annie was grateful for the slight nod to her modesty. She climbed out of her familiar shirt and khakis with a sinking feeling. If this didn't fit, they'd only make her try on another. Worst-case scenario, she'd end up in the peacock dress she'd worn already, with them wondering why it looked so crumpled.

The dress was quite heavy, with built-in boning at the waist and yards of expensive silk. The short, puffy sleeves hugged her arms quite tightly, but there was no way she could do up the long line of buttons down the back by herself. "Um…"

"Need help?" Vicki was right outside the door. She opened it without an invitation. "Oh, yes."

Annie felt hot and flustered under their rather stunned gazes. "I must look very silly."

"Nonsense. You look lovely." Katherine frowned. "What are we going to do with her hair?" Her eyes raked over Annie like she was a mannequin.

"Got to be an updo." Vicki squinted at her. "I have some pins and hairspray in my room. And some earrings."

They buttoned her into the dress, which fit almost perfectly. The original owner must have been quite chunky by Victorian standards, if this fit her corseted waist. The bodice hugged Annie's cleavage in an embarrassing but flattering way, especially after Katherine convinced her to abandon her bra. Vicki fussed over her hair, creating tiny finger coils that framed her temples, and Katherine lent her a pair of pewter ballet flats.

"Won't I be overdressed?" The silk skirt fell to the floor.

"A lady can never be overdressed." Katherine eyed her with approval. "Especially not when she looks fabulous. Goodness, I'd never have guessed you had such a lovely figure. You should show it off more."

Great. Now they'd probably get her a French maid's uniform to wear while performing her duties.

"Maybe we'd better make sure Sinclair looks presentable." Vicki glanced toward the door.

"Oh, don't worry about him. He always looks good.

Horribly unfair. I don't know how he stays so tanned, either. He always seems to have his face in his laptop."

"I suspect Sinclair of having a secret life." Vicki snuck a wink at Annie, who pretended not to notice.

"Where he's out lying in the sun?"

"Or running along the beach with the wind in his hair." Vicki laughed. "I have a feeling most people only see a tiny part of the real Sinclair."

"Hmm." Katherine looked doubtful. "Well, as long as the other parts are going to give me a grandchild before I get too old and decrepit, that's fine. He doesn't know he's going with Annie instead yet, does he?"

"I haven't breathed a word. I think we should stay out of the way until the last minute, then surprise him with her." Annie cringed, but had long given up trying to shape the evening's events. All she could do now was brace herself.

Three hours later, the sound of Sinclair's tread on the stairs made her gut clench into a fist. He'd been in his room almost since lunch, supposedly working. He hadn't heard about Vicki's supposed headache. Or that he was about to see his housekeeper dressed like some sacrificial virgin—except without the virgin part.

"Come, stand here. I can't wait to see his face." Vicki prodded her into position in the alcove between the living room and the front hallway. Annie wished she could warn him somehow. What look would they all see on his face? Horror, quite likely. Then maybe disgust.

"Sinclair, darling, do come into the living room for a cocktail before you go." His mom winked at Annie.

"Is Vicki ready?" His world-weary tone carried

through the house along with the sound of his footfalls on the old oak boards.

"Not exactly." Vicki crossed her arms and looked smug. She held a finger over her lips. Annie wished she could dive behind the sofa. Her heart rate increased as Sinclair's movements grew closer. By the time he reached the door, her heart was pounding so hard she worried the whalebone stays in her bodice might burst and release her braless breasts just in time for his entrance.

"Come in, Sinclair." She heard his mom from outside the room.

"Why's everyone acting so strange?" His deep voice sent a ripple of anticipation—richly mingled with dread—right through her.

He rounded the corner and looked up, at her. Frozen to the spot and unable to think at all, let alone utter a word, she watched his reaction. Astonishment, sure. Disbelief. Her face heated as he took in her hair, her earrings, the subtle makeup Vicki had painstakingly applied. Then his gaze dropped lower, almost imperceptibly grazing her cleavage and the nipped-in waistline of the dress. Her breasts swelled against the snug neckline, responding to the desire that flashed in his eyes. Or was that alarm?

"Annie, you look stunning." His compliment sounded cool and composed, as if he'd expected to see her standing there dressed for the party.

"Vicki isn't well," she rushed to explain. "And they didn't think you'd go if you were alone, so they insisted that I…" She wanted to let him know this wasn't her idea.

"Vicki's loss is my gain."

His expression was unreadable. She reminded herself it was simply a polite response, something he might say to a friend of his mother's. No doubt he didn't want to betray his horror to the others or they'd suspect there was some reason he felt uncomfortable going with her. Beyond the obvious reason that she was supposed to be waxing the furniture, not waltzing with the boss.

"It seemed such a shame to waste the invitation." Katherine picked a speck of imaginary lint from his spotless tux. "And why shouldn't Annie get to have some fun for a change? You will make sure she has a good time, won't you?"

"Of course." He didn't take his eyes off Annie. "It would be my pleasure."

There was an oddly flat tone to his voice.

I'm sorry. She tried to say it with her eyes. He must be appalled at the prospect of spending the evening with her. Maybe he thought she'd try to rekindle the flame of lust that had singed them both so badly.

"Why don't we all have a gin and tonic?" Vicki moved toward the drinks cabinet.

"No, thanks." Sinclair and Annie said it in unison. A moment of awkward silence turned into a nervous laugh. "We should get going," said Sinclair. He probably wanted to get out of there and get this whole charade over with as quickly as possible.

Annie gathered her impressive skirts. Hopefully she wouldn't trip over them and fall flat on her face. She headed for the side door, through the kitchen, but Katherine pulled open the formal front door they rarely used. "This way tonight. You look far too elegant to sneak out the side door." She now had to negotiate the rather uneven brick steps, and an equally hazardous slate walkway, and was almost breaking a sweat by the time they reached the driveway. Sinclair's black BMW gleamed golden in the low rays of sunlight sneaking through the tall hedges. She walked toward it until she realized there was a silver Bentley sitting a little farther up the drive.

"We're being driven to the event." He spoke coolly. "Mom is always very cautious about drinking and driving."

A uniformed driver emerged and held open one of the rear doors. Annie's spirits sank when she realized they wouldn't be alone even long enough for her to plead innocence in this whole caper. She managed to climb in, pulling her long skirt behind her and arranging it around her legs.

Sinclair entered on the other side and sat next to her. The rear seat was spacious enough to leave room for another person between them, but the space quickly filled with tension.

The driver climbed into his seat and started the engine, then started to speak with a heavy Brooklyn accent. "I'll be waiting there for you tonight, so you can leave any time you want. Sounds like quite the party, from the talk at the depot. Everyone wants a limo tonight. We could have rented this one three times over." Annie pictured people scrambling to rent fabulous limousines before the town ran dry of them. Who knew such problems existed?

Sinclair glanced sideways at her. Probably wondering why she was there instead of Vicki.

"Vicki complained of a headache since lunch." She felt the need to explain in a way that wouldn't reveal the whole situation to the rather chatty driver. "She seemed really keen for me to come."

"She's never had so much as a hangnail in all the years I've known her." He met her gaze. Her breath hitched at the warmth in his dark eyes. "I suspect she has an ulterior motive."

"I was wondering about that." She fingered the beading at her waistline. "It was all her idea."

"Doesn't surprise me in the least."

Annie hesitated. It was hard to be secretive and frank at the same time. But she did wonder if Sinclair had laughingly told Vicki about their...misadventure. "I didn't say anything to her at all, about, you know."

He frowned for a moment. "Of course you didn't." She waited for him to say that he'd also kept quiet. "She probably has her own agenda. Maybe she's trying to avoid someone who'll be there."

Annie nodded. "Could be." She couldn't figure Vicki out at all, but if she'd teased her about liking Sinclair, she wouldn't be surprised if she'd done the same to him.

Apparently he wasn't going to reveal anything either way.

He looked breathtakingly handsome in his tux. The crisp, white shirt collar emphasized the hard, bronzed lines of his chin and cheekbones. She'd have loved to drink in the vision of him but had to make do with surreptitious glances.

She risked another sneak peak, enjoying the set of his broad shoulders against the luxurious leather seat of the car. "Your mom looks better every day."

"Yes, thank God. She really does seem to be on the mend. The doctors said it will be months before she's fully recovered, though. Her liver and kidneys shut down and her immune system almost gave up. She's very lucky to be here. This whole thing with the cup is keeping her at home, too, which is good. Normally she's traveling all over the world, which the doctors told her not to do until her immune system is up to speed. I'm sure that's the only reason she's not in Scotland storming the baronial halls of that particular Drummond."

Annie laughed. "I can't believe how much stuff is in that one attic. It could take a lifetime to go through it." She glanced at the driver. Maybe it wasn't wise to reveal their treasure trove to a total stranger.

"That's good. It will keep Mom safely in Dog Harbor longer." His wry smile sent a flash of warmth to her heart. He settled his broad hand on the soft seat and for a second she imagined it resting on her thigh, only inches away, hidden beneath the dress's layer of silk.

"It's downright strange how well that dress fits you. Almost like it was made for you."

"Weird, huh? The original owner would have worn all kinds of undergarments to get it this shape. I just have a narrow waist." She shrugged. "It seems wrong to wear something that's really an antique. It must ruin the fabric. But Vicki kept saying that clothes are for wearing, not storing in boxes. And she is an antiques dealer so I suppose she knows what she's talking about." At least she wasn't trying to steal them and sell them on eBay.

"I agree. And maybe it was made for you, if the unseen powers of the universe that my mother's grown so fond of are really at work." His dark gaze sent a shiver of strange emotion though her. Did those same mysterious forces throw them into each others' arms? Maybe they were meant to be together and Vicki was a cleverly disguised fairy godmother who'd conjured her into this finery so she could go to the ball with her prince.

Which meant this Bentley might turn into a pumpkin at midnight.

"What are you laughing at?"

"I don't know. Trying to dissolve the tension." She snuck a glance at the driver, wondering if he was a rat transformed into a man by the wave of a magic wand. She didn't want him to know she wasn't supposed to be here. For all he knew, she was some heiress, out on a date with wealthy bachelor Sinclair Drummond.

How was he going to introduce her to people? *This is Annie Sullivan, my housekeeper* probably wouldn't go over too well. *This is my old friend Annie? Let me introduce you to the love of my life?* Another stray giggle bubbled in her chest.

Being so close to him made her giddy. Her skirt poufed out until it was resting on the leg of his black pants, caressing his thigh. Her fingers longed to do the same. He looked so relaxed and at ease. Maybe he was happy to be here with her? Maybe he'd secretly orchestrated the whole thing, with Vicki as his accomplice, so he could take her to the ball as his date without alarming his still-weak mom?

One look at his somber face in profile, staring out the window, purged that thought from her mind. He'd probably rather be anywhere than here, with her. He hadn't even responded to her comment about dissolving tension, perhaps preferring a sturdy barrier of angst between them to easy intimacy. She had to stay focused on getting through this evening with a minimum of humiliation and hurt, and that meant keeping her emotions firmly under wraps.

They arrived at the beachfront mansion in less than ten minutes, and the Bentley pulled into the circular driveway in a line of cars depositing their occupants in front of a large stone house. Artfully placed lighting lit up the night and sparkled off the elegant gowns and pearly smiles of the glamorous people around them. The driver helped Annie out of the car and she thanked him.

Sinclair rounded the car and took her arm in his. The increased closeness made her feel panicky. What if she couldn't resist the urge to throw her arms around his neck and kiss him? Experience had already proven she could go completely mad in his presence.

"Don't be nervous. They're all just human under the crazy outfits." Sinclair's rough whisper in her ear startled her, then made her chuckle. How sweet of him to try to relax her.

"I may well have the craziest outfit here." Her big, pale dress stood out amongst a lot of sleek dark gowns.

Sinclair stopped and looked at her for a moment as if contemplating whether this was true. More cars pulled in and guests swirled around them. "You're the most stunning woman here, and you look unbelievably beautiful in that dress."

The murmur of conversations and the purr of expensive engines faded into silence as his words took over her brain. Had he really said that, or had she imagined it? His dark eyes rested on hers for a second longer, stealing the last of her breath. For a second she thought she might fall down unconscious.

"Sinclair, darling!" Reality sucked her back into its jaws as a very tall blonde woman threw her arms around Sinclair. They bumped into Annie, almost knocking her to the ground. "And my husband was worried you wouldn't come. I knew you'd grace us with your austere and magnificent presence." She kissed him on both cheeks. Annie simply stared.

"And who is this damsel on your arm this evening?" The blonde peered at Annie with large, blue eyes.

"I'm pleased to be escorting the lovely Annie Sullivan."

"A pleasure to make your acquaintance, Miss Sullivan." The hostess shook her hand firmly. "You look familiar. Have we met before?"

Annie hesitated. She'd likely served this woman finger sandwiches or taken her coat for hanging. But she couldn't tell. These very rich, emaciated blonde women all looked alike after a while. "Perhaps."

"Do head around to the tent and enjoy some drinks. Henry's madcap festivities will be starting soon but we need everyone a little tipsy first."

"Happy anniversary, Jessica." Sinclair smiled. Then he took Annie's arm again and led her along a path lit with glowing lanterns toward the rear of the house. Strains of music floated on the air, mingling with the tinkle of polite laughter. "She's an old friend of my mom's," Sinclair murmured, once they were out of earshot.

"Thanks for not introducing me as your housekeeper. Though I don't know why that would be embarrassing, since it is my job after all."

"You're not here as my housekeeper. You're here as my date." He gave her a stern look. She wasn't sure whether to take it seriously. Was this a date with the Annie who'd writhed on the spare bed with him, or the one who was under orders to pretend it had never happened? His arm linked with hers felt proprietary, like he was taking charge of the situation, which was fine with her. She never felt Sinclair would try to take advantage of her.

What a shame.

A waiter swept toward them with a tray of champagne glasses. Sinclair took one and handed it to her. The glass was cold against her hand, in sharp contrast to her hot skin. People swirled around them on the large terrace. Hanging lanterns illuminated the night enough for them to make each other out, but the garden beyond was cloaked in velvety darkness. The unknown. A band, tucked away somewhere, launched into a swingy jazz number that made the very air throb with anticipation.

She took the tiniest sip of her champagne, and the bubbles tickled her tongue. Sinclair took a manlier drink from his glass. Muted light played across his hard features. His eyes glittered, dark and unreadable, as they rested on her face.

"I've never seen a woman look more radiant, Annie." He spoke plainly, with no hint of joking or exaggeration.

Her bodice suddenly felt tight as her chest swelled. "I don't think I've seen a man look more handsome." She tried to laugh off his comment with an offhand one of her own.

But Sinclair didn't even seem to notice what she said. He frowned. "Why do you hide your beauty?"

"I don't hide anything. You see me every day, or at least when you're out at the house. I'm hardly wearing a mask. That's the real me. This is the one that Vicki decorated for the party."

He took a sip of his champagne. "You're right, of course. And in fact, I think you're even more beautiful when you're not dressed up like a visiting princess." His words sank in and her breath stuck in her throat.

"It's refreshing to see someone who isn't afraid to be her natural self and not try to enhance something that's already lovely."

She blinked. "I'm sure the folks at L.L. Bean will be glad to hear that." She managed a smile. "I bet they'd hate to hear I was abandoning my familiar khakis and Oxford shirts for vintage prom dresses."

"Then I'm with them. I like the authentic Annie."

"Your mom didn't think I'd fit in these dresses. I think the general consensus is that my usual look makes me appear shapeless."

"I heartily disagree, but on the other hand it does leave something to the imagination." A tiny smile crossed his mouth. "And some surprises to discover."

Was he flirting with her? It certainly felt like flirting, not that she had much experience to rely on.

"I think you've discovered most of my surprises." There, she'd said it. She'd been burning to bring up that afternoon. There was no way she could get through this night pretending it had never happened.

"I doubt that very much." His gaze lingered on hers for a moment, heating her blood. "In fact I feel confident that I only scratched the surface."

The silence thickened with the suggestion that he'd like to return for another journey of discovery. Annie sucked in a breath, which wasn't easy in her tight bodice. She'd certainly be up for a voyage into the dark and mysterious lands of Sinclair, but only if it wasn't another accident. She wasn't sure she could handle trying to pretend something like that never happened again.

On the other hand, if it was mutually desired, and mutually agreed upon…

She sipped her champagne and the bubbles tickled

the tip of her tongue again. "What kind of activities do they have planned for tonight?"

"Are you nervous?" Humor shone in his eyes.

"A little. Especially since they want us half-cocked before we start. That sounds rather dangerous."

"I promise I'll protect you." He raised his glass and sipped, looking at her steadily over the rim.

A sense of clear and present danger swelled in the air. "It's entirely possible that you're exactly what I need protecting from. After all, we didn't need too much encouragement that one time."

His gaze darkened slightly. "True. Tonight I'll be a gentleman if it kills me."

"Shame." She said it boldly, not wanting him to think she wasn't interested. She'd already gone out on a limb, so why not keep going until it snapped? Maybe the champagne was making her reckless.

A smile played around his eyes, crinkling the skin in that way she found so adorable. "If you don't want me to be a gentleman, I'm sure that can also be arranged."

"Good. I think I'd prefer a dashing rake." Now she was flirting.

"Is that so? In that case, let's top off your champagne so I can more easily take advantage of you." He gestured to a passing waiter, who readily obliged. How had she drunk more than half a glass already?

"Sinclair, how did you sneak past me? I've been lying in wait for you all night." A tall brunette materialized out of the night air and breathed in his ear. "Your mother told me you're in town for the summer. I do hope you'll have time to come out on my new yacht."

"Dara, this is Annie, Annie, Dara." Annie thrust out a hand so that at least one of them couldn't be accused of rudeness. Dara had barely glanced at her. Now she reluctantly gave her a limp handshake. At least Annie didn't recognize her from any social events at the house. "I'm going to be very busy this summer. Annie has me all tied up." He spoke with a straight face, but a hint of suggestion in his voice.

Dara's mouth opened like a fish. "Really." She took a longer look at Annie. "Well, if you change your mind." She flounced off, looking distinctly irritated.

"That was fun." Sinclair sipped his champagne and surveyed her with narrowed eyes.

"You're naughty."

"And enjoying it. Let's dance."

It wasn't a question. His sudden, sturdy grip around her waist swept her toward a wooden dance floor set up under an elegant canopy on the lawn. They moved through a crowd of laughing, chatting people, and handed their glasses to one of the many waiters before climbing onto the dance floor just as a song was ending. The band was a big jazz ensemble with a stunning singer. "Oh, my God, is that Natalie Cole?"

"Probably."

Laughing, Annie let him pull her into his arms as the singer started into a sultry number about a broken heart. He wound one hand firmly around her and took her hand with the other, and pulled her into a dance. Her feet followed his effortlessly, as if she already knew the steps. The thundering drumbeat and mellow pulse of the saxophone flowed through her, drawing her around the dance floor as if she did this every day. She could feel the smile glowing on her face as Sinclair twirled her through the crowds, her long dress flying out around her. His gaze stayed fixed on hers the whole time, capturing her attention and daring her to look away.

Her breaths came faster and faster as the pace of the song picked up and they swept across the floor with bold dance steps. Sinclair's muscular hands guided her, making her feel pliable and athletic, almost fluid, moving in time to the music.

The singer launched into an impassioned plea to her lover, begging him to come back and make her whole. Annie let herself ride on the wave of emotion her voice created among the dancers. Her heart seemed to pound in time with the bold blasts from the trumpet as the song rose to a crescendo and Sinclair held her tighter against his chest.

Their faces grew closer, gazes still locked in a mute challenge. He was taller than her, but if he leaned down he could kiss her right on the lips.

Her mouth started to quiver in anticipation. Surely he couldn't tantalize her like this and not kiss her? Her entire body felt alive with desire for him, her nipples pressing relentlessly against the tight bodice of her dress. The song ended with a sudden flourish and she waited in an agony of excitement for his lips to touch hers.

Seven

But they didn't.

He pulled back from her, shoved a hand through his hair and glanced across the dance floor. Annie stood there stunned. The flowing motion had ceased so abruptly that she felt like a fish suddenly thrown up on dry sand, wondering what happened. Blinking, she stepped back, trying to regain her composure. She bumped into someone and had to turn and apologize. When she turned back, Sinclair was staring into the distance with a face like honed granite.

"What is it?" She had to say something, if only to reassure herself that she still had the power of speech.

"Nothing." He frowned. "Let's go get some air."

It was hard to imagine that they weren't getting air already, since they were outdoors. As they walked across the lawn, fresh glasses of champagne in their hands, Annie realized that the "lake" was actually Long

Island Sound, stretching out before them in a gleaming
sheet, with the full moon glowing on its surface like an
oversized silver Christmas ornament.

"Do you think they booked this moon along with
the band?"

"Quite likely." He looked out over the water. "Whatever they paid, it was worth the money." He sipped his
champagne, silent for a moment. He looked anything
but relaxed. The buildup to their non-kiss had tightened all her muscles and sent blood flowing to places
she wasn't usually aware of. She was on edge and fired
up with anticipation that had no place to go, and he
looked the same.

Should she tell him she didn't regret their wild afternoon in bed? Right now she didn't. It had awakened
her to a new sensual side of herself.

"What is your ambition in life, Annie?" He turned
to her suddenly, fixing her with the full force of his
dark gaze.

Was this some kind of test? If she answered wrong
would his estimation of her plummet even lower? "To
own my own home." She answered with the simple
truth. It was a small dream, and an old-fashioned one,
but it had guided her decisions ever since she'd left
home at age twenty-one.

"Why don't you buy one?" He frowned slightly.

She laughed. "They cost money."

"You earn a good salary."

"Yes, living in *your* home and taking care of it. If I
moved I'd be out of a job."

"So your job in my house is preventing you from
fulfilling your dream?"

"Not at all. I'm saving the money so that when I'm

ready I can buy it. I'm not nearly there yet, in case you're worried about your floors going unpolished." She meant it as a joke, but it came out almost scolding. "It's just something I've always wanted. I grew up in a big house filled with people. My grandmother's house." Her Connecticut was very different from the one Sinclair had lived in with his ex-wife Muffy. There were no shady lawns or million-dollar mansions on her street, in one of the grimmer parts of the old industrial city. "My parents and sister still live there. It's like a trap or something. My sister moved away when she got married and had a child, but now she's divorced and back there again. My dad's been on disability for decades and just watches TV all day. He could work if he wanted to, but he'd rather just sit around. My mom, on the other hand, works all day and night just to get out of the house." She raised a brow. "That's probably what I'd be doing, too, if I was still there. I want to have my own space where I can do what I like."

"And that's your only goal?" Apparently that wasn't enough for Sinclair Drummond. Which was hardly surprising, given all he'd already achieved in his own life.

"I'm thinking more about my career. I'm planning to take evening classes and learn about running a business. I'd like to be self-employed eventually. Maybe even own a shop. Being a housekeeper isn't a highly transferrable career in this day and age." She smiled.

"I suppose it's not easy to find someone with more houses than they have need of." He looked as if he was going to smile, but he didn't. If anything he looked pained. Perhaps he'd been hoping she'd prove herself worthy of him with a grand ambition. He must be cruelly disappointed by her simple aspirations.

"What's your dream?" She'd never have dared to ask him if they weren't here tonight, in the silver-edged darkness.

Sinclair hesitated for a moment. Frowned. "I don't know anymore. I used to want a family life, children, all that, but now I know that's not for me."

"How do you know that? You've never tried." Her indignation made her sound abrupt.

"To have a family you have to be married, and my two efforts in that direction have demonstrated that I'm not a suitable husband."

"Maybe they weren't suitable wives." She cocked her chin.

"Not for me, apparently." He looked out over Long Island Sound. "I won't make that same mistake again."

"That seems a real shame. You're far too young to swear off relationships. Besides, you can easily afford a few more divorces." Her joke was meant to defuse the tension, but the haunted look he gave her only ratcheted it higher. "Not that you'd ever have another, of course."

"I guarantee that I won't. Since I have no intention of getting married again." He drained his champagne glass and stared out over the dark water. "You should marry."

"What? Why?" His odd statement shocked her. The idea that he even had any thoughts on the subject made her uneasy.

"You're nurturing and thoughtful. You'd be a good mother. Someone would be very lucky to have you as a partner." He glanced at her, then looked away again, as if something on the black-velvet horizon held his attention.

"You make me sound rather dull. Not the kind of

person who goes to elegant dances wearing a vintage dress." She teased him. He was right, of course.

"Not at all, because quite obviously you are the kind of person who lights up the night at an occasion like this." His gaze swept quietly over her, stirring a flurry of arousal. His eyes lingered on her lips, which twitched involuntarily, still hungry for the kiss they never got.

She really needed to distract herself from wanting to kiss him. Although her body thought it was a good idea, her mind knew better. It would only make her life more complicated. After all, he'd made it clear he didn't want a relationship with her—or anyone—so where could it lead?

Still, why did he have to have such a sensual mouth? His lips were quite full, with a graceful arch on the top, in tantalizing contrast to the masculine jut of his cheekbones and jaw, and the aristocratic profile of his nose. Frankly, his lips begged to be kissed.

And having kissed him once, she knew just how soft and yet how firm they'd be as she pressed her lips against them.

"So, why don't you want to marry again?" That line of questioning should kill any hint of romance.

He raised a brow. "Isn't it obvious?"

"Because your marriages failed? I'd imagine that would be off-putting, but it didn't stop Elizabeth Taylor." She smiled. "I bet if you found the right person you'd get it right this time."

I could be that right person.

Her brain spat out the thought entirely against her will. She spat it right back. She was trying to crush her romantic aspirations toward Sinclair, not stoke them.

"Maybe you need to figure out exactly what went

wrong. Did you ever do that?" She was pretty darn curious, for sure.

"It's easy. We wanted different things. My first wife, Muffy..." He hesitated.

Of course she was called Muffy. She probably wore pink twinsets with little whales embroidered on them.

"We were together all through college and did everything together. We got married the summer after graduation, and both of our families were thrilled. We bought a lovely house in Connecticut and I thought we'd live happily ever after. Then she decided she wanted to pursue a doctorate in modern languages at Yale, then she wanted to become a professor, then she wanted to take a position at a university in Peru, and by that point we'd realized we were two different people on entirely different courses and we went our separate ways. She teaches at a university in Argentina. It seemed like she changed into a completely different person after I married her."

"You never considered moving away with her?"

"No. I have my life here, my business. I don't want to spend my time traveling around the world." He looked out over the Sound. "I decided right then that I'd never get serious about someone who's just starting out in life and has no idea what they want yet. One of the things I liked about Diana was that she had her own established PR business and had built a full life for herself. I was pretty confident she wasn't going to throw it all away and move to Tibet to join a monastery." He smiled wryly. "And that was where our problems started."

"She joined a monastery?" Annie's eyes widened.

"No. Her life was so full that there was no room for me and my life in it. I didn't want to fly around

the country each weekend going to weddings and parties and visiting friends and clients. If I didn't do those
things, I didn't see my wife. Still, I was determined to
make it work so I let her do her thing while I did mine."
He frowned. "I started to believe that was how successful marriages worked. I didn't have a very good example to follow. My parents led almost entirely separate
lives during my childhood. That's one of the reasons
we have several houses." He sighed. "But Diana found
someone else."

"Oh." She knew that already. Her infidelity had been
the grounds for the divorce. "I'm sorry."

"So, you see, I'm too inflexible. I wasn't willing to
live their lives and they weren't willing to live mine.
Maybe I should just get a dog?" He raised an eyebrow,
and humor sparkled in his eyes.

"I don't know. That's a big commitment. All that
walking. And what if you want to go to the beach and
he wants to go to the park?" She giggled. There was
something strangely intimate in Sinclair trusting her
with the story of his failed relationships. She felt closer
to him than ever before.

"You're right. And I travel a lot."

"You'd have to get your housekeeper to walk it." She
tilted her head. "Housekeepers can handle that kind of
responsibility."

"Sounds like I need a housekeeper more than I need
a wife."

"Lucky thing you already have one." She sipped her
champagne. "And apparently she's a housekeeper with
benefits." She raised a brow.

Sinclair's shocked expression made her regret her
little jibe. Then his face softened and the look he gave

her made her stomach do a somersault. "Which proves, I suppose, that just having a housekeeper isn't enough." His voice was gruff, rich with all the emotion he kept buried beneath his chiseled and polished surface.

"You're a unique individual." She tried to look arch, like the heroine in a regency novel. Though she wasn't really sure what arch looked like so she probably didn't pull it off. "You need a very special housekeeper." Clearly she was tipsy. Or the dress had once again unleashed a part of her that dared to do things the usual Annie wouldn't dream of.

"What are you two doing all the way over here?" A voice beckoned to them across the lawn. "Come back to civilization for some oysters."

"Oysters." Sinclair laughed. "Just what we need."

"Aren't they supposed to be an aphrodisiac?"

"Exactly. Do you and I really need an aphrodisiac?" His gaze lingered on her face long enough to heat her skin.

No. We don't need one. Desire flashed between them like electric current, and he'd just admitted he could feel it. "I've never tried oysters."

"Never? Then let's go fix that terrible omission." He held his arm out for her to take it. A gesture that was formal but breathtakingly intimate at the same time. When she slid her arm through his, she could swear she felt the heat of him through his elegant suit, though maybe she imagined it. She was so overstimulated by his presence that she couldn't trust her senses anymore. She knew that a muscled body, capable of passion and abandon no one here would have expected, lay beneath his formal attire. Did anyone here imagine what had gone on between them?

Couples strolled on the lawn and the terrace, arm in arm like them, laughing. Everyone seemed to be paired up, but that was the theme of the party. Caterers in black-and-white uniforms moved among them, brandishing silver platters piled high with oyster shells. Tables for two had sprung up all over the lawn like mushrooms after a rain, each set with two delicate patterned plates and oyster forks. A bucket of fresh champagne stood beside each table, and chairs decorated with ribbons beckoned each couple to sit. Sinclair pulled out a chair for her and she arranged her wide skirt around her legs.

Three sauce bowls, each with a tiny spoon, sat in the middle of the table, next to a dish of lemon wedges. Sinclair poured them each a flute of champagne. The opened oysters glowed intriguingly in the moonlight in their mother-of-pearl-lined shells. He picked up a shell and spooned one of the sauces onto it. "Open your mouth."

She obeyed, her stomach clenching slightly, either because of the strange food or the prospect of Sinclair feeding it to her—or both. He tipped the shell toward her mouth and she gently sucked. The cool, oceany taste of the oyster met with a pleasantly sharp explosion of picante sauce on her tongue.

"Swallow."

She swallowed, blinking at the strange sensation of the smooth oyster sliding down her throat. "That was different."

Sinclair smiled. "Now you feed me one."

"My duties as a housekeeper keep expanding in strange directions." She glanced flirtatiously at him. She wasn't sure why she kept reminding him—and herself—that he was her employer, but somehow it seemed preferable to having them both forget again. It made whatever romance they did share feel more...real.

"You're not here as my housekeeper." Sinclair obviously didn't find comfort in her words. "But feed me an oyster anyway." His voice contained a hint of suggestion that made her skin tingle with awareness. She reached for the plate and took one of the pearly shells. She surveyed the sauces. One looked tomatoey, like a cocktail sauce. One was thinner and a little darker, probably hot sauce. The other had herbs floating in it— garlic? She decided to go classic and squeezed a spritz of lemon onto the fish, then held it out. Sinclair's lips struggled with a slight smile as he opened them for her to tip the contents of the shell into his mouth. Her fingers trembled but she managed to hold it steady as he slurped the oyster gracefully into his mouth and swallowed it. "Delicious."

The satisfied look on his face suggested that it wasn't only their appetizer that he spoke about. Some strange place way below her belly button shimmied in response. Was this the aphrodisiac effect of the oysters?

"Your turn." Their champagne sat untouched as he fed her another oyster, then she fed him. Then he caught hold of her fingers that proffered the shell and kissed them, sending sparks of arousal dancing up her arm.

"You're glowing tonight." He spoke softly, serious.

"Like the oyster shells." She said the first thing that came to mind. His compliment shocked and embarrassed her.

Those adorable smile crinkles showed around his eyes. "In most of the women I know, modesty sounds like they're fishing for compliments. In you it's far more annoying because I suspect you really mean it." He kissed her fingertips again before letting them go.

"No one growing up in my family could suffer from a swelled head for long."

He leaned forward. "I don't know anything about your family, except that you need to buy your own house so you don't have to live with them anymore."

She laughed. "They're not that bad. Just loud and bossy and funny. They're nice, really, except Granny when she's in one of her moods. She's the dictator of the family and what she says, goes."

"Partly because she owns the house everyone lives in."

"Exactly." She smiled. "You have personal experience with how that works."

"I don't have moods," he protested. His eyes glittered with amusement.

"Not often, anyway," she teased. "But if you did I'd have to put up with them, wouldn't I?"

"Definitely not. I don't encourage people to slink about like mute sheep. I wouldn't have much of a business if everyone yessed me to death."

"I suppose you're right." She had tiptoed around him for a long time. Maybe that's why he hadn't seemed to notice her before. Judging from his past wives, he was attracted to rather strong-minded women—even if he couldn't actually stay married to them. "I'll make a point of being more assertive. Then again, I'm not sure I need to be, since I do everything my way and you all seem to be happy anyway."

A smile crept across his mouth. "Sounds like the ideal state of affairs. Obviously your way is perfect."

He tilted his head slightly, and held her gaze with those relentless dark eyes. "For me, anyway."

Annie's chest tightened inside her elegant gown. This sounded like some kind of major declaration. Or was it simply dinner-party chatter? She didn't have enough experience to tell the difference. And Sinclair's eyes were having a very unsettling effect on her.

He lifted both of their glasses and handed one to her. "To perfection. Long may it reign in castle Drummond." She smiled and clinked her glass against his. The champagne contrasted pleasurably with the smooth saltiness of the oyster.

"Castle Drummond. I like that. The house doesn't have a name, does it?"

"We've always called it Dog Harbor, after the town. It should, though. Anything that's hung in there for three hundred years should have a name."

"Especially if it's built of wood. I can't believe those ceiling beams in the attic. That house was built to stand the test of time. Do you think part of that old cup is really up there somewhere?"

He shrugged. "Could well be. It has no value or function that would encourage anyone to sell it over the years, so unless it was thrown away at some point, it's probably in there somewhere."

He fed her another oyster, and she shivered slightly as the cool, liquidy flesh slid down her throat. The tender look in his eyes made the gesture seem almost protective. *Don't get carried away! This is just one night.*

It was hard not to, though. She picked up another oyster and fed it to him. He held her gaze as he pulled it into his mouth, and a corresponding flash of awareness lit up her secret places. Energy was gathering here, swirling around them, drawing them closer together.

A waiter arrived at the table with an empty wine bottle and a broad smile. Annie and Sinclair both looked at him curiously. Then he pulled out two leaves of delicate paper and two golden pencils. "You are hereby invited to write a message to each other. Preferably something you'd never dare say out loud. You may share the message before you place it in the bottle—or not. All the bottles will be released into the ocean to travel around the world and take your messages to each other with them."

Annie blinked. What would she never dare say out loud?

I'm crazy about you.

He probably knew that anyway.

Sinclair was frowning at his piece of paper. He glanced up at her with an odd look in his eyes. "Let's write something and not show each other."

"Okay." Anxiety fluttered in her stomach. What if he said they wouldn't look, then at the last minute they had to because of some party game? She picked up her pencil and chewed it thoughtfully. "At least they're not making us write rhyming couplets."

"True, though that might be fun." He paused for a moment, then started writing, looking intently at his paper.

She couldn't read the words, partly because a single candle on the table was their only light beyond the moon, and partly because his writing was worse than most doctors'. She turned to the blank square that sat mockingly on the table. A quick glance revealed that other guests at the tables around them were writing or even already squeezing their rolled-up papers into the neck of the bottle. "What if it ends up in the Great Pacific Plastic Patch?"

"What if it ends up in the hands of a lonely castaway on a remote Pacific island and gives him the strength to survive another month?"

"You apparently have a more romantic imagination than me." She snuck a glance at him. He'd rolled his paper into a thin cylinder, held between his thumb and finger. "And now I'm really curious about what you wrote."

He smiled mysteriously. "Maybe one day I'll tell you." His gaze lingered on her face for a moment, making heat rise under her skin.

Sinclair, I think you're a very handsome and thoughtful man who deserves to live happily ever after (preferably with me). She wrote the last part so tiny there was no way anyone could read it. *P.S. I love you.*

She rolled the message up fast and shoved it into the neck of the bottle before anyone could pry it from her fingers and make her read it aloud. Her hands trembled with the power of writing exactly what she wanted to, and not settling for saying the sensible thing. If it came back to haunt her someday, so what? Right now she was living a dream, if only for a night.

Did she really love him? She had no idea. Lack of experience again. She'd certainly never admired and adored a man as much as she did Sinclair. And a simple glance in her direction from him made her palms sweat. If that wasn't love it was something pretty close.

Sinclair pushed his message into the bottle and jammed in the cork their hosts had provided.

The waiter appeared again, and asked them to follow him. Annie rose from her chair, gathered her skirts, and she and Sinclair joined the other couples now walking across the broad sweep of lawn toward the Sound.

The moon cast an ethereal silver glow over the landscape. The lawn was a lush carpet underfoot and the slim beach at the shoreline glittered like crushed diamonds. Protected from the Atlantic by Long Island, the waveless water shimmered like a pool of mercury. Behind them the house resembled a fairy palace, its many windows lit and lanterns festooning the terraces.

As they grew closer she could see rowboats, almost like Venetian gondolas, lined up along a long, wooden dock. They bobbed slightly on the calm water. Attendants dressed in black brocade helped each couple into their own personal boat and gave the oars to the men, before pointing to a small, tree-cloaked island far out in the water.

"We're supposed to row out there in the dark?" Each gondola had a lantern, hung from a curlicue of wrought iron, at its stern.

"It'll be an adventure." Sinclair's low voice stirred something inside her. He took her hand, his skin warm and rough against hers. Her pulse quickened as they walked along the dock, amid laughs and shouts of mock distress from the other boaters. Sinclair and the staff helped her into the boat and seated her on a surprisingly comfortable plush seat, while Sinclair took up his place at the oar locks.

"Do stop at Peacock Island for refreshments." An elegantly attired man gestured toward the clump of trees dotted with lanterns, barely visible in the black night.

Sinclair pulled away from the dock with powerful

strokes, soon overtaking even the first boat to leave, and heading out into the quiet darkness of the sound.

Yet another bottle of champagne, beaded with tiny droplets of condensation, sat in a silver bucket at the prow of the boat. Annie resolved to keep her hands off it. Too much champagne might make her do something she would regret.

"The island is that way," she said, as he rowed swiftly past it, their wake lapping toward its shores.

"I know. I'm taking us somewhere else."

Eight

Sinclair enjoyed the pull of the oars in the heavy water. It felt good to move his muscles. The tension building between Annie and him all evening was beginning to tip from pleasurable to punishing.

Annie looked out over the side of the boat, staring at the long ribbon of the shore. The cool moonlight played across her features. He loved her face. She had a freshness about her that always caught his eye. Bright eyes, her mouth so quick to smile, that adorable nose with its faint sprinkling of freckles. Even in her extravagant gown and evening makeup she looked innocent and unworldly.

Was that what attracted him? Perhaps he was so jaded and tired of the world's movers and shakers that her quiet beauty and sweetness became irresistible.

Then there was her body. The voluminous skirt did nothing to hide his memory of her gorgeous, shapely legs…wrapped around his waist. The fitted bodice cupped her small, full breasts in a way that made his blood pump faster. Her gold-tinged hair was swept up into a knot, with a few strands escaping to play about her cheeks and momentarily hide her pretty blue eyes.

Was it really a good idea to take her to a private dock, away from the prying eyes of strangers? Probably not.

But he pulled away at the oars, as sure of his destination as he'd ever been.

"It's so quiet out here. I love it." Her voice drifted toward him, then she turned, all sparkling eyes and lush, full lips. "It's nice being away from the lights on the shore. We can see the stars." She looked up, and the moon glazed her face with its loving light.

Sinclair looked up, too, and almost startled at the bright mantle of stars—hundreds of them, millions—filling the dark sky above them. "I don't think I've looked up at the stars in years."

She laughed, a heartwarming sound. "And they've been up there all the time, shining away, waiting for you to remember them."

"I guess I've forgotten a lot of things. They say you get wiser as you get older, but I'm not so sure."

"We're not at the age where you get wiser yet. You have to go through other stages first, like the ones where you dream too big, then have your hopes crushed and get scared."

"What are you scared of?" She seemed so self-contained, in her neat domestic world, it was hard to imagine her being afraid of anything.

She shrugged, then hugged herself for a second. "Life not working out the way I hope it will. I think we're both in the phase of life where you start to realize it's now or never for a lot of things."

"You sound like my mom. She thinks if I don't have children this calendar year the Drummonds will vanish from the face of the earth and we'll both grow old and wizened alone together."

"I guess that's what she's scared of. I don't suppose you ever grow wise enough to stop worrying about some things. What are you afraid of?"

She fixed her steady blue gaze on him, expecting nothing less than the truth.

"Failure." He responded with honesty. "For all my success in business, I haven't succeeded where it matters most."

She looked at him, her eyes filled with understanding. "You want to have a family, and you're worried you never will."

"At this point I'm pretty sure I never will." She was so easy to talk to. He didn't feel the need to put on an impenetrable facade with her. "I've already tried twice and I know when to admit failure. If my marriage prospects were a publicly traded company I'd be dumping the stock." A smile crept to his mouth, despite his dismal confession. "Wouldn't you?"

"No." She hesitated, and a smile danced in her eyes. "But I'd be looking at how to enhance my business strategy for an increased chance of success. Perhaps a new approach to management, with more carefully selected principals."

He laughed. "You mean I need better taste in women."

She shrugged. Moonlight sparkled off her smooth skin. "Worth a try, at least."

Was Annie the right woman for him? The question hung in the still night air. No doubt she was wondering the same. No one sensible would recommend that a man of his background and position look for love with an "uneducated housekeeper"—but Annie was so much more than the sum of those two dismal words. What she lacked in formal education she'd obviously made up for with reading widely and observing closely. His previous marriages had proved that choosing a highly educated and ambitious mate was not necessarily a recipe for success.

"Where are we headed?"

Her question startled him. "I don't know. I only know that I enjoy your company immensely. And I think you're the sweetest, most beautiful woman I've ever met."

She stared for a moment, than laughed softly. "I appreciate your frank answer, but I meant, where are we rowing to? The lights from the party are totally out of sight."

"Don't worry. I know the Sound like the back of my hand. Rather better, in fact. Who really knows the back of their hand, anyway?" He smiled mysteriously.

"You still haven't answered my question." She tried to look stern, but a smile tugged at her lips. "Some people would be very nervous about being sailed off with in the dark with no idea where they're going."

"Are you nervous?"

"A little."

He wanted to reach out and reassure her, but couldn't take his hands off the oars. "We're going to the private dock of a friend of mine. I keep a boat there, in fact. It's just around this next headland." He gestured out into the darkness. You couldn't see anything now but dark, shimmering water and the broad cloak of stars over their heads, but he knew the curve of the coast like the face of an old friend.

At last the wooded shore beckoned, and he steered the boat into the familiar sheltered cove, where broad stone steps joined the water to the vast lawn of his friend's Victorian summer house. The house itself was shrouded in darkness, but moonlight illuminated the stone terraces with their sheltered seating areas. He docked the boat and tied it to one of the big, cast iron mooring rings. Annie giggled as he helped her to her feet so she could make a bold leap out of the boat, with her skirts gathered in one hand.

She glanced around. "I feel like we've landed at the Taj Mahal."

"I think that's what the architect intended. My friend's great-great-grandfather imported tea from India and wanted to recreate the pavilions of Assam here on Long Island." He led her through a stone archway to a row of cushioned seats that lined one side of the terrace.

"This should be more comfortable than the boat." He helped her sit down on the plush cushions. An ornately painted pavilion sheltered them from the moonlight, which filtered through the trees around them.

"I'm slightly worried that you brought me here to take advantage of me." She raised a slim brow.

"I brought you here so we could be alone together. That doesn't seem to be possible even in my own house right now."

"I think it's sweet the way you're taking care of your mom. They always say you can tell everything you need to know about a man by the way he treats his mother."

"Then maybe I'm not quite so dastardly as legend would have you believe."

She paused and looked at him. "I already know you're kind and thoughtful."

He laughed. "Maybe not as much as you think. It's possible that you have good reason to be worried for your virtue. Any man would be hard-pressed to resist the temptation of being alone in the dark with you."

In the privacy of the pavilion he let his hungry gaze roam over her, drinking in her soft skin, her gentle eyes, her lush, full mouth. Even her throat looked beautiful, and he fought the urge to kiss the curve of her neck, which sloped down to her pert, high breasts encased so enticingly in the silvery silk.

"As a woman, I have to admit I'm fighting my primal instincts to keep my hands off you, too." A mischievous smile danced in her eyes. "You look very hot in a tux."

He chuckled. "I can't encourage you to fight your instincts. I'm sure it's far healthier to indulge them."

"So you think I should give in to the urge to loosen your tie and collar?"

"I'm not sure if that's a good idea." A slow smile crept across his mouth. "But there's only one way to find out."

His muscles tightened as she reached up and tugged at one side of his silk bow tie. He could smell the subtle scent of her skin. He loved that she never wore perfume, and why would she? Her natural aroma was as intoxicating as the finest fragrance.

Her fingertips brushed his skin as she unbuttoned his collar, and sent a shiver of rich desire rolling through him. This really wasn't a good idea. He'd regretted sleeping with her the first time. It felt fantastic while they were writhing around on the bed together, but only moments later he was gripped by an agony of regret.

Why?

Right now he couldn't think of one good reason why he shouldn't be intimate with Annie Sullivan. They were both mature adults and in charge of their own destiny. He wasn't forcing her into anything. She seemed to be enjoying this as much as he was, if her dazzled expression was anything to go by.

And if he could gauge her desire by the way her mouth was moving slowly, but inexorably toward his...

Their lips met in a slow collision, like two thunderstorms meeting out over the ocean. Rain and hail and lightning exploded inside him at the touch of her skin to his. His hands flew out and gripped her with force, holding her close as he'd ached to for days.

Her hot breath on his skin set his senses on fire. Her fingers reached into his hair, down his neck, over his shirt, moving with fevered anxiety echoed in his own body. Before he could stop himself he'd undone some of the buttons on the back of her dress and slid his fingers inside. Instead of historical corsetry they met smooth, bare skin.

"Are you naked under this dress?"

"Maybe." He could hear the smile in her voice. "You'll have to explore to find out."

Her invitation tantalized him and worked like fresh oxygen on the flames of desire ripping through him. Undoing the buttons had loosened the shaped bodice, which softened its grip on her breasts.

Annie wasn't shy about undressing him. She pushed his jacket off and unbuttoned his shirt with an intent concentration that made him want to laugh. "You must be hot after all that rowing," she murmured as an excuse. The way she licked her lips, as if anticipating a treat, suggested a more delicious ulterior motive.

Already he was hard as the stone piers on the dock. The heat flushing his skin had more to do with anticipation than exertion. Having cracked open Annie's demure shell once—or did he simply peel it away?—he knew that a sensual and passionate woman lay beneath her quiet and compliant exterior.

She tugged his shirt from his pants with a flourish and pulled it off, exposing his chest and arms to the balmy night air. "Doesn't that feel better?"

"It does." He kissed her gently. "Especially because now I can do this." He pulled her closer, until her breasts spilled against the muscle of his chest, her taut nipples grazing his skin and shifting his arousal into high gear.

Their kiss deepened as they pressed against each other, skin to skin, surrounded by the whisper of trees and the gentle lapping of the water against the dock. For the first time in months—no, the second time—Sinclair felt a sense of peace and contentment well up inside him. Right here, right now, everything was perfect. Their kiss tasted like honey and fruit and champagne, tantalizing his taste buds and every other part of him.

Why did he feel this way with only Annie? He couldn't remember enjoying the company of a woman so much. Was it pure sexual attraction?

He didn't think so. There was something more substantial about the pleasure he felt in her company, but he couldn't put his finger on what it was.

He pulled back from their kiss, letting the night air cool his mouth before lowering it to her breasts. Her skin glowed in the silver moonlight, making her look like an ancient statue in a tempting state of undress. He licked her nipples, and enjoyed the little murmur of pleasure that escaped her lips. Her fingers roamed over the muscles of his back and arms, sparking little rivers of sensation that flowed through his body, and increasing the pressure building inside him like water behind a dam.

When Annie's hands slid inside the waistband of his pants he flinched, responding powerfully to the increased sensation. "I want to make love to you." It sounded so old-fashioned the way he said it, but he couldn't think of a better way to express his desires or intentions.

"And I want you to make love to me." She breathed it in his ear, hot and sultry. "Again."

His eyes slid closed as memories of their first encounter met and mingled with the sensations and emotions of the present. He fumbled with the last of the buttons on her dress and it fell and pooled around her feet before she stepped out of it, wearing nothing but a delicate pair of flesh-toned panties. She looked totally unselfconscious, a glorious, timeless study in feminine beauty, standing on the hand-hewn limestone of the terrace. The moon dressed her in light and shadow that emphasized the full curve of her breasts and the sweet pear shape of her behind. He could sit and stare at her for an hour.

But, growing impatient, and with a glint in her eye, she slid his belt out of the buckle and soon he was also naked in the moonlight.

"Are you sure we're alone here?" She glanced suddenly over her shoulder, into the dark woods on the edge of the lawn.

"There's probably a crowd of admirers in the trees." He let his fingers skate over the curve of her waist.

"You're kidding." Her eyes widened.

"But they'll keep our secrets. They have other things to do, like feather their nests, and bury their acorns in the tree trunks."

Her look of alarm mellowed into a smile. Then her expression grew more serious. "Is this going to be another secret?"

Her gaze hinted at a well of sadness beneath her lovely exterior. Guilt stabbed him for the way he'd pushed her aside after their surprise encounter. He'd been shocked at his own behavior. He was barely even divorced and already he'd pulled another woman into his bed. His emotions had been jolted out of the deep freeze and he didn't know how he felt about anything. His first and only impulse had been to run and keep on running.

But all that running had led him right back here into Annie's welcoming arms. "Only if you want it to be."

She looked at him, her eyes clear and bright. "I don't like secrets."

"Me, either. Usually they make me worry about the SEC and insider trading accusations." He watched the smile creep back onto her face. "But in this case it just seems unnecessary. We're adults."

"There's no arguing with that." She surveyed his body with a mischievous twinkle in her eye. "You're certainly all man."

His arousal pulsed stronger. His hands rested at her waist, and he pulled her gently to him and kissed her lips. "And you're all woman." He sighed as he ran his hands over the sweet curve of her backside. His erection pressed gently against the soft skin of her stomach, and throbbed with anticipation at finding an even more inviting and intimate hiding place.

Annie spread herself out on the elegant fabric, sheltered from the stars by an elaborate canopy. Her body looked like an invitation to sin, of the most enjoyable kind. Right now he must be the luckiest man alive.

Then a dark thought crossed his mind. "Now is probably not the ideal time to mention this, but I don't have a condom."

"Better now than afterwards." She simply smiled and shifted herself into an even more delectable pose. "But don't worry. I still have it covered."

Thank heaven. He wasn't sure if even a bracing plunge in Long Island Sound could take the edge off his current state of erotic tension. "That doesn't surprise me, since you're always prepared for everything."

He climbed over her on the wide, cushioned sofa, sinking against her warm skin and drinking in her subtle fragrance. Her arms wrapped around his back, holding him close as she layered kisses over his face. He sighed at the luxurious sensation of her body in his arms, and the ever growing ache inside him so close to being soothed.

Being with Annie felt utterly different from any encounter in his life before and he really had no idea why. Naturally a thinker, he'd usually be able to puzzle it out, but right now he didn't want to think at all. It was enough to just feel—in his body and in his heart.

He entered her slowly, kissing her inviting mouth. They moved together in a hypnotic rhythm, her soft sighs music that made his heart fill with joy. He loved the sensation of her hands on his body, even her nails digging into his flesh as the fever of their passion gripped her.

Lithe and agile, she moved with him on the lush, upholstered sofa. Astride him, she took him to new heights of agonized pleasure. Just when he thought he couldn't stand another second without exploding, she pulled back, a sly smile on her face, and shifted so that he was on top of her again.

He managed to roll over without losing his safe place deep inside her. Every inch of his body, every muscle and corpuscle, throbbed with intensity. Half of him wanted to climax and end the delicious agony, the other half wanted it to continue forever. To keep them both suspended in a blissful half-life of sensual pleasure.

Would they both regret this in the morning, when the champagne would wear off and the silver moonlight be replaced by blinding rays of harsh sun?

"I won't regret this."

Her rasped words startled him. She'd spoken as if she could read his thoughts. "I won't, either."

"Whatever happens next, we'll always have this moment." With her legs wrapped around his waist and her arms tight around his neck, Annie held him with force. The heat of her arousal, compounded with his own, threatened to make sparks in the air. "And I won't forget it."

A threat or a promise, her words drove him those last few miles out into the realm where worldly cares and concerns evaporated and there was nothing but right now. They shared a climax so forceful it almost threw them onto the stone terrace, and he had to brace with his arms to keep them on the cushions.

Panting, gasping and holding on for dear life, they

floated back down to earth together, chests heaving against each other.

"Why does that feel so good?" Annie's question, after a long silence, made him laugh.

"Because if it didn't there wouldn't be any people on earth. If having sex was like brushing your teeth people wouldn't bother."

"You don't brush your teeth?" Her eyes sparkled with both passion and humor.

"I'm the kind of person who does stuff out of a sense of duty."

"I like that about you."

"I can tell. You're the same. I bet you never go to bed without brushing your teeth."

"Am I that easy to read?" She pouted, or tried to, despite the smile tugging at her mouth.

"Yes, you're an open book."

Her smile faded slightly and a thoughtful look darkened her gaze. "Am I really? Did you know all along that I've…had a thing for you?"

He didn't know that. It hadn't crossed his mind that she felt that way about him. She'd simply been an excellent employee to him. How did you say that without sounding rude? "Something rendered me blind to your charms until our trip up to the attic. I don't know why, because you've been the same ravishing beauty—cunningly disguised by L.L. Bean—haunting my house for years."

She frowned slightly. "How odd that the trip up to the attic changed everything."

"My mom would say it's fate. Something mystical is happening." He spoke in a deliberately mysterious tone.

Annie glanced around, still holding tight to his body.

"I kind of feel that way, too. I'm not sure I would have ever dared to do…something like this before."

"Have hot, wild sex on a stranger's patio?"

"Pretty much. And with my boss, too. In fact I can't believe we're lying here naked under the moon."

"I know. There's a chill in the air." He pretended to hold her closer, like a blanket.

"Is there? I can't feel it. But then I'm glowing all over, thanks to you."

She *was* glowing. Her eyes, her skin, her whole spirit radiated joy, good health and happiness. And he had the power to increase or destroy that happiness.

A dark shadow crept across his heart. He didn't know how to keep a woman happy. He could make it past the wedding, past the honeymoon, and then, somehow, it all fell apart.

But maybe, with Annie, it could be different.

He jolted upright. Was he seriously thinking about embarking on another relationship so soon after the disastrous failure of his second marriage? And if he wasn't, what the heck was he doing here with this beautiful and sweet woman naked in his arms?

"What's the matter?" The concern in her voice wrung his soul.

"I'm not naturally suited to living in the present."

She stroked his cheek. Her serious expression didn't mock his doubts and worries. She seemed to silently accept them. "I usually live in the future. I go through the motions in the present, rinsing lettuce and making beds, but my mind and spirit are way ahead in 'one day' land."

He frowned. He was good at living on the edge and going with the flow in business, but his personal life was a whole other story. "I suspect I tend to lag behind in 'if only' territory."

"Then there's obviously no hope for us, is there?" She spoke brightly, but there was an undercurrent of sadness to her tone.

"Either that, or we'll have to save each other and only live in the present from now on." A fresh flame of hope—or was it simply desire—roared through him, and he took her mouth in a fierce kiss. She kissed him back hard, gripping him as if sheer strength and determination could hold them here, at least for a few moments longer.

When their lips finally parted he felt breathless and light-headed.

"I hate to live in the future as usual, but we'd better get back to the party before it ends or our driver will wonder what happened to us." Annie's soft voice tugged him back to the present.

"You're right." He stretched, easing against Annie's warm body. "Though it pains me to put clothes back on when I feel so comfortable without them."

"I like putting my dress back on. I never know what's going to happen when I put on one of the dresses from that trunk."

"Or maybe you do know what's going to happen now. There's a definite theme." He traced the line of her jaw with his thumb. Her lip quivered as he drew close. "Involving me taking the dresses off."

They put their clothes on and climbed—gingerly—into the boat. The journey back to the party seemed so much quicker than the trip out, maybe because of the way the current was flowing. Or maybe because he hated to see their evening together end. He had an unsettling feeling that everything would be different once they got back to the mundane world of other people and their cares.

Annie sat at the prow of the boat, looking out over the dark water, which was choppy now, rippled with undercurrents and invisible forces that broke up its formerly smooth surface.

"What's that?" She looked up suddenly at a bright light in the sky, rising like a comet behind the dark shadows of the woodland along the shore.

"It's a Chinese lantern. They're popular at parties now. You light the wick inside and the paper lantern floats up, and drifts in the sky until it finally burns up."

As they rounded the last bend in the river, the sky seemed to fill with lanterns, drifting higher and floating out into the night.

"They're beautiful." Annie watched, mesmerized. "But they seem so dangerous. They could touch down somewhere and start a fire."

The water all around them did nothing to cool the fire burning in his heart. This time was going to be different. His tryst with Annie would turn into a real relationship, and they'd figure out how to live together in a way that didn't cramp each other's style and threaten to turn them into different people. Maybe they'd even marry and have a family.

Sinclair drew in a deep, hard breath. He was getting carried away. Better just to pull on the oars and keep going, and let the future take care of itself.

"Do I look okay?" Annie turned to him as they drew nearer to the shore, fingers tucking her hair back into its bun.

"You look ravishing." She was even more beautiful

with the final polish gone from her dress and makeup. More natural and sexy. "I hope no one will realize that I've been ravishing you this whole time."

She gave him a seductive smile. "That will be our secret. I don't think anyone ever needs to know we were such rude guests." She gasped. "We never even went to the island!"

"Never mind. We'll tell them we got lost."

In a way, that was how he felt. He'd wandered off the usual course of his life, got lost in Annie, and found himself in a wondrous new land of possibilities.

"I can't wait to get lost again."

"Me, either." But he frowned. He couldn't shed the nagging doubt that this wild and perfect evening might be his last taste of paradise on earth.

You don't know how to live. His second wife's words echoed in his brain. *You're always worrying about your duties and responsibilities. You have no idea how to have fun.* She'd have been horrified to leave the "fun" of the party for the secret world of the waterfront pavilion. He suddenly wanted to laugh at the realization that he'd come to this party out of obligation. Much like the stupid croquet game he'd played to humor his mom and help her recovery. And she'd thrust Annie on him in her borrowed finery, knowing his sense of duty would make him take her to the party.

Sometimes a sense of duty could be a beautiful thing.

When they got home, Annie immediately crept back to her bedroom like one of the twelve dancing princesses. If this affair with Sinclair was about to turn into a real relationship, then everyone would know about it sooner or later, but four in the morning was not the best time to declare their newfound passion.

She frowned. Why did the princesses in the fairy tale have to be so secretive and sneak off to their princes every night? Why couldn't they just marry them and live happily ever after? She didn't remember ever seeing a good explanation for that in the story. Maybe they weren't princesses at all, but housekeepers who had to get up early and scrub the floors before dawn, and who'd be in trouble if anyone found out they were skimping on sleep while wearing out their shoes.

Sinclair had made the evening so perfect. From the moment he'd been surprised with her as his partner for the evening, he'd been romantic, charming and adorable. He'd treated her like a princess and made her fall even more hopelessly in love with him.

When they stepped out of their accustomed roles, he was so easy to talk to, and so much more interesting than the men she'd been on dates with. He seemed to know at least a little about everything under the sun, which allowed her to stretch her own mind. She tried her best to fill in the gaps in her education by devouring books and magazines on every subject, and it was fun to realize that he'd acquired a lot of his knowledge the same way. Maybe they weren't so different after all?

Annie smiled as she read a message she found on her pillow: *Don't you dare get up until noon!* Katherine Drummond had signed it *Kate* in an intimate flourish. She set the piece of monogrammed notepaper on the nightstand with a sigh and slid beneath her covers. Sinclair unleashed something absolutely wild inside her, and filled her with hope for a future she'd never dared to reach for. Would they tell everyone tomorrow at breakfast? Would he pledge his undying love for her in front of his mom and Vicki over her handmade omelets?

She couldn't help a strange, nagging feeling that something entirely different would happen.

Nine

Annie came very close to obeying the command in Katherine's note. Though she'd set her alarm for seven, she had no recollection of switching it off when she finally woke again near eleven-thirty.

She sat upright. Had she really made love with Sinclair again last night? It grew hard to separate dreams from reality lately. Or nightmares. What kind of crazy person slept with her boss for no good reason other than that he was gorgeous and she couldn't resist him?

The champagne was at least partly to blame, but what happened to her self-control when she was alone with him? She groaned. She could remember word for word the intimate and romantic conversations they'd had afterward, but now their sentiments seemed fanciful. The kind of thing that sounds perfectly reasonable by moonlight but silly in the cold light of day.

I won't regret this. She'd said it then, and believed it

completely. But now, as she lowered her feet onto the cold wood floor and pondered how he'd react when he saw her, she wasn't so sure.

She showered and dressed, wondering what everyone had eaten for breakfast. At least now she could busy herself with lunch and stay hidden in the kitchen for a while. Heart thudding, she let herself out of her room and walked quickly down the corridor.

"Back in your khakis already." Vicki's voice made her jump. She turned to see Vicki marching along the hall behind her brandishing a newspaper. "What would the editors at *Women's Wear Daily* think?"

"I doubt they'd have any thoughts on the subject." She tried to sound casual yet polite, and it came out sounding forced. *Women's Wear Daily* was just one of several papers that filled the mailbox since Vicki's arrival.

"Ah, but that's where you're wrong." Vicki swept past her into the kitchen and spread the paper out on the kitchen island.

Annie froze at the sight of a double-page spread with three huge pictures of her at the dance last night. "What?" She squinted at them. The headline jumped out at her. "Mystery Woman in Mystery Dress." "Why would they print this?"

"Because you had everyone talking last night." She crossed her arms and looked triumphant. "And apparently you and Sinclair missed dinner."

Dinner? She hadn't even noticed that they never ate it. They went right from oysters to... She could see how the aphrodisiac rumors got started.

"This being the fashion press, they're even more

curious about who designed your gown than who was in it."

"Whoever designed it is long dead." Annie moved closer, increasingly fascinated by the pictures. One showed her dancing with Sinclair, his arms around her waist and her skirt in a whirl that showed how big the skirt was, even without a crinoline. Another showed them walking across the terrace. Then there was a three-quarter picture showing Sinclair with his arm around her waist, which seemed poured into the fitted gown.

"They don't know that. They're thinking it's by the next Balenciaga." She laughed loudly. "This is the most fun I've had in months!"

"Where's Sinclair?" She said it softly. Had he seen these pictures that boldly proclaimed their romantic liaison to the world?

"He's been on the phone most of the morning. Work, I suppose. He's such a stick-in-the-mud. But it looks like you shook him loose last night. He's almost radiant in that last picture."

Annie's breath caught as she saw the expression on his face. A close-up of them dancing, her dress floating out behind her and her arms on his shoulders. And an expression of…rapture on his handsome face.

"We had a really good time." She said it so quietly that it sounded eerie, like an apology.

"I can see that." Vicki grabbed a glass from a shelf and filled it with iced water from the dispenser on the fridge. "Exactly as I intended."

"You faked the headache, didn't you?"

She laughed. "I'm a martyr to them, and don't you tell anyone otherwise. You needed to go to that ball, young lady. I *had* a ball waving my magic wand over you, and look how well it turned out." She beamed with such obvious good cheer that Annie almost began to like her. "And this won't be the last of it. I bet you're on Page Six as well. You'll be the talk of all New York."

Annie blinked. How would Sinclair react to all this? Like the old-school aristocrat he was, he seemed skilled at avoiding publicity, despite his illustrious career and many high-profile friends. She'd searched online for him more than once, when he hadn't visited the house in a while and she just felt like seeing his face. A few photos from parties and a corporate portrait were all she found. She didn't imagine he'd be happy to see these pictures plastered all over the papers.

Especially once they figured out that the woman in his arms was his own housekeeper. "Sinclair is going to be upset."

"Who cares? He needs to live a little. And I think the two of you make an adorable couple." She tapped the picture of them dancing. "Tell me that isn't romantic."

Annie's heart squeezed at the image of herself and Sinclair, staring intently at each other as they whirled around the dance floor as if no one else existed and the music was being played only for them. Last night they had found their own little world together, and inhabited it so fully they forgot about the consequences.

"I hope he won't be embarrassed." She chewed her nail absently for a moment, then pulled her hand back. "I think we both got carried away by the atmosphere of the evening."

"Good. Sinclair needs to get carried away more often. I'll make sure his mom and I are out late tonight." She gave Annie a knowing look and swept out of the room, leaving the pages open on the island. Annie quickly closed the paper and tucked it out of sight in the pantry. She didn't want anyone—especially Sinclair—to come in and think she'd been gloating over it.

Heavy footfalls on the stairs made her hands shake as she shredded chicken into a salad. Given that Katherine and Vicki were both built and moved like gazelles, it could be only one person. Heart bumping, she quickly dried her hands and tucked a stray lock of hair into her bun.

Last night had been so magical, so breathtaking. It was a dream come true in every sense of the word, and even the pictures in the paper had captured that. Would electricity jump between them as he entered the room? She felt her temperature rise, and started to take off her light sweater when he entered the doorway. How should she greet him? With a cheery hello? Maybe even a kiss…?

His expression stopped her cold. The angles of his chiseled face looked harder than she'd ever seen them. He filled the door frame, all broad shoulders and hard planes. His onyx gaze met hers with the force of a blow.

She swallowed. Her romantic fantasies shriveled up and went to hide under the island. "I had a really nice time last night." She was going to say how she felt, damn it, and not let mystery and suspense rule the air. She wasn't going to let him sweep their fantasy evening under the rug this time. If nothing else, they'd at least talk about it. "But I'm guessing you don't feel the same."

He shoved a hand through his hair. It looked as if he'd done that a few times already. "Annie." He came into the kitchen and closed the door. Which could have been an intimate gesture, but his tense physique and stony expression made it unsettling instead. He hesitated, as if searching his brain for what to say.

"Don't tell me to forget last night happened. I won't do it again." She heard the tone of desperation in her own voice. "I can't." She gripped her sweater in her fist, digging her nails into the fabric.

"Last night was…" His broad brow furrowed. "It was wonderful." He met her gaze, and the pain in his dark eyes rooted her to the spot.

"Then why do you look so unhappy?" Part of her wanted to rush to him and throw her arms around him. The other, more experienced and sensible part, wanted to wrap her arms around herself and shield her heart from whatever was coming.

"Something's happened."

"Is it your mom?" Panic rushed her. She hadn't seen Katherine yet, and had just assumed she was up and out of the house already. "What's wrong?"

"Not my mom." His frown deepened. "My ex-wife, Diana."

She blinked. He hadn't even spoken to her in months, as far as she knew. They'd had an acrimonious divorce, with lawyers and angry words, despite the short duration of their marriage. "Is she ill?"

"No." He inhaled and blew it out. "She's pregnant."

"Oh." The word fell from Annie's lips as her heart sank a full inch in her chest. "And it's yours." Why else would it be such a big deal?

"Yes. She's due to give birth any day now. She said she didn't want to tell me, since our marriage was ending, but now that she's drawing close to delivery she felt the need to tell the truth."

Or the need to apply for child support. Annie kept

her unkind thought to herself. But she couldn't help saying another. "Hasn't she been involved with some-one else?" The gossip was that his wife had cheated on him. She didn't know the whole story. "Couldn't it be the other man's baby?" She braced herself for Sinclair's reaction. It wasn't a kind thing to suggest.

"I just spoke to her on the phone. She swears the story was just an excuse for the divorce, and that the baby is mine."

"She wants to reconcile?" She couldn't help doubt creeping into her voice.

Sinclair's pained expression gave her the answer. "No, she doesn't. But she's due any day now. If it is my baby, I need to be there for the birth."

A tiny flame of hope leaped in her chest at the word *if*. Obviously he wasn't entirely sure the child was his.

"Why didn't she tell you before now, if she's so far along?"

Sinclair frowned. "She said she didn't want me to know about it." The hurt in his eyes stole her breath. "That she wanted to raise it on her own."

Frustration rose in Annie's craw. "So why don't you let her do that?"

"I'd never forgive myself if our child grew up in a broken family without me making every effort to fix it."

"You don't have to marry her again to make it okay. Plenty of people live in separate households and play a full role in raising their children." Was he really going to walk away from her after all their declarations of last night?

"I know. But it's who I am, I suppose." That inscru-table dark gaze met hers. "I have to try."

"I understand." Of course he'd want to do the "right

thing" and be an old-fashioned *Leave It to Beaver* dad. He was hardly the type to feel fulfilled by taking the kids out for pizza and a movie twice a month. "I hope it all works out." That last part was a lie. But maybe in time she'd have the generosity of spirit to truly wish that for him. Right now she wanted to curl into a ball and sob.

Sinclair shoved a hand through his hair. "I just got off the phone with her. She's living in Santa Barbara right now. I'm going to fly there this afternoon."

"Oh." So much for their evening of romance tonight, with Vicki whisking Katherine away. Annie cursed herself for the selfish thought. Sinclair's life would be thrown into turmoil by this, no matter what happened.

And her own life?

No one cared about that very much.

"I'm so sorry this had to happen, especially now." Sinclair looked genuinely agitated. "I'd never have… taken advantage of you again last night if I'd had any idea."

His words cut her like a dagger. "You didn't take advantage of me." She tried to keep her voice cool. "I was a willing participant." *More fool, me.* Then again, it wasn't his fault this had happened. Or was it? He didn't have to rush to his ex-wife's side and try to rekindle their romance. He could just as easily have explained it all, then given her a big romantic kiss.

But life didn't work like that. At least, hers didn't. She pulled the paper out of the pantry. "Did you see this?" She flipped to the double-page spread of their romantic evening.

Sinclair snatched it from her. "Damn."

Annie shriveled a little bit more. "I didn't notice them

taking the pictures." She was too wrapped up in their oh-so-temporary romance.

"Me, either." He flipped to the front cover. "What kind of paper is this, anyway?"

"It's a fashion thing. Vicki gave it to me. She gets a copy every day."

"She would." He put it down, folded so their pictures were hidden. "Let's hope the story doesn't leak to the mainstream press."

"Yeah." It was hard to even speak. He really did want to sweep their glorious evening under the rug. Pain welled up inside her. She could only pray that he'd leave before it spilled out as tears.

"I'll go pack. Don't bother making me lunch. I'm leaving for the airport in ten minutes."

Already they were back to a business relationship. She nodded, keeping her mouth shut tight. Inside she was slowly dying.

"I'm sorry, Annie." His voice was gruff, a little stiff. She wasn't sure whether he was trying to put on a brave front or whether he simply didn't feel anything. She was beginning to suspect the latter.

"Me, too." She folded the paper and put it back into the pantry, glad to get away from that cold, dark stare. When she turned back, he was gone.

She leaned on the island, trying to catch her breath after holding in her emotions so tightly. She wanted to scream, to cry out in pain and frustration. But she didn't. She'd dared to live the dream for one beautiful night. She should be proud of herself for being bold and brave enough to live life to the fullest. Expecting more was just greedy.

She took her sweet time making the salad, anxious

to be sure Sinclair was gone before she ventured out of the kitchen to set the table or call the others to lunch.

"Oh, crap." Vicki's voice made her jump so violently she spilled some of the sea salt she was sprinkling on the garlic bread. "Sinclair blows it again."

Annie shrugged. Didn't turn around. She didn't want Vicki to know how hurt she was. She didn't understand at all why Vicki kept trying to push her and Sinclair together. Right now she felt like a mouse that had been played with too hard and long by a cat. She wasn't in the mood to provide any more entertainment.

"It's bad luck. Sinclair looks like he's seen a ghost."

"Has he left yet?" Annie glanced out the window. She couldn't see his car from here.

"Just drove out of here like he had a hellhound on his heels."

She finally turned to look at Vicki. "Why does he want to reconcile when his ex-wife doesn't?" The question burned in her brain. She didn't know what kind of relationship they had. Though if Diana had gone through almost an entire pregnancy without telling him, they could hardly be close.

"Sinclair is a diehard romantic. He probably believes a baby can fix everything. Diana isn't, though. She's about as emotional as this radish." She plucked a radish from the bunch on the counter, and bit into it.

Annie's heart was breaking. It seemed such a waste. She and Sinclair could have been happy together, but now he was going back to a woman who'd only hurt him.

"Why did Sinclair fall in love with her?" It felt good to get the question off her chest.

Vicki shrugged. "She's beautiful. Very manipulative and controlling. She probably told him what he wanted to hear." She raised a brow. "At least until after they were married."

"Why wouldn't she tell him she was pregnant until now?"

"I suppose it didn't suit her. Maybe she had someone even richer and more handsome up her sleeve." She shook her head. "Though frankly that's hard to imagine. Sinclair's a real catch."

"Then how come you don't want him for yourself?" Annie could hardly believe how bold and blunt she was being. Maybe because she had nothing left to lose. "I can tell that you don't."

Vicki laughed. "Sinclair's far too good for me. He'd be thoroughly wasted." Her violet eyes took on a wistful look. "Sinclair really is one in a million, and I don't say that because of his wealth and flashy looks. He's a truly good person, principled to the core, who only wants to do the right thing."

"So how come he keeps screwing up?"

Vicki stared at her for a moment, then snorted with loud laughter. "You're showing a whole other side of yourself today, Annie. And your guess is as good as mine. Why are men stupid? It's the eternal question of women."

Annie rankled at Vicki calling Sinclair stupid. He was as intelligent as a person could get. On the other hand, he had very poor taste in women. Except for her. Or was she just another example of him falling into the arms of someone utterly wrong for him?

Her insides felt raw and empty and her brain worked too hard to grapple with events that didn't make any sense at all. Poor Sinclair, doomed to make the same mistake again. And poor her, left alone to lick her wounds.

Vicki played with the clasp on her heavy silver bracelet. "Oh, well. He's gone now. All good things must come to an end, though this certainly wasn't the end I had in mind. I'm sorry for encouraging you." The look she shot her was genuinely apologetic. "I hope I haven't screwed things up for you."

"Not any more than they already were." Annie let out a sigh. She couldn't stay now. There was no way she could continue to work here after making love to Sinclair for a second time and being unceremoniously dumped again. It didn't matter how good his reason was, she needed to save herself from this situation. That would mean leaving Katherine Drummond in the lurch, but she could hire someone else to buy her fresh greens and bake quinoa muffins for the rest of the summer. "I'd better put lunch out."

"I'll bring the plates."

Lunch was a grim affair. Annie wasn't sitting at the table, of course, but hovering nearby. Katherine, usually talkative and full of plans, was oddly silent. She looked paler than she had lately. Apparently the news of her new grandchild was not quite as happy as it could have been. "Oh, poor Sinclair," she said at last, after toying with her chicken salad for a while. "That woman will never make him happy."

"She won't." Vicki was the only one with an appetite. She helped herself to more salad and bread. "So we'll have to hurry up and put this damn cup back together and get the fates back on the right track."

Katherine gave a small laugh. "I'm beginning to think it's just a story and that there's no cup at all.

We've been through nearly every box and basket and strange multi-strapped valise in that attic. We've certainly found some interesting things, but nothing that looks like one-third of a three-hundred-year-old Scottish cup."

Vicki lacked her usual sparkle. "Maybe the three brothers reunited and put it back together, and this is as good as it gets."

"They didn't, though." Katherine frowned at her untouched glass of sparkling water. "Aaron Drummond, the son of our ancestor, kept a diary and he wrote several times about his father's disappointment at never reuniting with his brothers. He was moaning about it on his deathbed."

"Bummer. Why didn't they get back together?"

"According to his diary, one of the brothers was arrested for stealing, escaped from prison and became a pirate, harassing vessels from Virginia to Florida. Then he disappeared. The third brother made his fortune trapping beavers, then went back to Scotland and bought back the ancestral home. They're still there. I suppose an Atlantic crossing wasn't the kind of journey you'd make just to visit family, back then. So they never even saw each other again. Our ancestor built the oldest part of this house, and our branch of the family has owned it ever since, so if his piece of the cup is anywhere at all, it's here."

"And maybe it will stay here for another three hundred years." Vicki sighed and broke off a piece of bread. "As for reuniting all three pieces, I don't imagine the pirate ancestor took very good care of his piece, anyway."

"According to contemporary stories he had gold and treasure buried all up and down the East Coast. Not here, though. He never came near New York. Maybe he didn't want to face his brother after he became an outlaw." She stared at her glass for a moment.

"It would be interesting to at least get the other relatives searching for the other pieces. Maybe you could offer a reward to sweeten the pot?"

"A reward? As far as I know, the other Drummond descendants are as wealthy as Sinclair. They'd hardly go digging up the garden for a few grand."

"Exactly." Vicki leaned forward. "They don't care about it because they think they have everything they need already. It might make more sense to get other people involved. Someone with a true financial incentive will hunt for the cup to earn the money, then the Drummonds will benefit from their hard work."

"Total strangers?" Katherine looked alarmed.

"It's an idea. Otherwise I'm worried we'll never find all three pieces."

From her vantage point near the sideboard, Annie noticed that calculating look creep back into Vicki's eyes. She wandered back into the kitchen. She couldn't care less about Vicki's nefarious plots at this point. She just needed to get lunch over with and give notice. Right now she felt numb as a zombie. She was about to quit her job of six years, had no place to go except the home—admittedly loving—she'd tried so hard to escape, and no prospect of any job at all.

"You're not going to quit, are you?" Vicki's voice sounded right next to her in the kitchen. How did this woman move around like a shadow?

"Why do you care?" Her emotions bubbled into her voice. "What does it matter? I'm sure you think I'm wasting my life dusting the sideboards here, anyway."

"Well, that is true." Vicki frowned. "I guess I just don't want it to be my fault."

"Trust me. It isn't. I've been thinking about moving on with my life and this is the final kick in the pants I needed, so you can enjoy the rest of the summer guilt-free. Though I would appreciate it if you looked out for Katherine. I promised Sinclair I'd take care of her, but…" Her chest tightened at the prospect of letting him down. She didn't like to go back on her word. On the other hand, it was time she put herself first for once. She'd been a doormat for too long, and these people were all adults who could take care of themselves, or at least pay someone else handsomely to do it.

"Of course." Vicki looked totally serious. "I'll make sure she has the most relaxing and healthful summer of her life." She exhaled. "What a mess. I hope Sinclair doesn't do anything really stupid, like marry Diana again."

"Whatever he does, it's none of my business. Now if you'll excuse me, I need to speak with Katherine."

Ten

Sinclair pulled his rented car out of the Santa Barbara airport with a drumbeat of dread in his heart. He didn't relish the sight of his ex-wife's face. He'd learned, gradually, that its perfect contours and smooth skin were not the result of a peaceful temperament or even good breeding, but rather the skill and tenacity of an army of surgeons and technicians with expertise in everything from sandblasting to spray tans. Terrified of wrinkles, she slept with a paste of cream around her eyes and neck. Even her lustrous dark hair wasn't natural. She had hanks of someone else's hair woven into it every three weeks. A bitter taste rose in his mouth at the prospect of ever having to kiss those silicone-plumped lips again.

Pain stabbed his heart at the memory of Annie's natural beauty. Her pale skin with its light sprinkling of freckles over her nose and cheeks. Her hair, which at first appeared to be light brown, but in a shaft of light revealed itself as a mass of red-gold silk. Her natural features, so pretty in their slight unevenness, and the crinkles that danced around her eyes when she smiled. Her slender, natural body with its ripe, soft curves and eager affection.

Regret soaked through him at the memory of how he'd treated her. Hungry with need that had clawed at his insides for two weeks, he'd peeled her beautiful dress off her and ravished her under the moonlight, with barely a sprinkling of pleasantries to smooth the way. He'd never felt such powerful desire for any woman and he still didn't understand it. Something about Annie reached deep inside him and held on tight.

So to have to tell her, this morning, that they couldn't be together, was agonizing. Cruel to her, torture for him. He let out a curse. Frustration crackled in his veins. He'd come so close to what seemed like happiness, only to have it snatched away again.

Maybe he was cursed. His mom was right and the whole damn family line was doomed to a miserable existence in a marriage of quiet resentment, like the one he'd witnessed between his own parents.

The cold grip of dread grew stronger as he pulled up in front of Diana's house. It seemed only a few months ago that they'd chosen it—well, she had, he hadn't liked the ornate Mediterranean exterior much, but at that point he was still trying to make his new bride happy. He'd been glad to give it to her in the divorce and say goodbye to both at the same time.

Muscles taut, he rang the doorbell. No answer. He rang again. Three cars sat in the driveway, so someone was home. At last he heard footsteps on the stone-tiled hallway and the door was flung open. "Sinclair!" The alarmed tone and the appalled look on his ex-wife's face gave him all the welcome he'd been expecting.

"I had to come see you."

"Why? I told you not to come." She made no move to invite him in. She filled the doorway almost completely, her huge belly hidden behind a veritable toga of ivory silk. Her face was bloated and puffy, which, combined with her heavy makeup, made her look like something from a horror movie.

Stop these ugly thoughts. She's the mother of your child.

"Why? Because we're having a child together."

"No, we're not." She glanced behind her. He thought he saw someone move in the large kitchen at the far end of the foyer. "*I'm* having a baby. We're divorced, in case you've forgotten. Still, since you're here, you better come in."

Her voice had an acid tone he hadn't heard before. Maybe now the divorce was final she didn't feel the need to cajole him into giving her more of what she loved most—money.

"If I'm the father…" Yes, he had doubts. But those weren't enough to keep him away. An innocent baby deserved the benefit of the doubt. "Then I intend to play a full and active role in our child's life, and we'll need to establish at the very least an honest working relationship." Any ideas of getting back together with her had fled at the sight of her angry, bitter stare.

"What's up, babe?" A gruff male voice echoed from the back of the house.

She swallowed and glanced behind her again.

"Who's that?" Sinclair's hackles rose. Was she living with someone already? Right now the thought of another man raising his child made his chest hurt.

"That's Larry. Larry, come meet Sinclair." She regarded him coolly as a hulking brute of a man, aged about twenty-two and with bleached blond hair, appeared behind her.

Larry nodded and took up a bodyguard-like position behind Diana.

"May I come in?" It rankled having to ask for an invitation into the house he'd bought for them to share.

"I suppose you'll have to." Diana turned, caftan flaring, and walked along the highway to an overdecorated living room. "Though you won't need to stay long. I told you our marriage is over."

"Not if we're having a child together. Why didn't you mention the pregnancy during the divorce?"

She twisted a big ring on one of her fingers. "I didn't want you feeling like you owned a part of me." She lifted her proud chin. "That you had rights over my future."

"Then why now?" None of this made sense.

She gestured to her large belly. "My livelihood depends on me being able to attend parties and interface with people. I confess I didn't realize how much a pregnancy would impact that. Obviously I can't be seen in public right now."

He wanted to laugh—or at the very least, agree. Instead he just felt sad. "So this is all about money. You don't want me in your child's life—you just want me to bankroll your existence while you take care of it."

"Pretty much." Her hard stare made his chest constrict.

"Have you taken a DNA test?"

"Yes, I told you that on the phone."

It was the reason he'd come here so fast. But now that he was here, something about the situation smelled like a week-dead New York City subway rat. "Let me see the results."

"I don't know where they are." She crossed her arms in the valley between her swollen breasts and her enormous belly.

"So you just expect me to take your word for it that they show the baby is mine?"

"I know you don't want a messy court case. And really, a little child support is peanuts to you. Just pay it and leave me alone. I'll let you see the child whenever you want."

Something in her eyes made him want to push further. "I need to see the test results." Diana wasn't a liar. If anything she was honest to a fault. There must be a reason she wouldn't show him the results.

"You do not. I'm nine months pregnant. Nine months ago we were still married," she snarled angrily. "The baby's yours. Do the math."

"That assumes that you weren't cheating on me during our marriage, when you've already admitted that you were."

"I only said that because New York doesn't have no-fault divorce, so somebody has to cheat." That's what she'd claimed at the time. He hadn't believed her then, either. "I conceived while still married, and you're the father."

"I no longer intend to take your word for anything. You'll have to take another test."

"I'm not putting the baby at risk by having a needle stabbed into my womb at this late stage." Her eyes bulged as she stared at him, and her swollen breasts looked as if they might pop right out of her toga. Which was not an appetizing thought.

"Then I'll wait here until it's delivered. One of the advantages of owning your own company is that you can do as you please, and from the look of you, I won't have to wait here long." If it was his baby he'd swallow his resentment and anger and make the best of the situation. If it wasn't…?

"Annie!" Her grandmother's big, soft arms encased her in a hug that made her want to collapse and rest. "Why've you been a stranger so long?"

"I was home for Christmas." That sounded pathetic. "I've just been wrapped up in…stuff." She'd quit her job in Dog Harbor yesterday and left early this morning, with most of her belongings in cardboard boxes that had been very awkward to carry on the train.

"How long are you staying?" Her grandmother pushed her back so she could survey her. "You look pale as a slab of squid. You're not sick, are you?"

She shook her head and tried to smile. "I'm fine." Just heartsick. "I'd like to stay until I find a new job. If you'll all have me back, that is."

Granny Pat's mouth opened wide for a moment. "You quit your job?"

She nodded. "It was time. I'd been there six years and was stuck in a rut."

Her grandmother grimaced. "Not a great time to find a job, hon. Your sister's been looking with no luck."

"I know. But I couldn't help it." She tried for a casual shrug.

"Something else is wrong." Her grandma's pale blue eyes narrowed. "I can always tell."

"There was…someone." Tears welled up inside her and she willed them not to spill from her eyes. "But that's over now." Thankfully the story had never moved into the mainstream process.

"Oh." Granny Pat folded her arms to her ample bosom again. "Poor baby. You tell Granny Pat where he lives and I'll go shake some sense into him."

Annie had to laugh. "If only it were that easy."

"Well, come in and park your stuff. We've been piling junk in your old room, but we'll move it out on the double."

The junk didn't have anywhere else to go, though, so that night she found herself in bed surrounded by grocery boxes full of garage-sale "treasures" that her mom and grandma had accumulated over the past few years. Maybe if she looked through them hard enough she'd find one-third of an old Scottish cup. Her bed was lumpy, and single. Being back in it felt like the grimmest admission of failure.

Sinclair was probably back between the sheets with the dreaded Diana, eagerly awaiting the arrival of his firstborn. She stared up at the ceiling, where cobwebs had formed around the 1970s light fixture, and tried not to miss her peaceful bedroom back in Dog Harbor, with the trees rustling outside and the call of owls in the early morning. That was all in the past and it was up to her to make her own future now. Tomorrow she'd enroll for fall courses at the community college. She had ample savings that she'd been piling up to build her little dream house, and she could live on them for some time, even if it meant eating her own dream for a while.

She really didn't want to know what was going on with Sinclair and his ex. He'd flown back to her without a moment's hesitation, which plainly showed how shallow and insignificant any feelings he had for Annie truly were. After all, he freely admitted to barely noticing her until she put the Victorian dress on. What he felt for her was obviously no more than temporary lust, easily forgotten once the heat of the moment wore off.

The mattress springs screeched as she climbed out of her bed. Sunlight poured unceremoniously through the ugly nylon curtains with their garish flowers. She'd grown used to the subtle and textured décor of the very rich, and now she'd probably be cursed with expensive tastes for the rest of her life.

She wasn't going to sit around waiting for life to happen. She splashed water on her face at the sink and patted her skin dry. She was going to make it happen. Maybe she wouldn't take the world by storm like the kind of women Sinclair was attracted to, but she'd forge her own dreams into reality, one little bit at a time.

"Do we get any of those dreamy eggs you're so good at?" Her dad's voice boomed up the stairs. She laughed. No chance of a day off here. Unlike Sinclair's house, where she was alone much of the time, she'd have a constant source of "clients" for her well-honed culinary skills. At least that would give her something useful to do, instead of hanging around moping in her old room.

"Coming!" She dressed quickly and went downstairs, but when she got to the kitchen, no one was around. They'd show up soon enough once cooking smells filled the air. She cracked some eggs into a bowl and heated the pan, then peeled some strips of bacon off the big slab from the butcher and put them in to sizzle.

Sinclair didn't like bacon, and she'd gone off it, too, since living in his house. Which was all the more reason to start eating it again.

You came here to leave Sinclair behind and move on. She slapped the cooked bacon onto a plate and tipped eggs into the hot pan. Sinclair would never eat eggs fried in bacon grease.

Why was she still thinking about him? Frustration made her growl aloud, and she racked her brain for something else to focus on. She should think about her future. What kind of job she'd actually like to do, instead of rushing to take whatever came first. Maybe she should work in someone else's store to see if owning her own was really a good dream to hold on to. She flipped the eggs over. The truth was she didn't know what she wanted.

Sinclair had probably forgotten all about her. Easy come, easy go. She'd certainly been easy in every way, as far as he was concerned. Every silly magazine article she'd read on the subject said that was a bad idea. Men weren't interested in what was readily available. They'd rather chase after the unattainable. But she had no self-control where Sinclair was concerned.

"Why can't I stop thinking about Sinclair?" Her words echoed off the kitchen walls.

"Because you're in love with him?" Her sister Sheena's voice made her whirl around. She hadn't told anyone, especially Sheena, about her romantic misadventures.

"I am not."

"Are, too." Her sister lolled in the doorway with a big smirk on her face. "You're so secretive, but I've learned to see past your cool expression."

"Why do I feel like I'm thirteen again?" Her big sister always had a superior attitude.

"I have no idea. What I hate is that you still look like you're thirteen. You need more stress in your life."

"Trust me, I have more than enough." She turned the eggs out onto a plate. "Why don't you take some breakfast and leave me alone." She moved to the door and called out, "It's ready."

"Nah. I'll take some breakfast and keep hounding you." She picked up a plate and helped herself to some bacon. "So, is he hot?"

Annie crossed her arms. "I have no idea what you're talking about."

"Yes, you do. You were talking about him when I came in." Her sister's smirk broadened. "So don't try and pretend there isn't anyone. Isn't your boss called Sinclair?"

"He was."

"Then he changed his name to Spike?" Her sister lifted a brow in that infuriating way.

"No. He's still called Sinclair. He's just not my boss anymore." Her stomach dropped a little as she said it. She still couldn't believe her life had turned upside down in such a short time. The loss of her job hadn't sunk in at all, even though it was her who'd quit.

"So, you're in love with him, but he doesn't love you." Sheena picked up a piece of crispy bacon in her fingers and bit it.

"Something like that," she muttered. "I really don't want to talk about it."

"You were talking about it before I came in, so I think you need to get it off your chest. Is he in love with someone else?"

"No. I don't think he's ever been in love with anyone and I don't think he ever will be." She said it with clear conviction that suddenly flooded her brain. "He's been married twice and I don't think he loved either of his wives. I think he was just looking for the right package. I think his whole life is about trying to be organized, efficient and perfect. I don't think he's capable of emotions at all." Her own feelings clawed at her insides.

"Damn. I wasn't sure you were, either, but now I'm beginning to see different." Sheena crunched another piece of bacon. "I always envied you your independence."

"I used to enjoy my independence." Her voice cracked. "And I hope I'll enjoy it again once I get him out of my mind."

"What does he look like?" Her sister lolled in the door frame, munching on her bacon like it was popcorn at the movies.

"What does it matter?" She sat at the table and tried to summon the appetite to eat.

"Is he tall, dark and handsome, by any chance?"

"Yes. Of course." She managed to swallow a bite of eggs. "He's gorgeous."

"Broad shoulders? Tight ass?"

"Go away."

"Does he dress like a preppy country-club type?"

"Yes." She frowned. "How did you know that?"

"Well, I'm describing the guy who's out on the front stoop sweet-talking Granny Pat." She walked in and scooped an egg onto her plate. "Mmm, nice and greasy. Just the way I like 'em."

Annie froze. "What?"

"Bacon grease. Really makes the eggs taste good."

"No. I mean, what did you say about someone talking to Granny?" She could hardly get the words out. She realized she was gripping her knife and fork like weapons.

"This dude drove up in a big shiny car. Asked if an Annie Sullivan lives here." Her sister pretended to be engrossed in her egg.

Annie rose to her feet, almost knocking her chair to the ground. "He's looking for me?"

"Yeah." Sheena chewed slowly, while Annie's blood pressure rose. "He had the address, but you know how our house has no number on it."

Annie raced out of the kitchen. Heart in her throat, she opened the front door and walked out onto the porch. Granny Pat and Sinclair both swiveled to watch her. Her eyes met Sinclair's.

He walked toward her. In a white shirt, open at the collar, and dark pants, he looked dashing and elegant, in stark contrast to the dreary street with its peeling houses and rusting minivans. "Thank God I found you."

His deep voice rocked her and his words chased her soul. He sounded like a lover who'd searched to the ends of the earth for his one and only.

Except that she knew better. "I couldn't stay. Not after the second time."

"This young man has traveled nonstop from California to see you." Granny Pat smiled at him. "Wasn't even sure if you'd be here."

Curiosity pricked her. Sinclair climbed the porch steps in an athletic stride. He stopped just short of her and she could feel the tension radiating off his body. She felt strangely calm. She'd already walked away from him and from their whole affair—you couldn't even call it an affair—and resolved to get on with her life. His sudden appearance on her family's doorstep seemed surreal.

His brows lowered. "I made a terrible mistake."

"Only one?" So cool, her comment seemed to have come from someone else's mouth. Maybe she was angry. Six years of pining followed by two weeks of the greatest pleasure and cruelest torture she could imagine. It could leave any girl on edge.

"I missed you."

I missed you, too. She didn't say it. She hadn't really had the luxury of missing him. She'd been too busy scrambling to reorient her life and figure out what to do next. She knew that if she stopped to think about the life she'd left behind everything would rise up and overwhelm her, so she'd kept her mind and hands busy every minute since she left.

"I couldn't believe you were gone."

"You thought I would just put up with anything you threw at me? I'm pretty tough, but you going back to your ex-wife was too much for me. Not that we had a relationship or anything. I didn't have a chance to develop that illusion." She'd never enjoyed the luxury of thinking she and Sinclair had a future for an entire twenty-four hours. The harsh light of dawn had always managed to dissolve her dream into a mist of memory and regret.

His brow furrowed. "I shouldn't have gone. I should have stayed with you."

"But you didn't." She didn't want to hear his apology. It didn't mean anything now. Whatever they'd shared— so briefly—was over and gone forever. "Everything happens for a reason." His ex must have told him she wasn't interested in getting back together—otherwise he'd probably still be there, trying to do the "honorable thing."

"Diana only wanted money. The baby isn't mine. She had done a DNA test, so she didn't lie about that, but she did lie when she said the baby was mine. The test proved it isn't. I left for the airport as soon as I heard, and I had my mom and Vicki track down your old résumé with your home address on it. You told me your family still lived here and I hoped I'd find you here."

She nodded. Of course. Still, a sliver of pain did prick her. Not so much for her own frustrated longing, but that Sinclair had once again tried to form a bond and been rejected.

Then she wanted to curse herself for caring. What about her own feelings? No one cared about those.

"I have feelings for you, Annie."

His sudden response to her thoughts touched a raw place inside her.

"I've always had feelings for you, Sinclair. They've brought me nothing but pain."

Emotion flickered over his chiseled features. "I know I'm to blame. I've been blind for so long."

She wanted to agree with him. But what would that accomplish? The pained expression in his eyes tugged at her heartstrings. Even now, after everything that had happened, she ached to run into his arms and tell him how happy she was to see him. He'd come all the way to Connecticut to find her. And apparently to reveal his true feelings for her.

But why? Would he beg her to come back and jump between the sheets with him? Or did he need her to take care of his house and his mother? She had no intention of doing either. "What do you want from me, Sinclair?"

Annie bit her lip and steeled herself to say no to whatever he hoped to talk her into.

Sinclair reached into the pocket of his pants. Annie's eyes grew wider as he pulled out a large, sparkling ring.

Annie felt her legs grow wobbly. Surely he wasn't…?

He was going to propose. Thoughts swirled around Annie's mind like hurricane-force winds. Years of idle dreaming and foolish fantasy were coalescing in this crazy moment on the front porch. The man of her dreams held a sparkling diamond the size of a muscatel grape and was about to ask her to be his wife.

And she was about to say no.

With an expression of intense concentration, Sinclair held the ring between his thumb and forefinger. She heard his intake of breath as he looked up to meet her eyes. "Annie, will you marry me?"

Eleven

The ring felt hard and sharp between Sinclair's finger and thumb. The sun, high overhead, hit its faceted surface, throwing out daggers of light. His words hung in the air as the seconds stretched out and he waited for her response.

Not the smile he'd hoped for. Nor the sigh, or the embarrassed laugh. Instead, his beautiful Annie looked… pained.

"Maybe you two need some privacy." Her grandmother's voice penetrated the slight fog of disbelief that accompanied her lack of response. Her broad chin lowered its tilt slightly. Then her cheerful expression darkened and she peered at Annie. "Is there something I should know?" She gave a pointed look at Annie's waist.

"No!" Annie's lightning-fast response made his neurons snap. Her abrupt refusal felt like a slap, and a response to his proposal, even though she was only replying to her grandmother's question. "Let's go inside." She didn't look at him.

Still holding the ring, he followed her through the front door. Another girl about Annie's age stood nearby, but Annie didn't introduce her. She walked down the hallway and he followed her into a large living room with high ceilings. She gestured for him to sit, and he lowered himself onto the worn, overstuffed sofa. She sat on an armchair about ten feet away, and the distance between them felt wide as Long Island Sound.

The ring stuck out, still throbbing with light, a sore thumb of frustrated hope and wounded feelings. "You must think my proposal is premature, because we haven't really…dated."

"Yes, that's true." She blinked. Her expression was blank, as if she didn't feel any of the emotion that crashed and sloshed around in him like the ocean in a gale. "You don't really know me."

"But I do." Hope surged in his chest at the chance to explain himself. "I've known you for six years. I feel closer to you after that one night we spent together than to anyone else in my life. Surely you feel the connection between us."

He saw emotion light her blue eyes. "Yes, I felt it." She frowned. "But that doesn't mean we're meant to be together. We don't have anything in common. If I wasn't your employee we'd never have even met."

"We have a lot in common." He spoke quietly. "It's my fault for being oblivious to it for years, but I can see now that we look at the world in a very similar way."

"I guess that's why I've done such a good job of running your house the way you like it." He wanted to agree heartily, but the way she said it sounded more like an accusation than an agreement.

"I don't want you to run my house anymore. I want you to run my life."

Her eyes widened. "Like a glorified personal assistant?"

"No." Frustration ripped through him. Why was he such a disaster when it came to matters of the heart? A bull in a china shop was subtle by comparison. "I want you to be my life partner, my constant companion… my soul mate."

She sat there, so sad and still. The surface of her eyes suggested emotion traveling behind them, but her face revealed nothing. "You can't become someone's soul mate. If we were soul mates we'd have realized it a long time ago."

He closed his fist around the ring and squeezed until the facets dug into his palm. He cursed himself for being an idiot. How had he managed to live for six years with the perfect woman under his roof—or at least one of his roofs—and not realized she was the one he'd been waiting for?

Instead he'd been dating—and marrying—people who were all wrong.

"Never mind the mumbo jumbo about soul mates." He leaned forward, urgency spurring his muscles. "I want you, Annie. Something deep inside me, I don't know what it's called—" He thumped his chest with his clenched fist, driving the ring harder against his hurting flesh. "Something tells me I need you. I don't want to go home without you." His words rang with all the raw emotion that soaked through him, and he prayed she'd feel the urgency and truth of his words.

A sudden tear sparkled in one of her eyes, filled her lower lid for a moment, then dropped across her cheek. His chest ached. Had he hurt her further with all his declarations?

She still said nothing.

"What is it, Annie? Have I said the wrong thing?" He heard his own voice crack.

"We're from totally different backgrounds. As you can see." She made a wooden gesture indicating the room. Her voice sounded flat. Only her eyes betrayed any emotion beneath the surface.

"Our backgrounds aren't important at all. All my life I've tried to make a relationship work with women from backgrounds identical to mine, and look how that turned out. Where you come from doesn't matter. It's what you want to accomplish in your life, how you want to live it and who you want to share it with that counts."

Her eyes were dry, that single tear now only a bright trail across her cheek. She stared at him for a moment without blinking. Then she looked away, past him. "It wouldn't work."

"Why not?" He sprang to his feet. Why couldn't he make her see sense?

Annie looked at him quietly for a moment. "Because you don't love me."

Her words dropped like a stone to his heart. Had he said all these things, even asked her to marry him, without once telling her that he loved her?

"I do love you." He drew in a breath to the bottom of his lungs. "I love you with all my heart." He strode across the room and crouched at her feet. Unable to resist, he snatched her hands out of her lap and held them. The big ring tumbled to the floor. "I didn't know what love was until I took you in my arms. I feel like I've been skating over the surface of life until now. I thought I was seeing life in color and smelling its scents and hearing its music, but I wasn't. I've been watching life on television, and suddenly I'm alive and can feel and see and taste all those things I've watched from afar for so long."

He heard his voice getting loud. Her hands trembled in his and he held them closer. "I've never felt this way before, or even knew that I could. It's taken me all this time to figure out what's going on with me. When I got to California I felt like someone had cut my heart out with a knife. All I could think about was coming back to you." His chest swelled with emotion. "Because I love you, Annie. I do love you."

Twin tears sprang to her eyes and rolled down her cheeks. "I believe you. I really do." Her voice trembled. "Oh, Sinclair. If only I believed we could be happy together."

"Never mind about that." He held her hands tight as hope soared in his heart. "We could be unhappy together. As long as we're together. I can't bear to be without you, Annie."

She laughed, and the light that had dimmed returned to her eyes, a brilliant sparkle that made the diamond now lying somewhere on the floor seem like a chunk of old glass by comparison. "You know, now you're making some sense. Being unhappy together actually sounds achievable."

"Better than being unhappy apart." He felt laughter bubbling in his chest. "And who knows, maybe we'll learn to smile from time to time."

"I wouldn't divorce you, you know." Her face wore

that strange, calm expression again. She had an air of total self-assurance that filled his heart with joy.

"I wouldn't let you." He softened his fierce grip on her hands long enough to lift them to his lips. The scent of her skin made him tremble. "Damn, Annie. I've missed you so much it hurts."

"I've missed you, too." Emotion glistened in her gaze. "I didn't want to admit it. It was just one more thing to keep to myself. Kind of like falling in love with you over the past six years."

"I could kick myself for wasting so much time. I promise I'll make it up to you. If you'll give me the chance."

She bit her lip, which shone red against her pale skin. "I am feeling reckless today."

"Wait. Let me start over. Don't move a muscle." Still holding both her hands in one of his, he groped toward the floor with the other. His fingers met the cold metal of the ring and he snatched it back up. "You never did answer my question." He hesitated for a moment, gathering the strength to ask again. "Annie Sullivan, I love you in a way I never dreamed possible, and I want to spend the rest of my life at your side. Will you marry me?"

"I will." She said it quickly and quietly, eyes sparkling bright.

He felt like letting out a cheer. Instead he slid the engagement ring onto her finger. The fit was snug, perfect.

"What a stunning ring." She stared at it. "Those look like rubies." The big, cushion-cut diamond was ringed by smaller, dark pink stones.

"I believe so. It's a Drummond family ring, so it

might be cursed, but it's not as if we're trying to be happy together."

She looked at him, eyes sparkling with humor. "Yes, that is a relief. Really takes the pressure off. How horribly did the last person to wear it die?"

"Hmm." He pretended to consider. "Actually she's still alive. My mom said it's too beautiful to sit in a safe, so she suggested I give it to you."

"Your mom knew you were going to propose to me?" Her eyes grew huge.

"She made me promise not to screw it up." He squeezed her hands gently, taking care not to crush the ring against her skin. "She said she won't speak to me if I come back without you."

Annie stared, blinking, her lips slightly parted. The urge to kiss her swelled inside him. "You did say yes, didn't you?" He spoke softly, afraid to break the spell that seemed to bind them together.

"Yes, yes I did." Her mouth held him riveted, soft and lush, saying the words he needed to hear. His lips met hers and their arms wound around each other. The feel of her body in his arms made a sigh rise through his chest, where it got lost in their kiss. Having Annie in his arms felt so right. He could stay right here and kiss her forever.

A knock sounded at the door, and he managed to pull away from Annie enough to look behind him and see the source. "Come in?" It was more a question than a command. The door opened slowly to reveal the rather red faces of her grandmother and a woman about Annie's age.

"Were you listening at the keyhole?" Annie jumped to her feet.

Her grandmother scrambled slowly upright, with the help of the door frame. "I needed to make sure he wasn't taking advantage of you." She pushed her glasses back up her nose.

"And what's your excuse?" Annie asked of the younger woman.

"Curiosity." A sly smile crept across her face. "And we were right to be curious. It got pretty interesting."

Annie put her hands on her hips. "So I suppose there's no need for me to make an announcement of any kind."

They looked from her to Sinclair and back. "We'd still like one." Her grandmother looked cheerfully expectant.

"Annie and I would like to announce that we're getting married."

"Can I be maid of honor?"

Annie had her arms around his waist. "Sinclair, this is my sister, Sheena. Sheena, we didn't say that we're having a big wedding. Just that we're getting married. For myself I'd prefer as little pomp and ceremony as possible."

"What's this I hear about someone getting married?" A short, plump man appeared behind the women.

Annie's grandmother stared at him. "Oh, my lord, the excitement has drawn your father away from his television. Wonders will never cease. Your daughter's getting married." She gestured to Sinclair. "To this fine young man." She leaned toward him. "His BMW is parked outside."

Her father blinked and scratched his forehead. "Goodness. I break from my show for a plate of eggs, and now I've lost the plot entirely. I suppose congratulations are in order." He stepped forward and shook Sinclair by the hand.

"I promise you I'll take good care of her."

"I'm not sure I need taking care of. I'm usually the one taking care of everyone else," Annie protested.

"Then it's time you took a break." Sinclair slid his arm around her waist. "And I think you should start with a nice, long vacation."

Annie shoved her belongings back into her flimsy suitcase again. It wasn't hard to convince Sinclair that they needed to visit his mom before flying off to parts unknown. Katherine Drummond was still in a vulnerable state and the events of the last week were enough to stress even a healthy person.

She splashed water on her face before heading back down into the maelstrom of her family. Her mom had come home from work and screamed when she heard the news. They'd all crowded around Sinclair's car and left fingerprints on the shiny paint. He'd handled their probing questions with grace and charm, but she couldn't wait to get out of here and back to the relative calm of Dog Harbor.

But how would it feel to be there as a guest instead of an employee? Not even a guest. What was she?

"I feel very old-fashioned, like I've come to carry you away from your family and take you back to my castle." Sinclair stood in the doorway. "I'm sure the Drummond ancestors would approve."

"And I didn't even have to lay seige. If only we could sail my car across Long Island Sound we'd be there in about fifteen minutes. Shame we actually have about a four-hour drive."

* * *

Scenery whipped by outside the window as they talked about Sinclair's other houses, the ones she'd never seen: the ski chalet in Colorado, an old beach-front mansion in northern California, and the hunting lodge in upper Michigan. They decided to be married in the garden of Dog Harbor, preferably within the month, with only people they considered true friends in attendance.

When they pulled into the driveway, the house looked different. She couldn't put her finger on what had changed. The chimneys still loomed above the gabled roof, windows sparkled in the late afternoon sun, and the lawn glowed green on either side of the gravel drive.

"Welcome home," Sinclair whispered in her ear. "Look. No one's here but us. I told my mom and Vicki to make themselves scarce for a few days. We have some catching up to do."

"I know what you mean. We're short at least six months of dating."

"We'll make up for lost time." His sultry gaze made her shiver. Desire and anticipation roared through her at the prospect of being alone with Sinclair—her new fiancé.

She still couldn't believe it.

"Don't move. I need to carry you over the threshold." Sinclair had rounded the circular drive and pulled up in front of the house. He leaped from the car and opened her door before she had time to protest. Dangling the key in his teeth, he slid his arms under her and lifted her out of the car. She gave a little scream as he ran for the house. "You don't mind if I hurry, do you? I'm feeling impatient."

"Not at all." She clung to his neck as he bounded up the stairs, and fumbled with the keys while balancing her in one strong arm.

She whispered in his ear. "Where's the housekeeper when you need her?"

"She's indisposed." He kicked open the door and threw his keys on the sideboard, then carried her over the marble threshold into the wide foyer. "On a permanent basis." His hot breath tickled her skin, sending ripples of sensation to her toes.

"Hey, what's that?" Something sitting in the middle of the dining room table had caught her eye as he headed past on the way to the stairs.

"What?"

"Take a detour into the dining room. I think there's a note on the table."

"It better be a short one," he growled playfully. "I have other priorities." He swung into the dining room, nuzzling her cheek. "What the heck is that?" A scarred wooden box sat in the middle of the table. Next to it, a sheet of white paper was scrawled with the words, *We found it.*

"The cup? I think you'd better put me down."

"What if I don't want to put you down?" He kissed her ear, and heat flooded her core. "I have more important things to do than mess with an old cup." He lifted her onto the dining room table, and kissed her with force. All the excitement that had built up during their long drive blossomed into the longest and fiercest kiss she'd ever known. Sinclair's powerful fingers plucked at the buttons on her shirt and soon slid it back over her shoulders. She tugged his polo shirt over his head, revealing his hard chest with that intoxicating sprinkling of dark hair that led below his belt buckle. Her fingers fumbled with the buckle while Sinclair breathed kisses over her face and neck, and licked her nipples into hard peaks.

Her belly trembled under his touch as he unzipped her pants and slid them down over her legs, leaving her sitting on the polished antique table in her bikini underwear. She giggled. "Should we really be doing this here?"

"Absolutely." Sinclair stepped out of his pants. The force of his desire was clearly visible and only heightened her own. Lips gently pressed to hers, he entered her slowly but surely, filling her and making her gasp with pleasure. The table proved surprisingly sturdy as Sinclair took them both on a sensual journey at its edge. Then, just as she felt her climax draw near, he lifted her up and carried her, striding swiftly, into the formal living room, where he spread her on the brocade chaise longue.

"I think we're scandalizing the furniture." She sighed at the sensation of sinking into the soft, upholstered surface, with Sinclair's warm, heavy weight on top of her.

"It could use some excitement." He licked her lips, making her gasp. "I know I needed some."

He sank deeper, and she melted under him, giving herself over to the sensation that lapped through her. For once she didn't have to worry about what would happen next, or what kind of a terrible mistake she was making. She was meant to be here, right now, in Sinclair's arms. Her heart felt so full. All the hope and fear she'd been storing for so long spilled over into passion. She

gripped Sinclair as they moved together, rising and falling with him and holding him as tight as she could until
their climax threw them deep into the chaise, breathing in heavy unison.

"Am I dreaming?" she said, when she could finally
catch enough breath.

"If you are, I am, too. Let's not wake up." His eyelashes brushed her cheek as he lay against her.

"We never looked in the box."

"What box?" His chest rose and fell and beads of
perspiration stood out on his proud forehead. "Oh, yes.
That box. I'm sure whatever it is can wait."

"Apparently we couldn't." She bit her lip, trying to
stop a smile sneaking across her face.

"Speak for yourself. I could have easily gone for a
cool dip in the Sound instead." His eyes opened just
enough for her to see them twinkle with mischief.

"Liar." She slid a fingertip down the groove of his
spine and he shivered slightly in response. "But I'm glad
you have no self-control where I'm concerned. Otherwise we might have gone on tiptoeing around each other
for another six years."

"That would have been a tragedy." He grazed her
cheek with his teeth. "Come on. Let's go see what the
big mystery is." He climbed off the sofa and pulled her
gently to her feet. She insisted on grabbing a couple of
white linen tablecloths from the pantry on the way back
to the dining room, so they looked like ancient Romans
as they surveyed the aged wooden box again.

Sinclair stood back. "You first. You're the newest
member of the Drummond family."

"Not yet."

"Doesn't matter. The curse starts working as soon

as you agree to marry a Drummond." A sneaky dimple appeared in his cheek.

"All right. Since I'm doomed anyway." She lifted the lid, which creaked loudly. Inside was a moth-eaten piece of tartan cloth, folded around something. She pulled the object out—it was heavy—and held it in her hands. She placed it on the table and peeled back the cloth, sending a small cloud of dust into the air. Her nose tickled with the desire to sneeze. The cloth fell away to reveal a very dark, tarnished rod of metal. "Huh? That's not what I was expecting. I thought it would be one-third of the infamous cup."

"Maybe it is." Sinclair reached into the folds of the fabric and drew it out. The surface was scored with patterns, and each end had a sort of claw on it. "This could be the stem."

"And the other pieces are the base and the cup? I never thought of that." He placed the cool metal rod in her hands, and she turned it. "These ends do look like they could attach to something else. I wonder where they found it?"

"I wonder *when* they found it. And if it coincides with me finally having the good sense to pursue the one woman I need by my side." He looked at her, his dark gaze serious. Her heart fluttered at the depth of emotion she read in his face.

"I love you, Sinclair."

"I love you, too, and thank heaven I had the sense to realize that before it was too late. Welcome home, Annie." He laid another warm kiss on her lips. "And welcome to the ancient line of Drummonds."

Epilogue

"Katherine, you shouldn't have." Annie pulled tissue paper from the big box. "It's not even Christmas yet."

"I don't have to wait for special occasions to give my grandson a few things." The balsam tree she and Sinclair had cut and brought home together already had piles of wrapped boxes and gift bags that reached as high as its lower branches.

"It might help if you wait until your grandson is actually born." Sinclair's gruff voice moved behind her as he slid his arms around Annie's waist—which was growing larger every day. Her skin tingled under his affectionate touch, even through her winter clothes.

"I'm naturally impatient, darling. You know that. And Annie understands, don't you?"

Annie pulled yet another adorable tiny outfit—French, of course—with a pattern of little sailboats, from the box. Followed by a matching hat and booties.

"Of course I do. It's impossible not to be excited about the arrival of a new person in our midst."

"The newest Drummond shall want for nothing. Do you think it would be silly to buy a sled in the sales?" Snow had been falling steadily for two days and they were all snowed into a very quiet and sleepy Dog Harbor.

"Definitely silly." Sinclair laughed. "He won't be able to sled until at least the winter after next. Besides, we found about eight antique sleds up in the attic. Those are probably faster and sturdier than anything you'll find in a toy store."

"I'm just so excited. It's hard to stop myself. I'm sure I'll calm down once the doctor gives me the okay to travel again. He said to wait a full year since my illness. That's another four months! It's driving me to distraction that I can't fly to Scotland and shake the young laird into looking for more of the cup."

"Why can't you go to Florida and harass the Drummond down there?" Sinclair kissed Annie gently on the cheek as she folded the baby outfit and laid it on the sofa. "That's only a domestic flight."

"Vicki insisted on going." Katherine shrugged her slim shoulders. "She seemed really interested. I think she knows people down there."

"Or she wants to win the reward she convinced you to offer for finding the cup piece." Sinclair topped up their glasses of eggnog.

"Sinclair! Vicki doesn't need money. Her family made a fortune in…something or other. I forget what."

"Never mind. I hope she does find it. I think more Drummonds deserve to be as happy as we are."

"See, I knew you could be happily married. You just

needed to pick the right woman." Katherine beamed at Annie.

"That's what I told him myself." Annie smiled at Sinclair.

"And I've never seen the house look so glorious at Christmastime." Fragrant pine decorated the balusters and fireplaces, and ornaments of all kinds had been brought out of the attic and polished before finding their new places in the house and on the tree.

"That's because we usually go to the Colorado house." Annie surveyed her handiwork. She'd always dreamed of decorating the house for Christmas. Like the lovely wedding they'd held on the lawn under fall-spangled trees, it was a dream come true. Sometimes her heart felt so full it was hard to keep her emotions contained. Or maybe that was just the pregnancy hormones. "Next year will be even more special, when we have a child to share it with."

Katherine rose from her seat and hugged Annie with tears in her eyes. "You've made me so happy already." She turned to Sinclair. "And I should scold you for making myself and Annie wait so long for you to come to your senses."

Sinclair sipped his eggnog. "I'm a slow study. I get there in the end, though. I can't believe I never thought of living here full-time before."

"The house feels quite different now it's a real home." Annie smiled at the warm and festive living room. "Before I felt a bit like I was always getting ready for a theatrical production."

"Now you're just living in one every day." Sinclair winked.

"Nonsense." Katherine reached for a walnut and the

ornate Victorian nutcracker. "Annie's kept everything very low-key and tasteful."

"I love being surrounded by all the beautiful old things the family has gathered over the years. This is such a special place. I suppose that's why the Drummonds have always kept it."

"I look forward to spending the rest of my life here." Sinclair slid his arm around her shoulders, sending a shiver of warmth through her. "With you."

Annie sighed. "Me, too. Leaving this house was almost as hard as leaving you." She nudged him. "I can happily stay here forever."

"Sinclair told me you're planning to open a shop." Katherine peeled her cracked walnut and ate it with delicate fingers.

"Yes." She smiled at Sinclair, butterflies still rising in her stomach at the thought of her grand plan. "It's going to sell local handmade crafts and foods. I plan to make some of them myself, too. I won't open for another year, though. I'm still taking business classes and developing my plan." She patted her belly. "And I'll be very busy for a while."

"I knew finding the cup would change our luck." Katherine glowed with satisfaction. She seemed to have fully recovered from her illness. "Where is our piece, by the way? I still don't know how we figured out that was a stem. It was just rattling around in the bottom of that box with a bunch of eighteenth-century tobacco pipes. It wouldn't look good if we track down the other two and we'd lost ours again."

Annie laughed. "It's up on the fireplace next to that glass bottle."

"Why do you have an empty wine bottle on the mantel?"

She shrugged. "It washed ashore one day and we decided to keep it." She and Sinclair had been walking on the beach one morning, looking out over the Sound and talking about the future, when they'd spotted a wine bottle bobbing in the surf. Sinclair had waded in to grab it and—surprise, surprise!—there were two tiny pieces of paper rolled up in the bottom.

The paper had been washed completely clean by water leaking in through a cracked cork, so while they were certain it was debris from the party they'd attended, they had no idea if it was their own fond wishes that had rinsed off or someone else's. They resolved to put their thoughts into words.

Sinclair had said "Annie, I never knew what I was looking for until I found you in my arms." And she told him of her hope that he would live happily ever after, preferably with her. They'd put the mysterious notes back into the bottle and placed it up high next to the cup piece that had—just maybe?—lifted centuries of bad luck and finally brought them together.

* * * * *

PRINCESS IN THE MAKING

BY
MICHELLE CELMER

Bestselling author **Michelle Celmer** lives in southeastern Michigan with her husband, their three children, two dogs and two cats. When she's not writing or busy being a mum, you can find her in the garden or curled up with a romance novel. And if you twist her arm really hard, you can usually persuade her into a day of power shopping.

Michelle loves to hear from readers. Visit her website, www.michellecelmer.com, or write her at PO Box 300, Clawson, MI 48017, USA.

To Patti, who has been an invaluable source of support
through some rough times.

One

From a mile in the air, the coast of Varieo, with its crystal blue ocean and pristine sandy beaches, looked like paradise.

At twenty-four, Vanessa Reynolds had lived on more continents and in more cities than most people visited in a lifetime—typical story for an army brat—but she was hoping that this small principality on the Mediterranean coast would become her forever home.

"This is it, Mia," she whispered to her six-month-old daughter, who after spending the majority of the thirteen-hour flight alternating between fits of restless sleep and bouts of screaming bloody murder, had finally succumbed to sheer exhaustion and now slept peacefully in her car seat. The plane made its final descent to the private airstrip where they would be greeted by Gabriel, Vanessa's... it seemed silly and a little juvenile to call him her boyfriend, considering he was fifty-six. But he wasn't exactly her fiancé either. At least, not yet. When he asked her to marry him she hadn't said yes, but she hadn't said no either. That's what this visit would determine, if she wanted to marry a man who was not only thirty-two years her senior and lived halfway around the world, but a *king*.

She gazed out the window, and as the buildings below grew larger, nervous kinks knotted her insides.

Vanessa, what have you gotten yourself into this time?

That's what her father would probably say if she'd had the guts to tell him the truth about this visit. He would tell her that she was making another huge mistake. And, okay, so maybe she hadn't exactly had the best luck with men since…well, *puberty*. But this time it was different.

Her best friend Jessy had questioned her decision as well. "He seems nice now," she'd said as she sat on Vanessa's bed, watching her pack, "but what if you get there and he turns out to be an overbearing tyrant?"

"So I'll come home."

"What if he holds you hostage? What if he forces you to marry him against your will? I've heard horror stories. They treat women like second-class citizens."

"That's the other side of the Mediterranean. Varieo is on the European side."

Jessy frowned. "I don't care, I still don't like it."

It's not as if Vanessa didn't realize she was taking a chance. In the past this sort of thing had backfired miserably, but Gabriel was a real gentleman. He genuinely cared about her. He would never steal her car and leave her stranded at a diner in the middle of the Arizona desert. He wouldn't open a credit card in her name, max it out and decimate her good credit. He wouldn't pretend to like her just so he could talk her into writing his American history term paper then dump her for a cheerleader.

And he certainly would never knock her up then disappear and leave her and his unborn child to fend for themselves.

The private jet hit a pocket of turbulence and gave a violent lurch, jolting Mia awake. She blinked, her pink bottom lip began to tremble, then she let out an ear-piercing wail that only intensified the relentless throb in Vanessa's temples.

"Shh, baby, it's okay," Vanessa cooed, squeezing her chubby fist. "We're almost there."

The wheels of the plane touched down and Vanessa's heart climbed up into her throat. She was nervous and excited and relieved, and about a dozen other emotions too jumbled to sort out. Though they had chatted via Skype almost daily since Gabriel left Los Angeles, she hadn't been face-to-face with him in nearly a month. What if he took one look at her rumpled suit, smudged eyeliner and stringy, lifeless hair and sent her right back to the U.S.?

That's ridiculous, she assured herself as the plane bumped along the runway to the small, private terminal owned by the royal family. She had no illusions about how the first thing that had attracted Gabriel to her in the posh Los Angeles hotel where she worked as an international hospitality agent was her looks. Her beauty—as well as her experience living abroad—was what landed her the prestigious position at such a young age. It had been an asset and, at times, her Achilles' heel. But Gabriel didn't see her as arm dressing. They had become close friends. Confidants. He loved her, or so he claimed, and she had never known him to be anything but a man of his word.

There was just one slight problem. Though she respected him immensely and loved him as a friend, she couldn't say for certain if she was *in love* with him—a fact Gabriel was well aware of. Hence the purpose of this extended visit. He felt confident that with time—six weeks to be exact, since that was the longest leave she could take from work—Vanessa would grow to love him. He was sure that they would share a long and happy life together. And the sanctity of marriage was not something that Gabriel took lightly.

His first marriage had spanned three decades, and he claimed it would have lasted at least three more if cancer hadn't snatched his wife from him eight months ago.

Mia wailed again, fat tears spilling down her chubby, flushed cheeks. The second the plane rolled to a stop Vanessa turned on her cell phone and sent Jessy a brief text, so when she woke up she would know they had arrived safely. She then unhooked the straps of the plush, designer car seat Gabriel had provided and lifted her daughter out. She hugged Mia close to her chest, inhaling that sweet baby scent.

"We're here, Mia. Our new life starts right now."

According to her father, Vanessa had turned exercising poor judgment and making bad decisions into an art form, but things were different now. *She* was different, and she had her daughter to thank for that. Enduring eight months of pregnancy alone had been tough, and the idea of an infant counting on her for its every need had scared the crap out of her. There had been times when she wasn't sure she could do it, if she was prepared for the responsibility, but the instant she laid eyes on Mia, when the doctor placed her in Vanessa's arms after a grueling twenty-six hours of labor, she fell head over heels in love. For the first time in her life, Vanessa felt she finally had a purpose. Taking care of her daughter, giving her a good life, was now her number one priority.

What she wanted more than anything was for Mia to have a stable home with two parents, and marrying Gabriel would assure her daughter privileges and opportunities beyond Vanessa's wildest dreams. Wouldn't that be worth marrying a man who didn't exactly…well, *rev her engine?* Wasn't respect and friendship more important anyway?

Vanessa peered out the window just in time to see a limo pull around the building and park a few hundred feet from the plane.

Gabriel, she thought, with equal parts relief and excitement. He'd come to greet her, just as he'd promised.

The flight attendant appeared beside her seat, gesturing to the carry-on, overstuffed diaper bag and purse in a pile at Vanessa's feet. "Ms. Reynolds, can I help you with your things?"

"That would be fantastic," Vanessa told her, raising her voice above her daughter's wailing. She grabbed her purse and hiked it over her shoulder while the attendant grabbed the rest, and as Vanessa rose from her seat for the first time in several hours, her cramped legs screamed in protest. She wasn't one to lead an idle lifestyle. Her work at the hotel kept her on her feet eight to ten hours a day, and Mia kept her running during what little time they had to spend together. There were diaper changes and fixing bottles, shopping and laundry. On a good night she might manage a solid five hours of sleep. On a bad night, hardly any sleep at all.

When she met Gabriel she hadn't been out socially since Mia was born. Not that she hadn't been asked by countless men at the hotel—clients mostly—but she didn't believe in mixing business with pleasure, or giving the false impression that her *hospitality* extended to the bedroom. But when a king asked a girl out for drinks, especially one as handsome and charming as Gabriel, it was tough to say no. And here she was, a few months later, starting her life over. Again.

Maybe.

The pilot opened the plane door, letting in a rush of hot July air that carried with it the lingering scent of the ocean. He nodded sympathetically as Mia howled.

Vanessa stopped at the door and looked back to her seat. "Oh, shoot, I'm going to need the car seat for my daughter."

"I'll take care of it, ma'am," the pilot assured her, with a thick accent.

She thanked him and descended the steps to the tarmac, so relieved to be on steady ground she could have dropped to her knees and kissed it.

The late morning sun burned her scalp and stifling heat drifted up from the blacktop as the attendant led her toward the limo. As they approached, the driver stepped out and walked around to the back door. He reached for the handle, and the door swung open, and Vanessa's pulse picked up double time. Excitement buzzed through her as one expensive looking shoe—Italian, she was guessing— hit the pavement, and as its owner unfolded himself from the car she held her breath…then let it out in a whoosh of disappointment. This man had the same long, lean physique and chiseled features, the deep-set, expressive eyes, but he was *not* Gabriel.

Even if she hadn't done hours of research into the country's history, she would have known instinctively that the sinfully attractive man walking toward her was Prince Marcus Salvatora, Gabriel's son. He looked exactly like the photos she'd seen of him—darkly intense, and far too serious for a man of only twenty-eight. Dressed in gray slacks and a white silk shirt that showcased his olive complexion and crisp, wavy black hair, he looked more like a *GQ* cover model than a future leader.

She peered around him to the interior of the limo, hoping to see someone else inside, but it was empty. Gabriel had promised to meet her, but he hadn't come.

Tears of exhaustion and frustration burned her eyes. She *needed* Gabriel. He had a unique way of making her feel as though everything would be okay. She could only imagine what his son would think of her if she dissolved into tears right there on the tarmac.

Never show weakness. That's what her father had drilled into her for as long as Vanessa could remember. So she took a deep breath, squared her shoulders and greeted the prince with a confident smile, head bowed, as was the custom in his country.

"Miss Reynolds," he said, reaching out to shake her hand. She switched Mia, whose wails had dulled to a soft whimper, to her left hip to free up her right hand, which in the blazing heat was already warm and clammy.

"Your highness, it's a pleasure to finally meet you," she said. "I've heard so much about you."

Too many men had a mushy grip when it came to shaking a woman's hand, but Marcus clasped her hand firmly, confidently, his palm cool and dry despite the temperature, his dark eyes pinned on hers. It lasted so long, and he studied her so intensely, she began to wonder if he intended to challenge her to an arm wrestling match or a duel or something. She had to resist the urge to tug her hand free as perspiration rolled from under her hair and beneath the collar of her blouse, and when he finally did relinquish his grip, she experienced a strange buzzing sensation where his skin had touched hers.

It's the heat, she rationalized. And how did the prince appear so cool and collected when she was quickly becoming a soggy disaster?

"My father sends his apologies," he said in perfect English, with only a hint of an accent, his voice deep and velvety smooth and much like his father's. "He was called out of the country unexpectedly. A family matter."

Out of the *country?* Her heart sank. "Did he say when he would be back?"

"No, but he said he would be in touch."

How could he leave her to fend for herself in a palace full of strangers? Her throat squeezed tight and her eyes burned.

You are not going to cry, she scolded herself, biting the inside of her cheek to stem the flow of tears threatening to leak out. If she had enough diapers and formula to make the trip back to the U.S., she might have been tempted to hop back on the plane and fly home.

Mia wailed pitifully and Marcus's brow rose slightly.

"This is Mia, my daughter," she said.

Hearing her name, Mia lifted her head from Vanessa's shoulder and turned to look at Marcus, her blue eyes wide with curiosity, her wispy blond hair clinging to her tearstained cheeks. She didn't typically take well to strangers, so Vanessa braced herself for the wailing to start again, but instead, she flashed Marcus a wide, two-toothed grin that could melt the hardest of hearts. Maybe he looked enough like his father, whom Mia adored, that she instinctively trusted him.

As if it were infectious, Marcus couldn't seem to resist smiling back at her, and the subtle lift of his left brow, the softening of his features—and, oh gosh, he even had dimples—made Vanessa feel the kind of giddy pleasure a woman experienced when she was attracted to a man. Which, of course, both horrified and filled her with guilt. What kind of depraved woman felt physically attracted to her future son-in-law?

She must have been more tired and overwrought than she realized, because she clearly wasn't thinking straight.

Marcus returned his attention to her and the smile disappeared. He gestured to the limo, where the driver was securing Mia's car seat in the back. "Shall we go?"

She nodded, telling herself that everything would be okay. But as she slid into the cool interior of the car, she couldn't help wondering if this time she was in way over her head.

She was even worse than Marcus had imagined.

Sitting across from her in the limo, he watched his new rival, the woman who, in a few short weeks, had managed to bewitch his grieving father barely eight months after the queen's death.

At first, when his father gave him the news, Gabriel thought he had lost his mind. Not only because he had fallen for an American, but one so young, that he barely knew. But now, seeing her face-to-face, there was little question as to why the king was so taken with her. Her silky, honey-blond hair was a natural shade no stylist, no matter how skilled, could ever reproduce. She had the figure of a gentlemen's magazine pinup model and a face that would inspire the likes of da Vinci or Titian.

When she first stepped off the plane, doe-eyed and dazed, with a screaming infant clutched to her chest, his hope was that she was as empty-headed as the blonde beauties on some of those American reality shows, but then their eyes met, and he saw intelligence in their smoky gray depths. And a bit of desperation.

Though he hated himself for it, she looked so disheveled and exhausted, he couldn't help but feel a little sorry for her. But that didn't change the fact that she was the enemy.

The child whimpered in her car seat, then let out a wail so high-pitched his ears rang.

"It's okay, sweetheart," Miss Reynolds cooed, holding her baby's tiny clenched fist. Then she looked across the car to Marcus. "I'm so sorry. She's usually very sweet natured."

He had always been fond of children, though he much preferred them when they smiled. He would have children one day. As sole heir, it was his responsibility to carry on the Salvatora legacy.

But that could change, he reminded himself. With a pretty young wife his father could have more sons.

The idea of his father having children with a woman like her sat like a stone in his belly.

Miss Reynolds reached into one of the bags at her feet, pulled out a bottle with what looked to be juice in it and handed it to her daughter. The child popped it into her mouth and suckled for several seconds, then made a face and lobbed the bottle at the floor, where it hit Marcus's shoe.

"I'm so sorry," Miss Reynolds said again, as her daughter began to wail. The woman looked as if she wanted to cry, too.

He picked the bottle up and handed it to her.

She reached into the bag for a toy and tried distracting the baby with that, but after several seconds it too went airborne, this time hitting his leg. She tried a different toy with the same result.

"Sorry," she said.

He retrieved both toys and handed them back to her.

They sat for several minutes in awkward silence, then she said, "So, are you always this talkative?"

He had nothing to say to her, and besides, he would have to shout to be heard over the infant's screaming.

When he didn't reply, she went on nervously, "I can't tell you how much I've looked forward to coming here. And meeting you. Gabriel has told me so much about you. And so much about Varieo."

He did not share her enthusiasm, and he wouldn't pretend to be happy about this. Nor did he believe even for a second that she meant a word of what she said. It didn't take a genius to figure out why she was here, that she was after his father's vast wealth and social standing.

She tried the bottle again, and this time the baby took it. She suckled for a minute or two then her eyelids began to droop.

"She didn't sleep well on the flight," Miss Reynolds said, as though it mattered one way or another to him. "Plus, everything is unfamiliar. I imagine it will take some time for her to adjust to living in a new place."

"Her father had no objection to you moving his child to a different country?" he couldn't help asking.

"Her father left us when he found out I was pregnant. I haven't seen or heard from him since."

"You're divorced?"

She shook her head. "We were never married."

Marvelous. And just one more strike against her. Divorce was bad enough, but a child out of wedlock? What in heaven's name had his father been thinking? And did he honestly believe that Marcus would ever approve of someone like that, or welcome her into the family?

His distaste must have shown in his face, because Miss Reynolds looked him square in the eyes and said, "I'm not ashamed of my past, your highness. Though the circumstances may not have been ideal, Mia is the best thing that has ever happened to me. I have no regrets."

Not afraid to speak her mind, was she? Not necessarily an appropriate attribute for a future queen. Though he couldn't deny that his mother had been known to voice her own very potent opinions, and in doing so had been a role model for young women. But there was a fine line between being principled and being irresponsible. And the idea that this woman would even think that she could hold herself to the standards the queen had set, that she could replace her, made him sick to his stomach.

Marcus could only hope that his father would come to his senses before it was too late, before he did something ridiculous, like *marry* her. And as much as he would like to wash his hands of the situation that very instant, he had promised his father that he would see that she was settled in, and he was a man of his word. To Marcus, honor was not only a virtue, but an obligation. His mother had taught him that. Although even he had limits.

"Your past," he told Miss Reynolds, "is between you and my father."

"But you obviously have some strong opinions about it. Maybe you should try getting to know me before you pass judgment."

He leaned forward and locked eyes with her, so there was no question as to his sincerity. "I wouldn't waste my time."

She didn't even flinch. She held his gaze steadily, her smoky eyes filled with a fire that said she would not be intimidated, and he felt a twinge of...something. An emotion that seemed to settle somewhere between hatred and lust.

It was the lust part that drew him back, hit him like a humiliating slap in the face.

And Miss Reynolds had the audacity to *smile*. Which both infuriated and fascinated him.

"Okay," she said with a shrug of her slim shoulders. Did she not believe him, or was it that she just didn't care?

Either way, it didn't make a difference to him. He would tolerate her presence for his father's sake, but he would never accept her.

Feeling an unease to which he was not accustomed, he pulled out his cell phone, dismissing her. For the first time since losing the queen to cancer, his father seemed truly happy, and Marcus would never deny him that. And only because he believed it would never last.

With any luck his father would come to his senses and send her back from where she came before it was too late.

Two

This visit was going from bad to worse.

Vanessa sat beside her sleeping daughter, dread twisting her stomach into knots. Marcus, it would seem, had already made up his mind about her. He wasn't even going to give her a chance, and the idea of being alone with him until Gabriel returned made the knots tighten.

In hindsight, confronting him so directly probably hadn't been her best idea ever. She'd always had strong convictions, but she'd managed, for the most part, to keep them in check. But that smug look he'd flashed her, the arrogance that seemed to ooze from every pore, had raked across her frayed nerves like barbed wire. Before she could think better of it, her mouth was moving and words were spilling out.

She stole a glance at him, but he was still focused on his phone. On a scale of one to ten he was a solid fifteen in the looks department. Too bad he didn't have the personality to match.

Listen to yourself.

She gave her head a mental shake. She had known the man a total of ten minutes. Was she unfairly jumping to conclusions, judging him without all the facts? And in doing so, was she no better than him?

Yes, he was acting like a jerk, but maybe he had a good reason. If her own father announced his intention to marry a much younger woman whom Vanessa had never even met, she would be wary too. But if he were a filthy rich king to boot, she would definitely question the woman's motives. Marcus was probably just concerned for his father, as any responsible son should be. And she couldn't let herself forget that he'd lost his mother less than a year ago. Gabriel had intimated that Marcus had taken her death very hard. He was probably still hurting, and maybe thought she was trying to replace the queen, which could not be further from the truth.

Looking at it that way made her feel a little better.

But what if he disliked her so much that he tried to come between her and Gabriel? Did she want to go through life feeling like an intruder in her own home? Or would it never feel like home to her?

Was this just another huge mistake?

Her heart began to pound and she forced herself to take a deep breath and relax. She was getting way ahead of herself. She didn't even know for certain that she wanted to marry Gabriel. Wasn't that the whole point of this trip? She could still go home if things didn't work out. Six weeks was a long time, and a lot could happen between now and then. For now she wouldn't let herself worry about it, or let it dash her excitement. She was determined to make the

best of this, and if it didn't work out, she could chalk it up
to another interesting experience and valuable life lesson.

She smiled to herself, a feeling of peace settling over
her, and gazed out the window as the limo wound its way
through the charming coastal village of Bocas, where
shops, boutiques and restaurants lined cobblestone streets
crowded with tourists. As they pulled up the deep slope to
the front gates of the palace, in the distance she could see
the packed public beach and harbor where everything from
sailboats and yachts to a full-size cruise ship were docked.

She'd read that the coastal tourist season stretched from
April through November, and in the colder months the
tourist trade moved inland, into the mountains, where
snowboarding and skiing were the popular activities. According to Gabriel, much of the nation's economy relied
on tourism, which had taken a financial hit the last couple of years.

The gates swung open as they approached and when the
palace came into view, Vanessa's breath caught. It looked
like an oasis with its Roman architecture, sprawling foun-
tains, green rolling lawns and lush gardens.

Things were definitely starting to look up.

She turned to Marcus, who sat across from her looking impatient, as though he couldn't wait to be out of the
car and rid of her.

"Your home is beautiful," she told him.

He glanced over at her. "Had you expected otherwise?"

Way to be on the defensive, dude. "What I meant was,
the photos I've seen don't do it justice. Being here in person is really a thrill."

"I can only imagine," he said, with barely masked sarcasm.

Hell, who was she kidding, he didn't even *try* to mask
it. He really wasn't going to cut her a break, was he?

She sighed inwardly as they pulled up to the expansive marble front steps bracketed by towering white columns. At eighty thousand square feet the palace was larger than the White House, yet only a fraction of the size of Buckingham Palace.

The instant the door opened, Marcus was out of the car, leaving it to the driver to help Vanessa with her things. She gathered Mia, who was still out cold, into her arms and followed after Marcus, who stood waiting for her just inside the massive, two-story high double doors.

The interior was just as magnificent as the exterior, with a massive, circular foyer decorated in creamy beiges with marble floors polished to a gleaming shine. A ginormous crystal chandelier hung in the center, sparkling like diamonds in the sunshine streaming through windows so tall they met the domed ceiling. Hugging both sides of the curved walls, grand staircases with wrought iron railings branched off to the right and the left and wound up to the second floor. In the center of it all sat a large, intricately carved marble table with an enormous arrangement of fresh cut exotic flowers, whose sweet fragrance scented the air. The impression was a mix of tradition and modern sophistication. Class and a bit of excess.

Only then, as Vanessa gazed around in wonder, did the reality of her situation truly sink in. Her head spun and her heart pounded. This amazing place could be her home. Mia could grow up here, have the best of everything, and even more important than that, a man who would accept her as his own daughter. That alone was like a dream come true.

She wanted to tell Marcus how beautiful his home was, and how honored she felt to be there, but knew it would probably earn her another snotty response, so she kept her mouth shut.

From the hallway that extended past the stairs, a line of

nearly a dozen palace employees filed into the foyer and Marcus introduced her. Celia, the head housekeeper, was a tall, stern-looking woman dressed in a starched gray uniform, her silver hair pulled back into a tight bun. Her three charges were similarly dressed, but younger and very plain looking. No makeup, no jewelry, identical bland expressions.

Vanessa smiled and nodded to each one in turn.

"This is Camille," Celia told her in English, in a flat tone that perfectly matched her dour expression, signaling for the youngest of the three to step forward. "She will be your personal maid for the duration of your stay."

Duration of her stay? Were they anticipating that she wouldn't be sticking around? Or more to the point, hoping she wouldn't?

"It's nice to meet you, Camille," she said with a smile, offering her hand.

Looking a little nervous, the young woman took it, her eyes turned downward, and with a thick accent said, "Ma'am."

The butler, George, wore tails and a starched, high collar. He was skin and bones with a slight slouch, and looked as though he was fast approaching the century mark…if he hadn't hit it already. His staff consisted of two similarly dressed assistants, both young and capable looking, plus a chef and baker, a man and a woman, dressed in white, and each looking as though they frequently tested the cuisine.

Marcus turned to George and gestured to the luggage the driver had set inside the door. Without a word the two younger men jumped into action.

A smartly dressed middle-aged woman stepped forward and introduced herself as Tabitha, the king's personal secretary.

"If there is anything you need, don't hesitate to ask,"

she said in perfect English, her expression blank. Then she gestured to the young woman standing beside her, who wore a uniform similar to those of the maids. "This is Karin, the nanny. She will take care of your daughter."

Vanessa was a little uncomfortable with the idea of a total stranger watching her baby, but she knew Gabriel would never expose Mia to someone he didn't trust implicitly.

"It's very nice to meet you," Vanessa said, resisting the urge to ask the young woman to list her credentials.

"Ma'am," she said, nodding politely.

"Please, call me Vanessa. In fact, I've never been one to stand on formality. Everyone should feel free to use my first name."

The request received no reaction whatsoever from the staff. No one even cracked a smile. Were they always so deadpan, or did they simply not like her? Had they decided, as Marcus had, that she wasn't to be trusted?

That would truly suck. And she would have to work extra hard to prove them wrong.

Marcus turned to her. "I'll show you to your quarters."

Without waiting for a reply, he swiveled and headed up the stairs to the left, at a pace so brisk she nearly had to jog to keep up with him.

Unlike the beige theme of the foyer, the second floor incorporated rich hues of red, orange and purple, which personally she never would have chosen, but it managed to look elegant without being too gaudy.

Marcus led her down a long, carpeted hall.

"So, is the staff always so cheerful?" she asked him.

"It's not enough that they'll cater to your every whim," Marcus said over his shoulder. "They have to be happy about it?"

With a boss who clearly didn't like her, why would they?

At the end of the hallway they turned right and he opened the first door on his left. Gabriel told her that she would be staying in the largest of the guest suites, but she hadn't anticipated just how large it would be. The presidential suite at the hotel where she worked paled in comparison. The main room was big and spacious with high ceilings and tall windows that bracketed a pair of paned French doors. The color scheme ran to muted shades of green and yellow.

There was a cozy sitting area with overstuffed, comfortable-looking furniture situated around a massive fireplace. There was also a dining alcove, and a functional desk flanked by built-in bookcases whose shelves were packed with hardback books and knickknacks.

"It's lovely," she told Marcus. "Yellow is my favorite color."

"The bedroom is that way." Marcus gestured toward the door at the far end of the suite.

She crossed the plush carpet to the bedroom and peeked inside, her breath catching. It was pure luxury with its white four-poster king-size bed, another fireplace and a huge, wall-mounted flat screen television. But she didn't see the crib Gabriel had promised.

The weight of her sleeping daughter was starting to make her arms ache, so she very gently laid Mia down in the center of the bed and stacked fluffy pillows all around her, in case she woke up and rolled over. She didn't even stir.

On her way back to the living area Vanessa peered inside the walk-in closet where her bags were waiting for her, and found that it was large enough to hold a dozen of her wardrobes. The bathroom, with its soaking tub and glass-enclosed shower, had every modern amenity known to man.

She stepped back into the living space to find Marcus standing by the door, arms crossed, checking his watch impatiently.

"There's no place for Mia to sleep," she told him, and at his blank expression added, "Gabriel said there would be a crib for her. She moves around a lot in her sleep, so putting her in a normal bed, especially one so high off the ground, is out of the question."

"There's a nursery down the hall."

There was an unspoken "duh" at the end of that sentence.

"Then I hope there's a baby monitor I can use. Otherwise, how will I hear her if she wakes in the middle of the night?" Though Mia slept through most nights, Vanessa was still accustomed to the random midnight diaper changes and feedings, and an occasional bad dream.

He looked puzzled. "That would be the responsibility of the *nanny*."

Right, the nanny. Vanessa had just assumed the nanny was there for the times when Mia needed a babysitter, not as a full-time caregiver. She wasn't sure how she felt about that. Vanessa worked such long hours, and was away from home often. Part of this trip was about spending more time with her daughter.

"And where does the nanny sleep?" she asked Marcus.

"Her bedroom is attached to the nursery," he said, in a tone that suggested she was asking stupid questions. In his world it was probably perfectly natural for the staff to take full responsibility for the children's care, but she didn't live in his world. Not even close. Surely he knew that, didn't he?

She would have to carefully consider whether or not she wanted the nanny to take over the nightly duties. She didn't want to be difficult, or insult Karin, who was probably more than capable, but when it came to Mia, Vanessa didn't fool around. If necessary, she would ask Marcus to move the crib into her bedroom, and if he had a problem with that, she would just sleep in the nursery until Gabriel returned. Hopefully it wouldn't be more than a few days.

"If there's nothing else you need," Marcus said, edging toward the door. He really couldn't wait to get away, could he? Well, she wasn't about to let him off the hook just yet.

"What if I do need something?" she asked. "How do I find someone?"

"There's a phone on the desk, and a list of extensions."

"How will I know who to call?"

He didn't roll his eyes, but she could see that he wanted to. "For a beverage or food, you call the kitchen. If you need clean towels or fresh linens, you would call the laundry…you get the point."

She did, although she didn't appreciate the sarcasm. "Suppose I need you. Is your number on there?"

"No, it isn't, and even if it were, I wouldn't be available."

"Never?"

A nerve in his jaw ticked. "In my father's absence, I have a duty to my country."

Why did he have to be so defensive? "Marcus," she said, in a voice that she hoped conveyed sincerity, "I understand how you must be feeling, but—"

"You have no *idea* how I'm feeling," he ground out, and the level of animosity in his tone drew her back a step. "My father asked me to get you settled in, and I've done that. Now, if there's nothing else."

Someone cleared their throat and they both looked over to see the nanny standing in the doorway.

"I'll leave you two to discuss the child's care," Marcus said, making a hasty escape, and any hope she'd had that they might be friends went out the door with him.

"Come in," she told Karin.

Looking a little nervous, the girl stepped inside. "Shall I take Mia so you can rest?"

She still wasn't sure about leaving Mia in a stranger's care, but she was exhausted, and she would have a hard time relaxing with Mia in bed with her. If Vanessa fell too deeply asleep, Mia could roll off and hurt herself. And the last thing she needed was Marcus thinking that not only was she a money-grubbing con artist, but a terrible mother as well.

"I really could use a nap," she told Karin, "but if she wakes up crying, I'd like you to bring her right to me. She's bound to be disoriented waking up in a strange place with someone she doesn't know."

"Of course, ma'am."

"Please, call me Vanessa."

Karin nodded, but looked uncomfortable with the idea.

"Mia is asleep on the bed. Why don't I carry her, so I can see where the nursery is, and you can bring her bag?"

Karin nodded again.

Not very talkative, was she?

Vanessa scooped up Mia, who was still sleeping deeply, and rolled her suitcase out to Karin, who led her two doors down and across the hall to the nursery. It was smaller than her own suite, with a play area and a sleeping area, and it was decorated gender-neutral. The walls were pale green, the furniture white and expensive-looking, and in the play area rows of shelves were packed with toys for children of every age. It was clearly a nursery designed for guests, and she supposed that if she did decide to stay, Mia would get her own nursery closer to Gabriel's bedroom.

The idea of sharing a bedroom with Gabriel, and a bed, made her stomach do a nervous little flip-flop.

Everything will work out.

She laid Mia in the crib and covered her with a light blanket, and the baby didn't even stir. The poor little thing was exhausted.

"Maybe I should unpack her things," she told Karin.

"I'll do it, ma'am."

Vanessa sighed. So it was still "ma'am"? That was something they would just have to work on. "Thank you."

She kissed the tips of her fingers, then gently pressed them to Mia's forehead. "Sleep well, sweet baby."

After reiterating that Karin was to come get her when Mia woke, she walked back to her suite. She pulled her cell phone out of her bag and checked for calls, but there were none. She dialed Gabriel's cell number, but it went straight to voice mail.

She glanced over at the sofa, thinking she would sleep there for an hour or so, but the bed, with its creamy silk comforter and big, fluffy pillows, called to her. Setting her phone on the bedside table, she lay back against the pillows, sinking into the softness of the comforter. She let her eyes drift closed, and when she opened them again, the room was dark.

Three

After leaving Miss Reynolds's suite, Marcus stopped by his office, where his assistant Cleo, short for Cleopatra—her parents were Egyptian and very eccentric—sat at her computer playing her afternoon game of solitaire.

"Any word from my father?" he asked.

Attention on the screen, she shook her head.

"I'm glad to see that you're using your time productively," he teased, as he often did when he caught her playing games.

And obviously she didn't take him seriously, because she didn't even blink, or look away from the cards on the screen. "Keeps the brain sharp."

She may have been pushing seventy, but no one could argue that she wasn't still sharp as a pin. She'd been with the royal family since the 1970s, and used to be his mother's secretary. Everyone expected she would retire after the queen's death, and enjoy what would be a very generous pension, but she hadn't been ready to stop working. She claimed it kept her young. And since her husband passed away two years ago, Marcus suspected she was lonely.

She finished the game and quit out of the software, a group photo of her eight grandchildren flashing on to her computer screen. She turned to Marcus and caught him in the middle of a yawn and frowned. "Tired?"

After a month-long battle with insomnia, he was always tired. And he wasn't in the mood for another lecture. "I'm sure I'll sleep like a baby when *she* is gone."

"She's that bad?"

He sat on the edge of her desk. "She's awful."

"And you know this after what, thirty minutes with her?"

"I knew after five. I knew the second she stepped off the plane."

She leaned forward in her chair, elbows on her desk, her white hair draped around a face that was young for her years, and with no help at all from a surgeon's knife. "Based on what?"

"She only wants his money."

Her brows rose. "She told you that?"

"She didn't have to. She's young, and beautiful, and a single mother. What else would she want from a man my father's age?"

"For the record, your highness, fifty-six is not that old."

"For her it is."

"Your father is an attractive and charming man. Who's to say that she didn't fall head over heels in love with him."

"In a few *weeks?*"

"I fell in love with my husband after our first date. Never underestimate the powers of physical attraction."

He cringed. The idea of his father and that woman... he didn't even want to think about it. Though he didn't doubt she had seduced him. That was the way her kind operated. He knew from experience, having been burned before. And his father, despite his staunch moral integrity, was vulnerable enough to fall under her spell.

"So, she's really that attractive?" Cleo asked.

Much as he wished he could say otherwise, there was no denying her beauty. "She is. But she had a child out of wedlock."

She gasped and slapped a hand to her chest. "Off with her head!"

He glared at her.

"You do remember what century this is? Women's rights and equality and all that."

"Yes, but *my* father? A man who lives by tradition. It's beneath him. He's lonely, missing my mother and not thinking straight."

"You don't give him much credit, do you? The king is a very intelligent man."

Yes, he was, and clearly not thinking with his brain. No one could convince Marcus that this situation was anything but temporary. And until she left, he would simply stay out of her way.

Vanessa bolted up in bed, heart racing, disoriented by the unfamiliar surroundings. Then, as her eyes adjusted to the dark and the room came into focus, she remembered where she was.

At first she thought that she'd slept late into the night, then realized that someone had shut the curtains. She grabbed her cell phone and checked the time, relieved to see that she had only slept for an hour and a half, and there were no missed calls from Gabriel.

She dialed his cell number, but like before it went straight to voice mail. She hung up and grabbed her laptop from her bag, hoping that maybe he'd sent her an email, but the network was password protected and she couldn't log on. She would have to ask someone for the password.

She closed the laptop and sighed. Since she hadn't heard a word from Karin, she could only assume Mia was still asleep, and without her daughter to take care of, Vanessa felt at a loss for what to do. Then she remembered all the bags in the closet waiting to be unpacked—basically her entire summer wardrobe—and figured she could kill time doing that.

She pushed herself up out of bed, her body still heavy with fatigue, and walked to the closet. But instead of finding packed suitcases, she discovered that her clothes had all been unpacked and put away. The maid must have been in while she was asleep, which was probably a regular thing around here, but she couldn't deny that it creeped her out a little. She didn't like the idea of someone else handling her things, but it was something she would just have to get used to, as she probably wouldn't be doing her own laundry.

She stripped out of her rumpled slacks and blouse and changed into yoga pants and a soft cotton top, wondering, when her stomach rumbled, what time she would be called for dinner. She grabbed her phone off the bed and walked out to the living room, where late afternoon sunshine flooded the windows and cut paths across the creamy carpet. She crossed the room and pulled open the French doors. A wall of heat sucked the breath from her lungs as she stepped out onto a balcony with wrought iron railings and exotic plants. It overlooked acres of rolling green grass and colorful flower beds, and directly below was the Olympic-size pool and cabana Gabriel had told her about. He put the pool in, he'd bragged, because Marcus had been a champion swimmer in high school and college, and to this day still swam regularly. Which would account for the impressively toned upper body.

But she definitely shouldn't be thinking about Marcus's upper body, or any other part of him.

Her cell phone rang and Gabriel's number flashed on the screen. Oh, thank God. Her heart lifted so swiftly it left her feeling dizzy.

She answered, and the sound of his voice was like a salve on her raw nerves. She conjured up a mental image of his face. His dark, gentle eyes, the curve of his smile, and realized just then how much she missed him.

"I'm so sorry I couldn't be there to greet you," he told her, speaking in his native language of Variean, which was so similar to Italian they were practically interchangeable. And since she was fluent in the latter, learning the subtle differences had been simple for her.

"I miss you," she told him.

"I know, I'm sorry. How was your flight? How is Mia?"

"It was long, and Mia didn't sleep much, but she's napping now. I just slept for a while too."

"My plane left not twenty minutes before you were due to arrive."

"Your son said it was a family matter. I hope everything is okay."

"I wish I could say it was. It's my wife's half sister, Trina, in Italy. She was rushed to the hospital with an infection."

"Oh, Gabriel, I'm so sorry." He'd spoken often of his sister-in-law, and how she had stayed with him and his son for several weeks before and after the queen died. "I know you two are very close. I hope it's nothing too serious."

"She's being treated, but she's not out of danger. I hope you understand, but I just can't leave her. She's a widow, and childless. She has no one else. She was there for me and Marcus when we needed her. I feel obligated to stay."

"Of course you do. Family always comes first."

She heard him breathe a sigh of relief. "I knew you would understand. You're an extraordinary woman, Vanessa."

"Is there anything I can do? Any way I can help?"

"Just be patient with me. I wish I could invite you to stay with me, but…"

"She's your wife's sister. I'm guessing that would be awkward for everyone."

"I think it would."

"How long do you think you'll be?"

"Two weeks, maybe. I won't know for sure until we see how she's responding to the treatment."

Two weeks? Alone with Marcus? Was the universe playing some sort of cruel trick on her? Not that she imagined he would be chomping at the bit to spend quality time with her. With any luck he would keep to himself and she wouldn't have to actually see Marcus at all.

"I promise I'll be back as soon as I possibly can," Gabriel said. "Unless you prefer to fly home until I return."

Home to what? Her apartment was sublet for the next six weeks. She lived on a shoestring budget, and being on unpaid leave, she hadn't had the money for rent while she was gone. Gabriel had offered to pay, but she felt uncomfortable taking a handout from him. Despite what Marcus seemed to believe, the fact that Gabriel was very wealthy wasn't all that important to her. And until they were married—if that day ever came—she refused to let him spoil her. Not that he hadn't tried.

The wining and dining was one thing, but on their third date he bought her a pair of stunning diamond earrings to show his appreciation for her professional services at the hotel. She had refused to take them. She had drooled over a similar pair in the jewelry boutique at the hotel with a price tag that amounted to a year's salary.

Then there had been the lush flower arrangements that began arriving at her office every morning like clockwork after he'd flown back home, and the toys for Mia from local shops. She'd had to gently but firmly tell him, no more. There was no need to buy her affections.

"I'll wait for you," she told Gabriel. Even if she did have a place to go home to, the idea of making that miserably long flight two more times with Mia in tow was motivation enough to stay.

"I promise we'll chat daily. You brought your laptop?"

"Yes, but I can't get on the network. And I'll need plug adaptors since the outlets are different."

"Just ask Marcus. I've instructed him to get you anything that you need. He was there to greet you, wasn't he?"

"Yes, he was there."

"And he was respectful?"

She could tell Gabriel the truth, but what would that accomplish, other than to make Gabriel feel bad, and Marcus resent her even more. The last thing she wanted to do was cause a rift between father and son.

"He made me feel very welcome."

"I'm relieved. He took losing his mother very hard."

"And it's difficult for him to imagine you with someone new."

"Exactly. I'm proud of him for taking the change so well."

He wouldn't be proud if he knew how Marcus had really acted, but that would remain hers and Marcus's secret.

"Your room is satisfactory?"

"Beyond satisfactory, and the palace is amazing. I plan

to take Mia for a walk on the grounds tomorrow, and I can hardly wait to visit the village."

"I'm sure Marcus would be happy to take you. You should ask him."

When hell froze over, maybe. Besides, she would much rather go exploring on her own, just her and Mia.

"Maybe I will," she said, knowing she would do no such thing.

"I know that when you get to know one another, you'll become friends."

Somehow she doubted that. Even if she wanted to, Marcus clearly wanted nothing to do with her.

"I left a surprise for you," Gabriel said. "It's in the top drawer of the desk."

"What sort of surprise?" she asked, already heading in that direction.

"Well, it won't be a surprise if I tell you," he teased. "Look and see."

She was already opening the drawer. Inside was a credit card with her name on it. She picked it up and sighed. "Gabriel, I appreciate the gesture, but—"

"I know, I know. You're too proud to take anything from me. But I *want* to do this for you."

"I just don't feel comfortable spending your money. You're doing enough already."

"Suppose you see something in the village that you like? I know you have limited funds. I want you to have nice things."

"I have you, that's all I need."

"And that, my dear, is why you are such an amazing woman. And why I love you. Promise me you'll keep it with you, just in case. I don't care if it's five euros or five thousand. If you see something you really want, please buy it."

"I'll keep it handy," she said, dropping it back in the drawer, knowing she would never spend a penny.

"I've missed you, Vanessa. I'm eager to start our life together."

"If I stay," she reminded him, so he knew that nothing was set in stone yet.

"You will," he said, as confident and certain as the day he'd asked her to marry him. Then there was the sound of voices in the background. "Vanessa, I have to go. The doctor is here and I need to speak with him."

"Of course."

"We'll chat tomorrow, yes?"

"Yes."

"I love you, my sweet Vanessa."

"I love you, too," she said, then the call disconnected.

She sighed and set her phone on the desk, hoping there would come a day when she could say those words, and mean them the way that Gabriel did. That there would be a time when the sort of love she felt for him extended past friendship.

It wasn't that she didn't find him attractive. There was no doubt that he was an exceptionally good-looking man. Maybe his jaw wasn't as tight as it used to be, and there was gray at his temples, and he wasn't as fit as he'd been in his younger years, but those things didn't bother her. It was what was on the inside that counted. And her affection for him felt warm and comfortable. What was missing was that...*zing.*

Like the one you felt when you took Marcus's hand?

She shook away the thought. Yes, Marcus was an attractive man, too, plus he didn't have the sagging skin, graying hair and expanding waist. He also didn't have his father's sweet disposition and generous heart.

When Gabriel held her, when he'd brushed his lips

across her cheek, she felt respected and cherished and safe. And okay, maybe those things didn't make for steamy hot sex, but she knew from personal experience that sex could be highly overrated. What really mattered was respect, and friendship. That's what was left when the *zing* disappeared. And it always did.

Men like Marcus thrilled, then they bailed. Usually leaving a substantial mess in their wake. She could just imagine the string of broken hearts he'd caused. But Gabriel was dependable and trustworthy, and that's exactly what she was looking for in a man now. She'd had her thrills, now she wanted a mature, lasting relationship. Gabriel could give her that. That and so much more, if she was smart enough, and strong enough, to let him.

Four

Marcus was halfway through his second set of laps that evening, the burn in his muscles shaking off the stress that hung on his shoulders like an iron cloak, when he heard his cell phone start to ring. He swam to the side of the pool, hoisted himself up onto the deck and walked to the table where he'd left his phone, the hot tile scorching his feet. It was his father.

He almost didn't answer. He was sure his father would have spoken to Miss Reynolds by now, and she had probably regaled him with the story of Marcus's less than warm welcome. The first thing on her agenda would be to drive a wedge between him and his father, which the king would see through, of course. Maybe not right away, but eventually, and Marcus was happy to let her hang herself with her own rope. Even if that meant receiving an admonishment from his father now. So he took the call.

"Father, how is Aunt Trina?"

"Very sick, son," he said.

His heart sank. He just wasn't ready to say goodbye to yet another loved one. "What's the prognosis?"

"It will be touch and go for a while, but the doctors are hoping she'll make a full recovery."

He breathed a sigh of relief. No one should ever have to endure so much loss in the span of only eight months. "If there's anything you need, just say so."

"There is something, but first, son, I wanted to thank you, and tell you how proud I am of you. And ashamed of myself."

Proud of him? Maybe he hadn't spoken to Miss Reynolds after all. Or was it possible that he'd already seen though her scheme and had come to his senses? "What do you mean?"

"I know that accepting I've moved on, that I've fallen in love with someone new—especially someone so young—has been difficult for you. I was afraid that you might treat Vanessa…well, less than hospitably. But knowing that you've made her feel welcome…son, I'm sorry that I didn't trust you. I should have realized that you're a man of integrity."

What the hell had she told him exactly?

Marcus wasn't sure what to say, and his father's words, his misplaced faith, filled him with guilt. How would he feel if he knew the truth? And why had she lied to him? What sort of game was she playing? Or was it possible that she really did care about his father?

Of course she didn't. She was working some sort of angle, that was how her kind always operated.

"Isn't her daughter precious?" his father said, sounding absolutely smitten. Marcus couldn't recall him ever using the word *precious* in any context.

"She is," he agreed, though he'd seen her do nothing

but scream and sleep. "Is there anything pressing I should know about, business that needs tending?"

"There's no need to worry about that. I've decided to fly my staff here and set up a temporary office."

"That's really not necessary. I can handle matters while you're away."

"You know I would go out of my mind if I had nothing to do. This way I can work and still be with Trina."

That seemed like an awful lot of trouble for a short visit, unless it wasn't going to be short. "How long do you expect you'll be gone?"

"Well, I told Vanessa two weeks," he said. "But the truth is, it could be longer."

He had a sudden, sinking feeling. "How much longer?"

"Hopefully no more than three or four weeks."

A *month*. There was no question that Trina—*family*— should come first, but that seemed excessive. Especially since he had a guest. "A month is a long time to be away."

"And how long did Trina give up her life to stay with us when your mother was ill?"

She had stayed with them for several months in the final stages of his mother's illness, then another few weeks after the funeral. So he certainly couldn't fault his father for wanting to stay with her. "I'm sorry, I'm being selfish. Of course you should be there with her. As long as she needs you. Maybe I should join you."

"I need you at the palace. Since Tabitha will be with me, it will be up to you to see that Vanessa and Mia have anything they need."

"Of course." He could hardly wait.

"And I know this is a lot to ask, but I want you to keep them entertained."

Marcus hoped he didn't mean that the way it sounded. *"Entertained?"*

"Make them feel welcome. Take them sightseeing, show them a good time."

The idea had been to stay away from her as much as humanly possible, not be her tour guide. "Father—"

"I realize I'm asking a lot of you under the circumstances, and I know it will probably be a bit awkward at first, but it will give you and Vanessa a chance to get to know one another. She's truly a remarkable woman, son. I'm sure that once you get to know her you'll love her as much as I do."

Nothing his father could say would make Marcus want to spend time with that woman. And no amount of time that he spent with her would make him "love" her. "Father, I don't think—"

"Imagine how she and her daughter must feel, in a foreign country where they don't know a soul. And I feel terrible for putting her in that position. It took me weeks to convince her to come here. If she leaves, she may never agree to come back."

And that would be a bad thing?

Besides, Marcus didn't doubt for an instant that she had just been playing hard to get, stringing his father along, and now that she was here, he seriously doubted she had any intention of leaving, for any reason. But maybe in this case absence wouldn't make the heart grow fonder. Maybe it would give his father time to think about his relationship with Miss Reynolds and realize the mistake he was making.

Or maybe, instead of waiting for this to play out, Marcus could take a more proactive approach. Maybe he could persuade her to leave.

The thought brought a smile to his face.

"I'll do it," he told his father.

"I have your word?"

"Yes," he said, feeling better about the situation already. "You have my word."

"Thank you, son. You have no idea how much this means to me. And I don't want you to worry about anything else. Consider yourself on vacation until I return."

"Is there anyplace in particular you would like me to take her?"

"I'll email a list of the things she might enjoy doing."

"I'll watch for it," he said, feeling cheerful for the first time in weeks, since his father had come home acting like a lovesick teenager.

"She did mention a desire to tour the village," the king said.

That was as good a place to start as any. "Well then, we'll go first thing tomorrow."

"I can't tell you what a relief this is. And if ever you should require anything from me, you need only ask."

Send her back to the U.S., he wanted to say, but he would be taking care of that. After he was through with her, she would be *sprinting* for the plane. But the key with a woman like her was patience and subtlety.

He and his father hung up, and Marcus dropped his phone back on the table. He looked over at the pool, then up to the balcony of Miss Reynolds's room. He should give her the good news right away, so she would have time to prepare for tomorrow's outing. He toweled off then slipped his shirt, shorts and sandals on, combing his fingers through his wet hair as he headed upstairs. He half expected to hear her daughter howling as he approached her room, but the hallway was silent.

He knocked, and she must have been near the door because it opened almost immediately. She had changed into snug black cotton pants, a plain pink T-shirt, and her hair was pulled up in a ponytail. She looked even younger this way, and much more relaxed than she had when she stepped off the plane. It struck him again how attractive she really was. Without makeup she looked a little less exotic and vampy, but her features, the shape of her face, were exquisite.

He looked past her into the suite and saw that she had spread a blanket across the carpet in the middle of the room. Mia was in the center, balanced on her hands and knees, rocking back and forth, shaking her head from side to side, a bit like a deranged pendulum. Then she stopped, toppled over to the left, and rolled onto her back, looking dazed.

Was she having some sort of fit or seizure?

"Is she okay?" Marcus asked, wondering if he should call the physician.

Miss Reynolds smiled at her daughter. "She's fine."

"What was she doing?" Marcus asked.

"Crawling."

Crawling? "She doesn't seem to be getting very far."

"Not yet. The first step is learning to balance on her hands and knees."

She apparently had a long way to go to master that.

Mia squealed and rolled over onto her tummy, then pushed herself back up and resumed rocking. She seemed to be doing all right, until her arms gave out and she pitched forward. Marcus cringed as she fell face-first into the blanket, landing on her button nose. She lifted her head, looking stunned for a second, then she screwed up her face and started to cry.

When Miss Reynolds just stood there, Marcus asked, "Is she okay?"

"She's probably more frustrated than injured."

After several more seconds of Mia wailing, when she

did nothing to comfort the child, he said, "Aren't you going to pick her up?"

She shrugged. "If I picked her up every time she got discouraged, she'd never learn to try. She'll be fine in a second."

No sooner had she spoken the words than Mia's cries abruptly stopped, then she hoisted herself back up on her hands and knees, starting the process all over again. Rocking, falling over, wailing…

"Does she do this often?" he asked after watching her for several minutes.

She sighed, as if frustrated, but resigned. "Almost constantly for the past three days."

"Is that…normal?"

"For her it is. She's a very determined child. She'll keep doing something over and over until she gets it right. She gets that from my father, I think."

He could tell, from the deep affection in her eyes, the pride in her smile as she watched her daughter, that Miss Reynolds loved the little girl deeply. Which made her attempts to con his father all the more despicable.

"I'm sorry," she said, finally turning to him. "Was there something you wan…" She trailed off, blinking in surprise as she took in the sight of him, as if she just now noticed how he was dressed. Starting at his sandals, her eyes traveled up his bare legs and over his shorts, then they settled on the narrow strip of chest where the two sides of his shirt had pulled open. For several seconds she seemed transfixed, then she gave her head a little shake, and her eyes snapped up to his.

She blinked again, looking disoriented, and asked, "I'm sorry, what did you say?"

He began to wonder if maybe he'd been mistaken earlier, and she really was a brainless blonde. "I didn't say anything. But I believe you were about to ask me if there was something that I wanted."

Her cheeks blushed bright pink. "You're right, I was. Sorry. Was there? Something you wanted, I mean."

"If you have a moment, I'd like to have a word with you."

"Of course," she said, stepping back from the door and pulling it open, stumbling over her own foot. "Sorry. Would you like to come in?"

He stepped into the room, wondering if perhaps she'd been sampling the contents of the bar. "Are you all right?"

"I took a nap. I guess I'm not completely awake yet. Plus, I'm still on California time. It's barely seven a.m. in Los Angeles. Technically I was up most of the night."

That could explain it, he supposed, yet he couldn't help questioning her mental stability.

She closed the door and turned to him. "What did you want to talk about?"

"I want to know why you lied to my father."

She blinked in surprise, opened her mouth to speak, then shut it again. Then, as if gathering her patience, she took a deep breath, slowly blew it out, and asked, "Refresh my memory, what did I lie about?"

Did she honestly not know what he meant, or were there so many lies, she couldn't keep track? "You told my father that I made you feel welcome. We both know that isn't true."

She got an "oh *that*" look on her face. "What was I supposed to tell him? His son, who he loves and respects dearly, acted like a big jer—" She slapped a hand over her mouth, but it was pretty obvious what she'd been about to say.

Marcus had to clench his jaw to keep it from falling open. "Did you just call me a *jerk?*"

She shook her head, eyes wide. "No."

"Yes, you did. You called me a *big jerk*."

She hesitated, looking uneasy. "Maybe I did."

"Maybe?"

"Okay, I did. I told you, I'm half asleep. It just sort of… slipped out. And let's be honest, Marcus, you were acting like a jerk."

He was sure people said unfavorable things about him all the time, but no one, outside of his family, had ever dared insult him to his face. Twice. He should feel angry, or annoyed, yet all he felt was an odd amusement. "Are you *trying* to make me dislike you?"

"You already don't like me. At this point I doubt anything I say, or don't say, will change that. Which I think is kind of sad but…" She shrugged. "And for the record, I didn't *lie* to Gabriel. I just…fudged the truth a little."

"Why?"

"He has enough on his mind. He doesn't need to be worrying about me. Besides, I can fight my own battles."

If he didn't know better, he might believe that she really did care about his father. But he knew her type. He'd dated a dozen women just like her. She was only after one thing—his legacy—and like the others, he would make sure that she never got her hands on it.

"I would hardly call this a battle," he told her.

She folded her arms, emphasizing the fullness of her breasts. "You would if you were me."

Marcus had to make an effort to keep his eyes on her face. But even that was no hardship. She was exceptionally attractive and undeniably sexy. A beautiful woman with a black heart.

Her eyes wandered downward, to his chest, lingering there for several seconds, then as if realizing she was staring, she quickly looked away.

She didn't strike him as the type to be shy about the male physique. Or maybe it was just his that bothered her.

"Look," she said. "You don't like me, and that's fine. I can even understand why. It's disappointing that you aren't going to give me a chance, but, whatever. And if I'm being totally honest, I'm not so crazy about you either. So why don't we just agree to stay out of each other's way?"

"Miss Reynolds—"

"It's *Vanessa*. You could at least have the decency to use my first name."

"Vanessa," he said. "How would you feel if we called a truce?"

Five

A truce?

Vanessa studied Marcus's face, trying to determine if his words were sincere. Instead, all she could seem to concentrate on was his damp, slicked-back hair and the single wavy lock that had fallen across his forehead. She felt the strongest urge to brush it back with her fingers. And why couldn't she stop looking at that tantalizing strip of tanned, muscular, bare chest?

"Why would you do that?" she asked, forcing her attention above his neck. He folded his arms over his chest and she had to wonder if he'd seen her staring. Was she creeping him out? If she were him, she would probably be creeped out.

"I thought you wanted me to give you a chance," he said.

But why the sudden change of heart? A couple of hours ago he could barely stand to be in the same room with her. She couldn't escape the feeling that he was up to something. "Of course I do, you just didn't seem too thrilled with the idea."

"That was before I learned that for the next few weeks, we're going to be seeing a lot of each other."

She blinked. "What do you mean?"

"My father thinks it would be a good idea for us to get to know one another, and in his absence has asked me to be your companion. I'm to show you and your daughter a good time, keep you entertained."

Oh no, what had Gabriel done? She wanted Marcus to give her a chance, but not by force. That would only make him resent her more. Not to mention that she hadn't anticipated him being so...

Something.

Something that made her trip over her own feet and stumble over her words, and do stupid things like stare at his bare chest and insult him to his face.

"I don't need a companion," she told him. "Mia and I will be fine on our own."

"For your safety, you wouldn't be able to leave the palace without an escort."

"My safety?"

"There are certain criminal elements to consider."

Her heart skipped a beat. "What kind of criminal elements?"

"The kind who would love nothing more than to get their hands on the future queen. You would fetch quite the ransom."

She couldn't decide if he was telling the truth, or just trying to scare her. Kidnappings certainly weren't unheard of, but Varieo was such a quiet, peaceful country. No handguns, very little crime. Gabriel hadn't mentioned any potential threat or danger.

And why would he when he was trying to convince

her to marry him? There was a reason royalty had body-guards, right?

Wait a minute. Who even knew that she was here? It wasn't as if Gabriel would broadcast to the country that eight months after his wife's death he was bringing his new American girlfriend in for a visit.

Would he?

"The point is," Marcus said, "my father wanted you to have an escort, and that person is me."

"What about Tabitha?"

"She's flying to Italy to be with my father. He takes her everywhere. Some people have even thought…" He paused and shook his head. "Never mind."

Okay, now he *was* trying to mess with her.

But how well do you really know Gabriel, that annoying voice of doubt interjected. He could have a dozen mistresses for all she knew. Just because he claimed to have been faithful to his wife didn't mean it was true. Maybe there was no sick sister-in-law. Maybe he was with another one of his girlfriends. Maybe there had been a scheduling conflict and he chose her over Vanessa. Maybe he—

Ugh! What are you doing?

She *trusted* Gabriel, and she hated that Marcus could shake her faith with one simple insinuation. And a ridiculous one at that. Maybe she hadn't known Gabriel long, but in that short time he had never been anything but honest and dependable. And until someone produced irrefutable evidence to the contrary, she was determined to trust him.

This wasn't another dumb mistake.

It wasn't Gabriel's fault that she'd had lousy luck with relationships, and it wasn't fair to judge him on her own bad experiences. If he wanted her to spend a couple of weeks getting to know his son, that's what she would do, even if she didn't exactly trust Marcus, and questioned his motives. She would just be herself, and hope that Marcus would put aside his doubts and accept her.

"I guess I'm stuck with you then," she told him.

Marcus frowned, looking as if she'd hurt his feelings. "If the idea of spending time with me is so offensive—"

"No! Of course not. That isn't what I meant." No matter what she said, it always seemed to be the wrong thing. "I really would like us to get acquainted, Marcus. I just don't want you to feel pressured, as if you have no choice. I can only imagine how awkward this is for you, and how heartbreaking it was to lose your mother. It sounds as if she was a remarkable woman, and I would never in a million years try to replace her, or even think that I could. I just want Gabriel to be happy. He deserves it. I think that would be much more likely to happen if you and I are friends. Or at the very least, not mortal enemies."

"I'm willing to concede that I may have rushed to judgment," he said. "And for the record, my father is not *forcing* me. I could have refused, but I know it's important to him."

It was no apology for his behavior earlier, but it was definitely a start. And she hoped he really meant it, that he didn't have ulterior motives for being nice to her. "In that case, I would be honored to have you as my escort."

"So, truce?" he said, stepping closer with an outstretched hand. And boy did he smell good. Some sort of spicy delicious scent that made her want to bury her face in his neck and take a big whiff.

No, she *definitely* didn't want to do that. And she didn't want to feel the zing of awareness when he clasped her hand, the tantalizing shiver as his thumb brushed across the top of her hand, or the residual buzz after he let go.

How could she zing for a man she didn't even like?

"My father will be sending me a list of activities he thinks you'll enjoy, and he's asked me to accompany you to the village tomorrow. If there's anything in particular you'd like to do, or someplace you would like to see, let me know and we'll work it into the schedule."

Honestly, she would be thrilled to just lie around by the pool and doze for a week, but she knew Gabriel wanted her to familiarize herself with the area, because how could she decide if she wanted to live somewhere if she didn't see it? "If there's anything I'll let you know."

"Be ready tomorrow at ten a.m."

"I will."

He nodded and walked out, closing the door behind him.

Vanessa sat on the floor beside her daughter, who had tired of rocking, and was now lying on her tummy gnawing contentedly on a teething ring.

The idea of spending so much time alone with Marcus made her uneasy, but she didn't seem to have much choice. To refuse would only hurt Gabriel's feelings, and make her look like the bad guy. At the very least, when the staff saw that Marcus was accepting her, they might warm up to her as well.

Vanessa's cell phone rang and she jumped up to grab it off the desk, hoping it was Gabriel.

It was her best friend Jessy.

"Hey! I just woke up and got your text," Jessy said, and Vanessa could picture her, sitting in bed in her pajamas, eyes puffy, her spiky red hair smashed flat from sleeping with the covers pulled over her head. "How was the flight?"

"A nightmare. Mia hardly slept." She smiled down at her daughter who was still gnawing and drooling all over the blanket. "But she seems to be adjusting pretty well now."

"Was Gabriel happy to see you?"

Vanessa hesitated. She didn't want to lie to Jessy, but she was afraid the truth would only add to her friend's doubts. But if she couldn't talk to her best friend, who could she talk to?

"There was a slight change of plans." She explained the situation with Gabriel's sister-in-law, and why he felt he had to be with her. "I know what you're probably thinking."

"Yes, I have reservations about you taking this trip, but I have to trust that you know what's best for you and Mia."

"Even if you don't agree?"

"I can't help but worry about you, and I absolutely hate the idea of you moving away. But ultimately, what I think doesn't matter."

To Vanessa it did. They had been inseparable since Vanessa moved to L.A. With her statuesque figure and exquisitely beautiful features—assets that, unlike Vanessa, she chose to cleverly downplay—Jessy understood what it was like to be labeled the "pretty" girl. She knew that, depending on the circumstances, it could be more of a liability than an asset. They also shared the same lousy taste in men, although Jessy was now in a relationship with Wayne, a pharmaceutical rep, who she thought might possibly be the *one*. He was attractive without being too handsome—since she'd found most of the really good-looking guys to be arrogant—he had a stable career, drove a nice car and lived in an oceanside condo. And aside from the fact that he had a slightly unstable and bitter ex-wife and a resentful teenaged daughter with self-cutting issues in Seattle, he was darn close to perfect.

Vanessa hoped that they had both found their forever man. God knows they had paid their dues.

"So, what will you do until Gabriel comes back?" Jessy asked, and Vanessa heard the whine of the coffee grinder in the background.

"His son has agreed to be my companion." Just the thought caused a funny little twinge in her stomach.

"Companion?"

"He'll take me sightseeing, keep me entertained."

"Is he as hot in person as he is in the photos you showed me?"

Unfortunately. "On a scale of one to ten, he's a solid fifteen."

"So, if things don't work out with Gabriel..." she teased.

"Did I mention that he's also a jerk? And he doesn't seem to like me very much. Not that I don't understand why." She picked a hunk of carpet fuzz from Mia's damp fingers before she could stuff it in her mouth. "Gabriel wants us to be friends. But I think I would settle for Marcus not hating my guts."

"Vanessa, you're one of the sweetest, kindest, most thoughtful people I've ever met. How could he not like you?"

The problem was, sometimes she was too nice and too sweet and too thoughtful. To the point that she let people walk all over her. And Marcus struck her as the sort of man who would take advantage of that.

Or maybe she was being paranoid.

"He's very...intense," she told Jessy. "When he steps into a room he's just so...*there*. It's a little intimidating."

"Well, he is a prince."

"And Gabriel is a king, but I've never felt anything but comfortable with him."

"Don't take this the wrong way, but maybe Gabriel, being older, is more like...a father figure."

"Jessy, my dad has been enough of a father figure to last a dozen lifetimes."

"And you've told me a million times how his criticism makes you feel like a failure."

She couldn't deny that, and Gabriel's lavish attention did make her feel special, but she wasn't looking for a substitute father. Quite the opposite in fact. In the past she always found herself attracted to men who wanted to control or dominate her. And the worst part was that she usually let them. This time she wanted a partner. An *equal*.

Maybe the main thing that bothered her about Marcus—besides the fact that he despised her—was that he seemed a bit too much like the sort of man she used to date.

"I don't trust Marcus," she told Jessy. "He made it clear the minute I stepped off the plane that he didn't like me, then a couple of hours later he was offering to take me sightseeing. He said he's doing it for his father, but I'm not sure I buy that. If he really wanted to please Gabriel, wouldn't he have been nice to me the second I stepped off the plane?"

"Do you think he's going to try to come between you and Gabriel?"

"At this point, I'm not sure what to think." The only thing she did know was that something about Marcus made her nervous, and she didn't like it, but she was more or less stuck with him until Gabriel returned.

"I have some good news of my own," Jessy said. "Wayne has invited me to Arkansas for a couple of days for his parents' fortieth anniversary party. He wants me to meet his family."

"You're going, right?"

"I'd love to. Do you realize how long it's been since I've met a man's family, since I've even wanted to? The thing is, they live in a remote area that doesn't have great cell coverage and I might be hard to get ahold of. I'm just a little worried that if you end up needing me—"

"Jessy, I'll be fine. Worst-case scenario, I can call my dad." Although things would have to be pretty awful for her to do that.

"Are you sure? I know you say everything is okay, but I still worry about you."

"Well, don't," she told Jessy. "I can handle Prince Marcus."

She just hoped that was true.

Six

Marcus was sure he had Vanessa pegged, but after spending a day with her in the village, he was beginning to wonder if his original assumptions about her were slightly, well...unreliable.

His first hint that something might be off was when he arrived at her door at 10 a.m. sharp, fully anticipating a fifteen- or twenty-minute wait while she finished getting ready. It was a game women liked to play. They seemed to believe it drew out the anticipation or gave them power, or some such nonsense, when in reality, it just annoyed him. But when Vanessa opened the door dressed in conservative cotton shorts, a sleeveless top, comfortable-looking sandals and a floppy straw hat, she was clearly ready to go, and with a camera hanging from a strap around her neck, a diaper bag slung over one shoulder and her daughter on her hip, she looked more like an American tourist than a gold digger angling for the position of queen.

His suspicions grew throughout the day while he witnessed her shopping habits—or lack thereof. Tabitha, with only the king's best interest at heart, had warned Marcus of the credit card his father had requested for Vanessa, and its outrageous credit limit. Therefore, Marcus requested his driver be at the ready in anticipation of armfuls of packages. But by midafternoon they had visited at least a dozen shops showcasing everything from souvenirs to designer clothing to fine jewelry, and though he'd watched her admire the fashions, and seen her gaze longingly at a pair of modestly priced, hand-crafted earrings, all she'd purchased was a T-shirt for her daughter, a postcard that she said she intended to send to her best friend in L.A. and a paperback romance novel—her one guilty pleasure, she'd explained with a wry smile. And she'd paid with cash. He had an even bigger surprise when he heard her speaking to a merchant and realized she spoke his language fluently.

"You never mentioned that you could speak Variean," he said, when they left the shop.

She just shrugged and said, "You never asked."

She was right. And everything about her puzzled him. She was worldly and well traveled, but there was a childlike delight and curiosity in her eyes with each new place she visited. She didn't just see the sights, but absorbed her surroundings like a sponge, the most trivial and mundane details—things he would otherwise overlook—snagging her interest. And she asked a million questions. Her excitement and enthusiasm were so contagious he actually began to see the village with a fresh pair of eyes. Even though they were tired and achy from lack of sleep.

She was intelligent, yet whimsical, and at times even a little flighty. Poised and graceful, yet adorably awkward, occasionally bumping into a store display or another shopper, or tripping on a threshold—or even her own feet.

Once, she was so rapt when admiring the architecture of a historical church, she actually walked right into a tourist who had paused abruptly in front of her to take a photo. But instead of looking annoyed, Vanessa simply laughed, apologized and complimented the woman on her shoes.

Vanessa also had an amusing habit of saying exactly what she was thinking, while she was thinking it, and oftentimes embarrassing herself or someone else in the process.

Though she was obviously many things—or at least wanted him to believe she was—if he had to choose a single word to describe her it would probably be...*quirky*.

Twenty-four hours ago he would have been content never to see her again. But now, as he sat across from her on a blanket in the shade of an olive tree near the dock, in the members-only park off the marina, watching her snack on sausage, cheese and crackers—which she didn't eat so much as inhale—with Mia on the blanket between them rocking back and forth, back and forth on her hands and knees, he was experiencing a disconcerting combination of perplexity, suspicion and fascination.

"I guess you were hungry," he said as she plucked the last cheese wedge from the plate and popped it in her mouth.

Most women would be embarrassed or even offended by such as observation, but she just shrugged.

"I'm borderline hypoglycemic, so I have to eat at least five or six times a day. But I was blessed with a fast metabolism, so I never gain weight. It's just one more reason for other women to hate me."

"Why would other women hate you?"

"Are you kidding? A woman who looks like I do, who can eat anything and not gain an ounce? Some people consider that an unforgivable crime, as though I have some

sort of control over how pretty I am, or how my body processes nutrients. You have no idea how often as a teenager
I wished I were more ordinary."

Acknowledging her own beauty should have made her
come off as arrogant, but she said it with such disdain, so
much self-loathing, he actually felt a little sorry for her.

"I thought all women wanted to be beautiful," he said.

"Most do, they just don't want *other* women to be beautiful too. They don't like competition. I was popular, so I
had no real friends."

That made no sense. "How could you be popular if you
had no friends?"

She took a sip of her bottled water than recapped it.
"I'm sure you know the saying, keep your friends close
and your enemies closer."

"And you were the enemy?"

"Pretty much. Those stereotypes you see in movies
about popular girls aren't as exaggerated as you might
think. They can be vicious."

Mia toppled over and wound up lying on her back
against his leg. She smiled up at him and gurgled happily,
and he couldn't help but smile back. He had the feeling she
was destined to be as beautiful as her mother.

"So, if the popular girls were so terrible, why didn't you
make friends who weren't popular?"

"Girls were intimidated by me. It took them a long time
to get past my face to see what was on the inside. And just
when they would begin to realize that I wasn't a snob, and
I started to form attachments, my dad would uproot us
again and I'd have to start over in a new school."

"You moved often?"

"At least once a year, usually more. My dad's in the
army."

He had a difficult time picturing that. He'd imagined

her as being raised in an upscale suburban home, with a pampered, trophy wife mother and an executive father who spoiled her rotten. Apparently he'd been wrong about many things.

"How many different places have you lived?" he asked.

"Too many. The special weapons training he did meant moving a lot. Overseas we were based in Germany, Bulgaria, Israel, Japan and Italy, and domestically we lived in eight different states at eleven bases. All by the time I was seventeen. Deep down, I think all the moving was just his way of coping with my mom's death."

The fact that she, too, had lost her mother surprised him. "When did she die?"

"I was five. She had the flu of all things."

His mother's death, the unfairness of it, had left him under a cloud so dark and obliterating, he felt as if he would never be cheerful again. Yet Vanessa seemed to maintain a perpetually positive attitude and sunny disposition.

"She was only twenty-six," Vanessa said.

"That's very young."

"It was one of those fluke things. She just kept getting worse and worse, and by the time she went in for treatment, it had turned into pneumonia. My dad was away at the time, stationed in the Persian Gulf. I don't think he ever forgave himself for not being there."

At least Marcus had his mother for twenty-eight years. Not that it made losing her any easier. And though he knew it happened all the time, it still struck him as terribly unjust for a child to lose a parent so young, and from such a common and typically mild affliction.

"How about you?" she asked. "Where have you lived?"

"I've visited many places," Marcus said, "but I've never lived anywhere but the palace."

"Haven't you ever wanted to be independent? Out on your own?"

More times than he could possibly count. When people heard *royalty,* they assumed a life of grandeur and excess, but the responsibilities attached to the crown could be suffocating. When it came to everything he did, every decision he made, he had to first consider his title and how it would affect his standing with the people.

"My place is with my family," he told Vanessa. "It's what is expected of me."

Mia gurgled and swung her arms, vying for his attention, so he tickled her under the chin, which made her giggle.

"If I'd had to live with my dad all these years, I would be in a rubber room," Vanessa said, wearing a sour expression, which would seem to suggest animosity.

"You don't get along?"

"With my father, it's his way or the highway. Let's just say that he has a problem with decisions I've made."

"Which ones, if you don't mind my asking?"

She sighed. "Oh, pretty much all of them. It's kind of ironic if you think about it. There are people who dislike me because I'm too perfect, but in my dad's eyes I've never done a single thing right."

He couldn't help thinking that must have been an exaggeration. No parent could be that critical. "Surely he's pleased now that you're planning to marry a king."

"I could tell him I'm the new Mother Teresa and he'd find a way to write it off as a bad thing. Besides, I haven't told him. The only person who knows where I am is my best friend Jessy."

"Why keep it a secret?"

"I didn't want to say anything to anyone until I knew for sure that I really was going to marry Gabriel."

* * *

"What reason would you have not to marry him?" Marcus asked, and Vanessa hesitated. While she wanted to get to know Marcus better, she wasn't sure how she felt about discussing the private details of her relationship with his father. But at the same time, she hated to clam up now, as this outing was definitely going better than expected. And as she sat there on the rough wool blanket in the shade, the salty ocean air cooling her sunbaked skin, her daughter playing happily between them, she felt a deep sense of peace that she hadn't experienced in a very long time.

The first hour or so had been a bit like tiptoeing around in a minefield, her every move monitored, each word dissected for hidden meaning. But little by little she began to relax, and so did Marcus. The truth is, he was more like his father than she'd imagined. Sure, he was a bit intense at times, but he was very intelligent with a quick wit, and a wry sense of humor. And though it was obvious that he wasn't quite sure what to make of her—which wasn't unusual as she always seemed to fall somewhere outside of people's expectations—she had the feeling that maybe he was starting to like her. Or at the very least dislike her less. And he clearly adored Mia, who—the little flirt—hadn't taken her eyes off him for hours.

"Unless you'd rather not discuss it," Marcus said, his tone, and the glint of suspicion in his dark eyes, suggesting that she had something to hide.

She fidgeted with the corner of the blanket. Even though her relationship with Gabriel was none of his business, to not answer would look suspicious, but the truth might only validate his reservations about her. "My relationship with Gabriel is…complicated."

"How complicated could it be? You love him, don't you?"

There was a subtle accusation in his tone. Just when

she thought things were going really well, when she believed he was having a change of heart, he was back to the business of trying to discredit her, to expose her as a fraud. Well, maybe she should just give him what he wanted. It didn't seem as though it would make a difference at this point.

"I love him," she said. "I'm just not sure I'm *in* love with him."

"What's the difference?"

Did he honestly not know, or did he think she didn't? Or was he possibly just screwing with her? "Your father is an amazing human being. He's smart and he's kind and I respect him immensely. I love him as a friend, and I want him to be happy. I know that marrying me would make him happy, or at least he's told me it will. And of course I would love for Mia to have someone to call Daddy."

"But?" Marcus asked, leaning back on his arms, stretching his long legs out in front of him, as if he were settling in for a good story.

"But I want *me* to be happy, too. I deserve it."

"My father doesn't make you happy?"

"He does but…" She sighed. There was really no getting around this. "What are your feelings about intimacy before marriage?"

He didn't even hesitate. "It's immoral."

His answer took her aback. "Well, this is a first."

"What?"

"I've never met a twenty-eight-year-old virgin."

His brows slammed together. "I never said that I'm…"

He paused, realizing that he'd painted himself into a corner, and the look on his face was priceless.

"Oh, so what you're saying is, it's only immoral for your father to be intimate before marriage. For you it's fine?"

"My father is from a different generation. He thinks differently."

"Well, that's one thing you're right about. And it's a big part of my problem."

"What do you mean?"

"I believe two people should know whether or not they're sexually compatible before they jump into a marriage, because let's face it, sex is a very important part of a lasting relationship. Don't you agree?"

"I suppose it is."

"You suppose? Be honest. Would you marry a woman you'd never slept with?"

He hesitated, then said, "Probably not."

"Well, Gabriel is so traditional he won't even kiss me until we're officially engaged. And he considers sex before the wedding completely out of the question."

"You seriously want me to believe that you and my father have never…" He couldn't seem to make himself say the words, which she found kind of amusing.

"Is that really so surprising? You said yourself he's from a different generation. He didn't have sex with your mom until their wedding night, and even then he said it took a while to get all the gears moving smoothly."

Marcus winced.

"Sorry. TMI?"

"TMI?"

"Too much information?"

He nodded. "A bit."

"Honestly, I don't know why I'm telling you *any* of this, seeing as how it's really none of your business. And nothing I say is going to change the way you feel about me."

"So why are you telling me?"

"Maybe it's that I've gone through most of my life being

unfairly judged and I'm sick of it. I really shouldn't care if you like me or not, but for some stupid reason, I still do."

Marcus looked as if he wasn't sure what to believe. "I don't *dis*like you."

"But you don't trust me. Which is only fair, I guess, since I don't trust you either."

Seven

Instead of looking insulted, Marcus laughed, which completely confused Vanessa.

"You find that amusing?" she asked.

"What I find amusing is that you said it to my face. Do you ever have a thought that you *don't* express?"

"Sometimes." Like when she hadn't told him how his pale gray linen pants hugged his butt just right, and the white silk short sleeved shirt brought out the sun-bronzed tones of his skin. And she didn't mention how the dark shadow of stubble on his jaw made her want to reach up and touch his face. Or the curve of his mouth made her want to...well, never mind. "When I was a kid, every time I expressed an idea or a thought, my father shot it down. He had this way of making me feel inferior and stupid, and I'm *not* stupid. It just took a while to figure that out. And now I say what I feel, and I don't worry about what other people think, because most of them don't matter.

When it comes to my self-worth, the only opinion that really matters is my own. And though it took a long time to get here, I'm actually pretty happy with who I am. Sure, my life isn't perfect, and I still worry about making mistakes, but I know that I'm capable and smart, and if I do make a mistake, I'll learn from it."

"So what will you do?" he asked. "About my father, I mean. If he won't compromise his principles."

"I'm hoping that if we spend more time together, I'll just know that it's right."

"You said it yourself, you're a very beautiful woman, and my father seems to have very strong feelings for you. I'm quite certain that with little effort you could persuade him to compromise his principles."

Was he actually suggesting she *seduce* Gabriel? And why, when Marcus said she was beautiful, did it cause a little shiver of delight? She'd heard the same words so many times from so many men, they had lost their significance. Why was he so different? And why did she care *what* he thought of her?

And why on earth had she started this conversation in the first place?

"I would never do that," she told Marcus. "I respect him too much."

Mia began to fuss and Vanessa jumped on the opportunity to end this strange and frankly *inappropriate* chat. No matter what she did or said, or how she acted, the situation with Marcus just seemed to get weirder and weirder.

"I should get her back to the palace and down for a nap. And I could probably use one too." She was still on L.A. time, and despite being exhausted last night, she'd slept terribly.

He pushed himself to his feet. "Let's go."

Together they cleaned up the picnic, and to Vanessa's

surprise, Marcus lifted Mia up and held her while she folded the blanket. Even more surprising was how natural he appeared holding her, and how, when she reached to take her back, Mia clung to him and laid her head on his shoulder.

Little traitor, she thought, but she couldn't resist smiling. "I guess she wants you," she told Marcus, who looked as if he didn't mind at all.

They gathered the rest of their things and walked back to the limo waiting in the marina parking lot. They piled into the air-conditioned backseat, and she buckled Mia into her car seat. She expected that they would go straight back to the palace but instead, Marcus had the driver stop outside one of the shops they had visited earlier and went inside briefly. He came out several minutes later carrying a small bag that he slipped into his pants pocket before climbing back in the car, and though she was curious as to what was in it, she didn't ask, for fear of opening up yet another can of worms. He'd probably picked out a gift for his girlfriend. Because men who looked the way he did, and were filthy rich princes, always had a lady friend—if not two or three. And according to Gabriel, his son was never short on female companionship.

Mia fell asleep on the ride back, and when they pulled up to the front doors to the palace, before Vanessa had a chance, Marcus unhooked her from the car seat and plucked her out.

"I can carry her," she told him.

"I've got her," he said, and not only did he carry her all the way up to the nursery, he laid her in her crib and covered her up, the way a father would if Mia had one. And somewhere deep down a part of Vanessa ached for all the experiences her daughter had missed in her short life. Because she knew what it was like to lose a parent, to miss that connection. She hoped with all her heart that Gabriel could fill the void, that these months without a father hadn't left a permanent scar on Mia.

"She was really good today," he said, grinning down at Mia while she slept soundly.

"She's a pretty easygoing baby. You saw her at her very worst yesterday."

Vanessa let Karin know to listen for Mia so she could take a quick nap herself—thinking this nanny business was sort of nice after all—then Marcus walked her down the hall to her room. She stopped at the door and turned to him. "Thank you for taking me to the village today. I actually had a really good time."

One brow lifted a fraction. "And that surprises you?"

"Yeah, it does. I figured it could go either way."

The corners of his mouth crept up into a smile and those dimples dented his cheeks. Which made her heart go pitter-patter. He was too attractive for his own good. And hers.

"Too honest for you?" she asked him.

He shrugged. "I think I'm getting used to it."

Well, that was a start.

"My father would like me to take you to the history museum tomorrow," he said.

"Oh."

One brow rose. "Oh?"

"Well, I'm still pretty exhausted from the trip and I thought a day to just lie around by the pool might be nice. Mia loves playing in the water and I desperately need a tan. Back home I just never seem to have time to catch any sun. And you don't need to feel obligated to hang out with us. I'm sure you have things you need to do."

"You're sure?"

"I am."

"Then we can see the museum another day?"

She nodded. "That would be perfect."

He started to turn, then paused and said, "Oh, I almost forgot."

He pulled the bag from the shop out of his pocket and handed it to her. "This is for you."

Perplexed, she took it from him. "What is it?"

"Look and see."

She opened the bag and peered inside, her breath catching when she recognized the contents. "But…how did you know?"

"I saw you admiring them."

He didn't miss a thing, did he?

She pulled the earrings from the bag. They were handcrafted with small emeralds set inside delicate silver swirls, and she'd fallen in love with them the instant she'd seen them in the shop, but at one hundred and fifty euros they had been way out of her budget.

"Marcus, they're lovely." She looked up at him. "I don't get it."

Hands hooked casually in his pants pockets, he shrugged. "If you had been there with my father, I don't doubt that he would have purchased them on the spot. It's what he would have wanted me to do."

She couldn't help but think that this meant something. Something significant. "I don't even know what to say. Thank you so much."

"What is it you Americans say? It's not a big deal?"

No, it was a *very* big deal.

It bothered her when Gabriel bought her things. It was as if he felt it necessary to buy her affections. But Marcus had no reason to buy her anything, other than the fact that he *wanted* to. It came from the heart. More so than any gift Gabriel had gotten her—or at least, that was the way she saw it.

Swallowing back tears of pure happiness—unsure of why it even mattered so much to her—she smiled and said, "I should go. Gabriel will be Skyping me soon."

"Of course. I'll see you tomorrow."

She watched him walk down the hall until he disappeared around the corner, then slipped into her room and shut the door behind her. Knowing how much it meant to Gabriel, she had really been hoping that she and Marcus could be friends. And now it seemed that particular wish might actually come true.

Marcus pushed off the edge of the pool for his final lap, his arms slicing through the water, heavy with fatigue due to the extra thirty minutes he'd spent in the pool pondering his earlier conversation with Vanessa. If what she said was true, and she and his father hadn't been intimate, what else could have possibly hooked him in? Her youth, and the promise of a fresh beginning, maybe?

Marcus's mother had confided once, a long time ago, that she and his father had hoped to have a large family, but due to complications from Marcus's birth—details she'd mercifully left out—more children became an impossibility. Maybe he saw this as his chance to start the family he always wanted but could never have. Because surely someone as adept at parenting as Vanessa would want more children.

Or maybe he saw what Marcus had seen today. A woman who was smart and funny and a little bizarre. And of course beautiful.

So much so that you had to buy her a present?

He reached the opposite end of the pool, debated stopping, then flipped over and pushed off one last time.

He really had no idea why he'd bought Vanessa the earrings. But as they were on their way back to the palace and he saw the shop, he heard himself asking the driver to stop, and before he knew what he was doing, he was inside, handing over his Visa card, and the clerk was bagging his purchase.

Maybe he and Vanessa had made some sort of...*connection*. But that wasn't even the point, because what he'd told her was true. If his father had seen her admiring the earrings he would have purchased them on the spot. Marcus did it to please his father and nothing more.

But the surprise on her face when she opened the bag and realized what was inside...

She looked so impressed and so grateful, he worried that she might burst into tears. That would have been really awful, because there was nothing worse than a woman in the throes of an emotional meltdown. And all for such a simple and inexpensive gift. If her only concern was wealth, wouldn't she have balked at anything but diamonds or precious gems? And if she were using his father, why would she admit that she wasn't in love with him? Why would she have discussed it at all?

Maybe, subconsciously, he'd seen it as some sort of test. One that she had passed with flying colors.

Marcus reached the opposite edge and hoisted himself up out of the water, slicking his hair back, annoyed that he was wasting any time debating this with himself.

He sighed and squinted at the sun, which hung close to the horizon, a reddish-orange globe against the darkening sky. The evening breeze cooled his wet skin. The fact of the matter was, though he didn't want to like Vanessa, he couldn't seem to help himself. He'd never met anyone quite like her.

From the table where he'd left it, his cell phone began to ring. Thinking it could be his father with an update about Aunt Trina, he pushed himself to his feet and grabbed the phone, but when he saw the number he cursed under his breath. He wasn't interested in anything his ex had to say, and after three weeks of avoiding her incessant phone calls and text messages, he would have expected that she'd gotten the point by now.

Apparently not. Leaving him to wonder what it was he'd seen in her in the first place. How could someone who had bewitched him so thoroughly now annoy him so completely?

Aggressive women had never really been Marcus's first choice in a potential mate. But sexy, sultry and with a body to die for, Carmela had pursued him with a determination that put other women to shame. She was everything he could have wanted in a wife, or so he believed, and because she came from a family of considerable wealth and power, he never once worried that she was after his money. Six months in he'd begun to think about engagement rings and wedding arrangements, only to discover that he'd been terribly wrong about her. And though the first week after the split had been difficult, he'd gradually begun to realize his feelings for her were based more on infatuation and lust than real love. His only explanation was that he'd been emotionally compromised by his mother's death. And the fact that she had taken advantage of that was, in his opinion, despicable. And unforgivable.

He shuddered to think what would have happened had he actually proposed, or God forbid *married* her. And he was disappointed in himself that he'd let it go as far as he had, that he'd been so blinded by her sexual prowess. And honestly, the actual sex wasn't that great. Physically, she gave him everything he could ask for and more, but emotionally their encounters had left him feeling…empty. Maybe it had been an unconscious need for a deeper connection that had kept him coming back for more, but now, looking back, he could hardly believe what a fool he'd been.

His text message alert chimed, and of course it was from her.

"Enough already," he ground out, turning on his heel and flinging his cell phone into the pool. Only when he looked up past the pool to the garden path did he realize that he had an audience.

Vanessa stood on the garden path watching Marcus's cell phone hit the surface of the water, then slowly sink down, until it was nothing but a murky shadow against the tile bottom.

"You know," she told Marcus, who clearly hadn't realized that she was standing there, "I have that same impulse nearly every day of my life. Although I usually imagine tossing it off the roof of the hotel, or under the wheels of a passing semi."

He sighed and raked a hand through his wet hair, the last remnants of evening sunshine casting a warm glow over his muscular arms and chest, his toned to perfection thighs. And though the Speedo covered the essentials, it was wet and clingy and awfully…well, revealing.

Ugh, what was she, *twelve?* It wasn't as if she hadn't seen a mostly naked man before. Or a completely naked one for that matter. Of course, none of them had been quite so…yummy.

Remember, this is your almost fiancé's son you're ogling. The thought filled her with guilt. Okay, maybe that was an exaggeration, but she did feel a mild twinge.

"That was childish of me," he said, looking as if he were disappointed in himself.

"But did it feel good?" she asked.

He hesitated, then a smile tilted the corners of his mouth. "Yeah, it did. And I needed a new one anyway."

"Then it's worth it."

"What are you doing out here?" He grabbed his towel from the table and began to dry himself. His arms, his pecs, the wall of his chest...

Oh boy. What she wouldn't give to be that towel right now.

Think son-in-law, Vanessa.

"Mia went down early, and I was feeling a little restless," she told him. "I thought I would take a walk."

"After all the walking we did today? You should be exhausted."

"I'm on my feet all day every day. Today was a cakewalk. Plus I'm trying to acclimate myself to the time change. If I go to bed too early I'll never adjust. And for the record, I am exhausted. I haven't slept well since I got here."

"Why not?" He draped the towel over the back of a chair, then took a seat, leaning casually back, with not a hint of shame. Not that he had anything to be ashamed of, and there was nothing more appealing than a man so comfortable in his own skin. Especially one who looked as good as he did.

"I keep waking up and listening for Mia, then I remember that she's down the hall. And of course I feel compelled to get up and go check on her. Then it's hard to get back to sleep. I thought a walk might relax me."

"Why don't you join me for a drink?" he said. "It might take the edge off."

She'd never been one to drink very often, and lately, with an infant in her care, she'd more or less stopped altogether. But now there was a nanny to take over if Vanessa needed her. Maybe it would be okay, just this once, to let her hair down a little.

And maybe Marcus would put some clothes on.

"Yeah, sure. I'd love one," she told him, and as if by magic, or probably ESP, the butler materialized from a set of French doors that led to…well, honestly, she wasn't sure where they led. She had gone out a side door to the garden, one patrolled by armed guards. She probably wouldn't have been able to find even that if Camille hadn't shown her the way. The palace had more twists and turns than a carnival fun house.

"What would you like?" Marcus asked.

"What do you have?"

"We have a fully stocked bar. George can make anything you desire."

She summoned a list of drinks that she used to enjoy, and told George, "How about…a vodka tonic with a twist of lime?"

George nodded, turned to Marcus, and in a voice as craggy and old as the man said, "Your highness?"

"The same for me. And could you please let Cleo know that I'll be needing a new phone, and a new number."

George nodded and limped off, looking as if every step took a great deal of effort.

Vanessa took a seat across from Marcus and when George was out of earshot asked, "How old is he?"

"I'm really not sure. Eighties, nineties. All I know is that he's been with the family since my father was a child."

"He looks as if he has a hard time getting around."

"He has rheumatoid arthritis. And though his staff does most of the real work these days, I assure you he's still quite capable, and has no desire to retire anytime soon. Honestly, I don't think he has anywhere else to go. As far as I'm aware, he's never been married. He has no children. We're his only family."

"That's kind of sad," Vanessa said, feeling a sudden burst of sympathy for the cranky old butler. She couldn't imagine being so alone in the world. Or maybe he didn't see it that way. Maybe his career, his attachments with the royal family and the other staff, were all the fulfillment he needed.

"If you'll excuse me a moment," Marcus said, rising from his seat. "I should probably go change before I catch a chill."

She had wanted him to put clothes on, but she couldn't deny being slightly disappointed. But the blistering heat of the afternoon did seem to be evaporating with the setting sun, and a cool breeze had taken its place.

While he was gone, Vanessa slipped her sandals off and walked over to the pool. She sat on the edge, dipping her feet in water warm enough to bathe in. She'd never been much of a swimmer—or into any sort of exercise, despite how many times her father had pushed her to try different sports and activities. She had the athletic prowess of a brick, and about as much grace. And firearms being his passion, he'd tried relentlessly to get her on the firing range. He'd gone as far as to get her a hunting rifle for her fourteenth birthday, but guns scared her half to death and she'd refused to even touch it. She'd often entertained the idea that he would have been much happier with a son, and had someone offered a trade, he'd have jumped at the chance.

As the last vestiges of daylight dissolved into the horizon and the garden and pool lights switched on, Vanessa noticed the shadow of Marcus's cell phone, wondering what—or *who*—had driven him to chuck it into the water. From what Gabriel had told her, Marcus was even-tempered and composed, so whatever it was must have really upset him.

She sighed, wondering what Gabriel was doing just then. Probably sitting at the hospital, where he spent the majority of his day. Trina was still very sick, but responding to the treatment, and the doctors were cautiously optimistic that she would make a full recovery. Though Vanessa felt selfish for even thinking it, she hoped that meant Gabriel would be home soon. She wanted to get her life back on track and plan her future, because at the moment she'd never felt more unsettled or restless. And it wasn't fair to Mia to keep her living in limbo, although to be honest she seemed no worse for wear.

"Your drink," Marcus said, and the sound of his voice made her jump.

She turned to find him dressed in khaki shorts and a pale silk, short sleeved shirt, that could have been gray or light blue. It was difficult to tell in the muted light.

"Sorry, didn't mean to startle you." He handed her one of the two glasses he was holding and sat next to her on the edge, slipping his bare feet into the water beside hers. He was so close, she could smell chlorine on his skin, and if she were to move her leg just an inch to the right, her thigh would touch his. For some reason the idea of actually doing it made her heart beat faster. Not that she ever would.

Eight

"I guess I was lost in thought," she said. "When I talked to Gabriel today he said that your aunt is responding to the treatment."

Marcus nodded, sipping his drink, then setting it on the tile beside him. "I spoke with him this afternoon. He said they're optimistic."

"I was kind of hoping that meant he would be home sooner. Which is pretty thoughtless, I know." She took a swallow of her drink and her eyes nearly crossed as it slid down her throat, instantly warming her insides. "Wow! That's strong."

"Would you care for something different?"

"No, I like it." She took another sip, but a smaller one this time. "It has kick, but the vodka is very...I don't know, smooth, I guess."

"George only stocks the best. And for the record, you're not thoughtless. I would say that you've been tremendously patient given the circumstances. Had it been me, considering my less than warm greeting, I probably would have turned around and gotten back on the plane."

"If it hadn't been for Mia, I might have. But another thirteen hours in the air would have done me in for sure."

Marcus was quiet for a minute, gazing at the water and the ripples their feet made on the surface. Then he mumbled something that sounded like a curse and shook his head.

"Is something wrong?" she asked him.

"Your proclivity toward brutal honesty must be rubbing off on me."

"What do you mean?"

"I probably shouldn't tell you this, and I would be breaking a confidence in doing so, but I feel as if you deserve the truth."

Vanessa's heart sank a little. "Why do I get the feeling I'm not going to like this?"

"My father told me that he would likely be three or four weeks. He didn't want you to know for fear that you wouldn't stay. It's why he wanted me to keep you entertained."

Her heart bottomed out. "But my visit will only be for six weeks. Which will leave us only two or three to get to know one another better."

What if that wasn't enough time?

Marcus shrugged. "So you'll stay longer."

Feeling hurt and betrayed, her nerves back on edge, Vanessa took another swallow of her drink. If Gabriel lied about this, what else was he lying about? "I can't stay longer. My leave from work is only six weeks. If I don't go back I'll get fired. Until I know for sure whether I'm staying here, I need that job. Otherwise I would have nothing to go back for. I have very little savings. Mia and I would essentially be on the streets."

"My father is a noble man," Marcus said. "Even if you decided not to marry him, he would never allow that to happen. He would see that you were taken care of."

"If he's so noble why would he lie to me in the first place?"

"He only did it because he cares for you."

It was a moot point because she would never take his charity. And even if she would, there was no guarantee that Gabriel would be so generous.

Marcus must have read her mind, because he added, "If he didn't see that you were taken care of, *I* would."

His words stunned her. "Why? As of this afternoon, you still believed that I'm using him."

"I guess you could say that I've had a change of heart."

"But, *why?*"

His laugh was rich and warm and seemed to come from deep within him. "You perplex me, Vanessa. You tell me that I should give you a chance, but when I do, you question my motives. Perhaps it's you who needs to give *me* a chance."

She had indeed said that. "You're right. I guess I'm just feeling very out of sorts right now." She touched his arm lightly, found it to be warm and solid under her palm. "I'm sorry."

He looked at her hand resting on his forearm, then up into her eyes, and said, "Apology accepted."

There was something in their sooty depths, some emotion that made her heart flip in her chest, and suddenly she felt warm all over.

It's just the vodka, she assured herself, easing her hand away and taking a deep swallow from her glass.

"Would you care for another?" Marcus asked.

She looked down and realized that her glass was empty, while his was still more than half full.

"I probably shouldn't," she said, feeling her muscles slacken with the warm glow of inebriation. It was the most relaxed she had felt in weeks. Would one more drink be such a bad thing? In light of what she'd just learned, didn't she deserve it? With Mia in the care of her nanny, what reason did Vanessa have to stop? "But what the hell, why not? It's not as if I have to drive home, right?"

Marcus gestured randomly and George must have been watching for it—which to her was slightly creepy—because moments later he appeared with a fresh drink. And either this one wasn't as strong, or the first had numbed her to the intensity of the vodka. Whatever the reason, she drank liberally.

"So, would I be overstepping my bounds to ask why you drowned your phone?" Vanessa said.

"A persistent ex-lover."

"I take it you dumped her."

"Yes, but only after I caught her in the backseat of the limo with my best friend."

"Ouch. Were they…you know…"

"Yes. Quite enthusiastically."

She winced. So he'd lost his mother, his girlfriend and his best friend. How sucky was that? "I'm sorry."

He slowly kicked his feet back and forth through the water, the side of his left foot brushing against her right one. She had to force herself not to jump in surprise.

"Each tried to pin it on the other. She's still trying to convince me that he lured her there under false pretenses, and once he had her in the car he more or less attacked her."

She let her foot drift slightly to the left, to see if it would happen again. "She cried rape?"

"More or less."

"What did your friend say?"

"That she lured him into the car, and she made the first move."

"Who do you believe?"

"Neither of them. In the thirty seconds or so that I was standing there in shock, she never once told him no, and she wasn't making any attempt to stop him. I think all the moaning they were both doing spoke for itself."

His foot bumped hers again, and a tiny thrill shot up from her foot and through her leg, settling in places that were completely inappropriate considering their relationship.

"Were you in love with her?" Vanessa asked him.

"I thought I was, but I realize now it was just lust."

"Sometimes it's hard to tell the two apart."

"Is that how it is with you and my father?"

What she felt for Gabriel was definitely not lust. "Not at all. Gabriel is a good friend, and I love and respect him for that. It's the lust part we need to work on."

Her candor seemed to surprise him. "And he knows you feel that way?"

"I've been completely honest with him. He's convinced that my feelings for him will grow. And I'm hoping he's right."

His foot brushed hers again, and this time she could swear it was intentional. Was he honestly playing footsies with her? And why was her heart beating so fast, her skin tingling with awareness? And why was she mentally willing him to touch her in other places too, but with his hands?

Because there is something seriously wrong with you, honey. But knowing that didn't stop her from leaning back on her arms and casually shifting her leg so her thigh brushed his.

Now this, what she was feeling right now, *this* was lust. And it was so wrong.

"I learned last week that her father's company is in financial crisis and on the verge of collapse," Marcus said, and it took Vanessa a second to realize that he was talking about his ex. "I guess she thought that an alliance with the royal family would have pulled him from the inevitable depths of bankruptcy."

"So you think she was using you?"

"It seems a safe assumption."

Well, that at least explained why he was so distrustful of Vanessa. He obviously looked at her and saw his ex. She shook her head in disgust and said, "What a bitch."

Marcus's eyes widened, and Vanessa slapped a hand across her mouth. Why couldn't she learn to hold her tongue? "Sorry, that was totally inappropriate of me."

Instead of looking angry, or put out, Marcus just laughed.

"No, it was more appropriate than you would imagine. And unfortunately she wasn't the first. But usually I'm better at spotting it. I think my mother's death left such a gaping hole, and I was so desperate to fill it I had blinders on."

"You want to hear something ironic? In my junior year of high school, I caught my boyfriend in the back of his car with my so-called friend."

His brow lifted. "Was it a limo?"

She laughed. "Hardly. It was piece of crap SUV."

"What did you do when you caught them?"

"Threw a brick through the back window."

He laughed. "Maybe that's what I should have done."

"I was really mad. I had just written his history term paper for him, and he got an A. I found out later from one of my 'friends' that he'd only dated me because I was smart, and in most of the same classes and willing to help him with his homework. I was stupid enough to do it for him. And let him copy off my tests. He played football, and if his grades dropped he would be kicked off the team. Pretty much everyone knew he was using me."

"And no one told you?"

"Suffice it to say they weren't my friends after that. My dad was reassigned a month later. It was one of the few times I was really relieved to be starting over."

"I hope you at least reported him to the headmaster," Marcus said.

"You have no idea how badly I wanted to go to our teachers and the principal and tell them what I'd been doing, that his work was really my work. Not only could I have gotten him kicked off the team, he would have been expelled."

"Why didn't you?"

"Because I would have been expelled too. And my father would have *killed* me. Not to mention that it was completely embarrassing. I should have known, with his reputation, he would never seriously date a girl who didn't put out unless he was after something else. Not that he didn't try to get in my pants every chance he got."

"You shouldn't blame yourself. You have a trusting nature. That's a good thing."

Not always. "Unfortunately, I seem to attract untrustworthy men. It's as if I have the word *gullible* stamped in invisible ink on my forehead, and only jerks can see it."

"Not all men use women."

"All the men I've known do."

"Surely not everyone has been that bad."

"Trust me, if there was a record for the world's worst luck with men, I would hold it. When Mia's dad walked out on me, I swore I would never let a man use me again. That I would never trust so blindly. But then I met Gabriel and he's just so...wonderful. And he treated me as if I were something special."

"That's because he thinks you are. From the minute he returned home he couldn't stop talking about you." He laid a hand on her arm, gave it a gentle squeeze, his dark eyes soft with compassion. "He's not using you, Vanessa."

Weird, but yesterday he was convinced she was using his father. When had everything gotten so turned around?

And why, as they had a heart-to-heart talk about his father—one that should have drawn her closer to Gabriel—could she only think about Marcus? Why did she keep imagining what it would be like to lay her hand on his muscular thigh, feel the crisp dark hair against her palm? Why did she keep looking at his mouth, and wondering how it would feel pressed against hers?

Maybe they both would have been better off if he kept acting like a jerk, because it was becoming painfully clear that Vanessa had developed a major crush. On the wrong man.

"Do you think someone can fall in love, real love, in a matter of two weeks?" Vanessa asked Marcus.

He could tell her that he believed falling in love so fast was nothing but a fairy tale, and that he thought his father was rebounding. What he felt for Vanessa was infatuation and nothing more, and he would realize that when he returned from Italy. Marcus knew if he told Vanessa that, she was confused and vulnerable enough that she might actually believe him. Which would discourage her, and fill her with self-doubt, and might ultimately make her leave. And wasn't that what he'd wanted?

But now, he couldn't make himself say the words.

Something had changed. He was instead telling her things that would make her want to stay, and for reasons that had nothing to do with his father's happiness, and everything to do with Marcus's fascination with her. She wasn't helping matters by encouraging him, by moving closer when he touched her, looking up at him with those expressive blue eyes. And did she have to smell so good? Most of the women he knew bathed themselves in cloying perfume, Carmela included, but Vanessa smelled of soap and shampoo. And he could smell that only because they were sitting so close to one another. *Too* close. If he had any hope of fighting these inappropriate feelings, he really needed to back off.

"I believe that when it comes to love, anything is possible," he told her, which wasn't a lie exactly. He just didn't believe it in this case. And the idea that she might be hurt again disturbed him more than he could have ever imagined possible. Maybe because he knew it was inevitable. He just hoped that when his father let her down, he did it gently. Or maybe after waiting for his father for so many weeks, she would grow frustrated and decide she didn't want to stay after all.

Now that Marcus had gotten to know her better, he wasn't any more sure of what to expect. He'd never met a woman more confusing or unpredictable. Yet in a strange way, he felt he could relate to her—understand her even— which made no sense at all.

But what baffled him most was how wrong he'd been about her, when he was so sure he'd had her pegged. He hadn't given his father nearly enough credit, had just assumed he was too vulnerable to make intelligent choices, and for that Marcus would always feel foolish.

George appeared at his side with two fresh drinks. Marcus took them and held one out to Vanessa. She looked in the glass she was still holding as if she were surprised to realize that it was empty.

"Oh, I really shouldn't," she said, but as he moved to give it back to George, added, "But it would be a shame to let the good stuff go to waste. No more after this though."

George shuffled off with their empty glasses, shaking his head in either amusement or exasperation, Marcus couldn't be sure which. None of the staff were sure what to think of her, and that was in large part Marcus's fault, as he'd made his feelings about her visit quite clear from the moment his father had broken the news. Now he knew that he'd unfairly judged her, and that was something he needed to rectify.

"Your dad said that when he met your mom it was love at first sight," she said. "And it was a big scandal because she wasn't a royal."

"Yes, my grandparents were very traditional. There was already a marriage arranged for him but he loved my mother. They threatened to disown him. He said it was the only time in his life that he rebelled against their wishes."

"That must have been difficult for your mom. To know that they hated her so much they would disown their own child."

"It wasn't her so much as the idea of her that they resented, but things improved after I was born. My father was an only child, so they were happy that she'd given my father a male heir."

"So your father wouldn't mind if you married a non-royal?"

"My parents have been very insistent my entire life that as sole heir it's imperative I also produce an heir, but they want me to marry for love."

"Like they did."

He nodded.

"What was your mom like?" she asked.

Just thinking of her brought a smile to his face. "Beautiful, loyal, outspoken—more so than some people thought a queen should be. She grew up in a middle-class family in Italy, so she had a deep respect for the common man. You actually remind me of her in a way."

She blinked in surprise. "*I* do?"

"She was brave and smart, and she wasn't afraid to speak her mind. Even if it got her into trouble sometimes. And she was a positive role model to young women."

"Brave?" she said, looking at him as though he'd completely lost his mind. "I'm constantly terrified that I'm doing the wrong thing, or making the wrong choice."

"But that doesn't stop you from *making* the choice, and that takes courage."

"Maybe, but I fail to see how I'm a role model to women. My life has been one bad move after another."

How could she not see it, not be proud of her accomplishments? "You're well traveled, intelligent, successful. You're an excellent mother, raising a child with no help. What young woman wouldn't look up to you?"

She bit her lip, and for a second he thought she might start crying. "That's probably the nicest thing anyone has ever said to me. Though I'm pretty sure that I don't deserve it. I'm a gigantic walking disaster waiting to happen."

"That's your father talking," he said.

"In part. But I can't deny that I've made some really dumb decisions in my life."

"Everybody does. How will you learn if you don't make occasional mistakes?"

"The problem is, I don't seem to be learning from mine."

Why couldn't she see what he did? Was she really so beaten down by her father's overinflated ideals that she

had no self-confidence left? And what could he do to make
her believe otherwise? How could he make her see how
gifted and special and unique she really was? "You don't
give yourself enough credit. If you weren't an extraordinary person, do you really think my father would have
fallen so hard for you so fast?"

Nine

Their eyes met and Vanessa's were so filled with hope and vulnerability, Marcus had to resist the urge to pull her into his arms and hold her. His gaze dropped to her mouth, and her lips looked so plump and soft, he couldn't help but wonder how they would feel, how they would taste.

The sudden pull of lust in his groin caught him completely off guard, but he couldn't seem to look away.

Carmela and most other women he'd dated favored fitted, low-cut blouses and skintight jeans. They dressed to draw attention. In shorts and a T-shirt and with no makeup on her face, her pale hair cascading down in loose waves across her shoulders, Vanessa didn't look particularly sexy. Other than being exceptionally beautiful, she looked quite ordinary, yet he couldn't seem to keep his eyes off her.

Vanessa was the one to turn her head, but not before he saw a flash of guilt in her eyes, and he knew, whatever these improper feeling were, she was having them too.

Vanessa rubbed her arms. "It's getting chilly, huh?"

"Would you like to go inside?" he asked.

She shook her head, gazing up at the night sky. "Not yet."

"I could have George bring us something warm to drink."

"No, thank you."

They were both quiet for several minutes, but there was a question that had been nagging him since their conversation this afternoon in the park. "You said that you were afraid two or three weeks wouldn't be long enough to get to know my father better. I'm wondering, what guarantee did you have that four weeks would be? Or six?"

She shrugged. "There was no guarantee. But I had to at least try. For him. And for Mia."

"What about you?"

"For me, too," she said, avoiding his gaze.

Why did he get the feeling her own needs were pretty low on the priority scale? The way he saw it, either you were physically attracted to someone or you weren't. There was no gray area. And it seemed a bit selfish of his father to push her into something she clearly was unsure about.

She took a swallow of her drink, then blinked rapidly, setting her glass on the tile beside her. "You know, I think I've had enough. I feel a little woozy. And it's getting late. I should check on Mia."

It was odd, but although he'd had no intention of spending the evening with her, now he wasn't ready for it to end. All the more reason that it should. "Shall I walk you back to your room?"

"You might have to. I'm honestly not sure I could find it by myself."

"Tomorrow I'll have Cleo print a map for you." Two days ago it wouldn't have mattered to him, now he wanted her to feel comfortable in the palace. It was the least he could do.

He set his drink down and pulled himself to his feet, the night air cool against his wet skin, and extended a hand to help her. It felt so small and fragile, and it was a good thing he was holding on, because as he pulled her to her feet, she was so off balance she probably would have fallen into the pool.

"Are you okay?" he asked, pulling her away from the edge.

"Yeah." She blinked several times then gave her head a shake, as if to clear it, clutching his hand in a death grip. "Maybe I shouldn't have had that last drink."

"Would you like to sit back down?"

She took several seconds to get her bearings, then said, "I think I should probably just get to bed."

His first thought, depraved as it was, was "Why don't I join you." But, while he could think it, and perhaps even wish it a little, it was something he would never say out loud. And even more important, never do.

Could this be more embarrassing?

Feeling like an idiot, Vanessa clung to Marcus's arm as he led her across the patio. So much for letting her hair down a little.

"On top of everything else, now you probably think I have a drinking problem," she said.

Marcus grinned, his dimples forming dents in both cheeks, and she felt that delicious little zing. Did he have to be so…*adorable?*

"Maybe if you'd had ten drinks," he said, stopping by the table so she could grab her phone and they could both slip into their sandals. "But you only had three, and you didn't even finish the last one. I'm betting it has more to do with the jet lag."

"Jet lag can do that?"

"Sure. So can fatigue. Are you certain you can make it upstairs? I could carry you."

Yeah, because that wouldn't be completely humiliating. Besides, she liked holding on to his arm. And she couldn't help wondering what it would be like to touch him in other places. Not that she would ever try. She probably wouldn't be feeling this way at all if it weren't for the alcohol.

Well, okay, she probably would, but never in a million years would she act on it. Even though he thought she was smart and brave and successful. Plus, he'd left out beautiful. That was usually the first, and sometimes the only thing, that people noticed about her. Gabriel must have told her a million times. Remarkably, Marcus seemed to see past that.

"I think I can manage," she told him.

Clutching her cell phone in one hand and his forearm in the other, she wobbled slightly as he led her across the patio, but as they reached the French doors, she stopped. "Could we possibly walk around the side, through the garden?"

"What for?"

She chewed her lip, feeling like an irresponsible adolescent, which is probably how everyone else in the palace would see her as well. "I'm too embarrassed to have anyone see me this way. The entire staff already thinks I'm a horrible person. Now they're going to think I'm a lush, too."

"What does it matter what they think?"

"Please," she said, tugging him toward the garden path. "I feel so stupid."

"You shouldn't. But if it means that much to you, we'll go in the side entrance."

"Thank you."

Actually, now that she was on her feet, she felt steadier, but she kept holding on to his arm anyway. Just in case. Or just because it felt nice. He was tall and sturdy and reliable. And warm. He made her feel safe. She tried to recall if any man had made her feel that way before and drew a blank. Surely there must have been someone.

They headed down the path, around the back of the palace to the east side. At least, she was pretty sure it was east, or maybe it was west. Or north. Suddenly she felt all turned around. But whichever way it was, she remembered it from earlier, even though it was a lot darker now, despite the solar lights lining the path.

They were halfway around the building when Vanessa heard a sound on the flagstones behind them and wondered fleetingly if they were being followed. Being an L.A. resident, her first instinct was to immediately whip out her phone in case she needed to dial 911, which was how she realized her cell phone was no longer in her hand. The noise must have been her phone falling onto the path.

She let go of Marcus's arm and stopped, squinting to see in the dim light.

"What's wrong," he asked. "Are you going to be sick?"

She huffed indignantly. "I'm not *that* drunk. I dropped my phone."

"Where?"

"A few feet back, I think. I heard it hit the ground."

They backtracked, scouring the ground for several minutes, but it wasn't on or even near the path.

"Maybe it bounced into the flower bed," she said, crouching down to peer into the dense foliage, nearly falling on her butt in the process.

Marcus shook his head, looking grim. "If it did, we'll never find it at night."

"Call it!" Vanessa said, feeling rather impressed with herself for having such a brilliant idea in her compromised condition. "When we hear it ring, we'll know where it is."

"Right," he said hooking a thumb in the direction of the pool. "I'll go fish my phone out of the water and do that."

"Oh yeah, I forgot about that. Can't you borrow one?"

"Or we could look for your phone tomorrow."

"No!" Maybe he could blithely toss his electronic equipment away, but she worked for a living. Nor did she have a secretary to keep track of her life. "Besides the fact that it cost me a fortune, that phone is my life. It has my schedule and all my contacts and my music. What if it rains, or an animal gets it or something?"

He sighed loudly. "Wait here and I'll go get a phone."

She frowned. "By myself, in the dark?"

"I assure you the grounds are highly guarded and completely safe."

"What about that certain criminal element who would love to ransom the future queen?"

He smiled sheepishly. "Maybe that was a slight exaggeration. You'll be fine."

She'd expected as much. He'd been trying to drive her away, to make her *want* to leave. And as much as it annoyed her, she couldn't hold it against him. Not after all the nice things he'd said about her. Which she supposed was a big part of her problem. Someone said something nice about her and she went all gooey.

"You should stay in the general vicinity of where you lost it," Marcus warned her. "Or this could take all night."

"I'll stay right here," she said, flopping down on the path cross-legged to wait, the flagstone still warm from the afternoon sun.

Marcus grinned and shook his head. She watched as he backtracked from where they'd come, until he disappeared around a line of shrubs.

She sat there very still, listening to sounds of the night—crickets chirping and a mild breeze rustling the trees. And she swore, if she listened really hard, she could hear the faint hiss of the ocean, that if she breathed deep enough, she could smell the salty air. Or maybe it was just her imagination. Of all the different places her father had been stationed over the years, her favorite bases had been the ones near the water. And while she loved living close to the sea, the coast of California was exorbitantly expensive. Maybe someday. Maybe even here. The palace wasn't right on the water, but it was pretty darn close.

After a few minutes of waiting, her butt started to get sore, so she scooted off the flagstone path into the cool, prickly grass. Falling backward onto the spongy sod, she looked up at the sky. It was a crystal-clear night with a half moon, and even with the lights around the grounds, she could see about a million stars. In L.A. the only way to see the stars was to drive up to the mountains. She and Mia's dad used to do that. They would camp out in the bed of his truck, alternating between making love and watching the stars. She couldn't be sure, but she suspected that Mia may have actually been conceived in the bed of that truck. An unusual place to get pregnant, but nothing about her relationship with Paul had been typical. She used to think that was a good thing, and one of their strengths, because God knew those "normal" relationships she'd had were all a disaster. Until she came home to find a "Dear Vanessa" letter and realized she was wrong. Again. He hadn't even had the guts to tell her to her face that he wasn't ready for the responsibility of a child, and they were both better off without him.

So normal was bad, and eccentric was bad, which didn't leave much else. But royal, that was one she'd never tried, and never expected to have a chance to. Yet here she was. Lying on the palace lawn on a cool summer night under a sky cloaked with stars.

Which she had to admit wasn't very royal of her. She wondered if Gabriel's wife, or even Gabriel, had ever sprawled out on the grass and gazed up at the sky. Or skipped in the rain, catching drops on their tongues. Or snowflakes. Had Gabriel and Marcus ever bundled up and built a snowman together? Had they given it coal eyes and a carrot nose? Had they made snow angels or had snowball fights? And would she really be happy married to someone who didn't know how to relax and have fun, do something silly? Would Mia miss out on an important part of her childhood? Because *everyone* had to be silly every now and then.

Or was she worrying for nothing? Suffering from a typical case of insecurity? Was she creating problems where none really existed? Was she trying to sabotage a good thing because she was too afraid to take a chance?

So much for her being brave, huh?

She pondered that for a while, until she heard footsteps on the path, and glanced over to see Marcus walking toward her, looking puzzled. He stopped beside her, hands on his slim hips, and looked down. "You okay?"

She smiled and nodded. "It's a beautiful night. I'm looking at the stars."

He looked up at the sky, then back down at her. "Are you sure you didn't fall down?"

She swatted at him, but he darted out of the way, grinning.

"Could you join me?" she said. "Unless you're not allowed."

"Why wouldn't I be?"

"I thought maybe it wasn't royal enough."

"You know, you're not making a whole lot of sense."

"Do I ever?"

He laughed. "Good point."

And that apparently didn't matter, because he lay down beside her in the grass, so close their arms were touching. And she liked the way it felt. *A lot.* She liked being close to him, liked the warm fuzzy feeling coupled with that zing of awareness, and that urge to reach over and lace her fingers through his. It was exciting, and scary.

But of course she wouldn't do it, because even she wasn't that brave.

"You're right," he said, gazing up at the sky. "It is beautiful."

She looked over at him. "You think I'm weird, don't you."

"Not weird, exactly, but I can safely say that I've never met anyone like you."

"I don't know if I'm royalty material. I don't think I could give this up."

"Lying in the grass?"

She nodded.

"Who said you have to?"

"I guess I just don't know what's acceptable, and what isn't. I mean, if I marry Gabriel can I still build snowmen?"

"I don't see why not."

"Can I catch rain and snowflakes on my tongue?"

"You could try, I suppose."

"Can I walk in the sand in my bare feet, and make mud pies with Mia?"

"You know, we royals aren't so stuffy and uptight that we don't know how to have fun. We're just people. We lead relatively normal lives outside of the public eye."

But normal for him, and normal for her, were two very different things. "This all happened so abruptly. I guess I just don't know what to expect."

Marcus looked over at her. "You know that if you marry my father, you'll still be the same person you are right now. There's no magic potion or incantation that suddenly makes you royal. And there are no set rules." He paused then added, "Okay, I guess there are some rules. Certain protocol we have to follow. But you'll learn."

And Gabriel should have been the one explaining that to her, not Marcus. It was Gabriel she should have been getting to know, Gabriel she needed to bond with. Instead she was bonding with Marcus, and in a big way. She could feel it. She was comfortable with him, felt as if she could really be herself. Maybe because she wasn't worried about impressing him. Or maybe she was connecting in a small way. The truth was, everything had gotten so jumbled and confused, she wasn't sure how she felt about anything right now. And she was sure the drinks weren't helping.

Everything will be clearer tomorrow, she told herself. She would talk to Gabriel again, and remember how much she cared about him and missed him, and everything would go back to normal. She and Marcus would be friends, and she would stop having these irrational feelings.

"I've been thinking," Marcus said. "You should call your father and tell him where you are."

His suggestion—the fact that he'd even thought it—puzzled her. "So he can tell me that I'm making another stupid mistake? Why would I do that?"

"*Are* you making a mistake?"

If only she could answer that question, if she could hop a time machine and flash forward a year or so in the future, she would know how this would all play out. But that would be too easy. "I guess I won't know for sure until things go south."

He exhaled an exasperated sigh. "Okay, do you *think* you're making a mistake? Would you be here if you were sure this was going to end in disaster?"

She considered that, then said, "No, *I* don't think I'm making a mistake, because even if it doesn't work out, I got to visit a country I've never been to, and meet new people and experience new things. I got to stay in a palace and meet a prince. Even if he was kind of a doofus at first."

He smiled. "Then it doesn't matter what your father thinks. And I think that keeping this from him only makes it seem as though you have something to hide. If you really want him to respect you, and have confidence in your decisions, you've got to have faith in yourself first."

"Wow. That was incredibly insightful." And he was right. "You're speaking from experience, I assume."

"I'm the future leader of this country. It's vital I convey to the citizens that I'm confident in my abilities. It's the only way they'll trust me to lead them."

"Are you confident in your abilities?"

"Most of the time. There are days when the thought of that much responsibility scares the hell out of me. But part of being an effective leader means learning to delegate." He looked at her and grinned. "And always having someone else to pin the blame on when you screw up."

He was obviously joking, and his smile was such an adorable one, it made her want to reach out and touch his cheek. "You know, you have a really nice smile. You should do it more often."

He looked up at the stars. "I think this is probably the most I've smiled since we lost my mother."

"Really?"

"Life has been pretty dull since she died. She made everything fun and interesting. I guess that's another way that you remind me of her."

The warm fuzzy feeling his words gave her were swiftly replaced by an unsettling thought. If she was so much like Marcus's mom, could that be the reason Gabriel was so drawn to her? Did he see her as some sort of replacement for the original?

Second best?

That was silly. Of course he didn't.

And if it was so silly, why did she have a sudden sick, hollow feeling in the pit of her stomach?

Ten

Remember what you told Marcus, Vanessa reminded herself. *Even if this doesn't work out, it's not a mistake.* The thought actually made her feel a tiny bit better.

"Oh, by the way…" Marcus pulled a cell phone from his shorts pocket. "What's your number?"

She'd actually forgotten all about her phone. She told him the number and he dialed, and she felt it begin to rumble…in the front pocket of her shorts! "What the—"

She pulled it out, staring dumbfounded, and Marcus started to laugh. "But…I heard it fall."

"Whatever you heard, it obviously wasn't your phone."

"Oh, geez. I'm sorry."

"It's okay." He pushed himself to his feet and extended a hand to help her up. "Why don't we get you upstairs."

As stupid as she felt right now, she was having such a nice time talking to him that she hated to actually go to her room. But it was late, and he probably had more important things to do than to entertain her in the short amount of evening that remained. He'd already sacrificed most of his day for her.

She took his hand and he hiked her up, but as he pulled her to her feet her phone slipped from her hand and this time she actually did drop it. It landed in the grass between them. She and Marcus bent to pick it up at the exact same time, their heads colliding in the process. Hard.

They muttered a simultaneous "Ow."

She straightened and reached up to touch the impact point just above her left eye, wincing when her fingers brushed a tender spot. Great, now she could look forward to a hangover *and* a concussion. Could she make an even bigger ass of herself?

"You're hurt," he said, looking worried, which made her feel even stupider.

"I'm fine. It's just a little tender."

"Let me see," he insisted, gently cradling her cheek in his palm, turning her toward the light for a better look. With his other hand he brushed her hair aside, his fingertips grazing her forehead.

Her heart fell to the pit of her stomach, then lunged upward into her throat. *Oh my god.* If her legs had been a little wobbly before, her senses slightly compromised, that was *nothing* compared to the head-to-toe, limb-weakening, mind-altering, knock-me-off-my-feet rush of sensation she was experiencing now. His face was so close she could feel his breath whisper across her cheek, and the urge to reach up and run her hand across his stubbled chin was almost irresistible.

Her breath caught and she got a funny feeling in the pit of her stomach. Then his eyes dropped to hers and what she saw in them made her knees go weak.

He wanted her. *Really* wanted her.

Don't do it, Vanessa. Don't even think *about it.*

"Does it hurt?" he asked, but it came out as a raspy whisper.

The only thing hurting right now—other than her bruised pride—was her heart, for what she knew was about to happen. For the betrayal she would feel when she talked to Gabriel tomorrow. But even that wasn't enough to jar her back to reality. She invited the kiss, begged for it even, lifted her chin as he dipped his head, and when his lips brushed hers…

Perfection.

It was the kind of first kiss every girl dreamed of. Indescribable really. Every silly cliché and romantic platitude all rolled in one. And even though it had probably been inevitable, they simply could not let it happen again. To let it happen at all had been…well, there was no justification for it. To say it was a mistake was putting it mildly. But the problem was, it didn't *feel* like a mistake. She felt a bit as though this was the first smart thing, the first *right* thing, she had done in years.

Which is probably why she was *still* kissing him. Why her arms were around his neck, her fingers curled into his hair. And why she would have kept on kissing him if Marcus hadn't backed away and said, "I can't believe I just did that."

Which made her feel even worse.

She pressed a hand to her tingling lips. They were still damp, still tasted like him. Her heart was still pounding, her knees weak. He'd *wrecked* her.

Marcus looked sick with guilt. Very much, she imagined, how she probably looked. She had betrayed Gabriel. With his own *son*. What kind of depraved person was she?

A slap to the face couldn't have sobered her faster.

"It's not your fault. I let you," she said.

"Why did you?" he asked, and she could see in his eyes that he wanted some sort of answer as to why this was happening, why they were feeling this way.

"Because…" she began, then paused. She could diffuse the situation. She could tell him that she was just lonely, or he reminded her so much of Gabriel that she was confused. But it felt wrong to lie, and there was only one honest answer to give him. "Because I wanted you to."

He took a second to process that, looking as though he couldn't decide if it was a good or a bad thing, if he should feel relieved that it wasn't all his fault, or even more guilty. "If it was something I did—"

"It wasn't!" she assured him. "I mean, it was, but it was me too. It was both of us. We're obviously just, confused, or…*something*. And it would probably be best if we don't analyze it to death. I mean, what would be the point? It doesn't matter why we did it. We know that we shouldn't have, and even more important, we know that it can't happen again. Right?"

"Right."

"So that's that?"

He was quiet for several long seconds and she waited for his confirmation, because they really needed to put an end to this now.

But instead of agreeing with her, Marcus shook his head and said, "Maybe not."

Though it seemed impossible that a heart could both sink and lift at the same time, hers managed it. "Why not?"

"Because maybe if we figure out why we did it, I'll stop feeling like I want to do it again."

Marcus watched Vanessa struggle for what to say next, feeling a bit as though he were caught up in some racy evening television drama. This sort of thing didn't happen in real life. Not in civilized society anyway. Men did not have affairs with their fathers' female companions, and that was exactly what he thinking of doing.

What was *wrong* with him?

She'd admitted that she was not *in* love with his father, nor was she physically attracted to him. And Marcus truly believed they would never marry. But until Vanessa's relationship with his father was completely over, he had no right to lay a finger on her. Even then a relationship with her could potentially come between him and his father.

Not that he even *wanted* a relationship. After Carmela, he had vowed to practice the single life for a while. Like his father he was probably just rebounding, and this strange fascination was probably fleeting. He would be wise to remember that.

Like father, like son, right?

"Marcus—"

"No, you're right," he interrupted. "This was a mistake. I promise it won't happen again."

"Okay," she said, but he couldn't tell if she was relieved, or disappointed. Or if she even believed him. He wasn't sure if he believed himself.

They walked in silence up to her room, and she must have sobered up, because she was steadier now. When they reached her door she turned to him.

"I had a really good time tonight. I enjoyed our talk."

"So did I."

"And…well, thank you."

He wasn't quite sure what she was thanking him for, but he nodded anyway.

Without a backward glance, she stepped into her room and closed the door, and for a full minute Marcus just stood there, plagued with the sensation that nothing had been resolved, feeling the overpowering urge to knock on her door. The only problem was, he had no idea what he wanted to say to her.

That should have been the end of it, but something wasn't right. He just couldn't put his finger on what.

You're losing your mind, he thought with a bitter laugh, then he turned and walked down the hall. He pulled out the cell phone from his pocket, with the private number that not even Cleo knew about, and tapped on the outgoing calls icon. Vanessa's number popped up. Though he wasn't sure why he did it, he programmed the number into his address book, then stuck the phone back in his pocket.

Tomorrow would be better, he assured himself. Considering how stressful the past few months had been, and the fact that he'd been sleeping—on a good night—four or five restless hours, it was no wonder he wasn't thinking clearly. His physician had offered a prescription for sleeping pills, but Marcus was against taking medication unless absolutely necessary. The meditation that Cleo had suggested hadn't helped much either. There were times, especially in the evening, when he felt a bit as if he were walking around in a fog.

Tonight I'll sleep, he told himself, then things would be clearer in the morning. Instead, he laid in bed, tossing and turning, unable to keep his mind off Vanessa and the kiss that never should have happened. He drifted in and out of sleep, his dreams filled with hazy images that made no sense, but left him feeling edgy and restless.

Marcus dragged himself out of bed at 6 a.m. with thoughts and feelings just as jumbled as the day before. He showered, dressed and had breakfast, then he tried to concentrate on work for a while, but his mind kept wandering back to Vanessa and Mia. George had informed him that they went down to use the pool around eleven, and though he found himself wanting to join them, he knew it was a bad idea. Thinking that it might help to get away for the afternoon, he called a few acquaintances to see if anyone was free for lunch, but everyone was either busy or didn't answer their phone. Instead he ate his lunch from a tray in his suite while he read the newspaper, but after he was finished he went right back to feeling restless.

"Laps," he said to himself. Swimming laps always relieved stress. He didn't even know for sure that Vanessa was still down there. It was past one-thirty, so wouldn't Mia be due for a nap? Besides, maybe it was best to confront these feelings head-on, prove to himself that he was strong enough to resist this.

He dressed in his swimsuit, pulled on a shirt and headed down to the pool. He stepped out into the blistering afternoon heat to find that Vanessa was still there, in the water, her hair pulled back in a ponytail, not a stitch of makeup on her face. In that instant the emptiness melted away, replaced by a longing, a desire to be close to her that made it difficult to breathe. And all he could think was, *Marcus, you are in big trouble.*

Vanessa carried Mia around the shallow end of the pool, swishing her back and forth while Mia plunged her little fists into the water, giggling and squealing, delighting in the fact that she was splashing them both in the face. After what had turned out to be a long and restless night, all Vanessa really wanted to do was collapse in a lounge chair and doze the afternoon away. Thinking, of course, about anything but last night's kiss. Which she could do if she called Karin, but Mia was having so much fun, Vanessa hated to take her out of the water.

Deep down she knew it was a good thing that Marcus had decided not to join them today. Still, she couldn't deny the jerk of disappointment every time she looked over at the door and he didn't come through it. Maybe, like her, he just needed a day or two to cool down. Or maybe it had nothing to do with that, and he just had more important things to do. Either way, by lunchtime she had resigned herself to the fact that he wasn't going to show. Of course that still hadn't stopped her from looking over at the door every five minutes, just in case.

"I guess today we're on our own," she told Mia.

"You two look like you're having fun."

Vanessa nearly jumped out of her skin at the unexpected voice, and whipped around to see Marcus walking toward the pool, wearing nothing but a shirt and a little black Speedo.

Holy cow.

Her heart plunged to her knees, then shot back up into her throat, and she snapped her mouth shut before her jaw had a chance to drop open. Did the man not own a pair of swim trunks? The baggy variety that hung to the knee?

"Hi there!" she said, hoping she came across as friendly, without sounding too enthusiastic. Mia, on the other hand, heard his voice and practically dislocated her neck trying to turn and see him, and when she got a glimpse of him she let out a screech and batted at the water excitedly.

Marcus sat on the edge of the pool, dipping his feet in the water, putting his crotch exactly at eye level, and with his knees slightly spread, it was difficult not to stare.

"It's a hot one," he said, shading his eyes to look up at the clear blue sky.

It certainly was, and she wasn't referring to the weather. Maybe wishing he were in the pool with them had been a bad idea. Her gaze wandered to his mouth, which of course made her think about that kiss last night, and what they might have done if they kept kissing. If she invited him into her room.

Disaster, that's what would have happened. As it stood, the damage they had done wasn't irreparable. She could write it off as a serious lapse in judgment. Another kiss, and that may have been no longer the case.

Mia on the other hand had no shame. She practically jumped out of Vanessa's arms trying to reach him.

Vanessa laughed. "I think she wants you to come in."

He pushed off the edge and slid into the water, looking even better wet. But on the bright side, she didn't have to look at as much of him.

Mia reached for him and Marcus asked, "May I?"

"Of course," she said, handing Mia over.

He held her tightly to his bare chest, as if he were afraid he might drop her, and all Vanessa could think was, *you lucky kid.* But Mia wiggled in Marcus's arms, trying to get closer to the water.

"If you turn her around and hook your arm across her belly she can play in the water," Vanessa told Marcus, and the second he turned her, she began to splash and squeal.

"It's okay if the water gets in her eyes?" he asked, looking concerned.

"Are you kidding, she loves it. She does the same thing in the bathtub. You wouldn't believe the mess she makes. When she's all soapy it's a lot like trying to bathe a squid."

"She's pretty slippery without the soap too," Marcus said, but he was grinning.

"If you want to put her in her floating ring she likes to be pulled around the pool. The faster the better." Vanessa grabbed the ring from the side and Mia shrieked.

Marcus laughed. "Let's give it a try."

Vanessa held the ring still while Marcus maneuvered her inside, which, with all of her squirming, was a bit like wrestling a baby octopus. When she was securely seated, he tugged her across the pool, swimming backward into the deeper water, then he spun her in circles and Mia giggled and swung her arms, beside herself with joy. It warmed her heart, but also broke it a little, to see Mia so attached to him.

She backed up against the edge of the pool and just watched them.

"She really does like this," Marcus said, looking as if he was having just as much fun.

"She loves being in the water. I wish I had more time to take her swimming, but our complex back home doesn't have a pool. I could take her to the hotel, but if I dare show my face on my day off, I inevitably get wrangled into working."

"Maybe she'll be a champion swimmer someday," Marcus said.

"Gabriel told me you used to compete."

"I was working toward a spot on the Olympic team, which meant intense training. I swam at least fifteen to twenty thousand meters a day, plus weight training and jogging."

"Wow, that is intense."

"Yeah, and it began to interfere with my royal duties, so I had to give it up. Now it's just a good way to stay in shape."

It certainly was, she thought, admiring all the lean muscle in his arms and shoulders. "It's sad that you weren't able to follow your dream."

"I was disappointed, but not devastated. My life was just meant for different things."

"It must have been really amazing growing up with all this," she said, looking up at the palace.

"Well, it didn't suck," Marcus said with a grin, all dimples and white teeth.

Vanessa laughed. Sometimes it was easy to forget that

he was a future king. He just seemed so…ordinary. Gabriel, though just as approachable, had a more serious and formal manner. His confidence, his sense of self-worth, had been intoxicating, and a little thrilling. Even if he had doubts about his abilities as king he would never admit them. And though Marcus possessed that same air of conviction, he wasn't afraid or ashamed to show vulnerability, and there was something unbelievably sexy about that. Especially for a woman like her, who was constantly second-guessing herself.

"The truth is, I was away at boarding school for the better part of my childhood," Marcus said. "But I did come home for school breaks and summer vacations."

"I'm not sure if I could do that," Vanessa said.

"Go to boarding school?"

"Send my child away to be raised by someone else. It would break my heart."

"In my family it's just what was expected, I guess. It was the same for my father, and his father before him."

"But not your mother, right? She didn't mind letting you go?"

"I know she missed me, but as I said, that's just the way things were. She had her duties as queen, and I had mine."

Vanessa had a sudden heart-wrenching thought. "If I marry your father, would I have to send Mia away to boarding school?"

For several seconds he looked as if he wasn't sure how to answer, or if she could handle the truth.

"I can only assume that's what he would want," he finally said.

"And if I refused?"

"She's your child, Vanessa. You should raise her the way you see fit."

But if Gabriel were to adopt her, then Mia would be

both of theirs. Which he had already said would be an eventuality. Until just this moment, she had only imagined that as a good thing. Now she wasn't so sure. What if they had contrasting views about raising children? And suppose they had a baby together? Would she have even less control then?

"I guess that's just another thing we'll have to discuss when he gets back," she said, then for reasons she didn't fully understand, heard herself ask, "How would you feel about sending your children away to school?"

Why would she ask such a thing when his opinions about child-rearing had no bearing on her life in the least?

"I guess I've never really considered that," Marcus said. "I suppose it would be something I would have to discuss with my wife."

She couldn't help but wonder if he was just giving her the PC answer, or if he really meant it. And honestly, why did it matter?

Eleven

Vanessa heard her phone ringing from the chair where she'd set her things. Thinking that it might be Gabriel, she pushed herself up out of the pool and rushed to grab it, the intense afternoon heat drying her skin in the few seconds it took to reach it. Her heart sank when she saw her father's number on the display. She had played over in her mind about a million times what she would say to him when he finally called, yet she was still too chicken to answer. She let the call go to voice mail, waited until her alert chimed, then listened to the message.

"Hey Nessy, it's Daddy," he said and she cringed, in part because she was a grown woman and he still referred to himself as Daddy, and also because she absolutely hated being called Nessy. It made her sound as though she belonged in a Scottish loch. "I thought I might catch you before you left for work. I just called to tell you that my platoon reunion will be in Los Angeles next week so I'm flying in."

Oh, crap. She closed her eyes and sighed.

"The reunion is a week from Friday night and I want time to see my grandbaby, so I'll be taking a flight early Thursday morning."

He wasn't coming there to see Vanessa, just Mia. Ironic considering he'd barely acknowledged her existence until she was almost three months old. Before then he referred to her as Vanessa's *latest mistake*. Knowing how disappointed he would be, she hadn't even told him she was pregnant until it was no longer possible to hide it. And when she had, he'd responded in that same tired, disappointed tone, "Vanessa, when will you learn?"

"I'll call with my flight information when I get it," his message said. "You can swing by and pick me up from the airport. See you soon!"

He never asked, he only demanded. Suppose she'd had other plans? Or was it that he just didn't care? It wasn't unlike him to visit on a whim and expect her to drop everything and entertain him. She had to endure that same old look of disappointment when she didn't cater to his every whim. It had always been that way, even when she was a kid. God forbid if she didn't get the laundry washed and ironed and the dishes done, not to mention the vacuuming and the dusting and the grocery shopping. And of course she was expected to maintain straight As in school. He ran a tight ship, and she had been expected to fall in line. And he wondered why she lit out of there the day she graduated high school. Which was, of course, another mistake.

This time she wouldn't be there to disappoint him… which in itself would be a disappointment, she supposed. The truth is, no matter what she did, in his opinion it would never be the right thing.

She sighed and dropped the phone back onto the chair, then looked up, surprised to find Marcus and Mia floating near the edge watching her.

"Everything okay?" he asked.

She forced a smile. "Sure. Fine."

"You're lying," he said.

She went for an innocent look, but was pretty sure it came out looking more like a grimace. "Why would you think that?"

"Because you're chewing on your thumbnail, and people generally do that when they're nervous."

She looked down to find she'd chewed off the tip of her left thumbnail. Damn. He didn't miss a thing, did he? And the way he was looking up at her, she began to wonder if choosing her bikini over the conservative one-piece had been a bad idea. She felt so…exposed, yet at the same time, she *liked* that he was looking at her. She *wanted* him to.

Vanessa, that is just so wrong.

"It's fine if you don't want to talk about it," he said.

She sat on the edge of the pool, dipping her feet in the water. "My father just left a message. He's coming to Los Angeles to visit next week."

"Does that mean you'll be leaving?"

The old Vanessa may have. She would have been worried about disappointing him yet again. But she was twenty-four years old, damn it. It was time to cut the umbilical cord and live her life the way she wanted. But she was the new Vanessa now, and that Vanessa was confident and strong and no longer cared what her father thought.

She hoped so at least.

"I'm not leaving," she told Marcus. "I'm going to call him back and tell him that I won't be there, and we'll have to reschedule for another time."

"And when he asks where you are?"

That was the tricky part.

"I'll tell him the truth." Maybe.

You're strong, she reminded herself. *You are responsible for your own destiny and what he thinks doesn't matter.*

And if she told herself enough times, she just might start to believe it.

Marcus stood behind Vanessa while she examined an exhibit at the museum, thinking that of all the visitors he had escorted there over the years—and there had been many—she showed by far the most intense interest. She didn't just politely browse while looking bored out of her skull. She absorbed information, reading every sign and description carefully, as if she were dedicating it to memory.

"You do realize that there's no quiz when we get back to the palace," he teased, as she read the fine print on a display of artifacts from the Varieo civil war of 1899.

She smiled sheepishly. "I'm taking forever, I know, but I just love history. It was my favorite subject in school."

"I don't mind," he told her, and he honestly didn't. Just like he hadn't minded spending the afternoon at the pool with her and Mia the day before. And not because of that hot pink bikini she'd worn. Okay, not completely because of the bikini. He just…liked her.

"I just wish Mia would sit in her stroller," Vanessa said, hiking her daughter, who had been unusually fidgety and fussy all day, higher on her hip. "She desperately needs a nap." But every time Vanessa tried to strap her into the stroller Mia would begin to howl.

"Why don't you let me hold her for a while," he said, extending his arms. Mia lunged for him.

"Jeez, kid!" Laughing, Vanessa handed her over, and

when Mia instantly settled against his shoulder, said, "She sure does like you."

The feeling was mutual. He even sort of liked having a baby around the palace. Although the idea that this little person could become his stepsister was a strange one. Not that he believed it would ever really happen. But did that possibly mean he was ready to start a family of his own? Eight months ago he would have said absolutely not. But so much had changed since then. He felt as if he'd changed, and he knew for a fact that it had everything to do with Vanessa's visit.

They walked to the next display, where Vanessa seemed intent on memorizing the name of every battle and its respective date. He stood behind her to the left, watching her, memorizing the curve of her face, the delicate shell of her ear, wishing he could reach out and touch her. He felt that way all the time lately, and the impulse was getting more difficult to ignore. And he knew, by the way she looked at him, the way her face flushed when they were close, the way her breath caught when he took her hand to help her out of the car, she felt it too.

When she was finished, she turned to Marcus, looked at him and laughed.

"What are you? The baby whisperer?"

He looked down at Mia to find that she was sleeping soundly on his shoulder. "Well, you said she needed a nap."

"You could try sitting her in the stroller now."

"I don't mind holding her."

"Are you sure?"

"Why risk waking her," he said, but the truth was, he just liked holding her. And he'd been doing it a lot more often. Yesterday he'd carried her on his shoulders as they strolled down the stretch of private beach at the marina—Vanessa wearing that ridiculous floppy hat—and Mia delighted in tugging on handfuls of his hair. Later they sat on a blanket close to the shore and let Mia play in the sand and splash in the salty water. Those simple activities had made him feel happier, feel more *human*, than he had in ages.

With Mia asleep in his arms, they turned and walked toward the next section of the museum.

"You're really good with her," Vanessa said. "Are you around kids much?"

"I have a few friends with young children, but I don't see them very often."

"The friends, or the children?"

"Either, really. Since we lost my mother I haven't felt much like socializing. The only time I see people now is at formal events where I'm bound by duty to attend, and children, especially small ones, are not typically included on the guest list."

She gazed up at him, looking sad. "It sounds lonely."

"What does?"

"Your life. Everyone needs friends. Would your mother be happy if she knew how you've isolated yourself?"

"No, she wouldn't. But the only true friend I had betrayed me. Sometimes I think I'm better off alone."

"I could be your friend," she said. "And having experienced firsthand what it feels like to be betrayed by a friend, you can trust that I would never do that to you."

Despite everything he'd learned of her the past three days, the blunt statement still surprised him. And he couldn't help but wonder if that might be a bad idea, that if being her friend would only strengthen the physical attraction he felt growing nearly every time he looked at her, every time she opened her mouth and all that honesty spilled out. Which is why he shouldn't have said what he said next.

"In that case, would you care to join me for dinner on the veranda tonight?"

The invitation seemed to surprise her. "Um, yeah, I'd love to. What time?"

"How about eight?"

"Mia goes to bed right around then, so that would be perfect. And I assume you mean the veranda in the west wing, off the dining room?"

"That's the one. I see you've been studying your map."

"Since I'm going to be here a while either way, I should probably learn my way around." She glanced at her watch, frowned and said, "Wow, I didn't realize how late it is. Maybe we should think about getting back."

"I'm in no hurry if you want to stay."

"I really do need to get back," she said, looking uncomfortable. "Gabriel promised to Skype me at four today, so…"

So she obviously was looking forward to speaking to him. And was that jealousy he was feeling? He forced a smile and kept his tone nonchalant. "Well then, by all means, let's go."

You have no reason to be nervous, Vanessa told herself for the tenth time since she'd left her room and made her way to the veranda. They'd spent all day together and though it had been a little awkward at times, Marcus had been a perfect gentleman, and she was sure tonight would be no exception. He probably only invited her to dinner because he felt obligated to entertain her. Or maybe he really did want to be friends.

And what a sophomoric thing that had been to say to him, she thought, offering to be his friend. As if he probably didn't already have tons of people lining up to be his friend. What made her so special?

Or was that just her way of subtly telling him that's all they could ever be. Friends. And she was sure that with time, she would stop fantasizing about him taking her in his arms, kissing her, then tearing off her clothes and making passionate love to her. Tearing, because he wasn't the kind of man to take things slow. He would be hot and sexy and demanding and she would of course have multiple orgasms. At least, in her fantasy she did. The fantasy she had been playing over and over in her head since he'd kissed her.

Get a grip, Vanessa. You're only making this harder on yourself.

She found the dining room and stepped through the open doors onto the veranda at exactly seven fifty-nine. Taper candles burned in fresh floral centerpieces on a round bistro table set for two, and champagne chilled in an ice bucket beside it. Beyond the veranda, past lush, sweetly scented flower gardens, the setting sun was a stunning palette of brilliant red and orange streaking an indigo canvas sky. A mild breeze swept away the afternoon heat.

It was the ideal setting for a romantic dinner. But this was supposed to be a meal shared between friends. Wasn't it?

"I see you found it."

She spun around to find Marcus standing behind her. He stood leaning casually in the dining room doorway, hands tucked into the front pockets of his slacks, his white silk shirt a stark contrast to his deep olive skin and his jacket the exact same rich espresso shade as his eyes. His hair was combed back but one stubborn wavy lock caressed his forehead.

"Wow, you look really nice," she said, instantly wishing she could take the words back. This is a casual dinner between *friends,* she reminded herself. She shouldn't be chucking out personal compliments.

"You sound surprised," he said with a raised brow.

"No! Of course not. I just meant…" She realized Marcus was grinning. He was teasing her. She gestured to the sleeveless, coral-colored slip dress she was wearing. She had wanted to look nice, without appearing blatantly sexy, and this was the only dress she'd brought with her that seemed to fit the bill. It was simple, and shapeless without looking frumpy. "I wasn't really sure how formal to dress."

His eyes raked over her. Blatantly, and with no shame. "You look lovely."

He said it politely, but the hunger in his gaze, and the resulting tug of lust deep in her belly, was anything but polite. And as exposed as she felt just then, she might as well have been wearing a transparent negligee, or nothing at all. And the worst part was, she liked it. She liked the way she felt when he looked at her. Even though it was so very wrong.

He gestured to the table. "Shall we sit?"

She nodded, and he helped her into her chair, the backs of his fingers brushing her bare shoulders as he eased it to the table, and she actually shivered. Honest to goodness goose bumps broke out across her skin.

Oh my.

She'd read in stories about a man making a woman shiver just by touching her, but it had never actually happened to her. In fact, she thought the whole thing sounded sort of silly. Not so much anymore.

"Champagne?" Marcus asked.

Oh, that could be a really bad idea. The last thing she needed was something to compromise her senses. They were compromised enough already. But the bottle was open, and she hated to let good champagne—and noting the label, it was *good* champagne—go to waste.

"Just one glass," she heard herself say, knowing she would have to be careful not to let one glass become two and so on.

Marcus poured it himself, then took a seat across from her. He lifted his glass, pinned his eyes on her and said, "To my father."

There was some sort of message in his eyes, but for the life of her, she wasn't sure what it was. Was toasting his father his way of letting her know the boundaries they'd established were still firmly in place, or did it mean something else entirely?

She'd just as soon they didn't talk about Gabriel at all. And rather than analyze it to death, she lifted her own glass and said, "To Gabriel." Hoping that would be the end of it.

She took a tiny sip, then set her glass down, and before she could even begin to think of what to say next, one of the younger butlers appeared with a gleaming silver tray and served the soup. He even nodded cordially when she thanked him. Karin definitely seemed to be warming to her as well, and Vanessa's maid had actually smiled and said good morning when she came in to make the bed that morning. They weren't exactly rolling out the red carpet—more like flopping down the welcome mat—but it was progress.

The soup consisted of bite-sized dumplings swimming in some sort of rich beef broth. And it was delicious. But that didn't surprise her considering the food had been exemplary since she arrived.

"You spoke with my father today?" he asked.

Ugh, she really didn't want to do this, but she nodded. "This afternoon."

"He told you that my aunt is still in intensive care?"

"He said she had a bad night. That her fever spiked, and she may need surgery. It sounds as if he won't be home anytime soon." Despite what she had hoped.

"He told me she's still very ill," Marcus said, then his eyes lifted to hers. "He asked if I've been keeping you entertained."

Oh, he had definitely been doing that.

"He asked if I've been respectful."

Her heart skipped a beat. "You don't think he…"

"Suspects something?" Marcus said bluntly, then he shook his head. "No. I think he's still worried that I won't be nice to you."

Oh, he'd been "nice" all right. A little too nice, some might say.

"He said you seemed reluctant to talk about me."

The truth was, she hadn't known what to tell Gabriel. She worried that if she said too much, like mentioning the earrings, or their evening stroll, Gabriel might get suspicious. She didn't know what was considered proper, and what was pushing the boundaries, so she figured it was better not to say anything at all. "I didn't mean to be elusive, or give him the impression I felt unwelcome."

"I just don't want him to think that I've neglected my duty," Marcus said.

"Of course. I'll be sure to let him know that you've been a good host."

They both quietly ate their soup for several minutes, then Marcus asked, "Have you spoken with your father yet?"

She lowered her eyes to her bowl. "Uh, nope, not yet."

She took a taste of her soup and when she looked up, he was pinning her with one of those brow-tipped stares.

"I *will*," she said.

"The longer you wait, the harder it will be."

She set her spoon down, her belly suddenly knotted with nerves. She lifted her glass and took another sip. "I know. I just have to work up the nerve. I'll do it, I just…I need to wait until the time is right."

"Which will happen when?"

When he was at the airport waiting for her to pick him up, maybe. "I'll do it. Probably tomorrow. The problem is, whenever I have the time, it's the middle of the night there."

The brow rose higher.

She sighed. "Okay, that's a lie. I'm a big fat chicken. There, I said it."

One of the butlers appeared to clear their soup plates. While another served the salad, Vanessa's phone started to ring. Would it be funny—not ha-ha funny, but ironic funny—if that were him right now.

She pulled it out of her pocketbook and saw that it wasn't her father, but Karin. As crabby as Mia had been today, maybe she was having trouble getting her to settle.

"Mia woke with a fever, ma'am."

It wasn't unusual for Mia to run a low-grade fever when she was teething, and that would explain her foul mood. "Did you take her temperature?"

"Yes, ma'am. It's forty point five."

The number confused her for a second, then she realized Karin meant Celsius. She racked her brain to recall the conversion and came up with a frighteningly high number. Over one hundred and *four* degrees!

She felt the color drain from her face. Could that be right? And if it was, this was no case of teething. "I'll be right up."

Marcus must have seen the fear in her eyes, because he frowned and asked, "What's wrong?"

Vanessa was already out of her chair. "It's Mia. She has a fever. A high one."

Marcus shoved himself to his feet, pulled out his phone and dialed. "George, please get Dr. Stark on the line and tell him we need him immediately."

Twelve

Other than a mild cold in the spring, Mia had never really been sick a day in her life. Imagining the worst, Vanessa's heart pounded a mile a minute as she rushed up the stairs to her suite, Marcus trailing close behind. When she reached the nursery she flung the door open.

Karin had stripped Mia down to her diaper and was rocking her gently, patting her back. Mia's cheeks were bright red and her eyelids droopy, and Vanessa's heart sank even lower as she crossed the room to her. How, in a couple of hours' time, could she have gotten so sick?

"Hey, baby," Vanessa said, touching Mia's forehead. It was burning hot. "Did you give her anything?"

Karin shook her head. "No, ma'am. I called you the minute she woke up."

Vanessa took Mia from her. She was limp and listless. "In the bathroom there's a bottle of acetaminophen drops. Could you get it for me, please?"

Karin scurried off and Marcus, who stood by the door looking worried, asked, "Is there anything I can do?"

"Just get the doctor up here as fast as possible." She cradled Mia to her chest, her hands trembling she was so frightened.

Karin hurried back with the drops and Vanessa measured out the correct dose. Mia swallowed it without a fuss.

"I don't know what this could be. She's barely ever had a cold."

"I'm sure it's nothing serious. Probably just a virus."

"I wonder if I should put her in a cool bath to bring her temperature down."

"How high is it?"

"Over one hundred and four."

His brows flew up.

"Fahrenheit," she added, and his face relaxed.

"Why don't you wait and see what the doctor says?"

She checked the clock across the room. "How soon do you think he'll be here?"

"Quickly. He's on call 24/7."

"Is he a pediatrician?"

"A family practitioner, but I assure you he is more than qualified."

She didn't imagine the royal family would keep an unqualified physician on call.

"Why don't you sit down," Marcus said, gesturing to the rocker. "Children can sense when parents are upset."

He was right, she needed to pull it together. The way the baby lay limp in Vanessa's arms, whimpering pathetically, it was as if she didn't have the energy to cry. She sat in the chair, cradling Mia in her arms and rocked her gently. "I'm sorry to have interrupted dinner. You can go back down and finish."

He folded his arms. "I'm not going anywhere."

Though she was used to handling things on her own when it came to her daughter, she was grateful for his company. Sometimes she got tired of being alone.

Dr. Stark, a kind-faced older gentleman, arrived just a few minutes later carrying a black medical bag.

He shook her hand and asked in English, "How old is the child?"

"Six months."

"Healthy?"

"Usually, yes. The worst she's ever had was a mild cold. I don't know why she would have such a high fever."

"She's current on her vaccinations?"

She nodded.

"You flew here recently?"

"Five days ago."

He nodded, touching Mia's forehead. "You have records?"

She was confused for a second, then realized he meant medical records. "Yes, in my bedroom."

"I'd like to see them."

Marcus held out his arms. "I'll hold her while you get them."

She handed her to him and Mia went without a fuss.

She darted across the hall to her room, grabbed the file with Mia's medical and immunization records, then hurried back to the bedroom. Marcus was sitting in the rocking chair, cradling Mia against his shoulder. Karin stood by the door looking concerned.

"Here they are," she said, and the doctor took the folder from her.

He skimmed the file then set it aside. "You'll need to lay her down."

Marcus rose from the chair and set Mia down on the changing table with all the care and affection of a father, watching with concern as the doctor gave her a thorough exam, asking random questions. When he looked in her ears she started to fuss.

When he was finished, Vanessa asked, "Is it serious?"

"She'll be fine," he assured her, patting her arm. "As I suspected, it's just an ear infection."

Vanessa was so relieved she could have cried. She picked Mia up and held her tight. "How could she have gotten that?"

"It could have started as a virus. A round of antibiotics should clear it right up. The acetaminophen you gave her should bring the fever down."

It looked as if it already had started to work. Mia's cheeks weren't as red and her eyes seemed less droopy. "Could that be why she was so crabby during the flight here?"

"I doubt it. Some children are just sensitive to the cabin pressure. It could have been hurting her ears."

It broke her heart to think that all the time they'd been in the air, Mia had been in pain and Vanessa hadn't even known it. "What can I do to keep it from happening in the future?"

"I would keep her out of the air until the infection clears, then, when you fly home, try earplugs. It will help regulate the pressure."

If she went home, that is. She glanced over at Marcus, who was looking at her. Was he thinking the same thing?

"Right now the best thing for her is a good night's rest. I'll have the antibiotics delivered right away. Just follow the directions. Call if she hasn't improved by morning. Otherwise I'll check her again in two days."

"Thank you, Dr. Stark," she said, shaking his hand.

"Shall I put her back in her crib?" Karin asked Vanessa after he left.

Vanessa shook her head. "I'm going to take her to my room, so you can have the night off. Thanks for calling me so quickly."

Karin nodded and started to walk to her room, then she stopped, turned back and said, "She's a strong girl, she'll be fine in no time." Then she actually smiled.

When she was gone, Vanessa turned to Marcus. He'd removed his jacket and was leaning against the wall, arms crossed. "Thank you," she said.

He cocked his head slightly. "For what?"

"Getting the doctor here so fast. For just being here with me. I don't suppose you have a portable crib anywhere around here. She rolls so much that I get nervous keeping her in bed with me."

Marcus pulled out his phone. "I'm sure we have one."

The medicine arrived fifteen minutes later and Vanessa gave her a dose, and within half an hour a portable crib had been set up in her bedroom. Vanessa laid Mia, who had fallen asleep on her shoulder, inside and covered her with a light blanket. She gently touched Mia's forehead, relieved to find that her temperature had returned almost to normal.

She walked back out into the sitting room where Marcus waited. It was dark but for a lamp on the desk. He stood by the French doors, the curtain pulled back, gazing into the night. Her first instinct was to walk up to him, slide her arms around his waist and lay her head against his back. She imagined that they would stay that way for a while, then he would turn and take her in his arms, kiss her the way he did the other night.

But as much as she wanted to—ached for it even—she couldn't do it.

"She's in bed," she said, and Marcus turned to her, letting the curtain drop. "I think she's better already."

"That's good."

The phone on her desk began to ring and she crossed the room to pick it up. It was Gabriel. Thank goodness he couldn't see her face or surely he would recognize the guilt there for the thoughts she had just been having.

"George called," he said, sounding worried. "He told me that Mia is ill."

"She woke with a fever."

"The doctor was there?"

"He came right away. It's an ear infection. He put her on antibiotics."

"What can I do? Do you need me to come home? I can catch a flight first thing in the morning."

This was it. She could say yes, and get Gabriel back here and be done with this whole crazy thing with Marcus. Instead she heard herself saying, "In the time it would take you to get here, she'll probably be fine. Her fever is already down."

"Are you sure?"

"Trina needs you more than I do. Besides, Marcus is helping," she said, glancing his way.

His expression was unreadable.

"Call me if you need anything, day or night," Gabriel said.

"I will, I promise."

"I'll let you go so you can tend to her needs. I'll call you tomorrow."

"Okay."

"Good night, sweet Vanessa. I love you."

"I love you, too," she said, and she did. She loved him as a friend, so why did she feel like a fraud? And why did she feel so uncomfortable saying the words in front of Marcus?

Well, duh, of course she knew why.

She set the phone down and turned to Marcus. He stood

by the sofa, his arms folded across his chest. "Your father," she said, as if he needed an explanation.

"He offered to come home?" he asked.

She nodded.

"You told him no?"

She nodded again.

He started walking toward her. "Why? Isn't that what you wanted?"

"It was...I mean, it *is*. I just think..." The truth was, she was afraid. Afraid that Gabriel would come home, see her face and instantly know what she was feeling for Marcus. He trusted her, *loved* her, and she'd betrayed him. And she continued to betray him every time she had an inappropriate thought about his son, but she just couldn't seem to stop herself. Or maybe she didn't want to stop. "Maybe we need some time to sort this out before he comes back."

"Sort what out?"

"This. Us."

"I thought there was no us. That we were going to pretend like it never happened."

That had seemed like a good idea yesterday, but now she wasn't so sure she could do that. Not right away, anyhow. "We are. I just...need some time to think."

He stepped closer, his dark eyes serious and pinned to hers. Her stomach bottomed out and her heart started to beat faster.

"Please don't look at me like that."

"Like what?"

"Like you want to kiss me again."

"But I do."

Oh boy. Her knees felt squishy. "You know that would be a really bad idea."

"Yeah, it probably would."

"You really shouldn't."

"So tell me no."

He wanted *her* to be the responsible one? Seriously?

"Have you not heard a thing I've said this week?"

"Every word of it."

"Then you know that you really shouldn't trust me with a responsibility like that, considering my tendency to make bad decisions."

His grin warmed her from the inside out. "Right now, I'm sort of counting on it."

Thirteen

Vanessa reached up and cupped Marcus's cheek, running her thumb across that adorable dimple, something she'd wanted to do since the first time she'd seen him smile.

This was completely insane, what they were about to do, because she knew in her heart that this time it wouldn't just be a kiss. But with him standing right in front of her, gazing into her eyes with that hungry look, she just couldn't make herself stop him. And her last thought, as he lowered his head and leaned in, as she rose up to meet him halfway, was how wrong this was, and how absolutely wonderful.

Then he kissed her. But this time it was different, this kiss had a mutual urgency that said neither would be having a crisis of conscience. In a weird way it felt as if they had been working toward this moment since the minute she'd stepped off the plane. Like somewhere deep down she just knew it had been inevitable. It was difficult to imagine that at one time she hadn't even liked him. A big fat jerk, that's what she'd thought him to be. She'd been so wrong about him. About so many things.

"I want you Vanessa," he whispered against her lips. "I don't care if it's wrong."

She pulled back to look him in the eyes. How could she have known this beautiful man only five days when right now it felt like an eternity?

And right now their feelings were the only ones that mattered to her.

She shoved his jacket off his shoulders, down his arms, and it dropped to the floor. She ran her hands up the front of his shirt, over his muscular chest, the way she had wanted to since he stood in her doorway that day with his shirt unbuttoned. And he felt just as good as she knew he would.

Marcus groaned deep in his throat. Then, as if the last bit of his control snapped, he kissed her hard, lifting her off her feet and pinning her to the wall with the length of his body. She gasped against his lips, hooked her legs around his hips, curling her fingers into the meat of his arms. This was the Marcus she had fantasized about, the one who would sweep her off her feet and take her with reckless abandon, and everything inside her screamed, "Yes!"

Marcus set her on her feet and grabbed the hem of her dress, yanking it up over her head—as close to tearing as he could get without actually shredding the delicate silk fabric. When she stood there in nothing but a bra and panties, he stopped and just looked at her.

"You're amazing," he said.

Not beautiful, but amazing. Was it possible that he really did see more in her than just a pretty face? When she looked at Marcus she saw not royalty, not a prince, but a man who was charismatic and kind and funny. And maybe a little vulnerable too. A man who was looking back at her with the same deep affection. Could it be that her feelings for Gabriel were never meant to be more than friendship? That Marcus was the one she was destined to fall in love with? Because as much as she'd tried to fight it, she was definitely falling in love with him.

She took his hand and walked backward to the sofa, tugging him along with her. A part of her said that she should have been second-guessing herself, or feeling guilty—and a week ago, she probably would have—but as they undressed, kissing and touching each other, it just felt right.

When he was naked, she took a moment to just look at him. Physically he was just as perfect as he could possibly be, but she didn't really care about that. It was his mind that fascinated her most, who he was on the inside.

She lay back against the sofa, pulling him down with her, so he was cradled between her thighs. He grinned down at her, brushing her hair back from her face. "You know that this is completely crazy."

"I know. I take it you don't do crazy things?"

"Never."

"Me neither." She stroked the sides of his face, his neck, ran her hands across his shoulders. She just couldn't stop touching him. "Maybe that's why this feels so good. Maybe we both need a little crazy."

"That must be it." He leaned down to kiss her, but just as his lips brushed hers, he stopped, uttering a curse.

"If you're about to tell me we have to stop, I'm going to be very upset," she said.

"No, I just realized, I don't have protection with me."

"You *don't?* Aren't princes supposed to be prepared at all times?" She paused, frowning. "Or is that the scouts?"

"I wasn't exactly planning for this, you know."

"Really?"

He laughed. "Yes, really. But then you walked into the room wearing that dress…"

"*That* dress? Are you kidding me? It's like the least sexy thing I own. I wore it so I *wouldn't* tempt you."

"The truth is, you could have been wearing a paper sack and I would have wanted to rip it off you. It's you that I want, not your clothes."

It was thrilling to know he wanted her that much, that he would be attracted to her even at her worst.

"I'm going to have to run back to my room," he said, not sounding at all thrilled with the idea.

"I'm on birth control, so you don't have to."

"Are you sure?"

"I'm sure. And now that we have that settled, could we stop talking and get to the good stuff?"

He grinned. "I thought women liked to talk."

"Yes, but even we have our limits."

She didn't have to ask twice, and lying there with him, kissing and touching, felt completely natural. There was none of the usual first time fumbling or awkwardness. And any vestige of reservations, or hint of mixed feelings that may have remained evaporated the instant he thrust inside her. Everything else in the world, any cares or worries or feelings of indecision that were always there somewhere in the back of her mind, melted away. She knew from the instant he began to move inside her—slow and gentle at first, then harder and faster, until it got so out of control they tumbled off the couch onto the rug—that this was meant to be. He made her feel the way a woman was supposed to feel. Adored and desired and protected, and *strong*, as if no one or no thing could ever knock her back down.

And she felt heartbroken, all the way down to her soul,

because as much as she wanted Marcus, she couldn't have him, and she was terrified that no man would ever make her feel this way again.

"We're totally screwed, aren't we?" Vanessa asked Marcus, lying next to him naked on the floor beside the sofa, her breath just as raspy and uneven as his own, glowing from what had been for him some of the best sex of his entire life. Actually no, it had been *the* best.

Maybe it was the anticipation that had made it so exciting, or the forbidden nature of the relationship. Maybe it was that she had no hang-ups about her looks or insecurities about her body, or that she gave herself heart and soul and held nothing back. It could have been that unlike most women, whatever she took, she gave back tenfold.

Or maybe he just really liked her.

At this point, what difference did it make? Because she was right. They were screwed. How could he possibly explain this to his father? "Sorry, but I just slept with the woman you love, and I think I might be falling in love with her myself, but don't worry, you'll find someone else."

There was a code among men when it came to girlfriends and wives, and that was even more true among family. It was a line a man simply did not cross. But he had crossed it, and the worst part was that he couldn't seem to make himself feel guilty about it.

"My father can't ever know," he said.

She nodded. "I know. And I can't marry him now."

"I know." He felt bad about that, but maybe it was for the best. He believed that Vanessa came here with the very best of intentions, but she obviously didn't love his father the way a wife loves a husband. Maybe by stepping between them Marcus had done them both a favor. Vanessa was so sweet and kind, he could imagine her compromising her own happiness to make his father happy. Eventually though, they would have both been miserable. In essence, he had saved them from an inevitable failed marriage.

Or was he just trying to rationalize a situation that was completely irrational?

She reached down and laced her fingers through his. "It's not your fault that this happened, so please don't ever blame yourself."

He squeezed her hand. "It's no one's fault. Sometimes things just…happen. It doesn't have to make sense."

She looked over at him. "You know that no matter how we feel, you and I, we can't ever…"

"I know." And the thought caused an actual pain in his chest. A longing so deep he felt hollowed out and raw. He had little doubt that Vanessa was the one for him. She was his destiny, she *and* Mia, but he could never have them. Not if he ever hoped to have a civilized relationship with his father. It was as if the universe was playing a cruel trick on them. But in his world honor reigned supreme, and family always came first. His feelings, his happiness, were inconsequential.

It wasn't fair, but when was life ever?

"I need to call him and tell him," Vanessa said. "That it's over, I mean. I won't tell him about us."

The minute she ended her relationship with his father, she would have to leave. There would be no justifiable reason to stay. And the idea that this was it, that Marcus would never be with Vanessa again, that he had to give her up so soon, made his heart pound and adrenaline rush. He wasn't ready to let her go. Not yet.

"That's not the sort of thing that you should do over the phone, or through Skype," he told her. "Shouldn't you wait until he returns?"

Her brow furrowed into a frown. "It just doesn't seem

fair to let him think that everything is okay, then dump him the second he gets back. That just seems…cruel."

And this was the woman he'd been convinced was a devious gold digger. How could he have been so wrong? Because he was an idiot, or at least, he had been. And he would be again if he let her go now.

"Do you really think now is the right time?" he said, grasping for a reason, any reason, to get her to stay. "He's so upset over my aunt."

She blinked. "I guess I hadn't really thought about it that way. That would be pretty thoughtless. But I don't think I can wait until he comes back. That could be weeks still."

"Then at least wait until she's out of intensive care."

"I don't know…"

Oh, to hell with this. Here she was being honest and he was trying to manipulate her.

"The truth is, I don't care about my father's feelings. This is pure selfishness. Because the minute you tell him, it's over, and I just can't let you go yet." He pulled her close, cupped her face in his hands. "Stay with me, Vanessa. Just a few days more."

She looked conflicted, and sad. "You know we'll just be torturing ourselves."

"I don't care. I just want a little more time with you." Not wanted. *Needed.* And he had never needed anyone in his life.

"We would have to be discreet. No one can know. If Gabriel found out—"

"He won't. I promise."

She hesitated a moment, then smiled and touched his cheek. "Okay. A few more days."

He breathed a quiet sigh of relief. Was this wrong in more ways than he could count, and were they just delaying the inevitable? Of course. And did he care? Not really.

He'd spent his entire life making sacrifices, catering to the whims of others. This one time he was going to be selfish, take something for himself.

"But then I have to go," she said. "I have to get on with my life."

"I understand." Because he did too, as difficult as that was to imagine. But for now she was his, and he planned to make the most of what little time they had left together.

"You did what?" Jessy shrieked into the phone, so loud that Vanessa had to hold it away from her ear. "I don't talk to you for a couple of days and this happens?"

Vanessa cringed. Maybe telling Jessy that she'd slept with Marcus, several times now, hadn't been such a hot idea after all. But if she didn't tell *someone,* she felt as if she would burst.

"You realize I was kidding when I suggested he could be a viable second choice," Jessy said.

"I know. And it's not something I planned on happening."

"He didn't, you know…*force* you."

"God no! Of course not. What is your hang-up about the men in this country being brutes?"

"I'm just worried about you."

"Well, don't be. Marcus would never do that. He's one of the sweetest and kindest men I've ever met. It was one hundred percent mutual."

"But you've barely known him a week. You don't sleep with guys you've known a week. Hell, sometimes you make them wait *months*."

"I know. And it's a wonder we held out as long as we did."

Jessy laughed. "Oh my God. Who are you and what have you done with my best friend?"

"I know, this isn't like me at all. And the weird thing is, if I could go back and do it differently, I wouldn't. I'm glad for what happened. And I'm glad I met him. It's changed me."

"In five days?"

"It sounds impossible, I know. I have a hard time believing it myself, but I just feel *different*. I feel…gosh, I don't know, like a better person, I guess."

Jessy laughed again. "You're sleeping with the son of the man you're supposed to marry, and you feel like a better person?"

It did sound weird when she said it like that. "It's hard to explain. And though I hate to admit it, I think what you said about Gabriel being a father figure was true. Nothing I do is good enough for my dad, and I guess in a way I transferred my feelings onto Gabriel. Deep down I knew that I didn't love him the way a wife should love a husband, that I never would. But he seemed to love me so much, and I didn't want to let him down. But then I met Marcus and something just…clicked. If it hadn't been for him, I may have made another terrible mistake."

"So you must really like him."

If only it were that simple. "That would be a major understatement."

Jessy was quiet for a second, then she said, "Are you saying that you *love* him? After *five* days?"

"Weird, huh?"

"How does he feel?"

She shrugged. "What does it matter?"

"It seems to me like it would matter an awful lot."

If only. "We can't be together. How do you think Gabriel would feel if I told him I was dumping him for his son? He might never forgive Marcus."

"You don't think Marcus would choose you over his father?"

"It doesn't matter because I would never ask him to. Nor would I want him to. Family and honor mean everything to Marcus. It's one of the things I love most about him."

"So, the thing you love most is what's keeping you apart."

"I guess so, yeah." And the thought of leaving, of giving him up, filled her belly with painful knots, and she knew that the longer she stayed the worse it would be when she left, yet here she still was. "This is making me sad. Let's talk about something else. How was your trip?"

"It was good," Jessy said, sounding surprised. "It was actually…fun."

"His family is nice?"

"Yeah. They're very small-town, if you know what I mean, and very traditional. Wayne and I had to sleep in separate rooms. They have this big old farmhouse with lots of land and though I've always been more of a city girl, it was really beautiful. Hot as hell though."

Vanessa smiled. "I'm really glad that it went well."

At least one of them was in a relationship that might actually work.

"I know you don't want to talk about it," Jessy said, "but can I just say one more thing about your affair with the prince?"

Vanessa sighed. "Okay."

"This is going to sound strange. But I'm proud of you."

It was Vanessa who laughed this time. "I slept with the son of the man I was planning to marry and you're *proud* of me?"

"You're always so hell-bent on making other people happy, but you did something selfish, something for yourself. That's a huge step for you."

"I guess I never thought of being selfish as a good thing."

"Sometimes it is."

"You know what the hardest part about leaving will be? Mia has become so attached to him, and he really seems to love her. I think he would be an awesome dad."

"You'll meet someone else, Vanessa. You'll fall in love again, I promise."

Vanessa wasn't so sure about that. In her entire life she'd never felt this way about anyone, she hadn't even known it was possible to love someone the way she loved Marcus. To need someone as much as she needed him, yet feel more free than she had in her life. And she just couldn't imagine it ever happening again. What if Marcus was it? What if he was her destiny? Was it also her destiny to let him go?

Fourteen

Vanessa woke to another message from her father, the third one that he had left in as many days, this one sounding more gruff and irritated than the last two.

"Nessy, why haven't you called me back? I called the hotel and they said you took a leave of absence. I want to know what's going on. Have you gotten yourself into trouble again?"

Of course that would be his first assumption, that she had done something wrong. What else would he think? She sighed, not so disappointed as she was resigned to the way things were. And a little sad that he always seemed to see the worst in her.

"Call me as soon as you get this," he demanded, and that's where the message ended. She dropped her phone on the bedside table and fell back against the pillows.

Beside her, Marcus stirred, waking slowly, the way he always did. Or at least, the last three mornings when they woke up together, he had. First he stretched, lengthening every inch of that long, lean body, then he yawned deeply, and finally he opened his eyes, saw her lying there next to him, and gave her a sleepy smile, his hair all rumpled and sexy. Creases from his pillow lined his cheek.

Watching this ritual had become her new favorite way to spend her morning. Even though what they were doing still filled her with guilt. She just couldn't seem to stay away.

"What time is it?" he asked in a voice still gravelly from sleep.

"Almost eight."

He rolled onto his back and laughed, the covers sliding down to expose his beautiful bare chest. "That makes last night the third night in a row that I slept over seven hours straight. Do you have any idea how long it's been since I got a decent night's sleep?"

"I'm that boring, huh?"

He grinned and pulled her on top of him, so she was straddling his thighs, his beard stubble rough against her chin as he kissed her. "More like you're wearing me out."

It had rained the past two days and Marcus had decided it would be best to spend them in the palace, in her suite. Wearing as little clothing as possible. They mostly just talked, and played with Mia, and when Mia took her naps, they spent the entire time making love. A few times Vanessa had even let Karin watch Mia for an extra hour or so, so they had a little more time together. And though it had been a week now, neither Vanessa nor Marcus had brought up the subject of her leaving, but it loomed between them, unspoken. A dark shadow and a constant element of shame that hung over what had been—other than Mia's birth—the best time of her life. She kept telling herself that when the time was right to leave, they would just know it. So far that time hadn't come, and deep down she wished it never would.

Marcus was it for her. He was the one, her *soul mate,* and of that she was one hundred and ten percent sure. For the first time in her life she had no doubts. She wasn't second-guessing herself, or worrying that she was making a mistake.

She wasn't exactly sure if he felt the same way. He seemed to, and he clearly didn't want her to leave, but did he love her? He hadn't actually said so. But to be fair, neither had she. At this point, what difference did it make? They were just words. Even if he did love her, his relationship with his father *had* to come first.

After that first time making love, she'd dreaded having to face Gabriel on Skype, sure that he would know the second he saw her face, but while she waited on her computer for over an hour, he'd been a no-show. She'd been more relieved than anything. He'd phoned the next day, apologizing, complaining of security issues, and said it might be better if they limited their calls to voice only. Which actually worked out pretty well for her. Already she could feel herself pulling away.

Their conversations were shorter now, and more superficial. And one day, when Marcus had taken them for a drive to see the royal family's mountain cabin—although to call the lavish vacation home a cabin was akin to calling the Louvre a cute little art gallery—she'd been out of cell range and had missed his call completely. She hadn't even remembered to check for a message. And though it was clearly her fault that they hadn't spoken, he had been the one to apologize the next day. He said he was swamped with work and tending to Trina, and he hadn't had a chance to call back.

She kept waiting for him to ask her if there was a problem, but if he had noticed any change in their relationship, he hadn't mentioned it yet. But Trina had been improving, and though she was still very weak, and Gabriel hadn't felt comfortable leaving her yet, it was only a matter of time.

And then of course she had her father to deal with.

"You look troubled," Marcus said, brushing her hair back and tucking it behind her ear.

He had an uncanny way of always knowing what she was thinking. "My dad called again."

He sighed. "That would explain it."

"He called the hotel and found out that I took a leave, so of course he's assuming that I'm in some sort of trouble. He demanded that I call him immediately."

"You should. You should have called him days ago."

"I know." She let out a sigh and draped herself across his warm, solid chest, pressing her ear to the center, to hear the thump of his heart beating.

"So do it now."

"I don't want to."

"Stop acting like a coward and just call him."

She sat up and looked down at him. "I'm acting like a coward because I *am* one."

"No, you aren't."

Yes, she was. When it came to dealing with her father anyway. "I'll call him tomorrow. I promise."

"You'll call him now," he said, dumping her off his lap and onto the mattress. Then he got up and walked to the bathroom, all naked and gorgeous, his tight behind looking so squeezable.

He stopped in the doorway, turned to her and grinned. "Now, I'm going to take a shower, and if you want to join me, you had better start dialing."

The door closed behind him, then she heard the shower switch on. Damn him. He knew how much she loved taking their morning shower together. He brought a change of clothes to her room every night so no one would see him the next morning wearing the same clothes from the night before. He also rolled around in his bed and mussed up the covers so it would look as if he'd slept there. It had to be obvious to pretty much everyone how much time they had been spending together, but if anyone suspected inappropriate behavior, they'd kept it to themselves.

Vanessa sighed and looked over at the bathroom door, then her phone. Well, here goes nothing.

She sat up, grabbed it and dialed her father's number before she chickened out. He answered on the first ring. "Nessy, where the hell have you been? I've been worried sick. Where's Mia? Is she okay?"

He'd been worried sick about both of them, or just Mia, she wondered. "Sorry, Dad, I would have called you sooner but I've actually been out of the country."

"Out of the country?" he barked, as if that were some unforgivable crime. "Why didn't you tell me? And where is my granddaughter?"

"She's with me."

"Where are you?" he said, sounding no less irate. She knew he was only acting this way because he was worried, and he hated not being in control of every situation every minute. If she gave him hourly reports of her activities he would be ecstatic. And usually when he spoke to her this way it made her feel about two inches tall. Right now, she just felt annoyed.

"I'm in Varieo, you know that little country near—"

"I *know* where it is. What in God's name are you doing there?"

"It's sort of…a work thing." Because she had met Gabriel at work, right?

"I thought you took a leave from the hotel. Or was that just a fancy way of saying they fired you?"

Of course he would think that.

Her annoyance multiplied by fifty. "No, I was not *fired,*" she snapped.

"Do not take that tone with me, young lady," he barked back at her.

Young lady? Was she *five?*

In that instant something inside of her snapped and she'd had enough of being treated like an irresponsible child. And if standing up for herself meant disappointing him, so be it. "I'm twenty-four, Dad. I'll take whatever tone I damned well please. And for the record, I deserve the same respect that you demand from me. I am sick to death of you talking down to me, and always thinking the worst of me. And I'm finished with you making me feel as if anything I do is never good enough for you. I'm smart, and successful, and brave, and I have lots of friends and people who love me. So unless you can think of something positive to say to me, don't bother calling anymore."

She disconnected the call, and even though her heart was thumping, and her hands were trembling, she felt... good. In fact, she felt pretty freaking fantastic. Maybe Marcus was right. Maybe she really was brave. And though she didn't honestly believe this would change anything, at least now he knew how she felt.

Her phone began to ring and she jerked with surprise. It was her dad. She was tempted to let it go to voice mail, but she'd started this, and she needed to finish it.

Bracing herself for the inevitable shouting, she answered. "Hello."

"I'm sorry."

Her jaw actually dropped. "W-what?"

"I said I'm sorry," he repeated, and she'd never heard

him sound so humbled. She couldn't recall a single time he'd ever apologized for anything.

"And I'm sorry I raised my voice," she said, then realized that she had done nothing wrong. "Actually, no, I'm not sorry. You deserved it."

"You're right. I had no right to snap at you like that. But when I didn't hear from you, I was just afraid that something bad had happened to you."

"I'm fine. Mia is fine. And I'm sorry that I frightened you. We're here visiting a...friend."

"I didn't know you had any friends there."

"I met him at the hotel. He was a guest."

"He?"

"Yes, he. He's..." Oh what the hell, why not just tell him the truth? Since she didn't really care what he thought at this point anyway. "He's the king."

"The *king?*"

"Yes, and believe it or not, he wants to marry me."

"You're getting married? To a king?" He actually sounded excited. He was finally happy about something she had done, and now she had to burst his bubble. Figures.

"He wants me to marry him, but I'm not going to."

"Why not?"

"Because I'm in love with someone else."

"Another king," he joked.

"Um, no."

"Then who?"

If he was going to blow his top, this would be the time. "I'm in love with the prince. His son."

"Vanessa!"

She braced herself for the fireworks. For the shouting and the berating, but it never happened. She could practically feel the tension through the phone line, but he didn't make a sound. He must have been biting a hole right through his tongue. And could she blame him? Sometimes even she couldn't believe what they were doing.

"You okay, Dad?"

"Just…confused. When did all this happen? *How* did it happen?"

"Like I said, he was visiting the hotel and we became friends."

"The king or the prince?"

"The king, Gabriel, and he fell in love with me, but I only ever loved him as a friend. But he was convinced I would grow to love him if I got to know him better, so he invited me to stay at the palace, but then he was called away when I got here. He asked Marcus—he's the prince—to be my companion and we…well, we fell for each other. Hard."

"How old is this prince?"

"Um, twenty-eight, I think."

"And the king?"

"Fifty-six," she said, and she could practically hear him chomping down on his tongue again. "Which was part of the reason I wasn't sure about marrying him."

"I see," was all he said, but she knew he wanted to say more. He was going to need stitches by the end of this conversation. But she gave him credit for making the effort, and she wished she had confronted him years ago. Though he probably hadn't been ready to hear it before now. Or maybe she was the one who hadn't been ready for this. Maybe she needed to make changes first.

"So, I assume you'll be marrying the prince instead?" he said.

If only. "I won't be marrying anybody."

"But I thought you love him."

"I do love him, but I could never do that to Gabriel. He's a really good man, Dad, and he's been through so much heartache. He loves me, and I could never betray him that way. I feel horrible that it worked out this way, as if I've let him down. Not to mention that it would most likely ruin his relationship with his son. I couldn't do that to either of them. They need each other more than they need me."

He was quiet for several seconds, then he said, "Well, you've had a busy couple of weeks, haven't you?"

Though normally a comment like that would come off as bitter or condescending, now he just sounded surprised. She smiled, feeling both happy and sad, which seemed to be a regular thing for her lately. "You have no idea."

"So I guess I won't be seeing you Thursday."

"No, but we should be flying home soon. Maybe we can make a quick stop in Florida on our way."

"I'd like that." He paused and said, "So you really love this guy?"

"I really love him. Mia does too. She's grown so attached to him, and she loves being here in the palace."

"Are you sure you're doing the right thing? By leaving, I mean."

"There isn't anything else that I can do."

"Well, I'll keep my fingers crossed that you work it out somehow. And Nessy, I know I've been pretty hard on you, and maybe I don't say it often enough, but I am proud of you."

She'd waited an awfully long time to hear that, and as good as it felt, her entire self-worth no longer depended on it. "Thanks, Dad."

"It's admirable what you're doing. Sacrificing your own happiness for the king's feelings."

"I'm not doing it to be admirable."

"I know. That's why it is. Give me a call when you're coming home and I'll get the guest room ready."

"I will. I love you, Dad."

"I love you too, Nessy."

She hung up and set her phone on the table, thinking that was probably one of the nicest things her dad had ever said to her, and one of the most civilized conversations they had ever had.

"Now aren't you glad you called?"

She looked up to find Marcus standing naked in the bathroom doorway, towel-drying his hair. She wondered how much of that he'd heard. Had he heard her tell her father that she loved Marcus?

"I confronted him about the way he makes me feel, and instead of freaking out, he actually apologized."

"That took guts."

"Maybe I am brave after all. I'm not naive enough to think it will be smooth sailing from here. I'm sure he'll have relapses, because that's just who he is, and I'll have to stand firm. But at least it's a start."

He dropped the towel and walked toward the bed. And my goodness he looked hot. The man just oozed sex appeal. It boggled the mind that a woman would be unfaithful to him. His ex must have been out of her mind.

He yanked the covers away and climbed into bed, tugging her down onto her back, spreading her thighs with his knee and making himself comfortable between them.

"Thank you," she said, running her hand across his smooth, just shaved cheek. "Thank you for making me believe in myself."

"That wasn't me," he said, kissing her gently. His lips were soft and tasted like mint. "I just pointed out what was already there. You chose to see it."

And without him she might never have. She was a different person now. A better person. In part because of him.

"There's one more thing," he said, kissing her chin, her throat, the shell of her ear.

She closed her eyes and sighed. "Hmm?"

"For the record," he whispered, "I love you, too."

Fifteen

After a week of torrential rain the weather finally broke and though Marcus would have been more than happy to spend the day in Vanessa's suite again, sunny skies and mild temperatures lured them back out into the world. A calm sea made it the perfect day for water sports, and since Vanessa had never been on a personal watercraft, he figured it was time she learned.

They left Mia with Karin, who he thought looked relieved to have something to do. Many of the young parents he knew took full advantage of their nannies—especially the fathers, to the point that they'd never even changed a diaper—but Vanessa was very much a hands-on parent. He had the feeling Karin was bored more often than not. And because Mia was usually with them, they always took the limo on their outings, so today he decided they would take *his* baby for a spin.

"This looks really old," Vanessa said, as he opened the

passenger door, which for her was on the wrong side of the car.

"It's a 1965. It was my grandfather's. He was a huge Ian Fleming fan."

"Oh my God! Is this—"

"An Aston Martin DB5 Saloon," he said. "An exact replica of the car 007 drove."

She slipped inside, running her hand along the dash, as gently as a lover's caress. "It's amazing!"

He walked around and climbed in. He started the engine, which still purred as sweetly as the day they drove it off the line, put it in gear and steered the car through the open gates, and in the direction of the marina. "I've always loved this car. My grandfather and I used to sneak off on Sundays and drive out into the country for hours. He would tell me stories about his childhood. He was only nineteen when his father died, and he would tell me what it was like to be a king at such a young age. At the time, I just thought it sounded exciting to be so important and have everyone look up to you. Only as I got older and began to learn how much hard work was involved did I begin to realize what a huge responsibility it would be. I used to worry that my father would die and I would be king before I was ready."

"How old was your father when he became king?"

"Forty-three."

She was quiet for a minute, then she turned to him and said, "Let's not go to the marina. Let's take a drive in the country instead. Like you and your grandfather used to do."

"Really?"

"Yeah. I would love to see the places he took you."

"You wouldn't be bored?"

She reached over, took his hand, and smiled, "With you, never."

"Okay, let's go."

He couldn't recall ever getting in a car with a woman and just driving. In his experience they preferred constant stimulation and entertainment, and required lavish gifts and attention. In contrast, Vanessa seemed to relish the times they simply sat around and talked, or played with her daughter. And as far as gifts go, besides the earrings—which she wore every day—he'd bought nothing but the occasional meal or snack. She required little, demanded nothing, yet gave more of herself than he could ever ask. Before now, he hadn't even known women like her existed. That he once thought she had ulterior motives was ridiculous to him now.

"Can I ask you a question?" she said, and he nodded. "When did you stop thinking that I was after your dad's money?"

And she was apparently a mind reader. "It was when we went to the village and you didn't once use the credit card my father left for you."

Her mouth dropped open in surprise. "You knew about that?"

"His assistant told me. She was concerned."

"Gabriel insisted that I use it, but the truth is I haven't even taken it out of the drawer. It didn't seem right. He gave me lots of gifts, and I insisted he take them back."

"Well, if the credit card hadn't convinced me, your reaction to the earrings really drove the message home."

She reached up to finger the silver swirls dangling from her ears. "Why?"

"Because I've never seen a woman so thrilled over such an inexpensive gift."

"Value has nothing to do with it. It's the thought that counts. You bought them because you wanted to, because you knew that I liked them. You weren't trying to buy my affections or win me over. You bought the earrings because you're a sweet guy."

He glared at her. "I am not sweet."

She grinned. "Yes, you are. You're one of the sweetest, kindest men I've ever met." She paused, gave his hand a squeeze. "You know I have to go soon. I've probably stayed too long already. I feel like we're tempting fate, like someone is going to figure out what we're doing and it will get back to Gabriel. I don't want to hurt him."

Though it was irrational, he almost wished it would. He didn't want to hurt his father either, but it was getting more and more difficult to imagine letting her go. He wasn't even sure if he could. "What if he did find out? Maybe you wouldn't have to leave. Maybe we could explain to him. Make him understand."

She closed her eyes and sighed. "I can't, Marcus. I can't do that to him. Or to you. If our relationship came between the two of you I would never forgive myself."

"We don't know for certain that he would be upset."

She shot him a look.

"Okay, he probably would, but he could get over it. In fact, when he sees how much it means to me, I'm sure he will."

"But what if he doesn't? That isn't a chance I'm willing to take."

If she were anything like the women he'd dated in the past, this wouldn't be an issue. She wouldn't care who she hurt as long as she got what she wanted. Of course, then he wouldn't love her. And he knew that once she'd made up her mind, nothing would change it.

Her stubborn streak was one of her most frustrating yet endearing qualities. He liked that she continually challenged him. She kept him honest. And he loved her too much to risk losing her respect.

* * *

After a three-hour drive that they spent talking about their childhoods and families, then a stop in a small village for lunch, Marcus drove them back to the palace. He walked with her up to the nursery, only to discover that Mia had just gone down for a nap.

"Just call me when she wakes up," Vanessa told Karin, then she turned to Marcus and gave him the *look,* the one that said she had naughtiness on her mind. He followed her across the hall, but stopped her just outside her suite door.

"How about a change of pace?"

"What did you have in mind?" she asked, looking intrigued.

"Let's go to my room."

The smile slipped from her face. "Marcus…"

"But you've never even seen it."

"If someone sees us go in there—"

"The family wing is very private. And if you want, we won't do anything but talk. We can even leave the door open. We can pretend like I'm giving you a tour of the family wing."

She looked hesitant. "I don't know."

Despite the risk of being discovered by a passing employee, he took her hand. "We haven't got much time left. Give me the chance to share at least a small part of my life with you."

He could see her melting before his eyes. Finally she smiled and said, "Okay."

What he hadn't told was that just the other day Cleo had confronted him about all the time they had been spending together.

"Talk to my father," he'd told Cleo. "He's the one who wanted me to keep her entertained."

Her brows rose. "Entertained?"

"You *know* what I mean."

She flashed him a told-you-so smile. "I take it you're finding that she's not as terrible as you thought?"

"Not terrible at all," he'd told her, diffusing the situation entirely. Because if she believed the relationship was platonic, no one on the staff, except maybe George, would question it. But he still didn't dare tell Vanessa about the exchange. Especially now.

Under the ruse of tour guide, Marcus led Vanessa through the palace to the family wing, and the employees they did encounter only bowed politely, and showed not even a hint of suspicion. When they got to his suite, the hall was deserted. He opened the door and gestured her inside.

"Wow," she said, walking to the center of the living room and gazing around. He stood by the open door watching her take it all in. "It's huge. As big as an apartment. You even have a kitchen."

"I insisted. I figured, if I have to live here in the palace, I need a space of my own."

"I like it. It's very tasteful, and masculine without being too overpowering." She turned to him. "Comfortable."

"Thank you. And my designer thanks you."

"How many rooms?"

"Master suite, office, kitchen and living room."

She nodded slowly. "It's nice."

"I'm glad you like it."

She dropped her purse on the leather sofa and turned to him. "Maybe you should close the door."

"But I thought we agreed—"

"Close the door, Marcus." She was wearing that look again, so he closed it. "Lock it too."

He locked it, and crossed the room to where she was standing. "Changed your mind, did you?"

She slid her hands up his chest, started unfastening the

buttons on his shirt. "Maybe it's the element of danger, but the closer we got to your room, the more turned on I got." She rose up on her toes and kissed him, yanking his shirt from the waist of his slacks. "Or maybe, when we're alone, I just can't keep my hands off you."

The feeling was mutual.

"I know it's wrong, but I just can't stop myself. Doesn't that make me a terrible person?"

"If it does, I'm a terrible person, too. Which could very well mean we deserve each other."

She tugged his shirt off, but before she could get to work on his belt, he picked her up and hoisted her over his shoulder. She let out a screech of surprise, then laughed.

"Marcus, what are you doing!"

"Manhandling you," he said, carrying her to the bedroom and kicking the door open.

"Not that I mind, but why?"

He tossed her down onto the bed, on top of the duvet, then he reached under her dress, hooked his fingers in the waist of her panties and yanked them down. "Because I am not *sweet*."

She grinned up at him. "Well, I stand corrected."

Then she grabbed him by the shoulders, pulled him down on top of her and kissed him.

Every time he made love to her he thought it couldn't possibly get better, but she always managed to top herself. She was sexy and adventurous, and completely confident in her abilities as a lover, and *modest* was a word not even in her vocabulary. She seemed to instinctively know exactly what to do to drive him out of his mind, and she was so damned easy to please—she had a sensitive spot behind her knees that if stroked just right would set her off like a rocket.

She liked it slow and sensual, hard and fast, and she

even went a little kinky on him at times. If there were an ideal sexual mate for everyone, there was no doubt in his mind that she was his. And each time they made love that became more clear.

Maybe, he thought, as she unfastened his pants, it was less about skill, and more about the intense feelings of love and affection they shared. But then she slid her hand inside his boxers, wrapped it around his erection and slowly stroked him, and his thoughts became all hazy and muddled. She made it so easy to forget the world around him, to focus on her and her alone. And he wondered what it would be like this time, slow and tender or maybe hot and sweaty. Or would she get that mischievous twinkle in her eyes and do something that would make most women blush?

Vanessa pushed him over onto his back and climbed on top of him, then she yanked her dress up over her head and tossed it onto the floor. Hot and sweaty, he thought with a grin—his particular favorite—and as she thrust against him, impaling herself on his erection, she was so hot and tight and wet, he stopped thinking altogether. And as they reached their climax together, then collapsed in each other's arms, he told himself that there had to be some way to talk her into staying.

And at the same time, his conscience asked the question: To what end?

Sixteen

Somewhere in the back of Marcus's mind he heard pounding.

What the hell was that? he wondered, and what could he do to make it stop? Then he realized, it was his door. Someone was knocking on his bedroom door.

His eyes flew open, and he tried to sit up, but there was a warm body draped across his chest. He and Vanessa must have fallen asleep. He looked over at the clock, and realized that it was past suppertime. Oh hell. No doubt Mia was awake by now.

He shook Vanessa. "Wake up!"

Her eyes fluttered open and she gave him a sleepy smile. "Hey."

"We fell asleep. It's late."

She shot up in bed and squinted at the clock, then she uttered a very unladylike curse. "Where's my phone? Mia must be awake by now. Why didn't Karin call me?"

The pounding started again as they both jumped out of bed.

"Who is that?" Vanessa asked, frantically looking around, he assumed, for her purse.

He tugged his pants on. "Stay here. I'll go see."

He rushed out to the living room, unlocked the door and yanked it open. Cleo's hand was in the air, poised to knock again.

"There you are!" she said.

"I was…taking a nap," he said, raking a hand through his tousled hair. "I haven't been sleeping well."

"Well, we have a problem. Poor Karin is frantic. Mia woke from her nap an hour ago but she can't find Vanessa. She's not answering her phone and I can't find her anywhere in the palace. I thought perhaps you knew where I might find her."

Was that suspicion in her eyes? "She probably went for a walk," Marcus said. "Maybe she forgot her phone."

"If she left the palace, security would know about it."

He opened his mouth to reply and she added, "But just in case, I had them check the gardens and she isn't out there. It's as if she disappeared."

"Give me a minute to get dressed and I'll find her."

Behind him Marcus heard an "oof!" then a loud crash. He swung around to find Vanessa on the floor by the couch, wrapped in a bed sheet, wincing and cradling her left foot. Beside her lay the floor lamp that had been standing there. Then he heard a noise from the hall and whipped back around to find that in his haste he'd pushed the door open, and Cleo could see the entire sordid scenario.

"Miss Reynolds," Cleo said, her jaw rigid. "Would you please call Karin and let her know that you are in fact fine, and haven't been abducted by terrorists?"

"Yes, ma'am," Vanessa said, her voice trembling, her cheeks crimson with shame.

Cleo turned to Marcus and said tightly, "A word in private, your highness?"

"Are you okay?" he asked Vanessa, who looked utterly miserable, and she nodded. "I'll be right back."

He stepped out into the hall, pulling the door closed behind him, and the look Cleo gave him curdled his blood.

"You lied to me?"

"What was I supposed to do? Tell you the truth? I can see how well that's going over."

"Marcus, what were you thinking?"

Had it been anyone but her berating him this way, he would have dismissed them on the spot. But Cleo had earned this right through years of loyal service. She was more an extension of family than an employee.

"Cleo, believe me when I say, we didn't plan for this to happen. And if it's any consolation, she's not going to marry my father."

"I should hope not! Your father deserves better than a woman who would—"

"This was not her fault," he said sharply, because he absolutely drew the line at any disparaging remarks against Vanessa. She didn't deserve it. "I pursued her."

"Look, Marcus," she said, touching his arm. "I know you're upset over Carmela, and maybe this is your way of getting revenge, but would you risk your relationship with your father for a—a cheap *fling?*"

"No, but I would for the woman who I've fallen hopelessly in love with."

She pulled her hand back in surprise. "You love her?"

"She's everything I have ever imagined I could want in a woman, and a few things I didn't even know I wanted until I met her. And she loves me too, which, considering my track record with women, is pretty damned astonishing. And the irony of it all is that those things I admire most about her are the reason we can never be together."

"You can't?"

"She thinks our relationship will come between me and my father, and she absolutely refuses to let that happen."

"You know that she's right."

"Sometimes I think that I don't even care. But she does, and as much as I'd like to, I would never go against her wishes."

Cleo shook her head. "I don't know what to say. I'm just...I'm so sorry things have to be this way."

"I can count on you to keep this conversation private," he said.

"Of course, Marcus."

He leaned down and kissed her papery cheek. "Thanks."

He stepped back into his suite, leaving her in the hall looking unbelievably sad.

Vanessa was dressed and sitting on the couch, putting her sandals on, when Marcus stepped back into the room. And from his expression she couldn't tell what had happened. "Marcus, I am so sorry."

"It's okay."

"I left my phone in my purse on the couch, that's why I didn't hear Karin calling me. Then I tripped on that stupid lamp. And I didn't mean to fall asleep."

"I fell asleep too. I take it Mia is okay."

"Fine. I figured we would need to talk, so I asked Karin to feed Mia her dinner and get her into bed for me."

He sat down on the couch beside her. "There's nothing to talk about. It's no one's fault."

No, they had plenty to talk about. "Cleo looked so... disappointed."

He sighed. "Yeah, she's good at that. But I explained the entire situation and she understands."

"That's not good enough."

"Vanessa—"

"I can't do this anymore, Marcus."

"I'm not ready for you to go."

"We knew this was inevitable. We kept saying that eventually the day would come that I'd have to leave. And I honestly think that it's here."

He squeezed her hand, gave her a sad smile. "I can't lose you. Not yet."

She shook her head. "My mind is made up. But I want you to know that this has been the happiest couple of weeks in my life, and I will never, as long as I live, forget you."

"Say you'll leave tomorrow. That you'll give me one more night."

She touched his cheek. It was rough from afternoon stubble. "I'm sorry. I just can't."

He leaned in to kiss her, and someone knocked on his door again. Marcus muttered a curse.

"Marcus, it's Cleo!"

"Come in!" he called, sounding exasperated, and he didn't even let go of her hand.

She opened the door and poked her head in. "I'm sorry to bother you again, but I thought you might like to know that your father's limo just pulled up out front. He's home."

Vanessa and Marcus uttered the same curse, at the exact same time, and bolted up off the couch.

"We'll be right down," he told Cleo, and snatched his shirt off the floor. He tugged it on and fastened the buttons, tucking it into his slacks. She was pretty sure he wasn't wearing any underwear, not that it made a difference at this point. Her hands were shaking so hard she was just glad she was already dressed.

He raked his fingers through his hair and asked, "You ready for this?"

She had always thought she was; now she wasn't so sure. She swallowed hard, shook her head.

"Me neither." He pulled her against him and kissed her. Long and slow and deep. Their last kiss. And he definitely made it a good one. Then he pulled away and said, "We'd better go."

They rushed down the stairs, Vanessa's legs feeling like limp noodles. That would be a sure way out of this disastrous situation. Trip on the stairs, tumble down and break her neck when she hit the marble floor below. Talk about taking the easy way out. But she managed to stay on her feet.

The instant her sandal hit the marble floor the front door swung open and Gabriel walked through. He was dressed casually in khaki pants and a polo shirt. Though she had expected him to look tired and pale from splitting his time between working and sitting at Trina's bedside, instead he looked tan and well rested, as if he'd been on an extended vacation.

He saw the two of them there and smiled. "Marcus, Vanessa."

He walked over and gave his son a hug, then shook his hand firmly. Then he turned to Vanessa.

"My sweet Vanessa," he said, taking her hands and grasping them firmly. "It's so good to see you."

She would have expected a much more enthusiastic greeting from a man who supposedly loved her. Or could it have just been that he didn't feel comfortable showing her physical affection in front of his son? That made sense. Whatever the reason she was actually grateful. If he had pulled her into his arms and kissed her passionately, that would have been awkward. And seeing Gabriel and Marcus there together, side by side, she realized that while they were definitely built similarly, and had the same dark tones, in looks Marcus actually favored his mother.

"I talked to you yesterday but you didn't say you were coming home," she told Gabriel.

"I thought I would surprise you."

Oh, she was definitely surprised.

"You have a bit of sunburn," Gabriel said, touching her chin lightly. "You've been getting outdoors."

Actually, she hadn't been out in the sun for days, how could she—? Beard burn, she realized, from the last time Marcus kissed her. So she lied and said, "Yes, we were outside just today."

"Where is Mia?" he asked.

"Upstairs, having her dinner."

"Good, good," he said, and something about his demeanor was just slightly...off. As if he were nervous. And she had never seen him nervous. Strangely enough, now that he was here in front of her, any trace of nerves she'd had were gone. She just felt sad. And though she would always love and respect him as a friend, any desire she may have had to marry him was gone. In this case absence did not make the heart grow fonder. She was too busy falling in love with someone else. And she couldn't put this off any longer. She had to end it now.

"Gabriel," she said, forcing a smile. "Can we talk? Privately, I mean."

"Yes, yes, of course. Why don't we go up to your suite." He turned to Marcus, whose jaw was so tight it could have snapped like a twig. "Please excuse us, son. We'll catch up later. I have news."

Marcus nodded. He was jealous, Vanessa could see it in his eyes, but he stayed silent. What choice did he have?

As they walked up the stairs together, Gabriel didn't even hold her hand, and he made idle chitchat, much the way he had during their recent phone conversations. When they got to her suite, she held her breath, scared to death that he might suddenly take her in his arms and kiss her, because the idea of pushing him away, of having to be so cruel, broke her heart. But he made no attempt to touch her, and when he gestured toward the sofa and asked her to sit down, he didn't even sit beside her. He sat across from her in the wing back chair. And he was definitely nervous. Had someone told him that they suspected her and Marcus of something inappropriate? And if he asked her for the truth, what should she say? Could she lie to him?

Or what if...*oh God*, was he going to *propose*?

"Gabriel, before you say anything, there's something I really need to tell you."

He rubbed his palms together. "And there's something I need to tell you."

"I'll go first," she said.

"No, it would be better if I did."

Vanessa leaned forward slightly. "Actually, it would probably be better if I did."

"No, mine is pretty important," he said, looking slightly annoyed.

"Well, so is mine," she said, feeling a little annoyed herself.

"Vanessa—"

"Gabriel—"

Then they said in perfect unison, "I can't marry you."

Seventeen

Marcus watched Vanessa and his father walk up the stairs together thinking, *what is wrong with this picture.*

If his father was happy to see her, why hadn't he kissed her? Why wasn't he holding her hand? And why had he looked so…nervous? He never got nervous.

"Something is up," Cleo said behind him, and he turned to her.

"So it's not just me who noticed."

"As giddy in love as he was when he came back from America, I thought he would sweep her into his arms the instant he walked in the door, then promptly drop to one knee to propose."

"Are you thinking what I'm thinking?" Marcus asked.

"He doesn't want to marry her."

Marcus was already moving toward the stairs when Cleo grabbed his sleeve.

"This doesn't mean he won't be angry, Marcus, or feel betrayed."

No, it didn't, but every time Marcus imagined Vanessa leaving he got a pain in his chest so sharp, it was as if someone had reached into his chest, grabbed his heart and was squeezing the life from him. The thought of watching her and Mia get on a plane, of seeing it take them away from Varieo forever, filled him with a feeling of panic so intense it was difficult to draw a breath.

He shrugged. "I don't care, Cleo. I can't do it. I can't let her go."

Cleo let go of his sleeve, and smiled up at him. "So what are you waiting for?"

He charged up the stairs to the second floor and raced down the hall to her room. Not even bothering to knock, he flung the door open. Vanessa was seated on the sofa, his father in the chair across from her, and the sudden intrusion surprised them both.

"Marcus," Vanessa said. "What are you doing here?"

"I need to have a word with my father," he told her.

His father frowned. "Is something wrong, son?"

"Yes and no. I guess it just depends on how you look at it."

Vanessa rose to her feet, shaking her head. "Marcus, don't—"

"I *have* to, Vanessa."

"But—"

"I know." He shrugged helplessly. "But I have to."

She sat back down, as if she'd gotten tired of fighting it too, and whatever happened, she was willing to live with the consequences.

"Marcus, can this wait? I really need to talk to Vanessa."

"No, it can't. What I need to tell you must be said right now."

His father looked to Vanessa, who sat there silently. "All right," he said, sounding annoyed. "Talk."

Marcus took a deep breath and blew it out, hoping his father would at least try to understand. "Remember when you thanked me for agreeing to spend time with Vanessa, and said in return, if I ever needed anything, to just ask?"

He nodded. "I remember."

"Did you really mean it?"

"Of course I did. I'm a man of my word. You know that."

"Then I need you to do something for me."

"Anything, Marcus."

"Let Vanessa go."

He drew back slightly, blinking in confusion. "Let her go? But…I just did. I just now told her that I couldn't marry her."

"That's not good enough. I need you to *really* let her go, forget you ever wanted to marry her."

He frowned. "Marcus, what on earth are you talking about? Why would I do that?"

"So I can marry her."

His father's mouth actually dropped open.

"You told me that Vanessa is a remarkable woman, and said that once I got to know her, I would love her. Well, you were right. I do love her." He turned to Vanessa. "More than she could possibly imagine. Too much to ever let her leave."

She smiled, tears filling her eyes. "I love you, too, Marcus."

He turned back to his father, who sat there looking stunned. "You have to understand that we didn't mean for this to happen, and we did fight it. But we just…" He shrugged. "We just couldn't help it."

"You had an affair," his father said, as if to clarify.

"This was no affair," Marcus said. "We fell in love."

"So," his father said, turning to Vanessa, "this is why you couldn't marry me?"

"Yes. I'm so sorry. But like Marcus said, we didn't mean for this to happen. At first, he didn't even like me."

His father slowly nodded, as though he were letting it sink in, but oddly enough, he didn't look angry. Maybe the depth of their betrayal had left him temporarily numb.

"We had agreed not to say anything, to end it," Marcus told him. "She was going to do the honorable thing and leave. Neither of us could bear the thought of hurting you. But I need her. Her and Mia."

His father just sat there, eyes lowered, slowly shaking his head, rubbing his palms together. Marcus glanced over at Vanessa who looked both sad and relieved, and a little worried. He could relate. Telling his father the truth had been hard as hell, but he knew that living a lie would have been so much worse. It would have weighed on him the rest of his life.

"Would you please say something?" Marcus said. "Tell me what you're thinking."

His father finally looked over to him. "I find it ironic, I guess."

"Ironic how?"

"Because I have a secret, too."

"The reason you couldn't marry me?" Vanessa asked.

He nodded. "Because I'm engaged to someone else."

For a second Vanessa just sat there, looking dumbfounded, then she laughed.

"You think that's funny?" Marcus asked.

"Not funny ha-ha, but funny ironic. I guess because I

was so focused on Marcus, I didn't really see it. Suddenly everything makes sense."

Marcus was completely confused. "See *what?*"

"Why he stopped Skyping, why his calls were less frequent and increasingly impersonal. You were falling in love with her."

"It was difficult to look you in the eye," his father said, "to just hear your voice. I felt so guilty. I knew I had to end it but I didn't want to hurt you."

"I know exactly what you mean!" she said. "You have no idea how relieved I felt when you said we couldn't Skype anymore. I was so scared that the second you saw my face you would know what I was thinking."

Gabriel smiled. "Me, too."

"Excuse me," Marcus said, raising his hand. "Would someone like to tell me who is it that you were falling in love with?"

Vanessa looked at him like he was a moron, and right now, he sort of felt like one. "It's your Aunt Trina."

Marcus turned to his father, and could see by the look on his face that it was true. "You're engaged to *Trina?*"

He nodded. "Almost losing her opened my eyes to my feelings for her."

He and Aunt Trina had always been close, but Marcus honestly believed their relationship had been platonic.

"We didn't mean for it to happen," his father said. "But after spending so much time together, we just knew. I guess you can understand how that goes."

"When mother was still alive, did you and Trina…?"

"Marcus, *no!* Of course not. I loved your mother. I *still* love her. And until recently I never thought of Trina as anything but a friend. I'm still not sure what happened, what changed, I just know that it's right." He turned to Vanessa. "I was going to tell you this, and apologize profusely for dragging you and your daughter halfway around the world, and for making promises I couldn't keep. It's not that I don't care for you deeply. It's because of you that I was able to open up my heart again. I was so lonely, and unhappy, and then I met you and for the first time in months I felt alive again. And hopeful. I wanted to hold on to that feeling, but deep down I think I knew that it wasn't going to last. I knew that we would never love each other the way a wife and husband should."

"I wanted to love you that way," she said. "I wanted to be that woman."

"You are that woman, Vanessa." He looked to Marcus and smiled. "Just not for me."

"So, you're not angry?" Marcus asked.

"When I'm guilty of the same thing? You two love each other. And you were going to forsake your feelings to protect mine."

"Well, that was the plan," Vanessa said, shooting Marcus a look, but she was smiling.

"Then how could I possibly be angry. Besides, I can't imagine anyone else I would rather have as my daughter-in-law. And at my age, I think I'd much prefer being a grandfather to Mia than a father. I know men my age do it all the time, but I'm just too old and set in my ways to start over."

And Marcus felt as if his life was just beginning. As if everything up until now had just been a rehearsal in preparation for the real thing. It was so perfect that for an instant he couldn't help wondering if they might still be asleep in his bed and this whole thing was just a dream.

Marcus reached his hand out to Vanessa, and she reached for him, and the instant their fingers touched he knew this was very real. And very right.

"Father, could you give us a moment alone?" he asked.

He rose from the sofa, a smile on his face. "Take all the time you need."

The door had barely closed behind him and Vanessa was in his arms.

Vanessa buried her face against Marcus's chest, holding on tight, almost afraid to believe this was really happening. That it had worked out. That somehow, by breaking the rules and doing the *wrong* thing, she got exactly what she wanted.

"Is it real?" she asked him. "Could we be that lucky?"

He tightened his hold on her and she heard him sigh. "It sure feels real to me. But I don't think luck had anything to do with it."

She pulled back to look at him. "Why did you do it, Marcus? You risked so much."

"When I thought of you and Mia leaving...I just couldn't stand it. And when I saw the way he greeted you, I just had a feeling that something was wrong."

"He still could have been angry."

"I know. But that was a chance I had to take."

"For me?"

"Of course." He touched her cheek. "I love you, Vanessa."

He'd said it before, but until now, she hadn't allowed herself to really believe it. It would have been too painful when he let her down. But now, all that love, all those feelings she had been holding back, welled up inside her and she couldn't have held them back if her life depended on it. "I love you, Marcus. So much. I honestly didn't know it was possible to feel this happy."

"Well, get used to it," he said, kissing her gently. "Because if you'll have me, I'm going to spend the rest of my life making sure you stay that way."

"That's a long time."

"Vanessa, to truly express how much I love you, how much I *need* you, it would take an eternity."

She smiled. "Then I guess I'll just have to take your word for it."

"Does that mean you'll stay here with me, that you'll be my wife and make me the happiest man alive?"

In all the different places she had lived, Vanessa had never felt as if she truly belonged, but here, in Varieo with Marcus, she knew without a doubt that she was finally home.

"Yes," she told him, never feeling more sure about anything in her life. "I definitely will."

* * * * *

TEMPORARILY HIS PRINCESS

BY
OLIVIA GATES

Olivia Gates has always pursued creative passions such as singing and handicrafts. She still does, but only one of her passions grew gratifying enough, consuming enough, to become an ongoing career—writing.

She is most fulfilled when she is creating worlds and conflicts for her characters, then exploring and untangling them bit by bit, sharing her protagonists' every heart-wrenching heartache and hope, their every heart-pounding doubt and trial, until she leads them to an indisputably earned and gloriously satisfying happy ending.

When she's not writing, she is a doctor, a wife to her own alpha male and a mother to one brilliant girl and one demanding Angora cat. visit olivia at www.oliviagates.com.

To everyone at Harlequin, RWA, *RT Book Reviews*,
NINC and *CataRomance* who helped me realize a
dream and get to a much better place.
No thanks are enough.

Prologue

Six years ago

Vincenzo froze as he heard someone fumbling open the door.

She was here.

Every muscle turned to rock, every nerve fired like a high-voltage cable. Then the door slammed with an urgent thud and frantic footsteps followed, each jarring his equilibrium with the force of an earthquake.

There'd been no alert from his guards. No doorbell had announced her arrival. She was the only one he'd ever given unlimited access and keys to his penthouse.

But he'd given her more than access to his personal space—he'd given her dominion over his priorities and passions. She'd been the only woman he'd fully trusted, believed in. Loved.

And it had all been a lie.

The spear embedded in his gut twisted. Rage. Mostly at himself.

Even after he'd gotten proof of her betrayal, he'd clung to the belief that it would be explained away. She'd had him that deeply in her power.

That alone should have alerted him something was seriously wrong. It wasn't in his nature to trust. He'd never let anyone come that close or become anywhere near that vital. As a prince of Castaldini, he'd always been suspicious of people's intentions. After he'd become *the* rising-star researcher in the cutthroat field of energy alternatives, he'd believed any hope of a genuine relationship was over.

Until her. Until Glory.

From the first glance, he'd reeled at the attraction that had kept intensifying. From the first conversation, he'd sunk into a well of affinity, the deepest he'd ever known. It had been magical, how they'd hungered, connected. She'd aroused his every emotion, appeased his every need—physical, intellectual and spiritual.

But he'd just been a means to an end. An end she'd achieved.

After the first firestorm of agony had almost wrecked him, logic had doused it with its sobering ice. Seeking retribution would have only compounded the damage. He'd decided to let pain consume him, rather than give her more than what she'd already snatched from him. He'd walked away without a word.

Not that she'd let him walk away.

Her nonstop messages had morphed from worried to frantic. With each one, his heart had almost exploded, first with the need to soothe her, then with fury at falling for her act yet again. Then had come that last message. A heart-stopping simulation of a woman going out of her mind fearing for her loved one's safety.

The pain had been so acute it had seared him with clarity.

He'd realized there could only be one reason behind her desperate persistence. Her plan must not be concluded yet. Even if she thought his avoidance meant he suspected her, she seemed to be willing to risk anything to get close to him again, to pull the strings of his addiction to her for the opportunity to finish what she started.

So he'd let her find out he'd returned. He'd known she'd zoom right over to corner him.

But though he'd planned this face-off, he wasn't ready. Not for the sight of her, or for what he had to do.

Mannaggia! He shouldn't have given her the chance to invade his life again for any reason. He just wasn't *ready....*

"*Vincenzo!*"

A pale creature, who barely resembled the vibrant one who'd captured him body and heart, burst into his bedroom.

She stumbled to a halt, eyes turbid and swollen with what so convincingly looked like incessant weeping, and stood facing him across the bedroom where they'd shared unimaginable pleasures for the past six months.

Before another synapse could fire, she exploded across the room. Before he could draw another breath, her arms were around him, clinging like a woman would to a life raft.

And he knew. He'd missed it all, every nuance of her. He'd yearn for her, the woman he'd loved but who didn't exist, until the end of his days.

His mind unraveled with the need to crush her back, breathe her in so he could breathe again. He struggled not to bury his aching hands in her hair, not to drag her face to his and take of her breath. His lips went numb, needing to feel hers, just one last time....

As if sensing his impending capitulation, she surged up, pulled his head down and stormed his face in kisses.

Temptation tightened around his throat like a noose. His hands moved without volition.

They stopped before they closed around her, his body going rigid as if guarding against a blow as what she'd been reiterating in that tremulous, strangled voice sank into his fogged awareness.

"My love, my love."

Barely suppressing a roar, he clamped her arms before she sucked him dry of will and coherence.

She reluctantly let him separate them, raised the face that had embodied his desires and hopes. Her heavenly eyes were drowning in those masterfully feigned emotions.

"Oh, darling, you're all right." She hugged him again, seamlessly changing from overwrought relief to agitated curiosity. "I went insane when you answered none of my calls. I thought something…terrible must have happened."

So that was her strategy. To play innocent to the last.

"Nothing happened."

Was that his voice? That inhuman rasp?

Pretending not to notice the ice that encased him, dread entered the eyes that hid her soullessness behind that facade of guilelessness. "Did you have another breach? Did your security isolate you this time until they could identify the leak?"

Was she that audacious? Or did she believe she was too ingenious to be exposed? If she *were* still secure in his obliviousness, she wouldn't conceive of any other reason he'd stay away while his security team investigated how his research results kept being leaked in spite of their measures.

Good. He preferred to play it that way. It gave him the perfect opportunity to play the misdirection card.

"There haven't been any breaches." He pretended a calm that had to be his greatest acting effort. "Ever."

Momentary relief was chased away with deepening confusion. "But you told me…" She stopped, at a loss for real this time.

Si, that was a genuine reaction at last. For he *had* told her—every detail of the incidents and the upheavals he'd suffered as his life's work was being systematically stolen. And she'd pretended such anguish at his losses, at her help-lessness to help him.

"Nothing I told you was true. I let decoy results get leaked. I had great pleasure imagining the spies' reactions when they realized *that,* not to mention imagining their punishment for delivering useless info. No one knows where or what my real results are. They're safe until I'm ready to disclose them."

Every word was a lie. But he hoped she'd relay those lies to her recruiters, hopefully making them discard it without testing it and finding out it *was* the real deal.

That chameleon hid her shock, seamlessly performing un-certainty with hurt hovering at its edges. "That's fantastic... but...why didn't you tell *me* that? You thought you were being monitored? Even...here?" She hugged herself, as if to ward off invasive eyes. "But a simple note would have saved me end-less anguish, and I would have acted my part for the spies."

He gritted his teeth. "Everyone got the version I needed them to believe, so my opponents would believe it along with them. Only my most trusted people got the truth."

She stilled. As if afraid to let his words sink in. "And I'm not among those?"

Searing relief scalded through him, that she'd finally given him the opening to vent some antipathy. "How could you be? You were supposed to be a brief liaison, but you were too clingy and I had no time for the hassle of terminating things with you. Not before I found an as-convenient replacement, anyway."

If he could believe anything from her anymore, he would have thought his words had stabbed her through the heart.

"R-replacement...?"

His lips twisted. "With my schedule, I can only afford sexual partners who jump at my commands. That's why you

were so convenient, being so…compliant. But such accom-
modating lovers are hard to come by. I let one go when I find
another. As I have."

Hurt blossomed in her eyes like ink through turquoise wa-
ters. "It wasn't like that between us…"

"What did you think it was? Some grand love affair? Whatever gave you that impression?"

Her lips shook, her voice now a choking tremolo. "You
did… You said you loved me.…"

"I loved your…performance. You did learn to please me
exceptionally well. But even such a…malleable sex partner
only…keeps up my interest for a short while."

"Was that all I am…was…to you? A sex partner?"

His heart quivered with the effort to superimpose the truth
over her overwhelming act. "No. You're right. A partner in-
dicates a somewhat significant liaison. Ours certainly wasn't
that. Don't tell me that wasn't clear from day one."

He could have sworn his words hacked her like a dull
blade. If he didn't have proof of her perfidy, the agony she
simulated would have torn down his defenses. Its perfection
only numbed him now, turning his heart to stone.

He wanted her to rant and rave and shed fake tears, giving him the pretext to tear harder into her. She only stared at
him, tears a precarious ripple in her eclipsed eyes.

Then she whispered, "If—if this is a joke, please, stop…"

"Whoa. Did you actually believe you were more to me
than a convenient lay?"

She jerked as if he'd backhanded her. His trembling hold
on restraint slipped another notch. He had to get this over
with before *he* started to rant, exposing the truth.

"I should have known you wouldn't take the abundant
hints. From the way you believed my every word it was clear
you lack any astuteness. You sure didn't become my execu-

tive projects manager through merit. But you're starting to anger me, acting as if I owe you anything. I already paid for your time and services with far more than either was worth."

Her tears finally overflowed.

They streaked her hectic cheeks in pale tracks, melting the last of his sanity, making him snarl, "Next time a man walks away, let him. If you'd rather not hear the truth about how worthless you were to him…."

"Stop…please…" Her hands rose, as if to block blows. "I know what I felt from you…it was real and intense. If—if you no longer feel this way, just leave me my memories…."

"Is that obliviousness or just obnoxiousness? Seems you've forgotten who I am, and don't know the caliber of women I'm used to. But it's not too late to give you a reality check. Your replacement is arriving in minutes. Care to hang around and get a sobering, humbling look at her?"

Her disbelief finally disintegrated and resignation seeped in to fill the vacuum it left behind.

She was giving up the act. At last. It was over.

He turned away, feeling like he'd just kicked down the last pillar in his world.

But she wouldn't let it be over, her tear-soaked words lodging in his back like knives. "I…loved you, Vincenzo. I *believed* in you…thought you an exceptional human being. Turns out you're just a sleazy user. And no one will ever know, since you're also a flawless liar. I wish I'd never seen you…hope one of my 'replacements' pays you back…for what you've done to me."

When his last nerve snapped, he rounded on her. "You want to get ugly, you got it. Get out or I won't only make you wish you'd never seen me, but that you'd never been born."

His threat had no effect on her; her eyes remained dead.

Then, as if fearing she'd fall apart, she turned and exited the room.

He waited until a muted thud told him she'd left. Then he allowed the pain to overwhelm him.

One

Vincenzo Arsenio D'Agostino stared at his king and reached the only logical conclusion.

The man had lost his mind.

He must have buckled under the pressure of ruling Castaldini while steering his multibillion-dollar business empire. *And* being the most adoring and attentive husband and father who walked the planet. No man could possibly weather all that with his mental faculties intact.

That must be the explanation for what he'd just said.

Ferruccio Selvaggio-D'Agostino—the bastard king, as his opponents called him, relishing it being a literal slur, since Ferruccio *was* an illegitimate D'Agostino—twisted his lips. "Do pick your jaw off the floor, Vincenzo. And no, I'm *not* insane. Get. A. Wife. ASAP."

Dio. He'd said it again.

This time Vincenzo found himself echoing it. "Get a wife."

Ferruccio nodded. *"ASAP."*

"Stop *saying* that."

Mockery gleamed in Ferruccio's steel eyes. "You've got only yourself to blame for the rush. I've needed you on this job for *years,* but every time I bring you up to the council they go apoplectic. Even Leandro and Durante wince when your name is mentioned. That playboy image you've been diligently cultivating is now so notorious, even gossip columns are beginning to play it down. And that image won't cut it in the leagues I need you to play in now."

"That image never hurt *you.* Just look where you are today. The king of one of the most conservative kingdoms in the world, with the purest woman on earth as your queen."

Ferruccio shrugged amusedly at his summation. "I was only known as the 'Savage Ironman' in reference to my name and business reputation, and my reported…hazard to women was beyond wildly exaggerated. I had no time for women as I clawed my way up from the gutter to the top, then I was in love with Clarissa for six years before she became mine. But your notoriety as one of the world's premier womanizers won't do when you're Castaldini's emissary to the United Nations. You've got to clean up your act and spray on some respectability to clear away the stench of the scandals that hang around you."

Vincenzo scowled up at him. "If it's depriving you of sleep, I'll tone things down. But I certainly won't 'get a wife' to appease some political fossils, aka your council. And I won't join your, Leandro's and Durante's trio of henpecked husbands. You're all just jealous you can't have my lifestyle."

Ferruccio gave him that look. The one that made Vincenzo feel hollow inside, made him feel like putting his fist through his king's too-well-arranged face. It was the pitying glance of a man who knew bone-deep contentment and found nothing more pathetic than Vincenzo's said lifestyle.

"When you're representing Castaldini, Vincenzo, I want the media only to cover your achievements on behalf of the kingdom, not your conquests' surgical enhancements or tell-alls after you exchange them for different models. I don't want the sensitive diplomatic and economic agendas you'll be negotiating to be overshadowed or even derailed by the media circus your lifestyle generates. A wife will show the world that you've changed your ways and will keep the news on the relevant work you'll be doing."

Vincenzo shook his head in disbelief. "*Dio!* When did you become such a stick in the mud, Ferruccio?"

"If you mean when did I become an advocate for marriage and family life, where have you been the last four years? I'm the living, breathing ad for both. And it's time I did you the favor of shoving you onto that path."

"What path? The one to happily ever after? Don't you know that's a mirage most men pursue to no avail? Don't you realize you've beaten impossible odds in finding Clarissa? That not a man in a million will find a fraction of the perfection you share with her?"

Ferruccio pursed his lips. "I don't know about those odds, Vincenzo. Durante found Gabrielle. Leandro found Phoebe."

"Only two more flukes. You all had such terrible things happen during your childhoods and youths, unbelievably good stuff has been happening later in life in compensation. Having lived a blessed life early on, I seem to be destined to have nothing good from now on, to even out the cosmic balance. I will never find anything like the love you all have."

"You're doing everything in your power *not* to find love, or to let it find you—"

Vincenzo interrupted him. "I've only accepted my fate. Love is not in the cards for me."

"And that's *exactly* why I want you to get a wife," Ferruccio interrupted back. "I don't want you to spend your life without the warmth and intimacy, the allegiance and certainty only a good marriage can bring."

"Thanks for the sentiment. But I can't have any of that."

"Because you haven't found love? Love *is* a plus, but not a must. Just look at your parents' example. They started out suitable in theory and turned out right for each other in practice. Pick someone cerebrally and once she's your wife, the qualities that logically appealed to you will weave a bond between you that will strengthen the longer you are together."

"Isn't that an inverted way of doing things? You loved Clarissa first."

"I thought I did, with everything in me. But what I felt for her was a fraction of what I feel for her now. Going by my example, if you start out barely liking your wife, after a year of marriage you'll be ready to die for her."

"Why don't you just acknowledge that you're the luckiest bastard alive, Ferruccio? You may be my king and I may have sworn allegiance to you, but it's not good for your health to keep shoving your happiness in my face when I already told you there's no chance I'll find anything like it."

"I, too, once believed I had no chance at happiness, either, that emotionally, spiritually, I'd remain vacant, with the one woman I wanted forever out of reach while I was incapable of settling for another."

Was Ferruccio just counterarguing with his own example? Or was he putting two and two together and realizing why Vincenzo was so adamant that he'd never find love?

Suddenly, bitterness and dejection ambushed him as if they'd never subsided.

Ferruccio went on, "But you're pushing forty…"

"I'm thirty-eight!"

"…*and* you've been alone since your parents died two *decades* ago…"

"I'm not alone. I have friends."

"*Whom* you don't have time for and who don't have time for you." Ferruccio raised his hand, aborting Vincenzo's interjection. "Make a new family, Vincenzo. It's the best thing you can do for yourself, and incidentally, for the kingdom."

"Next you'll dictate the wife I should 'get.'"

"If you don't decide on one on your own, *ASAP,* I will."

Vincenzo snorted. "Is that crown you've been wearing for the last four years too tight? Or is your head getting bigger? Or is it the mind-scrambling domestic bliss?"

Ferruccio just smiled that inexorable smile of his.

Knowing the kind of laserlike determination Ferruccio had, Vincenzo knew there was no refusing him.

Might as well give in. To an extent he found acceptable.

He sighed. "If I take the position…"

"*If* implies this is a negotiation, Vincenzo. It isn't."

"…*it* will be only for a year…"

"It will be until I say."

"A *year*. This isn't up for negotiation, either. There will be no more 'scandals' in the rags, so this wife thing…"

Ferruccio gave him his signature discussion-ending smile. "Is also nonnegotiable. 'Get a wife' wasn't a suggestion or a request. It's a royal decree."

Ferruccio had eventually buckled. On Vincenzo's one-year proviso. Provided that Vincenzo chose and trained his replacement to *his* satisfaction.

He hadn't budged on the "get a wife" stipulation. He'd even made it official. Vincenzo still couldn't believe what he was looking at. A royal edict ruling that Vincenzo must choose a suitable woman and marry her within two months.

This deserved an official letter from his own corporation telling Ferruccio not to hold his regal breath.

There was no way he'd choose a "suitable woman." Not in two months or two decades. There was no suitable woman for him. Like Ferruccio, he'd been a one-woman man. Unlike him, he'd blown his one shot on an illusion. After six years of being unable to muster the least interest in any other woman he was resigned to his condition.

Though he knew *resigned* wasn't the word for it. Not when every time her memory sank its inky tentacles into his mind, his muscles felt as if they'd snap.

He braced himself until this latest attack passed….

A realization went off in his head like a solar flare.

All these years…he'd been going about it all wrong!

Fighting what he felt with every breath had been the worst thing he could have done. After he'd realized none of it was going away, he should have done the opposite. He should have let it run its course, until it was purged from his system.

But it didn't matter that he hadn't done that before. Now was the perfect time to do it. And to let all those still-seething emotions work to his advantage for once.

A smile tugged at his lips, fueled by what he hadn't felt in six years, what he'd thought he'd never feel again. Excitement. Anticipation. Drive. Challenge.

All he needed now were some updates on Glory to use in this acquisition. He already had enough to make it a hostile takeover, but more leverage wouldn't hurt.

Wouldn't hurt *him*.

Now, *her*—that was a totally different story.

Glory Monaghan stared dazedly at her laptop screen.

She couldn't be seeing this. An email from *him*.

She drew a shaky hand across numb lips, shock reverberating in her every nerve.

Slow down. Think. It must be an old one....

No. This was new. She'd deleted his old emails. Though she had only two months ago. And by accident, too.

Yep, for six years, those emails had migrated from one computer to another with all of her vital data. She hadn't clicked a mouse to scrub her life clean of his degrading echoes. She hadn't gotten rid of one shred of him. Not his scribbled notes, voice messages or anything he'd given her or left at her place.

It *hadn't* been as pathetic as it sounded. It had been therapeutic. Educational. To analyze the mementos and the events associated with each, to familiarize herself further with the workings of the mind of a unique son of a bitch.

The lessons gained from such in-depth scrutiny had been invaluable. No one had ever come close to fooling her again. No one had come close again, period. No one had surprised her, let alone shocked her, since.

Leave it to that royal bastard to be the one to do it.

She resisted the urge to blink in hope that his email would disappear. She did squeeze her eyes, but opened them to find it still staring back at her. His unread message, somehow bolder and blacker than the other unread ones. As if taunting her.

The subject line read An Offer You Can't Refuse.

Incredulity swept inside her like a tornado.

But wait! Why was she thinking it was an actual email from Vincenzo? Some spammer with some lewd scam must have hacked into his account. Yeah. That was it. With a subject line like that, this had to be the only explanation.

Still…it was strange that Vincenzo hadn't deleted her from his list of contacts.

Whatever. This email belonged in the trash.

But before she emptied it, her hand froze on the button, an

internal voice warning, *Do that and go nuts wondering what that email was really all about.*

Okay. She had to concede that point. Knowing herself, she wouldn't be able to function today if she didn't know for sure.

But what if she opened it, only to find some nasty surprise? In the name of her quest for peace of mind, she should delete the damn thing.

God. That bastard was reaching through time and space, tugging at her like a marionette. Just an email with an inflammatory subject line had her spiraling down a vortex of agitation as if she'd never exited it.

Maybe she never had. Maybe she'd only been bottling it up, pretending to be back to normal. Maybe she did need some blow to jolt her out of her simulated animation. Maybe if this *was* an email from him, it would trigger some true resolution so she'd bury his memory once and for all.

She clicked open the email.

Her gaze flew to the bottom. There was a signature. His. This *was* from him.

All the beats her heart had been holding back spilled out in a jumbled outpour. And that was before she read the two sentences that comprised the message.

I can send your family to prison for life, but I'm willing to negotiate. Be at my penthouse at 5:00 p.m., or I'll turn the evidence I have in to the authorities.

At ten to five, Glory was on her way up to Vincenzo's penthouse, déjà vu settling on her like a suffocating cloak.

Her dry-as-sand eyes panned around the elevator she'd once taken almost every day for six months. The memories felt like they belonged to someone else's life.

Which wasn't too far-fetched. She'd been someone else then. After a lifetime of devoting her every waking hour to excelling in her studies, she'd reached the ripe age of twenty-three with zero social skills and the emotional maturity of someone a decade younger. She'd been aware of that, but hadn't had time to work on anything but her intellectual growth. She'd been determined she wouldn't have the life her family had, one of precarious gambles and failed opportunity hunting. She'd wanted a life of stability.

She'd worked to that end since she'd been a teenager, forgoing the time dump others called a social life. And she'd believed she'd been achieving her goal, graduating at the top of her class and obtaining a master's degree with the highest honors. Everyone had projected she'd rise to the top of her field.

But though she'd been confident her outstanding qualifications and recommendations would afford her a high-paying and prestigious job, she'd applied for a position in D'Agostino Developments not really expecting to get it. Not after she'd heard such stories about the man at the helm of the meteorically rising enterprise. In his corporation, Vincenzo D'Agostino had grueling standards. He interviewed and vetted even the mailroom staff. Then he had vetted her.

She still remembered every second of that fateful meeting that had changed her life.

His scrutiny had been denuding, his focus scorching, his questions rapid-fire and deconstructing. His influence had rocked her to her core, making her feel like a swooning moron as she'd sluggishly answered his brusque questions. But after only ten minutes, he'd risen, shaken her hand and given her a much more strategic position than she'd dared hope for, working at the highest level, directly with him.

She'd exited his office reeling at the shock of it all. She hadn't known it was possible for a human being to be so beautiful, so overpowering. She hadn't known a man could have her hot and wet just looking at her across a desk. She hadn't even been interested in a man before, so the intensity of her desire after one meeting had had her in a free fall of confusion.

But while she'd gotten a job she'd thought impossible, she'd thought the real impossibility would be him. Even if he hadn't had an absolute rule against mixing work and pleasure, she couldn't imagine he'd be interested in someone like her. Cerebrally, she knew she was pretty, but a man like him had stunning and sophisticated women swarming all over him, and she'd certainly been neither. Something he'd confirmed when he kicked her out of his life.

She'd been determined to stifle her fantasies so she wouldn't compromise her fantastic position. At least she had until he'd called an hour later, inviting her out to dinner.

Silencing her misgivings about his change of M.O. and its probable negative effects on her career, she stumbled over herself saying yes. She'd thrown discretion to the wind and hurtled full force into his arms, allowing her existence to revolve around him on every level, personal and professional.

Yeah, she'd hurtled all the way off the cliff of his cruelty and exploitation. And she could only blame herself. No law, natural or human-made, protected fools from their folly.

But there'd been one thing she'd learned from that ordeal. Vincenzo didn't joke. Ever. He was as serious as the plague.

In her eyes, it had been the one thing missing from his character back then. Of course, her eyes had been so filled with the plethora of his godlike attributes, she'd given the deficiency nothing but a passing regret. But that fact forced one belief on her. His email had been no prank.

She'd reached that conclusion minutes after she'd read it. After the first shock had passed, she'd gone through the range of extreme reactions until only rage remained.

A ping yanked her out of her murderous musings.

Forcing stiff legs to move, she stepped out into the hall leading to that royal slimeball's floor-spanning penthouse.

Nothing had changed. Which was weird. She'd thought he would have remodeled the whole building to suit the changing trends and his inflating status and wealth.

He'd once told her this opulent edifice in the heart of New York was nothing compared to his family home in Castaldini. He'd pretended he couldn't wait to take her there. His desire to take her there, and the prospect of visiting his home, had kept her in a state of constant anticipation and excitement.

But she hadn't been able to imagine anything more lavish than this place. His whole world had made her feel what Alice must have felt when she'd fallen into Wonderland. It *had* alerted her to how radically different they were, how it made no sense that they'd come together. But she'd ignored reason.

Until he'd thrown her out of his life like so much garbage.

Another wave of fury crashed over her as she stopped at his door.

He must be watching her through the security camera. He always had, barely letting her enter before sweeping her away on the rapids of his eagerness. Or so she'd thought.

She glared up at where the camera was hidden. She still had the key. Another memento she hadn't thrown away. He probably hadn't changed the lock. Why should he have? With enough guards to stop an army, she wouldn't have gotten here without his permission.

He probably expected her to ring the bell. Yeah, right. He might have dragged her here, but she was damned if he'd leave her waiting until he deigned to open the door.

She stabbed the key in, imagining the lock was his eye.

Her breath still hitched as the door clicked open, then again as she stepped inside.

He stood facing her at the end of the expansive sitting area, in front of the screen where he'd once displayed their video-taped sessions of sexual delirium as he'd drowned her in more.

Her heart clamored out of control as his steel-hued eyes struck her with a million volts of sexiness and charisma across the distance.

He'd once been the epitome of male beauty. Now he'd become impossibly more, his influence enhanced, his assets augmented.

Dressed in all black, he seemed taller than his six foot five, his shoulders even wider, his waist and hips sparser in comparison to a torso and thighs that had bulked up with muscle. His face was hewn to sharper planes and angles, his skin a darker, silkier copper, intensifying the luminescence of his eyes. The discreet silver brushing his luxurious raven hair at the temples added the last touch of allure.

But she wasn't only checking off his upgrades against what she'd known…too intimately. She was reacting to him in the same way, with the same intensity she had when she'd been younger, inexperienced and oblivious of his reality.

Weird, this disconnect between mental aversion and physical affinity.

She could barely breathe, and that was before he spoke, his voice deeper, strumming hidden places inside her with each inflection, with that trace accent, those rolling *r*'s…

"Before you say anything, yes, I do have evidence that would send your father and brother to prison from fifteen to life. But you must already be certain of that. That's why you're here."

Her momentary incapacitation cracked.

She moved steadily toward him, roiling rage fueling each step. "I know you're capable of anything. *That's* why I'm here."

His eyes smoldered as they documented her state. "I'll

dispense with the preliminaries then and get to the point of my summons."

She stopped feet away, scoffing, "Summons? Wow. Your 'princehood' has gone to your head, hasn't it? But then, you must have always been this pompous and loathsome, and I was the one who was too blind to notice."

Those sculpted lips that had once driven her to insanity twisted. "I don't have time now for your scorned-woman barbs, Glory. But once my objective is fulfilled, I might accommodate your need to vent. It will be...amusing."

Bringing herself under control, she matched his coolness. "I'm sure it will be. Sharks do relish blood. And that, along with anything I say to you or about you, isn't a barb. Just a fact. So let's stop wasting calories and get to the point of your 'summons.' What will it take so you won't destroy my family? If you want me to steal some top secret info from your rivals, I no longer work in your field, as I'm sure you know."

An imperious eyebrow rose. "Would you have, if you were?"

Her answer was unhesitating. "No."

Something streaked in his eyes, something that looked like...pain? What made it even more confusing was that it was tinged with...humor? Humor? Vincenzo? And now of all times?

"Not even to save your beloved family?"

She wanted to growl that they were no such thing.

Oh, sure, she loved them. But they drove her up the wall being so irresponsible. They were why she was now at this royal scumbag's mercy. He must have acquired some debts of theirs. And if he could send them to prison using those, they must be *huge*.

"No," she said, more forcefully this time. "I was just analyzing the only thing you might think I have to offer in return for your generous amnesty."

"That's not the only thing you have to offer."

For heart-scrambled moments it felt as if he meant…

No. No way. He'd told her in mutilating detail what an exchangeable "lay" she'd been. He'd discarded her and moved on to a thousand others. And he was known to never return to an already pollinated flower. He wouldn't go to these lengths, or any, to have her in his bed again.

Her glare grew harder. "I *can* offer you a much deserved skull fracture. Apart from that, I can't think of a thing."

This time, the humor filling his eyes and lips was unmistakable, shaking her more than anything else had.

"I'll pass on the kind cranial-reconstruction offer. But there is another alteration you can offer me that I vitally need." His lips quirked as if at a private joke. "ASAP."

"Will you stop wasting my time and just spit it out? What the hell do you 'need'?"

Unfazed by her fury, he calmly said, "A wife."

Two

"A wife?"

Glory heard herself echoing what Vincenzo had said.

But he couldn't have said *that*.

He only nodded, confirming that she'd parroted him correctly.

Dazed, she shook her head. "How can I offer you a wife?" A suspicion hit her between the eyes. "You're interested in someone I know?"

That lazy humor heated his eyes again. "Yes. Someone you know very well."

Nausea twisted her stomach as every woman she knew flashed through her mind. Many were beautiful and sophisticated enough to qualify for Vincenzo's demanding standards. Amelia, her best friend, in particular. But she was newly engaged. Was that why Vincenzo had her here, because he wanted her help to break up her friend's relationship so he'd…?

He interrupted the apoplectic fit in progress. "According to my king, I need an emergency reputation upgrade that only a wife can provide."

Her mind burned rubber calibrating the new info. "Your sexual exploits are giving Castaldini a bad name? That must be why King Ferruccio had to intervene. Did he issue you a royal decree to cease and desist?"

He gave a tranquil nod of that leonine head of his. "What amounted to that, *si*. That's why I'm 'getting a wife.'"

"Who knew? Even the untouchable Vincenzo D'Agostino has someone he bows down to. It must have stung bad, standing before another man, even if he is your lord and liege, being chastised like a kid and told what to do, huh? How does it feel to be forced to end your stellar career as a womanizer?"

One of those formidable shoulders jerked nonchalantly. "I'm ending nothing. I'm only getting a wife temporarily."

So he wasn't even pretending he'd change his ways. At least no one could accuse him of hiding what he was. No one but her. He'd hidden his nature and intentions ingeniously for the duration of their…liaison—what he'd made her believe had been a love affair to rival those of literature and legend.

She exhaled her rising frustration. "Of course she'd have to be temporary. All the power and money in the world, which you do have, wouldn't get you a woman permanently."

His uncharacteristic amusement singed her again. "You're saying women wouldn't fall over themselves to marry me?"

"Oh, I bet there'd be queues across the globe panting at the prospect. What I'm saying is any woman would end up paying whatever price to get rid of you once she got to know the real you. There's no way a woman would want you for life."

"Isn't it lucky then that I don't want one for anywhere near that long? I just need a woman who'll follow every rule of my temporary arrangement to the letter. But my problem isn't in finding the woman who'll accept my terms. It would be difficult to find one who won't."

"You're that conceited, you think all women would be so desperate for you, they'd accept you on any terms, no matter how short-lived and degrading?"

"That's not conceit. That's a fact. You being a case in point. You accepted me on no terms whatsoever. *And* clung so hard, I ended up needing to pull your tentacles out of my flesh with more harshness than I've ever had to employ before or since."

She stared at him, shriveling with remembered shame and again wondered…why all this malice? This fluency of abuse? When all she'd ever done was lose her mind over him….

He went on, his eyes cold. "But any woman, once she's carrying my name, might use my need to keep up appearances, the reason that drove me to marriage in the first place, to milk the situation for more. I need someone who can't even think it."

"Just hire a…mercenary then," she hissed. "One practiced enough to pretend to stand you, for a fixed time and price."

"A…mercenary is exactly what I'm after. But one who's not overtly…experienced. I need someone who's maintained an outwardly pristine reputation. I am trying to polish mine, after all, and it wouldn't do to put a chipped jewel in my already tarnished crown."

"Even an actual immaculate gem would fail to improve your gaudiness. But you should have called ahead. I certainly don't know anyone, well or not, who fits the category of… mercenary, let alone one so…experienced she simulates a spotless past. I don't even know someone reckless or desperate enough to accept you on any terms, for any length of time."

"You do know someone who fits all those criteria. You."

Vincenzo watched Glory as his last word drained every bit of blood and expression from her face. The face that had haunted him for six years. It was still the same, yet so different.

The last plumpness had vanished, exposing a bone structure that was a masterpiece of exquisiteness. It brought her every feature into stark focus, in a display of harmony and gorgeousness. Her complexion, due to her new outdoorsy lifestyle, was tanned a perfect honey, only shades lighter than her magnificent waterfall of tawny hair. Her skin gleamed with health, stretching taut over those elegant bones. Her eyebrows were denser, their arch defined and decisive, her nose more refined, more authoritative and her jaw cleaner, stronger.

But it was still those summer skies she had for eyes that struck him to his core. And those flushed lips. They looked fuller, as if they'd absorbed what had been chiseled off her cheeks. They were more sensuous even in their current severity. Just looking at them made every part of him they'd once worshipped and owned tense, tingle, clamor for their touch. Everything about her had him fighting to ease an arousal that had hardened to steel. And that was before his appraisal traveled down to her body.

That body that had held the code to his libido.

It was painfully clear it still did, now more than ever. But while her face had been chiseled, her body had filled out, the enhanced curves making her the epitome of toned femininity, a woman just hitting the stride of her allure and vigor. Her newly physical lifestyle really agreed with her.

Her navy pantsuit was designed to obscure her assets, but he had X-ray vision where she was concerned. And he couldn't wait until he confirmed his estimates with an unhindered visual and hands-on examination.

For now, he just wondered how those eyes of hers didn't display any tinge of the cunning the woman who'd once set him up should have. They only transmitted the indomitable edge of a warrior used to fighting adversaries who surpassed her in power a hundredfold. As she knew he did.

Or, at least they had until he'd said "You."

Her eyes now displayed nothing but absolute shock. If he didn't know better, he'd think she hadn't even considered that he'd been talking about her.

But of course she had. She was just in a class of her own when it came to spontaneous acting.

She blinked, as if coming out of a trance, shock giving way to fury so icy it burned him. "I don't care how big a debt my father and brother have. I'll pay it off."

He didn't see *that* coming. "You think what I have on them is a debt? You really think I'd have leverage so lame it could be nullified with money?"

"Quit posturing, you loathsome jerk. What *do* you have on them?"

He paused, testing, even tasting, his reaction to her insult. It felt like exhilaration, tasted tart and zesty. He immediately wanted more.

Dio. If he was hankering for more of her slurs, he must be queasier than he thought with all the deference he got in his official and professional roles. Not that he could imagine himself reveling in anybody else's verbal abuse.

His lips tugged as he contemplated his newfound desire to be bashed by her, knowing it would inflame her more. Which was just what he was after. "Oh, just a few crimes."

Her jaw dropped. "You'd go as far as framing them to get me to do your bidding?"

"I'm just exposing them. And only a fraction of their crimes at that. To save posturing on *your* end, read this." He bent, swiped a dossier off the coffee table between them and held it out to her. "Verify my evidence any way you like. I have more if you want. But that would be overkill. This is quite enough to see both in prison for embezzlement and fraud for maybe the rest of your father's life, and most of what's left of your brother's."

Her hand rose as if without volition, receiving the dossier. With one more dazed look, she relinquished his gaze, turned unsteadily and sank down onto the couch where he'd once taken her. He'd made love to her in every corner of this place. At least, *he'd* been making love. Love, or anything genuine, hadn't been involved on her end.

He watched her as she leafed through the pages with unsteady hands, that amazing speed-reading ability engaged, letting memories sweep through him at last.

How he'd loved her. Now he needed to exorcise her.

It felt as if hours had passed before she raised her gaze back to his, her eyes reddened, her lips trembling. What an incredible simulation of disbelief and devastation.

When she talked, her voice was thick and hoarse, as if she were barely holding back tears. "How long have you had… that?"

"That particular accumulation of damning evidence? Over a year. I have much older files retracing the rest of their crimes, in case you're interested."

"There was more?"

Anyone looking at her would swear this was the shock of her life, that she'd never suspected the men in her family could possibly be involved in criminal activities.

He huffed his disgust at the whole situation, and everyone involved in it. "They're both extremely good, I'll give them that. That's why no one else has caught them at it yet."

"Why have you?"

She was asking all the right questions. If he answered them all truthfully, they'd paint her the real picture of what had happened in the past. Which wouldn't be a bad idea. He was sick and tired of the pretense.

So he told her. "I've been keeping them under close scrutiny since the attempts to steal my research."

Her eyes rounded in renewed shock. "You suspected them?"

"I suspected everyone with access to me, direct or indirect."

A stricken look entered her eyes, as if she was just now realizing he must have suspected her, too. Of course, she was still under the impression that nothing of value had been stolen. When everything had been.

It had been so sensitive, even with all his security, he'd documented his results in bits and pieces that only he could put together. But they'd still been accessed and reconstructed and appeared in the hands of his rivals. Then he'd been given proof that the breach had originated from Glory.

But he'd insisted it must have been someone who had total access to Glory. Only her family had that. Needing to settle this without her knowledge, only thinking of her heartache if she found out, he'd confronted them. They'd broken under his threats, begged his leniency. He'd already decided to show them that, for Glory, but he'd said he'd only consider it if they gave him the details of their plan, their recruiters and any accomplices. If they didn't, he'd show no mercy. And they'd given him proof that it had been Glory. She'd been their only hope of getting to him.

And how she'd gotten to him.

She'd played him like a virtuoso. It hadn't even occurred to him to guard himself against her like he did with everyone else.

But a lengthy, highly publicized court case would have harmed more than helped him. Worse, it would have kept her in his life. So he'd groped for the lesser mutilation of cutting her off from his life abruptly, so the sordid mess wouldn't get any bigger.

Then something totally unexpected had happened. Also because of her.

As he'd struggled to put her out of his mind, he'd restarted his work from scratch, soon becoming thankful he had. What he'd thought was a breakthrough had actually been fundamentally flawed. If he hadn't lost the whole thing, he would have cost his sponsors untold billions of wasted development financing. But the real catastrophe would have been if the magnitude of confidence in his research had minimized testing before its applications hit the market. Lives could have been lost.

So her betrayal had been a blessing in disguise, forcing him to correct his mistakes and devise a safe, more cost-effective and streamlined method. After that, he'd been catapulted to the top of his field. Not that he was about to thank Glory for the betrayal that had led to all that.

Glory's choking words brought him out of the darkness of the past. "But they had nothing to do with your leaked research. And according to you, there *was* no leaked research."

"Not for lack of trying on the culprits' part. That I placed false results for them to steal doesn't exonerate them from the crime of industrial espionage and patent theft."

Her sluggish nod conceded that point. "But if you didn't pursue them then, they must have checked out. So why did you keep them under a microscope all this time?"

So she was still playing the innocence card. Fine. He'd play it her way. He had a more important goal now than exhuming past corpses. He'd get closure in a different way, which wouldn't involve exposing the truth. If she still believed she'd failed in her mission, he'd let her keep thinking that.

His lips twisted on ever-present bitterness. "What can I say? I follow my gut. And it told me they were shifty, and to keep an eye on them. Since I could easily afford to, I did. And because I was already following their every move, I found out each instance when they stepped out of line, even when others couldn't. I also learned their methods, so I could anticipate them. They didn't stand a chance."

A long moment of silence passed, filled with the world of hurt and disillusion roiling in her eyes.

Then she rasped, "Why haven't you reported them?"

Because they're your family.

There. He'd finally admitted it to himself.

Something that felt like a boulder sitting on his chest suddenly lifted. He felt as if he could breathe fully again, after years of only snatching in enough air to survive.

So this was how it felt to be free of self-deceptions.

It *had* sat heavily on his conscience, that he'd known of her family's habitual crimes and not done anything about it. He'd tried to rationalize why he hadn't, but it had boiled down to this: after all she'd done to him, he still hadn't been able to bring himself to damage her to that extent. He had been unable to cause her the loss of her family, as shoddy as they were. But even more, he couldn't have risked that they might have implicated her.

In spite of everything, he hadn't been able to contemplate sending her to prison.

Not that he was about to let her realize that she'd always had control over every irrational cell in his body.

He gave her one of the explanations he'd placated himself with. "I didn't see any benefit to myself or to my business in doing so." At her widening stare, he huffed. "I'm not just a mad scientist, not anymore. And then, scientists are among the most ruthless pragmatists around. Since the incidents six years ago, I've learned it always pays to have some dirt on everyone, to use when needed. Now the time has come for that nugget to deliver its full potential."

"And you think you can coerce me into marrying you, even temporarily, using their crimes?"

"Yes. It would make you the perfect temporary wife. You're the only woman who wouldn't be tempted to ask for more at the end of the contract's terms, or risk any kind of scandal."

Another silence detonated in the wake of his final taunt.

With eyes brimming, she sat up and tossed her head, making her shimmering hair shift to one side with an audible hiss.

He struggled not to swoop down on her, harness her by those luxurious tresses, ravage those lush lips, crush that voluptuousness under his weight and take her, make her writhe her pleasure beneath him, pour all of his inside her.

She exacerbated his condition with the lash of her challenge. "What if I told you I don't care what you do with said 'nugget'? If they did the things this file says they did, then they deserve to be locked up to pay for their crimes, and learn a lesson nothing else could teach them."

Elation at her defiance and disgust at the whole situation mingled in an explosive mix, almost making him lightheaded. "They may deserve it, but you still won't let them get locked up for a day, let alone years, if you can at all help it."

All anger and rebellion went out of her, dejection crashing in its place. Her shoulders slumped and her eyes dimmed.

He attempted to look unaffected by her apparent upheaval and defeat. *Apparent* being the operative word. In reality she must be rubbing her hands at the unexpected windfall and what she could negotiate out of it.

He exhaled. "It's a beneficial arrangement all around. Though your father and brother deserve to be punished, their punishment wouldn't serve any purpose. I…will compensate those they've embezzled from and defrauded." He'd nearly slipped and told her that he'd *already* compensated their victims, each in a way that made up for their losses, without connecting his actions to those, or to her family. "You will be spared the disgrace and heartache of having them imprisoned. My king and Castaldini will have me where they need me. And I will have the temporary image cleansing necessary for the job."

Her gaze froze on his face for a fraught moment until his heart started to thunder in his chest. And that was before a couple of tears arrowed down her flushed, trembling cheeks.

She wiped them away, as if pissed off with herself for letting him witness her weakness. Her turmoil seemed so real he felt it reverberating in his bones. But it couldn't be real. It had to be another act. But how could it be so convincing?

He should stop wondering. As far as his senses were concerned, her every breath and word and look were genuine. So he'd better stop pitting their verdict against that of his mind before they tore him down the middle in their tug-of-war.

She finally whispered, "How temporary is temporary?"

He exhaled heavily. "A year."

Her face convulsed as if at a stab of pain.

After swallowing with evident difficulty, she asked, "What would be the...job description?"

So she'd moved from rejection to defiance to setting terms. And somehow, though he was holding all the cards, it felt like she was the one setting the pace of this confrontation, steering its direction. No wonder. She'd been the best negotiator he'd ever had on his team, the most ordered, effective executive. He *had* loved her for her mind and abilities as much as everything else. He'd respected them, believed in them. Relied on them. Her loss had damaged every pillar in his world.

Pushing aside the bitterness that kept derailing him, he said, "I will be Castaldini's representative to the United Nations. It's one of the most exalted positions in the kingdom, and it is closely monitored and rated by Castaldinians before the rest of the world. My wife will need to share all of my public appearances, act as the proper consort in all the functions I attend, the gracious hostess in the ones I give, and the adoring bride in everything else."

Her incredulity rose with his every word. "And you think I am qualified for those roles? Why don't you just get someone from Castaldini, a minor princess or something, who'd jump at the chance for a temporary place in the spotlight, and who's been trained from birth in royal and diplomatic pretense? I'm sure no woman will cling or cause scandals when you want to cast her aside. You cast me aside without as much as a wrinkle in your suit."

No. Just a chasm in my heart. "I want no one else. And yes, you are qualified and then some. You're an unequaled expert in all aspects of the executive life with its due process and formalities. You're also quite the chameleon, and you blend perfectly in any situation or setting." Her eyes widened at that, as if she'd never heard anything more ridiculous in her life. Before she could voice her derision, he went on. "The jump to court and diplomatic etiquette and 'pretense' should be a breeze. I will tutor you in what you'll say and how you'll behave with dignitaries and the press. I'll leave the other areas of your education to Alonzo, my valet. And with your unusual beauty, and your…assets—" his gaze made an explicit sweep of said assets before returning to her once again chagrined eyes "—once Alonzo gets his hands on you, the tabloids will have nothing to talk about but your style and latest outfits. Your current occupation as a humanitarian crusader will also capture the imagination of the world, and add to my image as a clean-energy pioneer. We'll be the perfect fairy-tale couple."

What he'd once thought they could be for real.

His summation seemed to have as brutal an effect on her as it had on him. She looked as if regret that this could never be real crushed her, too.

Suppressing the urge to put his fist through the nearest wall, he gritted out, "I am also offering a substantial financial incentive to sweeten the deal. That's part of the offer I've already said you can't refuse."

She kept staring at him with what looked like disappointment pulsing in the depths of her eyes. She didn't ask how much. Still acting as if money meant nothing to her.

"Ten million dollars," he said, suppressing a sneer of disillusion. "Net of deductions or taxes. Two up front, the rest on completion of the contract term."

He bent, picked up the other dossier on the coffee table and came to stand over her where she sat limply on the couch. "That's the prenuptial agreement you'll sign."

When she didn't take the volume, he placed it on her lap.

"I'm giving you today to read through this. You're free to seek legal counsel, of course, but there's nothing in it to impact you whatsoever, if you abide by the letter of the terms. I will expect your acceptance tomorrow."

Without looking up from the dossier in her lap, she said, "Take it or take it, huh?"

"That about sums it up."

The gaze fixed on his filled with fury, frustration and… vulnerability.

Dio. Just a look from her and his whole being surged with need. To devour her, to possess her. To protect her.

Seemed his weakness where she was concerned was incurable.

And to think he'd hoped he'd realize that everything he'd felt for her was an exaggeration, that seeing her again would only make him wonder at how he'd once thought himself attracted to her. He'd hoped it would purge the memories that circulated in his system like a nondegradable mind-altering drug.

Instead, he'd found that what he remembered of her effect on him had been diluted by time. Either that or her effect had multiplied tenfold. He'd been aroused since he'd laid eyes on her again, was now in agony.

His only consolation was that she wanted him, too.

Si, of this he had no doubt. Not even she could have faked her body's responses. Their memory had controlled his fantasies all these years. Every manifestation of her desire, the scent of it, the taste of its honey on his tongue, the feel of its liquid silk on his fingers and manhood, the rush of her pleasure at the peaks that had rocked her beneath him, squeezed her around him and wrung him of explosive releases.

What would it feel like having her again with all their baggage, maturity and changes?

No need to wonder. For he'd made up his mind.

He *would* have her again.

Might as well make his intentions clear up front.

He caught her arm as she heaved up. Jolts arced from every fingertip pressing into firm flesh.

At her indignant glare, he bent and whispered in her ear, "When I take you to my bed this time, it will be far better than ever before."

Her flesh buzzed in his hand, her breath becoming choppy, her pupils dilating. Her scent rose to perfume the air, to fill his lungs with the evidence of her arousal.

Still, she said, "I will never sign to that."

"And I'd never ask you to. This has nothing to do with the deal. You have full freedom on this front. I'm only letting you know I want you in my bed. And you will come. Because you want to. Because you want me."

Her pupils fluctuated, her cheeks flushed. Proof positive of his claims.

She still scoffed, even if in a voice that had deepened to the timbre that used to arouse him out of his mind, as it did now. "You really have to see someone for that head of yours, before it snaps off your neck under its own weight."

He tugged on her arm, brought her slamming against him. A groan escaped him at the glorious feel of her against him from breast to knee. A moan of stimulation issued from her before she could stifle it.

The bouquet that had been tantalizing him since she'd walked in—her unique brand of femininity, that of sunshine-soaked days and pleasure-drenched nights—deluged his lungs. He had to get more, leave no breath unmingled with it.

He buried his face in her neck, inhaled her, absorbing her shudder into his. "I don't want you in my bed. I *need* you there. I've craved you there for six long years."

The body that had gone limp at contact with his stiffened, pushing away only enough to look confusedly up at him.

Feeling he'd said too much, he let her go before he swept her up and carried her to bed here and now.

Her face was a canvas of every turbulent emotion there was, so intense he felt almost dizzy at their onslaught.

And he found himself adding, "Passion was the one real thing we shared. You were the best I've ever had. I only ended it with you because you—" he barely caught back an accusation "—seemed to expect more than was on offer." He injected his voice with nonchalance. "But now you know what is on offer. You have every choice in becoming my lover, but none in being my princess."

Her gaze dropped to the dossier in her hand, which regulated their temporary relationship's boundaries and how it would end with a cold precision he was already starting to question.

Then she raised her eyes, the azure now dull and distant. "Only for a year."

Or longer. As long as we both want, he almost blurted out.

Catching back the impetuousness with all he had, he nodded. "Only for a year."

Three

"How long?"

Glory winced at her best friend's shrill stupefaction.

She was already regretting telling Amelia anything. But Glory had felt her head and heart might explode if she didn't tell someone. And it couldn't have been her mother. Glenda Monaghan would have a breakdown if she knew what her husband and son had been up to. Or what they were in danger of if Glory didn't go through with Vincenzo's "deal." The "take it or I send your family up the river for life" deal.

Glory smirked at her best friend's flabbergasted expression. "Don't you think you're going about this in reverse? You keep asking me a question right after I answer it."

Amelia rolled her long-lashed golden eyes. "Ex*cuse* me, Ms. Monaghan. We'll see how you'll fare when I come to you saying *I* was once on mouth-to-mouth-and-way-more terms with a prince of freaking Castaldini, who happens to be the foremost scientist and businessman in the clean-energy field, and that he now wants to marry me."

"Only for a year," Glory added, her heart twisting again.

Amelia threw her hands, palms up, at her. "There. You've said it again. So don't get prissy with me while I'm in shock. I mean…Vincenzo D'Agostino? Whoa!"

Glory emptied her lungs on a dejected sigh. "Yeah."

Amelia sagged down on the couch beside her. "Man. I'm trying to compose this picture of you with Prince Vastly Devastating himself, and I'm failing miserably."

Glory's exhalation was laced with mockery this time. "Thanks, Amie, so kind of you."

"It's not that I don't think you're on his level!" Amelia exclaimed. "Any man on any level would be lucky to have you look his way. But you haven't been making any XY chromosome carriers lucky since the Ice Age. You've been such a cold fish…." She winced then smiled sheepishly. "You *know* how you are with men. You radiate this 'do not approach or else' vibe. It's impossible to imagine you in the throes of passion with any man. But now I'm realizing your standards are just much higher than us mere mortal women. It's either someone of Vincenzo's caliber or nothing. Or—" realization seemed to hit Amelia, making her eyes drain of lightheartedness, then fill with wariness "—is it because it's Vincenzo or nothing? Is he the one who spoiled you for other men?"

Glory stared at her. She'd never thought of it this way.

After the brutal way Vincenzo had ended their affair, she'd been devastated, emotionally and psychologically. For the next year, she hadn't thought beyond stopping being miserable. After that, she'd poured all of her time and energy into changing her direction in life.

It had taken Vincenzo's kicking her out of his life, and out of her job, to make her realize the fatal flaw in her unwavering quest for security and stability. She'd known then that there could be neither, emotional or financial. If the man she'd thought to be her soul mate could destroy both with a few

words, she wouldn't count on anything again. She'd decided
to give her heart and skills to the world and hope they'd do
it more good than they'd done her.

The more she'd achieved, the more in demand she'd been.
For the past five years, she'd been constantly on the go, living out of a suitcase, setting up and streamlining multiple
humanitarian operations across the globe. If she'd wanted
intimacies, they would have had to be passing encounters.
And those just weren't for her.

But now, after Amelia's questions, she had to pause and
wonder. Had one of the major attractions of that whole lifestyle been the legitimate and continuous way of escaping
intimacies?

Glory loved her job, couldn't ask for anything more fulfilling on a personal or professional level. But it *had* given her no
respite, no time or energy for self-reflection or reassessment.
Had she unconsciously sought that flat-out pace to make herself too unavailable? Too consumed to even sense anything
missing? So she didn't have to face that she'd always be a
one-man woman? That for her, it *was* Vincenzo or nothing?

Amelia must have read the answer in Glory's silent stare,
for she, too, exhaled. "Did he break your heart?"

"No. He…smashed it."

Amelia frowned, expression darkening. "Okay, now I hate
the guy. I saw him a few times on TV, and I don't know how
I didn't peg him for a slimeball! I thought he sounded like
a pretty decent guy, no airs, and even with his reputation, I
remember wondering how he demolished the stereotype of
the royal playboy. I thought being a scientist saved him from
being a narcissistic monster. But I stand corrected."

The ridiculous urge to defend him overpowered Glory. "He
isn't…wasn't like that. He's—he's just… I don't know." She
shook her head in confusion. "It's like he's two—no, three
people. The man I fell in love with was like you describe

him—honorable, sincere and grounded in his public life, focused, driven and brilliant in his working one, and sensitive, caring and passionate in person. Then there was the man who ended things with me, cold and callous, even vicious. And finally there's the man I met today. Relentless and dominating, yet nothing like the man who took everything seriously, or the man who relished humiliating me."

"Humiliating you?" The edge to Amelia's rising fury was a blade against Glory's inflamed nerves. "And now he's asking you to marry him to fix his reputation? And don't say 'only for a year' again or I may have to break something. I can't believe I was excited at first! Tell him to take his short-term-lease-marriage offer and go to hell."

Glory had always thought Amelia as magnificent as a golden lioness. She now looked like one defending her cub. Her reaction warmed Glory even through the ice of her despondency. "You mean you wouldn't have told me to tell him that anyway?"

"No, I wouldn't have. I mean, you're not in the market for a regular marriage anyway, then comes Prince Very Delicious offering you a year in a fairy tale with a ten million dollar cash bonus. If he wasn't a scumbag who seems to have crippled you emotionally for life, I would have thought it a super deal for you. Now what I want to know is how *dare* he approach you of all people with his offer?"

Glory hadn't shared Vincenzo's reason for picking her. As the one "convenient"—not to mention compromised—enough for his needs. Again. She exhaled and escaped answering.

Amelia harrumphed. "But it doesn't matter what he's thinking. If he bothers you after you say no, I'll have my Jack have a word with his teeth."

Imagining Jack, a bear of a man and a bruiser, pitted against the equally powerful but refined great feline Vincenzo suddenly brought a giggle bursting out of her.

Pulling back from the edge of hysteria, Glory's laughter died on a heavy sigh. "I'm not looking for an intervention here, Amie. I only wanted to…share. I—" she barely swallowed back *have to* "—already decided to say yes."

Amelia gaped at her. Glory hadn't told her of Vincenzo's ultimatum, either. If she did, Jack and his whole rugby team would be after Vincenzo. Then Vincenzo would gather all those hulking wonders he had for cousins and it would probably lead to a war between the U.S. and Castaldini.…

She suppressed the mania bubbling inside her, and focused on overriding Amelia's vehement objections. "It'll only be for a year, Amie. And just think what I can do for all the causes I'm involved in with ten million dollars."

Amelia snorted. "Not much. That would barely supply a few clean-water stations. If you're foolish enough to put yourself within range of the man who hurt and humiliated you, I'd ask for a *hundred* million. He can afford it, and he's the one who needs to scrape a mile-deep of dirt from his image with your shining one. At least you'd be risking annihilation for a good enough cause."

Glory smiled weakly at the firebrand she had for a best friend. She'd met Amelia five years ago while working with Doctors Without Borders. They'd hit it off immediately—two women who'd worked all their lives to become professionals, then discovered, each through her own ordeal, that they needed a cause, not a career. As a corporate and international law expert, Amelia had made it possible for Glory to accomplish things she'd thought impossible. Amelia always insisted Glory's business and economic know-how were more valuable than law—in a world where money was a constant when everything else was mercurial.

"I wanted you to take a look at this.…" She reached for the hardcover prenuptial agreement as if reaching for a bomb. She dropped it in Amelia's lap as if it scalded her and attempted a wink. "That's mainly why I told you. To get your legal opinion on this little gem."

Amelia stared at the heavy volume in her lap with the gilded inscription proclaiming its nature. "I'd say this is a huge one. And from the looks and weight of it, I'm not sure *gem* is the right word for it, either. Okay, let's see what Prince Very Disturbing has to offer."

Unable to sit beside her as she read Vincenzo's terms, Glory got up and went to the kitchen.

While she searched for something to do, she tried telling herself that, considering the situation, the prenuptial shouldn't disturb her. She'd never seen one, and she had no knowledge of marriage laws. Maybe this language was standard within every marriage where one party outranks the other in position and wealth a thousandfold.

She wasn't poor, but financial ease had ceased to be a goal to her. She'd settled for having no debts, and a few inexpensive needs. But in comparison to Vincenzo with his Midas touch, she guessed she would rank as destitute. Maybe he had to consider his investors when he dealt with anything that could affect him financially. Maybe even his board of directors had a say in his financial decisions, and in today's world, marriage was one.

But did he have to go that far with the prenup, as if he was safeguarding himself from a hardened criminal? Or was it she who didn't know what was too far?

She'd made apple pie from scratch and baked it by the time Amelia entered the kitchen with the volume tucked beneath her arm, and a thundercloud hanging over her head.

Amelia slammed the prenup on the island with a huff of disgust. "The only thing he left out was the number of cutlery pieces that have to be accounted for before he gives you the 'latter portion of the monetary settlement at termination of contract term'!"

Glory's heart kicked her ribs. "It's that bad, huh?"

"Worse. This guy is making provisions for provisions, as if he's dealing with a repeat offender known for 'stealing kohl from the eye,' like I heard they say in Castaldini."

Just what Glory had been thinking.

Now that Amelia had confirmed her suspicion, her confusion deepened. Why all this? So a man in his position had much to lose, but *he* was forcing her to serve a sentence in lieu of her family. Could he really think she'd want to prolong it, or try to bribe him or cause any trouble at its end?

But those extensive precautions said that he did. Why? Because of her family's history? Didn't he already know she had nothing to do with her father's and brother's actions and choices? With his surveillance and investigations, he must know she'd had very little to do with them in the past years. She maintained close relations with her mother, who had nothing to do with her husband's and son's transgressions and stupidities. Or was Vincenzo just this paranoid with everyone?

He had been very cautious with people in general. She'd thought she'd been the exception, that he'd been totally open and trusting with her. Yeah, sure. Just like she'd thought he'd felt anything for her.

It had all been a lie. A mirage. This was the reality. That he'd never bothered to know anything about her. No, worse, that he thought the worst of her.

Amelia's harrumph brought Glory out of her musings. "You wanted my opinion? Based on a prenup like that, and the rest of this man's pattern of behavior? Go for a *billion* dollars, Glory. Up front. And right after the wedding, go for his balls."

After Amelia had given her verdict on Vincenzo's offer and Vincenzo himself, she'd insisted on going over the "submission contract." She'd spent the rest of the night dissecting it, and writing down in lawyer-speak what Glory would ask for instead. It was past two in the morning by the time Amelia left, and not of her own accord. Glory had to pretend to fall asleep on the couch to convince her she couldn't take anymore.

Not that she'd wanted to sleep. In fact, she'd known sleep would be an impossibility tonight. Maybe every night from now on. As long as Vincenzo was back in her life.

Her sleeping patterns had already been irrevocably changed since she'd first met him. First, with nights of longing, then ones interspersed with repeated lovemaking, then memories and miseries. She'd only had a measure of her old sleeping soundness restored when she'd maintained a schedule that knocked her out for the five or six hours she allotted for rest.

Right now she felt she was back in the bed of thorns of post-Vincenzo devastation. Even worse. Now she was caught in his maelstrom again, in a far more ambiguous relationship than ever before; she felt she was lying on burning coals.

But apart from the shock of her family's crimes and Vincenzo's outrageous "offer," what really shook her were those last minutes at his penthouse.

Everything inside her had surged so fiercely in response, it had incapacitated her. Outraged her. That after all the heartache and humiliation, he only had to touch her, to tell her he wanted her, that she'd been the best he'd ever had, to have her body come to life, proclaiming him its master...

A classic ringtone sundered the stillness of the night.

Jerking up in bed, her heart thundered, unformed dreads deluging her. Her mother. She'd been fragile since her last round of cancer treatments months ago. Something had happened....

She fumbled for the phone, almost dropping it when she

hit the button to answer. A deep-as-night voice poured into her brain.

"Are you awake?"

Gulping down aborted fright, anger flooded in to replace it, dripping into her voice. "It figures. You had to be one of those unfeeling, self-absorbed people who wake up others to ask if they're awake."

Dark amusement tinged his fathomless voice, making her almost see, taste, the smile that tugged at his lips. "You sound awake."

"I am now, thanks to a royal pain."

A bone-liquefying reverberation poured right into her brain, yanking at her responses. "So you still wake up ready."

He didn't say for what. He didn't need to. She'd been always ready for anything with him, on waking up in his arms. Even now, when her mind wanted only to roast him slowly over an open fire, her body obeyed his inexorable influence, readying itself with a languid throb of remembrance and yearning.

And that was before his voice dropped another octave as he whispered, "If I woke you up, I'm glad. I shouldn't be the only one who can't sleep tonight."

"Your conscience weighing on you?" Her voice, to her dismay, was rough and thick, aroused, nowhere as demolishing as she intended it to be. "Or have you long had that removed? Or has it always been genetically missing?"

His chuckle was louder this time, more enervating. "Its deployment hasn't been required in our current situation. As I mentioned before, my offer is beneficial to everyone, starting with you. Now enough of that. What did you decide?"

"You mean I *can* decide? Now, that's a new development."

"It's a few-hours-old one. I already made it unquestionable that it's up to you. I just couldn't wait till morning for your verdict."

"Good thing that you called, so *I* wouldn't have to wait to tell you that I never want to see or hear from you again."

"That's not on the menu of options open to you. Being my temporary princess is a done deal. And as such, you'll see plenty of me. I'm only inquiring if you've decided to see *all* of me."

Her huff was less exasperated with him than disgusted with the clench of longing at his lazy, overpowering seduction. "I guess you decided to develop a sense of humor and you had to start from scratch. I must have your late blooming to thank for this juvenile double-talk."

"I apologize for my trite attempts at euphemisms." He sounded serious all of a sudden. Just as she wondered if she'd finally managed to offend him, his voice plunged into the darkest reaches of temptation. "So when will you let me strip you naked, worship and own and exploit every inch of your mind-blowing new curves for my pleasure and yours? When will you let me kiss and caress you within an inch of your sanity, suckle and stroke you to a few screaming orgasms before sinking inside you and riding you into oblivion?"

Breath sheared out of her lungs, heartbeats fractured against her ribs. The surge of images crowded her mind's eye with memories of her desperation for his touch and assuagement.

She'd asked for that when she'd taunted him. Not that she'd thought he'd say...

"Mind-blowing new curves?"

She almost groaned. She couldn't believe that was what she'd latched on to in all the mind-melting things he'd just said. Seemed body-image issues were so hardwired that they'd override even the heart attack he'd almost given her. But she *had* put on weight she wasn't happy about and couldn't believe he found it appealing.

"Ah, *si, bellissima,* every inch of you has...appreciated.

You were always gorgeous down to your toes, but the years have ripened you into something impossibly…more. I ached the whole time you were at my penthouse to test and taste every remembered wonder, every new enhancement. I am now in agony to explore and devour every part of you. And I know you need every part of me, too, on you, in you. I can feel your arousal echoing mine even at this distance. But if you think you're not ready yet, I'll come…persuade you. I'll remind you what it was like between us, prove to you how much better it will be now we're both older and wiser and certain of what we want."

Fighting another surge of response and haywire heartbeats, she said, "Now that I'm older and wiser, you think I'll let you have me without guarantees, like when I was young and stupid?"

"You want a ring first? I can bring it with me right now."

"*No.* That's not what I meant…." She gulped, her head spinning. This was zooming beyond warp speed. Just a few hours ago she'd never thought she'd see him again. Now he was almost seducing her, over the phone no less, and she was a breath away from telling him to just hurry the hell over. "I didn't mean material guarantees. I meant guarantees of being treated with respect when you decide I'm no longer 'convenient.' I don't even have the advantage or excuse of obliviousness like I did when I believed you valued me."

A silent moment followed. Then an expressionless drawl. "Let's leave the past buried. We're different people now."

"Are we? Maybe you are, whatever the hell you are. But unlike you, I have one basic character, and I'm pretty much the same person I was six years ago. Just older and wiser, as you pointed out, and aware that what you're suggesting would cause long-term damage. And mentioning that, if I become your 'princess,' temporary or not…"

"*When* you become my princess. Very soon. Though, with

the necessary preparations, not soon enough. But say the word, and I'll be worshiping your glorious body within the hour—"

She cut him off before she combusted. "I demand to have a say in the details, since I have no choice in the fundamental stuff. If part of this charade is a ring, then I want to choose it. You'll have it back in the end, but I'm the one who's going to be wearing it, and 'only a year' is still a long time."

His voice suddenly lost the mind-scrambling sexiness and filled with a different passion. "Then you will choose your ring. And everything else you want. As my princess you can and will have everything you wish for."

Her heart squeezed into her throat. "Weird. I have a two-hundred-page volume detailing how I can't have anything."

Silence stretched over long seconds.

A forcible exhalation followed. "That volume is only to…" He stopped again. As if he couldn't find the right words. Which was even weirder. Vincenzo was never at a loss for words.

She decided to help him out. "Only to protect you from any opportunistic ideas I might develop at contract termination. So it's strange you're willing to be wide-open for those same ideas at its start. Not that I want anything from you, but I'm just observing the contradictions."

Another long silence answered her.

Then another heavy exhalation. "I changed my mind."

He did? He was taking back his offer of "everything"? Figured. That must have been his need to have sex talking. She must have managed to douse his desire and he was back to thinking straight, and taking back his reckless concessions.

Then he went on. "You don't have to sign if you find it excessive. And you don't have to make a decision now. And you *are* free to say no. Of course, I won't stop trying to persuade you. But for now, you can go back to sleep. I'll come for you tomorrow at five to pick the ring. Sorry if I woke you up."

The line went dead.

She pulled the phone from her ear, staring down at it.

What was that all about? Had that been a fourth man inhabiting his body?

What was she walking into? And with which man? Or would it be with all of them? With him changing from one to the other until he drove her mad with confusion, insane with wanting him—whoever he was—and self-destructing in the process?

Not that she had any choice. She'd enter his den, and wouldn't exit it for the next year. It was doubtful she'd exit in one piece.

No. Not doubtful.

Impossible.

Four

"Impossible!"

Vincenzo cocked his head at his valet's stupefaction. The fondness Alonzo always stirred in him relaxed lips that had been spastic with tension since his conversation with Glory last night.

Even over the phone, she'd seeped under his skin and into his system and confounded his common sense. He shouldn't have called her in the first place. But he'd been unable to stop. The indiscretion alone had been enough to expose his condition, but he hadn't left anything to her imagination, had told her in exhaustive detail he was burning for her.

Then at the first tinge of disappointment and indignation in her voice, he'd offered anything at all in hope of erasing it. He'd taken back every precaution his mind—not to mention his attorney—insisted were indispensable to protect him.

He jerked back to the moment as Alonzo, in a totally uncharacteristic action, grabbed him by the shoulders.

"Are you teasing me? Because I was lamenting the other day that it seemed both of us would end up shriveled-up bachelors? But…you never joke." Alonzo's vivid green eyes widened. "*Dio.* You mean it. You *are* getting married."

He hadn't told Alonzo why, or how. For reasons he wasn't up to facing, he wanted Alonzo to think this was real. And to treat the whole thing accordingly. To treat Glory accordingly.

"When? *How?*" Alonzo grabbed his own head in dramatic disbelief. "You met a woman, fell in love with her, decided to marry her, asked her and had her agree without my knowledge?"

That would have been an impossibility, indeed. Alonzo was almost his shadow, had been indispensable to him since his teens, even before he lost his parents, smoothing out his daily life, anticipating his needs and providing him with hassle-free, meticulous support and problem solving in everything that didn't involve work and most things that did. He'd only gotten Glory's visit under Alonzo's radar because he'd sent him on some needless errand. Not that Alonzo would have recognized her. In a weird coincidence, Alonzo had taken his one and only prolonged leave of absence during Vincenzo's affair with Glory. It was probably the reason she'd been able to breach him that totally.…

Oh, who was he fooling? He'd been the one and only reason. He'd left himself wide-open to her. And as she'd shrewdly commented, he was doing it again.

Clearly unaware of his turmoil, Alonzo pursued his own perplexity. "But most important, who?" Alonzo grimaced as if at an unsavory thought. "Please, don't tell me it's one of those women you parade for the paparazzi!"

This was another of the privacies that only Alonzo was privy to. That Vincenzo's reputation had been manufactured. By him. To keep hopeful and gold-digging women away. To keep women away, period. He'd found a ruthless playboy's image much more effectively off-putting than a reclusive scientist-prince's. Around a year after breaking up with Glory, he'd started hiring "escorts" wherever he went, to paint the image he wanted.

Not that he hadn't been with women outside his propaganda campaign. He'd tried. If not for long. After a few encounters had ended with him being unable to…rise to the occasion, he'd given up. Alonzo had even once asked if Vincenzo had changed his mind about his orientation, asking if he could take the glad tidings to the gay community that Vincenzo might be on the market soon.

Alonzo had been scandalized when Vincenzo had told him he'd just decided to take an open-ended leave of absence from sex. According to Alonzo, that was the most unnatural thing he'd ever heard. A virile man in his prime owed it to the world to give and receive pleasure to and from as many people as possible. Since he had no partner, of course.

But that had been the problem. While Vincenzo didn't have a partner, his body didn't know that. It had already been imprinted with Glory's code. And though his mind had rejected her, there'd been no reprogramming his body.

Now he decided to tell Alonzo what would appeal to the hopeless romantic in him. What had been true, if he didn't mention the parts that made it also ugly and painful.

"Her name is Glory Monaghan. She's an American who was once my executive consultant, and now she's consulting for major humanitarian operations. I fell in love with her during that time you went with Gio to Brazil. It ended…badly. Then Ferruccio slammed me with a royal decree to get married to clean up my image so I can be Castaldini's representative to the United Nations. And after all these years, and in spite of the way we parted, she was the only one I could think of. I sought her out again and found her hold on me is stronger than ever. Things…developed, and now…I'll marry her."

Alonzo's eyes, which had been reddening as he listened, now filled. "Oh, *mio ragazzo caro!* I have no words…no words…"

Vincenzo wondered if he'd ever get used to Alonzo calling him "dear boy." And he wondered if he was making a mistake by hiding the nature of his impending marriage.

Alonzo interrupted his heavy musings by doing something he hadn't done since Vincenzo was twelve. He pulled Vincenzo into a fatherly hug. Alonzo *had* been that to him, even more than his real father, though Bernardo D'Agostino had been an exceptional father, too.

Vincenzo accepted Alonzo's distraught joy, only wishing it was founded on something genuine, already starting to regret that he'd misled him.

Before he could make qualifications that would temper Alonzo's delight and expectations, and his subsequent letdown when things came to an inevitable end, Alonzo pulled back with a look of absolute anxiety on his face.

"Please tell me you're giving me enough time to prepare!"

Vincenzo shook his head, his lips once again tugging at how passionately Alonzo felt about everything. "Anyone hearing you would think it's your wedding, Alonzo."

"If only!" Alonzo's eyes filled with mockery and not a little resignation. "If Gio hasn't popped the question in fifteen years, he isn't about to do so now."

And for that, Vincenzo considered Giordano Mancini a major ass. Everyone knew Alonzo was his partner, but Giordano seemed to think that if he didn't openly admit it and didn't live with him he would avoid the prejudices that plagued same-sex relationships. As a businessman who came from a deeply traditional family, everyone turned a blind eye to his sexual orientation as long as he wasn't blatant about it.

Which outraged Vincenzo to no end. He considered Giordano a coward who shortchanged Alonzo to protect himself.

So same-sex marriages were still not accepted in Castaldini, but Vincenzo had told Gio he'd stand up for them, make sure everyone showed them every respect and courtesy, personally and professionally. His assurances hadn't been enough for Gio, and he'd convinced Alonzo that they didn't need a certificate or the world's acceptance to be happy. Or at least, Alonzo pretended to be convinced so he could stay with the man he loved. But his reaction now proved that he still yearned for the validation of his beloved's public proclamation, and the delight of preparing a ceremony to celebrate their bond.

Vincenzo's gaze settled heavily on Alonzo. Everyone thought Vincenzo couldn't be more different from the man, fourteen years his senior, who'd been his closest companion since he was ten. Only he knew how similar they were where it mattered. They were both detail-oriented and goal-focused. But most important, they suffered from the same fundamental ailment. Monogamy. The one thing stopping him from telling Alonzo to kick that guy out of his life was that Gio was equally exclusive.

At least so far. Vincenzo had made certain. If that ever changed, Gio wouldn't know what hit him.

"But it's worse." Alonzo's exclamation interrupted Vincenzo's aggressive thoughts. "It's *your* wedding. Do you know how long I've waited for this day?"

"I can subtract, Alonzo. Since you started droning that I should get married when I wasn't yet twenty. It's been two decades since you started longing to plan the elusive day."

"But it's elusive no more! I could kiss King Ferruccio for pushing you to make the decision."

"You just want to kiss Ferruccio under any pretext," he teased.

After that, Alonzo deluged him with questions, milking him for info on dates, preferences, Glory and everything besides, so he could start preparing the "Wedding of the Cen-

tury," as he was adamant it would be. He insisted he'd have
to get his hands on Glory ASAP so he'd get her input, and
construct the perfect "setting" for Vincenzo's royal jewel.

Alonzo only left him alone when he told him of his ring-
picking mission, for which he'd yet to prepare.

Alonzo almost skipped out of the room in his excitement
about the million things he had to arrange and the prospect
of his prince getting a princess at last.

Once alone, Vincenzo attacked planning the perfect ring
rendezvous with as much single-mindedness as he did his
most crucial scientific or business endeavors. But even with
his far-reaching influence, it still took hours to prepare things
to his satisfaction, leaving only two before his self-imposed
appointment with Glory.

He rushed into his bathroom, ticking off the things he
needed to do. To get ready for her.

Lust and longing seethed in his arteries as he entered the
shower cubicle, letting the hot water sting some measure of
relief into his tension. Not that it worked. He felt about to explode, as he had when he'd called Glory. He'd felt he might
suffer some lasting damage if he didn't spend the rest of the
night all over her, inside her, assuaging the hunger that had
come crashing to the fore at renewed exposure to her.

But although he was still in agony, he was glad she'd resisted him, and that he'd backed off. And he was fiercely satisfied that his domineering tactics had made her push back.
This was how he wanted it, wanted her, giving him the elation
of the struggle, the exhilaration of the challenge. And she'd
done that and more. She'd asked to pick her ring.

Suddenly, something that had been clenched inside him
since he'd lost his dream of a life with her unfurled. The plan
he'd started executing only twenty-four hours ago had been
derailed. It had taken on a life of its own. He no longer had
the least control over it or himself.

And he couldn't be more thrilled about it.

She's bewitched you all over again.

He smirked at that inner voice's effort to jolt him out of his intentions. It failed. He didn't care if she had. All his caution and self-preservation had only brought him melancholy and isolation. He was sick of them, of knowing that without her, he'd feel this way forever. It had taken seeing her again to prove that she was the only thing to bring him to life.

It might feel this way, but it's an illusion. It has always been.

He still didn't care. If the illusion felt that good, why not succumb to it? As long as he knew it was one.

What if knowing still won't protect you when it ends?

He frowned at the valid thought.

But no. Anything was better than the rut he was in. Apart from those months he'd had with her, all he'd done since he could remember was research, perform his business and royal duties, eat, exercise and sleep. Rinse and repeat in an unending cycle of emotional vacuum. Alone.

But when he had her again, he wouldn't be alone anymore. And he'd slake that obdurate sex drive of his with the only one who fueled and quenched it, who satisfied his every taste and need. For a year.

What if it isn't enough? What if you start this and sink so deep you can't climb out again? Last time you almost drowned. You barely survived, with permanent damage.

So be it. He was doing this. Letting go and gorging on every second of her. At whatever risk. He'd never have a real marriage, anyway. His only chance of that had been with her. Now that he'd already experienced the worst, he'd be prepared. At the end of the year, if he still wanted her as unstoppably as he did now, he'd negotiate an extension. And another, and another, until this unquenchable passion died out. It *had* to be extinguished at some point.

What if it only rages higher until it consumes you?

No, it wouldn't.

You're only hoping it won't. Against all evidence.

So what if it did consume him? After six barren years of safeguarding his emotions until they atrophied, of expanding his achievements until they'd swallowed up his existence, not to mention being bored out of his mind and dead inside, maybe it was time to live dangerously. Maybe being consumed wasn't such a bad idea. Or maybe it was, but so what?

He couldn't think of a better way to go.

And as long as he took her with him, he couldn't wait to hurl himself into the inferno.

Though she'd been counting down seconds, Glory's heart still rattled inside her rib cage like a coin inside an empty steel box when her bell rang at five o'clock sharp.

Smoothing hands damp with nervousness over the cool linen of her pants, she took measured steps to the door.

The moment she pulled the door open, she felt like she'd been hit by a car. And that was before she realized how Vincenzo looked. Exactly how he had looked the first time he'd shown up on her doorstep.

Her head spun, her senses stampeded with his effect now, with the reliving of his influence then.

A deepest navy silk suit, offset with a silver-gray shirt of the same spellbinding hue as his eyes, hugged the perfection of his juggernaut body. The thick waves of his hair were brushed back to curl behind his ears and caress his collar, exposing his virile hairline and leonine forehead. He even smelled of that same unique scent. Pine bodywash, cool seabreeze aftershave, fresh minty breath and the musk of his maleness and desire. His scent was so potent, she'd once believed it was an aphrodisiac. Her conviction was renewed.

Had he meant this? To show up on her doorstep like he

had that first day, only a minute after she'd said yes, making her realize he'd been already there? Dressed and groomed exactly like he had been then? The only difference was the maturity that amplified his beauty.

But there was another difference. In his vibe. His glance. His smile. A recklessness. A promise that there would be no rules and no limits.

Vincenzo? The man who had more rules and limits than his scientific experiments and developments? The prince who was forcing her to marry him to abide by his kingdom's social mores?

Maybe her perception was on the fritz. Which made sense. Vincenzo had always managed to blow her fuses. In spite of everything, all she wanted now was to drag him inside and lose herself in his greed and possession, have him reclaim her from the wasteland he'd cast her into, devour her, finish her...

"*Ringrazia Dio* for that way you look at me, *bellissima*...." He walked her back until he had her plastered against the wall. The sunlight slanting into her tiny but cheery foyer dimmed as his breadth blocked out the sun, the world. His aura enveloped her, his hunger penetrating her recesses, yanking at her. "As if you're starving for a taste of me. It would have been excruciating being the only one feeling this way."

Exactly what he'd said to her that first time.

He *was* reenacting that day.

That...that...*bastard!* What was he playing at?

Fury jerked her back from her sensuous stupor, infusing her backbone and voice with steel as she glared up at him. "You would have saved yourself the trip if you'd read my messages."

His hand moved, making her tense all over. His lips tugged as he touched her hair, smoothing it away from her cheek until she almost snatched his hand and pressed it against her flesh.

Then he made the feeling worse, bending to flay her with

his breath and words. "Oh, I read them. And chose to ignore them."

"Your loss." She almost gasped. "Their contents stand, whether you sanction them or not. I'm not going anywhere with you. Just give me whatever ring you have."

He withdrew to pour a devouring look down on her. "I would have gotten one if you'd said yes early this morning."

"Fine. When you get one, send it with one of your lackeys. And email instructions when you require I start advertising your image-cleansing campaign and wearing your 'brand.'"

His gaze melted her on its way down her body, taking in her casual powder-blue top and faded jeans, appreciation coloring the hunger there. "I see you believe you won't go out with me as you're not dressed for the occasion."

"There is no occasion, so I'm dressed in what suits a night at home. Alone."

This time, when his hand moved, it made contact with her flesh. A gossamer sweep with the back of his fingers down her almost combusting cheek. "You need to know that there are column A matters that are not open for negotiation. And then there are column B ones, where we either negotiate, or you can have whatever you like. Picking your ring is smack dab in column A."

Struggling so she wouldn't sink her teeth in his hand before dragging it to her aching breasts, she said, "Wow. You can even make a supposedly gallant gesture coercion."

"And reneging on our agreement is passive aggression."

"What agreement? You mean my stunned silence at your audacity in making an appointment without asking if I'm free?"

His pout was the essence of dismissal. "You're on vacation. I checked."

"I have a life outside of work. A personal life."

His self-satisfied grin made her palm itch for a stinging

connection with his chiseled cheek. "Not anymore. At least, none that doesn't involve me. Do get done with this tantrum so I can take you to pick your ring."

"It's you who's throwing a tantrum by insisting I pick it. Far from casting doubt on your impeccable taste when I asked to pick it, I was just trying to make a point, which I now see is pointless. I don't have any choice and pretending to have one in worthless stuff is just that—worthless. I've admitted it and moved on. So you don't have to prove your largesse by letting me grab a bigger rock, which is clearly what you think this is about."

All teasing evaporated from his eyes. "That didn't even cross my mind. I only want your taste not mine to dictate everything that will be intimate and personal to you."

"Wow. How considerate of you," she scoffed. "We both know you don't give a fig's peel about my opinion. And what intimate and personal things? This ring, and anything else you provide me with, is just a prop. What do I care what you deck me in? It's my role's costume and I'm returning everything at the end of this charade. And speaking of returning stuff, just so you're not worried I might 'lose' anything, or that you'll have to pay a steep premium on insuring it, just get me imitations. No one will dream anything you give me isn't genuine. And it would befit the fakeness of the whole setup."

The darkness on his face suddenly lifted. His eyes and lips resumed their provocation. "I must have been speaking Italian when I said this is nonnegotiable. Must be why we're having this breakdown in communications."

"Since I speak decent Italian—" she ignored his rising eyebrows; she wasn't telling him how and why she did "—it wouldn't have mattered which language you used. No is still my answer. It's the same in both languages."

His contemplation was now smoky, sensuous. "No is unacceptable. Are you prodding me into…persuading you?"

Knowing what kind of persuasion he'd expose her to, she slipped past the barrier of his bulk and temptation, staggered to her foyer's decorative storage cabinet and picked up the prenup. Her hands trembled as she turned and extended it to him.

He took it only when she thrust it against his chest, didn't even look at it, instead staring at her in that incapacitating way of his, his eyes like twin cloudy skies.

"I signed." Her voice was too breathless for her liking.

"I gave it to you to read. Signing would have been in duplicates, with both our legal counsels present."

She shrugged, confused at the note of disapproval—or was it disappointment?—in his voice. "Send me your copy to sign."

His gaze grew ponderous, probing. "Does that mean you didn't find it excessive?"

She huffed bitterly. "You know your Terms of Submission leave *excessive* in another galaxy. You only stop short of making provisions that I turn over the tan I acquire during my time in Castaldini."

"Then why did you sign? Why didn't you ask for changes?"

"You said it was nonnegotiable."

"I thought you'd have your attorney look at it, who'd tell you there's nothing in the world that isn't negotiable. I expected an alphabetized list of deletions and adjustments."

"I don't want any. I don't want *anything* from you. I never did. If you thought I'd haggle over your paranoid terms out of indignation or challenge or whatever, then you know nothing about me. But I already know that. You didn't consider me worth knowing, and I don't expect you to start treating me with any consideration now, when I'm just your smokescreen. So no, I don't care how far you go to protect yourself. This is what I want, too. It makes sure I'm out of your life, with no lingering ties whatsoever, the second the year is up."

Silence crashed in the wake of her ragged words.

Then he drawled, deep and dark, "A year is a long time."

Her pent-up breath rushed out. "Tell me about it. I just want to start serving my sentence with as little resistance as possible, so it will pass with as little damage as possible."

This time his gaze seemed to drill into her, as if to plumb the depths of her thoughts and emotions.

And she felt that he *could* read and sense everything she was thinking and feeling. Which was another new thing.

In the past, she'd always felt this…disconnection, except in the throes of passion. He'd been the classic absent-minded scientist, with his research occupying his fundamental being, only his superficial components engaged in everything else. Now it felt as if his whole being was tuned in to her. And that only deepened her confusion. What was he after?

Just as she tried to activate a two-way frequency to read him, he turned away, laying the prenup on her cabinet before turning back to her in utmost grace and tranquility.

"I'll wait while you put on something suitable for this momentous occasion. Any more stalling and I'll do it myself. I probably should since it's for my pleasure. I can also undress you first, for *our* pleasure. I remember in vivid detail how you used to enjoy both activities."

The avid look in his eyes said he'd carry out his silky threat at the slightest resistance. She couldn't risk it, since she might end up begging him not to stop at undressing her.

Exasperated with both of them in equal measure, her glare told him what would give her utmost pleasure now. Giving his perfect nose some crooked character.

Mumbling abuse, she stormed to her room, with his laughter at her back, sending her temperature into the danger zone.

Half an hour later, when loitering drove *her* to screaming pitch, she exited her room. She found him prowling her living area like a caged panther.

He stopped in midstep, taking in her new outfit. Or her old

one. The cream skirt suit with a satin turquoise blouse was… adequate. Even with stilettos and a purse coordinating with her blouse, it was nowhere near glamorous. But it was the only outfit she'd kept from her corporate days. Her wardrobe now consisted of a minimum of utilitarian clothes. Otherwise she would have never picked this suit. It was what she'd worn to her job interview with him. What she'd gone out with him in when he'd insisted on not wasting time changing. Fate was conspiring for her to take part in his déjà vu scenario.

She couldn't tell if he remembered the suit, since that devouring look he'd had since they'd met again remained unchanged.

Before he could say anything, she preempted him. "In case you find this lacking, too, tough. This is my one and only 'momentous occasion' outfit. You're welcome to check."

"It is a 'momentous occasion' outfit indeed. If only for being…nostalgic of one." So he remembered. Figured. He had a computer-like mind. Their time together must be archived in one of his extensive memory banks. "But we must do something about your wardrobe deficiencies. Your incomparable body must be clothed in only the finest creations. The masters of the fashion world will fall over each other for the chance to have your unique beauty grace theirs."

She just had to snort. "Uh…have you been diagnosed with multiple personality disorder yet? Incomparable body? Unique beauty? What do you call the persona that thinks that?"

He started eliminating the distance between them, intent radiating from him. "If I never told you how I find you breathtaking down to your pores, I need to be punished. Which you are welcome to do. In my defense, I was busy showing you."

"Yeah, before you showed me the door, and told me how interchangeable you found me with any female who wasn't too hideous but meek and willing enough."

"I lied."

His gaze was direct, his words clear, cutting.

Disorientation rolled over her. "You—you did?"

His nod was terse, unequivocal. "Through my teeth."

"Why?"

His lids squeezed, before he opened them, his gaze opaque. "I don't want to go into the reasons. But nothing I said had any basis in truth. Let's leave it at that."

"And to hell with what *I* want. But then, you're getting what you want no matter what I desire or what it costs me. Why do I keep expecting anything different? I must be insane."

He seemed to hold back something impulsive. An elaboration on his cryptic declarations?

But she *needed* something. *Anything.* If what he'd said to her, the words that had torn into her psyche like shrapnel all those years ago, had all been lies, why had he said them? To push her away? Had she been clinging so hard that he'd panicked…?

No. She wasn't rationalizing that son of a bitch's mistreatment. There was no excuse for what he'd done to her. And now he was doing worse. Reeling her closer even as he pushed her away. Confounding her then leaving her hanging. Depriving her of the stability of hating him, the certainty of why she did.

His eyes were blank as he took her coat from her spastic grip, disregarding her bitterness. "We'll have dinner first."

She sullenly let him help her on with her coat, moving away as his arms started to tighten around her. "You're not worried about putting cutlery in my reach?"

His gaze melted with an indulgence that hurt and confused her more than anything else. "I'll take my chances."

"You really expect me to eat after…all this?"

"I'll postpone serving dinner until you're very hungry. By

then, I also hope your appetite for food will overpower that of poking me in the eye with a fork."

With a look that said fat chance, she preceded him out of her condo.

She ignored him as he tried to hand her into the front passenger seat of a gemlike burgundy Jaguar he had parked in her building's garage. He gave up acting the gallant suitor and walked around to take the wheel.

So. No driver, no guards. He wasn't making their liaison public yet. Because he hadn't expected her to sign the prenup, hadn't considered it a done deal? No doubt he'd planned to coerce her some more during this "momentous occasion" until she did. She wondered what recalculation was going on inside that inscrutable mind now that she'd made further manipulation unnecessary.

During the drive, she sat barely breathing or moving so his scent and presence wouldn't scramble her senses even more. Then observations finally seeped into her hazy mind.

They were leaving the city.

When she was certain this was no roundabout way to any restaurant or jeweler, she forced herself to turn to him.

"Where are we going?"

Still presenting her with the perfection of his profile, he smiled. "To the airport."

Five

"The airport?"

At her croak, Vincenzo's smile widened. "We're going to have dinner on the jet. We'll fly to where the most exclusive collection of jewelry on the planet awaits you, so you can pick your ring, and anything else that catches your fancy."

He was so pleased with himself for stunning her again.

She was more than stunned. She was working on a stroke.

"And it didn't occur to you to ask if I'd agree to this hare-brained scheme of yours?"

His lips twitched at her venom. "A man going out of his way to surprise his fiancée doesn't tell her in advance of the details of his efforts."

Her jaw muscles hurt at his mention of *fiancée*. "Do save your 'efforts' for when you have a real fiancée."

"But you already said I can't have a real one for all the money and power in the world."

"Who knows? Lots of women have self-destructive tendencies. And I didn't say you couldn't get one, I said you wouldn't keep her."

His eyes twinkled with mischief before he turned onto a route she'd never seen into the airport, and she'd been here countless times. "Well, you're real enough for me. And for as long as I keep you, I get to go all-out to surprise you."

She harrumphed. "Save your energy. And save me from a stroke. I hate surprises. I haven't met one that wasn't nasty. Certainly never any from you."

He sighed. "I assure you, this trip is anything but."

"I don't care what it will be like. It's the concept I can't stand." She exhaled exasperatedly. "And to think I once thought you were part bulldozer."

He slowed down as he took a turn, his eyebrows rising in amused query. "You changed your mind?"

"Yes. You're the pure breed."

And he did something that almost made her head explode.

He threw *his* head back and let out a hearty guffaw.

When she felt he'd scrambled her nervous system forever, he turned to her, chuckles still reverberating deep in his endless chest, his smile wider than she'd ever seen it.

"Watch it with the laughter, Vincenzo," she mumbled, hating it that he affected her to extremes no matter what he was doing. "Doing something so unnatural to you can be dangerous. You'll dislocate a brain lobe or something."

His laugh boomed again. "*Dio,* I can get used to this."

"Your highness hasn't been exposed to sarcasm before? Figures, with all the syrupy ass-kissing you have everywhere you turn. Since you've been exposed to it from birth, you must have always had social juvenile diabetes."

"I was wrong. I'm already too used to getting lashed with your delightful tongue. I hope you won't ever hold it."

"I think it's a physical impossibility with you around."

He chuckled again, this time doing something even more

distressing. He reached out for her hand and brought it to his lips.

His lips. Those lips that had enslaved her with their possession, that had taught her passion and the pleasure her body was capable of experiencing. The moment they touched the back of her hand, her heart almost ruptured.

She snatched her hand back as if from open fire, agitation searing her insides. "I don't know what you're playing at…"

"I already told you my game plan." His eyes turned serious as he brought the car to a stop and turned to her. "But I've also come to a new decision. I no longer care how this started…"

"I do."

"…I only care that when I'm with you I feel…great. I haven't felt like that in… I don't even remember if I ever felt like that. You invigorate me. Your every word and look thrills me, and I don't intend to keep holding back and not show it. If you tickle my humor, and you do, constantly, I'll laugh. And I want you to do the same. Forget how we got to be here…"

"Because you blackmailed me."

"…and just make the best of it. If you enjoy my company…"

"I'm not a fan of Stockholm syndrome, thank you."

"…just allow yourself the enjoyment, don't stifle it and don't keep telling yourself why you should hold it back."

"Easy for you to say and do. You're not the one being threatened with your family's imprisonment and taken hostage for a year. *And* being kidnapped right now."

His eyes grew coaxing. "You are my partner in an endeavor I'm undertaking to serve my kingdom." The word *partner,* the term he'd once said would never apply to her, scratched like a talon against her heart. "You will help me bridge its distance from the world to benefit its people and the coming generations. And you're the fiancée I'm taking on a surprise trip. I will do everything in my power so you will enjoy it."

The wish that all that could be true overwhelmed her, closing her throat. "That's the facade hiding the ugly truth."

"It *is* the truth, if you don't dwell on the negative aspects."

"Negative aspects? Now, that's an innovative euphemism for *extortion*."

He didn't segue into a rejoinder this time. His gaze lengthened, grew distant, as if he was looking inward.

Seeming to come back to her, he exhaled. "Would you marry me if I took your family out of the equation?"

It was her turn to stare. "You mean I can say no and you wouldn't report them?"

"Yes."

He looked and sounded serious. Yeah. Sure.

"I don't believe you."

"Understandable. I don't believe myself, either." His headshake was self-deprecation itself. "But I do mean it."

"Is this a ploy to put me at ease? So I'll stop giving you a much deserved, not to mention much needed, hard time? So I'll stop resisting and 'come to your bed'?"

"Yes. No. Definitely." At her frown, he elaborated. "Yes, I want to put you at ease, though it's not a ploy. No, I don't want you to stop bashing me on the head. With the way I'm relishing it, I'm realizing how much I do need it. And I'm definitely anticipating you in my bed...." His arm snaked around her, pulled her into his heat and hardness, enervating her with the delight of his feel and scent. "I'm willing to do whatever it takes to have you racing me there as you used to."

Her head fell back as she stared at him, sounding as faint as she felt. "Even if it means not using your winning hand?"

"I already said it had nothing to do with our intimacies."

"How can I be sure you won't hurt my family if I say no?"

"How were you sure I wouldn't after you said yes? I guess you'll have to trust me."

"I don't." She'd trusted him before. Look where it had gotten her.

"We're even, then."

What? What did that mean?

Before she could voice her puzzlement, he pressed her harder, cupped her face, and her questions combusted at the feel of the warm, powerful flesh cradling hers. "Don't say anything now. Let's forget everything and go with the flow. Let me give us tonight."

Tonight. The word reverberated between them, sweeping through her, uprooting the tethers of her resolve and aversion. His lips were half a breath away, filling her lungs with his intoxication.

She hated that she yearned for his taste and urgency and dominance, but she did. How she did. The need screwed tighter, squeezing her vitals, strangling them. Everything that would assuage the craving gnawing her hollow was a tug away, on his lapel, his hair. Then he would give her everything she needed.

But she couldn't do it. Literally. She couldn't move a muscle. And he was giving her the choice of the first move. He wouldn't take that out of her hands, too. When that was where she needed him to leave her no choice.

Leave it to him to do the opposite of what she wanted.

Annoyance spurted, infusing her limpness with tension.

With a look acknowledging that he wouldn't get a cease-fire that easily, and with a last annihilating stroke across her stinging lips, he pulled back.

In moments he'd stepped down from the car and come around to her door. She almost clung to him for support as he handed her down. The coolness of twilight after the warmth

of the vehicle sprouted goose bumps all over her, adding to
her imbalance.

Then every concern evaporated as she gaped. Up.

They were beneath a massive jetliner that looked like a
giant alien bird of prey. This was his jet?

The next moment left no doubt as he took her elbow and
led her to the Air Force One–style stairs that led from the
tarmac to the inside of the jet.

Once inside, her jaw dropped further. She'd been on private
jets before, though never his. Another proof of how marginal
she'd been to him, when he'd been the center of her universe.
But any other jets she'd seen paled in comparison.

She turned sarcastic eyes up to him. "It's clear you believe in going the extra hundred million in pursuit of luxury."

He smiled down at her. "I wouldn't say I go that far."

She looked pointedly around. "I'd say you go beyond."

His smile remained unrepentant. "I travel a lot, with staff.
I have meetings on board. I need space and convenience."

"Tell me about your need for those." She waited until she
got a "so we won't stop dredging up the past, eh?" look, then
added more derision. "And you must have yet another castle
in the sky to accommodate both 'needs,' huh?"

"My family's being the first one on terra firma?"

"And the third being the futuristic headquarters in New
York. Next, I'll find out you have a space station and a couple
of pyramids. Hang on…"

She got out her phone.

He gave her a playful tug, plastering her to his side. "What
are you doing now?"

Squeezing her legs tighter against the new rush of heat,
she cocked her head up at him. "Just estimating how many
thousands of children this sickeningly blatant status symbol
could feed, clothe and educate for years."

He tipped his head back and his laughter boomed, sending her heartbeats scattering all over the jet's lush carpeting.

"*Dio,* will I ever come close to guessing what you'll say next?" He still chuckled as he led her through a meeting area, where staff hovered in the background, to the spiral staircase leading to the upper deck. "So you consider this jet too pretentious? A waste of money better spent on worthy causes?"

"Any personal 'item' with a price tag the length of a phone number ranges from ludicrously to criminally wasteful."

"Even if it's a utility that I use to make millions of dollars more, money I do use to benefit humanity at large?"

"By advancing science, protecting the environment and creating jobs? Yeah. You forget how I started my working life. I've heard all the arguments. And seen all the tax write-offs."

"But you started your working life with me, so you know I'm not in this to make money or to flaunt my power or status."

"Do I? Solid experience has taught me that I know nothing about the real you."

He didn't answer that as he walked her across an ultrachic foyer and through a door that he opened via a fingerprint-recognition module. It whirred shut as he let her lead him into what had to be the ultimate in airborne private quarters.

The sheer opulence hit her with more evidence of the world he existed in. The world he now maintained she could choose to enter, or not.

He guided her to one of the tan leather couches by huge oval windows and tugged her down with him. She hit the soft surface and it shifted to accommodate her body in the plushest medium she'd ever sat on. Not that she could enjoy the sensation with his body touching hers, making her feel split down the middle, with the half touching him burning and the other half freezing.

She tried to ignore him and her rioting senses by looking

around the grand lounge drenched in golden lights, earth tones and the serenity of sumptuousness and seclusion. At the far end of the huge space that spanned the breadth of the jet, a wall was decorated in intricate designs from the blend of cultures that made up Castaldini: Roman, Andalusian and Moorish. A double door led to another area. No doubt a bedroom suite.

A ghost of a touch zapped through her like a thousand volts. His finger feathering against her face, turning it to his.

"Regarding the 'real me,' as you put it," he said, his eyes simmering in the golden lighting. "If you insist you don't know him, let me rectify this." He sank deeper into the couch, taking her with him until their heads leaned on the headrest, their faces close enough for her to get lost in the pattern of his incredible irises. "The real me is a nerd who happens to have been born in a royal family then inherited lots of money. He owes not squandering said fortune on his research and impractical ideas to the teachers he's been blessed with, who tutored him in business practices, and directed his research and resources into money-making products and facilities. He, alas, never had the temperament or desire to become a corporate mogul."

"Yet 'he' became one, and as ruthless as they come." To her chagrin, her denunciation sounded like a cooing endearment.

"'He' basically found himself one. And I must contest the ruthless part. Though 'he' makes too much money, it's not by adopting cold-blooded bottom-line practices. It just happens that the methods those people taught him are that efficient."

Her own fundamental fairness got the best of her. "No one could have helped you make a cent, let alone such a sustained downpour, if you hadn't come up with something so ingeniously applicable and universally useful."

"And I wouldn't have gotten any of that translated into reality without those people."

Her heart hammered at his earnest words. At the memories they exhumed.

She'd once poured all her time and effort into providing him with a comprehensive plan for his future operations. He'd already had an exceptional head for business when he applied his off-the-charts IQ to it, but it hadn't been his specialty or his focus. And he *had* had some unrealistic views and expectations when it came to translating his science into practice. So she'd insisted on educating him in what would come after the breakthrough, how his R&D and manufacturing departments would sync and work at escalating efficiency and productivity to streamline operations and maximize profit.

That had been another of the injustices he'd dealt her as he'd discarded her, evaluating her only based on her sexual role, as if she'd never offered him anything else. That had cut deeper into her the more she'd dwelled on it. It had taken her a long time to recover her sense of self-worth.

She bet he didn't count her among those teachers fate had blessed him with.

A finger ran gently down her cheek. "You're at the top of the list of those people."

She blinked. He admitted that?

"I owe you for most of the bad decisions I didn't make before the good ones I did make."

Her heart stumbled, no longer knowing how hard or fast to beat, thoughts and emotions yo-yoing so hard she felt dizzy.

She shook her head as if to stop the fluctuations. "Is this admission part of your efforts to 'put me at ease'?"

"It's the truth."

"Not according to you six years ago. Or forty-eight hours ago."

His eyes misted with something like melancholy. "It's not the whole truth, granted." Now, what did *that* mean? "But I'm sick and tired of pretending this didn't happen, that there were no good parts. There were…incredible parts. And no matter why you offered me this guidance, you did offer it, and I did use it to my best advantage, so…*grazie mille, bellissima.*"

This time she gaped at him for what felt like an hour.

What did this confounding man want to do to her? Was he truly suffering from a multiple personality disorder? What else could explain his contradictions?

But he'd already said he wouldn't explain. So there was no use pursuing it.

Deciding not to give him the satisfaction of a response to his too-late, too-little thanks, she cast a look around. "I still think this level of luxury is criminal."

His smile dawned again, incinerating all in its path. "Sorry to shoot down your censure missiles, but this isn't my jet. It's the Castaldinian Air Force One." So her earlier observation was true! "Ferruccio put it at my disposal as soon as I told him of you, in his efforts to see me hitched…ASAP."

As he grinned as if at a private joke, something inside her snapped.

She whacked him on the arm, hard.

His eyebrows shot up in surprise that became hilarity, and then he was letting out peal after peal of laughter.

"Had your joke at my expense?" she seethed.

"I was actually basking in your abuse," he spluttered.

"Why didn't you say you developed masochistic tendencies in your old age? You don't need to manipulate me into obliging your perversion. The desire to shower abuse on your unfeeling head is my default setting." She'd bet her glare would have withered rock. That hunk of unfeeling male perfection only chuckled harder. She attempted a harder verbal volley. "That this jet isn't yours doesn't exonerate you. You probably have your own squadron that puts it to shame. But apparently you're so cheap you'd rather use state property and funds."

"Damned if I do and if I don't, eh?" He didn't seem too

upset about it, but looked like she'd just praised him heartily as he picked up her hand and brought it to his lips. "Sheathe your claws, my azure-eyed lioness."

She gritted her teeth as his lips moved against her knuckles. "Why? Didn't you just discover that you relish being ripped to shreds?"

He sighed his enjoyment. "Indeed. But it works better when you're slamming me over my real flaws. Being pretentious and exploitative isn't among my excesses and failings. If you think so then you haven't kept abreast with my pursuits."

That made her snort. "You mean you think it's possible to avoid those? When your face and exploits are plastered everywhere I go? You even come out of the faucet when I turn it on. My building has turned to your services for heating."

His laugh cracked out again.

In spite of wanting to smack him again, that sense of fairness still prodded her to add, "But among all that obnoxious overexposure, I do know your corporations have substantial and varied aid programs."

That seemed to surprise him. "The world at large doesn't know about this side of my activities. I wonder how you knew."

Her smirk told him two could play at withholding answers. "It's I who wonders what you're after with all the discreet philanthropy. Are you playing at being Bruce Wayne? If you are, all that's left is for you to don the cape, mask and tights..." She paused as his laughter escalated again then mumbled, "Since making you feel great is nonexistent on my list of priorities, I'll shut up now."

He leaned closer until his lips brushed her temple. He didn't kiss her, just talked against her flesh. "I'd beg you not to. I don't think I can live now without being bombarded by the shrapnel that keeps flying out of your mouth."

She kept said mouth firmly closed.

To incite another salvo—she was sure—his lips moved to the top of her cheekbone, in the most languid, heart-melting kiss.

She jumped to her feet, nerves jangling.

He was somehow on his feet before her, blocking her way. "If you're not going to abuse me, how about you use your mouth for something else?" He waited until her chagrin seethed and blasted out of her in a searing glare before adding in provocative pseudo innocence, "Eat?"

"It's safer for you if I'm not near cutlery tonight."

"Nonsense. I'm not in the least worried. What's the worst you could do with disposable ones?"

This was beyond weird. Had he always had a sense of humor, but just hadn't turned it on in her presence? Why did he have it perpetually on now?

Giving up trying to understand this baffling entity, yet refusing to give him an answer, she turned away, headed to the lavatory. She needed a breather before the next round.

When she came out, she faltered, trying to breathe around a lump that materialized in her throat.

He'd taken off his jacket. And had undone a few buttons on his shirt. And rolled up his sleeves.

It probably wouldn't affect her any more if he'd taken off all his clothes. Okay, it would, but this was bad enough. The imagination that was intimate with his every inch was filling in the spaces, or rather, taking off the rest of his clothes.

He smiled that slow smile of his, no doubt noting the drool spreading at her feet. Then he extended that beautifully formed—and from experience, very talented—hand in invitation.

She covered the space between them as if by his will alone, unable to stop devouring his magnificence.

Reality again outstripped imagination or memory. The breadth and power of his shoulders and chest had owed nothing to tailoring. They were even magnified now that they were covered only in a layer of finest silk. His arms bulged with strength and symmetry under the material that obscured and highlighted at once. Those corded forearms dusted with black hair tapered to solid wrists. His abdomen was hard, his waist narrow, as were his hips, before his thighs flowed with strength and virility on the way down to endless legs.

Magnificent wasn't even a fitting description.

He sat back down on the couch, patting where he wanted her to sit. On his lap.

She wanted to. To just lose her mind all over him, let him seduce her, own her, drain her of will and blow her mind with pleasure, again and again and again, for as long as it took him to have enough of her this time, and to hell with caution and the lessons of harsh experience.

Before she decided to take a flying jump into the abyss, he engulfed her hand in the warm power of his and gave a tug that was persuasion and urgency itself. She tumbled over him, her skirt riding up as her thighs splayed to straddle him.

The moment she felt him against her, between her legs, the rock hardness and heat of his chest and his erection pressing against her breast and core, arousal surged so fiercely she almost fainted. Then his lips opened over her neck, and she did swoon, melting over him.

His hands convulsed in the depths of her hair, harnessing her for his devouring as his mouth took pulls of her flesh, as if he'd suck her heartbeats, her essence into him. Her head fell back, arching her neck, giving him fuller access, surrendering her wariness and heartache to his pleasuring.

She needed this, needed him, come what may.

"You feel and taste even better than all the memories that tormented me, *Gloria mia*."

She jerked and moaned when he said her name the way he used to, Italianizing it, making it his. It inflamed her to hear it, maddened her. The way he moved against her, breathed her in, touched and kneaded and suckled her…it was all too much. And too little. She needed more. Everything. His mouth and hands and potency all over her, inside her.

"Vincenzo…"

The same desperation reverberating inside her emanated from his great body in shock waves. Then he heaved beneath her, swept her around, brought her under him on the couch, bore down on her with all of his greed and urgency. Spreading her thighs, he hooked them around his hips, pressed between them, his daunting hardness grinding against her entrance through their clothes. Her back arched deeply to accommodate him, a cry escaping from her very recesses, at the yearned-for feel of him, weight of him, sight of him as propped himself above her, his eyes molten steel with the vehemence of his passion.

"Gloriosa, divina, Gloria mia…"

Then he swooped down and his lips clamped on hers, moist, branding, his tongue thrusting deep, singeing her with pleasure, breaching her with need, draining her of moans and reason. Pressure built—behind her eyes, inside her chest, deep in her loins. Her hands convulsed on his arms, digging into his muscles, everything inside her surging, gushing, needing anything…anything he'd do to her. His fingers and tongue and teeth exploiting her every secret, his manhood filling the void at her core, thrusting her to oblivion….

"We'll be taking off in five minutes, *Principe*."

The voice rang in a metallic echo, not registering in the delirium. It was only when he stopped his plundering kisses that it crashed into her awareness, that it made sense.

He froze over her for a long moment, his lips still fused to hers. He moved again, took her lips over and over in urgent, clinging kisses as if he couldn't help himself, as if he was gulping what he could of her taste before he could have no more. Then muttering something savage under his breath, he severed their meld, groaning as if was scraping off his skin. It was how she felt, too, as his body separated from hers.

She lay back, stunned, unable to move. Dismay at the barely aborted insanity drenched her, even as need still hammered at her, demanding his assuagement. His heavy-lidded gaze regarded her in denuding intensity, as if savoring the sight of what he'd done to her. Then he reached for her, caressed and kneaded her as he helped her up on the couch.

He secured her seat belt before buckling his as the engines, which she realized had been on for a while now, revved higher and the jet started moving.

They were really taking off.

Everything was going out of control, too far, too fast.

And she had no idea where they were going. Figuratively and literally.

The latter had a definite answer. And in an existence that had no answers, past or future, she had to have at least that.

"Where are we going?"

At her unsteady question, he pulled her closer, his eyes blazing with unspent desire. "How about we keep it a surprise?"

"How about I go demand that your pilot drop me off?"

He tutted. "I see I have to surprise you with no warning next time."

"Since you can't take me somewhere without warning unless you develop teleportation, too..."

"Or kidnap you for real and keep you tied up and gagged on the way."

"...then get a *real* surprise when you finally untie and ungag me. Something broken or bitten off or both."

Looking even more aroused and elated, he gathered her tighter, put his lips to her ear, nipped her lobe and whispered, "We're going to Castaldini."

Six

Glory had one thought. That she wasn't going to repeat his words. No matter how flabbergasted she was that he'd said…

"Castaldini."

God. *No.* He was making her echo his declarations like a malfunctioning playback.

She pushed out of his arms, whacked him on both this time, as hard as she could.

"No, we're *not* going to Castaldini," she hissed.

He caught his lower lip in beautiful white teeth, wincing in evident enjoyment at her violence, rubbing the sting of her blow as if to drive it deeper, not away. "Why not?"

She barely held from whacking him again. "Because you conned me."

"I did no such thing."

"When you said we were flying, I assumed it would be to another city or at most another state."

"Am I responsible for your faulty assumptions? I gave

you all the clues, said I'm taking you where the most exclusive jewelry on the planet awaits you. Where did you think that was?"

"I didn't realize you were playing Trivial Pursuit at the time. And why go all this way for a ring? What's that hyperbole about Castaldinian jewelry? Is that exaggerated national pride where you claim everything in Castaldini is the best in history?"

"I don't know about everything, but I'm pretty sure Castaldini's royal jewels are as exclusive as it gets."

"Castaldini's royal j—" Her teeth clattered shut before she completed parroting this latest piece of astounding info. Shock surged back a moment later. "You can't be serious! I can't wear a ring from Castaldini's freaking royal jewels!"

"*You* can't be serious thinking my bride would wear anything else."

"I'm not your bride. I'm your decoy. And that only for a year. But as you said, a year can be a very long time. I can't take the responsibility for something that…that priceless…." She pushed his hands away when they attempted to draw her back into his embrace. "For God's sake, during the height of Castaldini's economic problems, before King Ferruccio was crowned, people were saying that if only Castaldini sold half of those jewels, they'd settle the national debt!"

"Oh, I did propose the solution. But Castaldinians would rather sell their firstborns."

"And you want me to wear a ring from a collection that revered, for any reason, let alone a charade? You expect me to walk around wearing a kingdom's legacy on my finger?"

"That's exactly what you'll do as my bride. In fact, you yourself will be a new national treasure. Now that's settled…"

"Nothing's settled," she spluttered, feeling she was in a whirlpool that dragged her deeper the more she struggled. "I won't go to Castaldini. Now tell your pilot to turn back."

A look came into his eyes that made her itch to hit him again. One of *such* patient reasonableness. "You knew you'd go to Castaldini sooner rather than later."

"I thought you said I could say no to your blackmail."

His nod was equanimity itself. "I said I wouldn't expose your family if you said no. But if you say yes, I'll make sure they will never be exposed."

Ice crept into her veins again. "Wh-what do you mean?"

"They've committed too many crimes. It's only a matter of time before someone finds out what I have. Marry me and I'll do everything in my power to wipe their trail clean."

"That's just another roundabout blackmail."

"Actually, it's the opposite. Before, I said I'd hurt them if you say no. Now I'm saying I'll help them if you say yes."

Her head spun, her thoughts tangling like a ball of twine after a wicked cat had gotten to it. He was the feline to her own cornered mouse.

"I don't see how that's different. And even if I say yes…"

He caught her hands, pressed them into the heat of his steel muscles. "Say it, *Gloria mia*. Give me your consent."

"Even if I do…"

"Do it. Say you'll be my bride."

She squirmed away from his intensity. "Okay, okay, yes. Dude, you're pushy."

He huffed mockingly. "Such eagerness. Such graciousness."

"If you think I owe you either, you're out of your zillion-IQ mind. And this doesn't mean anything's changed. Or that's it's not still under duress. It certainly doesn't mean I consent to going to Castaldini now."

He sat back, all tension leaving his body, a look of gratification sweeping across his breathtaking face. "Give me one reason why you're so against going."

She had to blink to clear the glaze of hypnosis from her eyes. "I can give you a volume as thick as your prenup."

"One incontestable reason should suffice. And 'because I don't want to' doesn't count."

"Of course what I want doesn't count. You made *that* clear."

His pout made her want to drag him down and sink her teeth into those lips that had just reinjected his addiction into her system. "I made it clear that I changed my mind, about many things. Be flexible and change yours."

"I don't owe you any flexibility, either. I let you steamroll me by letting me think this was going to be a short trip inside my country. I didn't sign on to leave it."

"As my bride, you will leave it. Though not forever."

"Yeah, only for a one-year term. But I get to choose when that will begin."

"I meant you'd always be free to return, to go anywhere. This time, you can go back to New York tomorrow if you wish."

"I don't want to leave New York in the first place. I can't just hop to another country!"

"Why not? You do that all the time in your work."

"Well, this isn't work. And speaking of work, I can't drop everything with no notice."

"You're on vacation, remember?"

"I have other things to do besides work."

"Like what?" He met her fury with utmost serenity.

"Okay, I changed my mind, too. You're not a bulldozer. You're an ocean. You'd erode mountains. No, a tsunami. You uproot everything, subside only with everything submerged under your control."

He chuckled. "As much as I enjoy having you dissect and detail my vices, food is becoming a pressing issue. I had the chef prepare favorite dishes from Castaldini for you to sample."

Her hands itched to tweak that dimpled cheek, hard. "Don't change the subject."

Ignoring her, he undid his seat belt, then leaned into her, undoing hers. "You really shouldn't risk me getting any hungrier—in every way."

Her gaze slid to the evidence of one hunger and...whoa.

She tore her gaze up, only to slam into his watchful, knowing, enticing one. Gasping with the need to explore him, she said, "Even in food you're giving me no choice."

He separated from her lingeringly, pushing buttons in a panel by the couch. It was still only when he stood up that she realized they were cruising steadily.

"I am. *My* choice is to feast on you and to hell with food. I'm giving you the choice to avoid what you really want by choosing food, for now."

She bit back a retort. It would be silly to deny his assessment, when only the pilot's announcement had saved her from being wrapped around him naked right now, begging for—and taking—everything.

Exasperated with both of them, she ignored his inviting hand to rise and walk to where he indicated. Behind a screen of gorgeous lacelike woodwork at the far end of the lounge by the closed quarters was a stunning table-for-two setup.

Though everything in the compartment felt like authentic masterpieces, with the distinctive designs of seventeenth- or eighteenth-century Castaldini, the furniture was discreetly mounted on rails embedded in the fuselage. Exquisite, delicately carved, polished mahogany chairs were upholstered in burgundy glossy-on-matte floral-patterned silk. The matching round table was draped in the most intricate beige tape-lace tablecloth she'd ever seen, set over longer burgundy organza, with its pattern echoing the stunning hand-painted china laid out on top. Lit candles, crystal glasses, a vase with a conflagration of burgundy and cream roses, linen napkins, silver cutlery and a dozen other accents—all monogrammed with the royal insignia of Castaldini—completed the breathtaking arrangement.

She looked up at him as he slid the chair back for her. "I somehow can't imagine King Ferruccio here."

His eyebrows rose as he sat across her. "You mean you still think it's my jet?"

It hadn't occurred to her to doubt that or anything else he'd said. She'd believed his every word, declaration and promise.

Which was only more proof that fools never, ever learned.

She sighed. "It's not that. The rest of the jet is so grand, befitting a king and then some. But *this* setting is too…"

"Intimate?" he chimed in when she made a stymied gesture around the dreamily lit space. "Your senses are on the money. This section was designed by Clarissa as her and Ferruccio's mile-high love nest."

Glory's simmering heat shot up, imagining all the pleasure that could be had here, and feeling she was intruding on someone's privacy. "You sure he's okay with you invading it?"

"He scanned my fingerprint into the controls."

"Let me put it this way, then. Are you sure he cleared it with Queen Clarissa?"

"What I'm sure of is if he didn't, he'd love to be punished for his unsanctioned actions."

Her lips twitched as she imagined the regal figure of King Ferruccio being spanked by his fair queen. "Another D'Agostino with a fetish for female abuse?"

"Ferruccio would let Clarissa step dance all over him and beg for more. But since she's part angel, she doesn't take advantage of his submissive affliction where she's concerned."

His expression softened as he talked about his queen and cousin. Though she'd been a princess first, the previous king's daughter, not much had been known about Clarissa before she became the illegitimate king's queen. Ever since their marriage, she'd become one of the most romantic royal figures in history. Glory had heard only great things about her.

It still twisted her gut to feel Vincenzo's deep fondness for the woman, to witness evidence that he was capable of such tender affections. What he hadn't felt for her. What she hadn't aroused in him.

Oblivious to her sudden plunge in mood, he smiled. "And speaking of access…"

He pushed a button on a panel by the huge oval window to his side. The door of the lounge whispered open. In moments, half a dozen waiters dressed in burgundy-and-black uniforms, with the royal emblem embroidered on their chests in gold, walked in a choreographed queue into the dining compartment.

She smiled back at them as they began arranging their burdens on the table and on the service station a few feet away. Even though domes covered the trays, the aromas struck directly to her vacant-since-she-read-Vincenzo's-email stomach, making it lament loudly.

His lips spread at the sound, his beauty supernatural in the candlelight. "Good to know you've worked up another appetite." The word *another* came out like a caress to her most intimate flesh. He was playing her body like the virtuoso he was. "Bodes well for your being more interested in food than using me for target practice."

"I see you failed to acquire harmless tableware. But you like living dangerously, don't you?" She picked up a fork, gauging its weight and center of gravity as if to estimate a perfect throw. "I mean, silver? Isn't that deadly to your kind?"

He sat back in his chair, spreading his great body, as if to let her to take aim wherever she pleased. "If I was the kind you refer to, wouldn't I be 'undying' dangerously?"

And she realized something terrible.

She was…enjoying this. This duel of words and wills. She found it exhilarating.

It shocked her because she'd never experienced anything quite like it. Certainly never with him. She'd once loved him with all her heart, lusted after him until it hurt, but she'd never really *enjoyed* being with him. Enjoyment necessitated ease, humor, and those and so much more had been missing from his life. He'd been too tense, too *in*tense, in work and in passion. She'd felt only towering yet turbulent emotions while he was around.

Now, this new him was just plain…*fun*.

Fun? The man who was more or less kidnapping her and making her marry him temporarily under terrible conditions and for all the wrong reasons while seducing her out of her mind just because he could?

Yeah. He was doing all that. And was still fun with a capital *F*. It made everything she felt for him even fiercer.

Had she caught his masochistic tendencies? Or maybe she was developing Stockholm syndrome after all?

Again unaware of her turmoil, he pursued their latest topic. "In the interest of not turning to dust if you fling something my way while you attempt to crack open the crab…" He took the fork from her, gathered the rest of her cutlery and placed them on the tray of a retreating waiter.

Admitting that there was no denying, or fighting, the enjoyment, she decided to go with the flow. As he'd recommended earlier, in what felt like another life.

She eyed him in derision. "You could have left me the spoon. It poses minimal danger, certainly a lesser one than the mess I'll make as I slurp soup directly from the bowl and wipe sauce off the plate with my fingers."

"Mess away." Another button had his chair circling the table, bringing him a breath away. "I'll lick you clean."

Leaving her struggling with another bout of arrhythmia, he leaned across her then lifted silver covers bearing Castaldini's royal insignia in repoussé, uncovering serving plates and bowls simmering over gentle flames. Her salivary glands gushed with the combination of aromas—his and the food's. He filled a bowl with heavenly smelling soup, garnishing it with dill and croutons. Then he reached across the table for his spoon.

Dipping it in the steaming depths, he scooped a spoonful then brought it to his lips. Pursing them slowly, sensuously, he blew a cooling breath over the thick creaminess. It rippled, just like the waves of arousal inside her.

Her nerves reverberated like plucked strings as he drew her to his side, no longer knowing if she felt her heart or his booming inside her rib cage. Then he lifted the spoon to her lips. They opened involuntarily, accepting his offering. She gulped down the delicious, rich liquid, moaning at the taste, at his ministrations. *Vincenzo was feeding her.*

Then he was kissing her, plumbing her depths with wrenching possession, as if he'd drink her up, gulping down her moans as they poured from her, growling the fervor of his endearments and enjoyment inside her. *"Meravigliosa, deliziosa…"*

Her stomach made another explicit protest.

He pulled back, his eyes on fire, his smile teasing. "So the flesh is willing, but the stomach is even more so. Will you stop looking so delicious so I can feed you?"

Unable to do anything but keep her head against his shoulder and her body ensconced in the security and delight of his, she sighed. "So, it's my doing now?"

"Everything is your doing, *gloriosa mia.* Everything."

For all the indulgence in which he'd said that, it confused her. For it didn't feel like a joke. Yet all she could do was surrender to his pampering and marvel at what a difference a few hours could make. She'd started this bent on resisting to the end. Now look at her. Her mind was shutting down, her will raising the white flag. And why not?

This, whatever this was, wouldn't last. But she knew that this time. She'd been forewarned, should be forearmed against any pain and disillusion. And it felt so good. The best she'd ever felt. Why not just revel in it?

Even at the cost of untold damages later? Maybe it couldn't be survived this time?

She gazed into his gorgeous eyes, let his spell topple the last pillar of her sanity, and had to face what she'd never wanted to admit. She'd missed him like she would a vital organ. The accumulated longing was only exacerbated by the new appreciation that was taking her over.

So yes. She'd take this journey with him. At any cost.

"We'll be landing in minutes, *Principe*."

The announcement made Glory do a triple take over Vincenzo's shoulder at the wall clock in the distance.

It was nine hours since they'd come on board already?

Time had never flown so imperceptibly. So pleasurably. She hadn't felt sleepy all through the flight, only deliciously languorous yet energized at once, each passing minute electrified, alive.

And here they were. Landing in a place she'd never been, and till forty-eight hours ago had thought, for too many reasons, she'd never be. His homeland. A land of vivid legend and unique tradition.

Castaldini.

She'd been so engrossed in Vincenzo and their newfound affinity she hadn't once looked outside the window as the pilot had periodically announced the landmarks they were flying over. She was now draped half over Vincenzo, one leg held in a possessive hand over his thighs, her face inches from his as they lay back on a now-reclined couch, gazing at each other, luxuriating in chatting and bickering and just relishing the hell out of each other.

Giving her thigh a gentle squeeze, he leaned in for another of those barely leashed kisses that had been scrambling her coherence, then withdrew with a regretful sigh. "Though I think some fuses inside me will burn out when I do, I have to take my hands off you. You need to see this. Castaldini from the air is breathtaking."

He untangled them and took her with him as he sat up, opening the shutter on the window behind them. He stood behind her as she rose to her knees and bent forward to peer down at his homeland. But she registered nothing but him as he pressed against her, one hand pulling her back into his hardness, the other moving the mass of her hair aside to caress her back and buttocks. All she wanted was to thrust back at him, beg him to end the torment that had been building for hours, years, plunge inside her as she knelt like that, vulnerable, open. She wished he would plummet them into delirium as they descended into his domain and the limited time they'd have together.

He bent over her until he was covering her back then suckled her earlobe, pouring his seduction right into her brain. "See this, *gloriosa mia?* This is where I'm going to make you mine again, this land that's as glorious as you are."

Everything inside her throbbed like an inflamed nerve, screaming for his invasion, his domination. "So you took your hands off me, only to substitute them with your whole body."

"Don't tell me, tell your body." His hand twisted in her hair, harnessing her as he suckled her neck, thrust against her, mimicking the act of possession. "It's operating mine remotely. It must want to keep my fuses intact, needs them fully functional." She was way past contesting this. With the way she'd been responding to his every touch, inviting more, she wondered how he hadn't taken her yet. Or why. He nipped her jaw, which sent another shock wave of need spasming in her core. "Now look."

It took moments to focus on the sight beneath her through the crimson haze of arousal. The place where she would come to life again, in his arms, in his orbit, however briefly.

And it was as he'd said. Breathtaking. Glorious.

The island gleamed like a collection of multifaceted jewels in the early afternoon sun. Jade masses of palm and olive trees, ruby and garnet rooftops on amber and moonstone houses, obsidian roads. White-gold beaches surrounded everything and were hugged in turn by the gradations of a turquoise-and-emerald Mediterranean.

Her chest tightening with elusive longing, she turned amazed eyes to him. "How can you leave this place, and stay away so long?"

Relief flared in his eyes, as if he'd been worried about her response. As if she could feel anything but wonder at beholding this magnificence.

"Wait until you see it at ground level." He turned her around, sat both of them down, buckled them in and brought her hands to his lips with a contemplative sigh. "But you're right. I was here too little for too many years."

"And now you're taking the UN post, you're going to be anywhere but here." And they wouldn't be here for their year of marriage.

As if feeling her disappointment, he shook his head. "We'll come here often and stay as long as possible each time. We can stay for a good while now. Would you like that?"

Vincenzo was asking her if she'd like to stay? When he hadn't bothered to ask if she'd like to come in the first place? Was that part of his "put her at ease" campaign?

If it was, it was succeeding. Spectacularly.

She melted back, luxuriating in his solicitude, no matter

its motives. She hadn't worked up the courage to take an active part in this seduction, but having him this close made her dizzy with the need to touch and taste him. His skin made her drool, polished as bronze, soft as satin. And it was like that everywhere. She knew. She'd once explored him inch by inch. She couldn't wait to binge on his flawlessness again.

But having taken the decision to give in to the insanity, she knew she'd have the mind-blowing pleasure soon. Sighing with the relief of surrender, she looked into his expectant eyes, loving the anxious expectation she saw there.

"As long as I can get a better toothbrush than the one in the jet's welcome pack."

Elation blazed in his eyes before he crushed her lips in an assuaging yet distressing kiss, groaning inside her. "Next time we're here, or on my jet—yes, I have only one—we're going to do our dueling and eating and bantering in bed. I hope you know what it cost me to not take you there this time."

"Because it's your king and queen's bed?"

"*Bellissima,* I'll have to refresh your memory that when it comes to taking you, I don't care where we are."

As if she needed her memory refreshed. She'd spent years wishing it erased. He'd once taken her at work, in the park, in his car, everywhere—the only uncharacteristic rule breaking he'd done back then. But...

"Then why didn't you?"

Winding a thick lock of her hair around his hand, he tugged her closer, whispered against her cheek, "Because I want to wait. For the ring. For our wedding night."

After that she had no idea what she said or what happened. Agitated all over again at being hit with the reality of what she was doing, she functioned on auto as they landed in what must have been the royal airport and disembarked.

A Mercedes was awaiting them at the bottom of the stairs.

The driver saluted Vincenzo with a deep bow, gave him the key then rushed to another car. Then Vincenzo was driving them out of the airport on a road that ran by the shore.

She gazed dazedly at the picturesque scenery as the powerful car sped on the smoothest black asphalt road she'd ever been on. She didn't ask where they were going. Now that she'd given up resisting, she wanted him to surprise her, and she had no doubt he'd keep doing that. This time she'd enjoy it. Having no expectations, knowing the worst was to come, freed her, allowing her to live in the moment.

For someone who worried every single second she was awake, and most of the moments she slept, too, it was an unknown sensation. Like free fall. And she was loving it more by the second.

Vincenzo bantered with her nonstop, acting the perfect tour guide, pointing out landmarks and telling her stories about each part of the island. He said he'd take her to Jawara, the capital, and the royal palace, later. For now, he wanted to show her something else.

Letting the magic of this land with its balmy weather and brilliant skies seep through her, she soaked up his information and consideration. Then coming around a hill, in the distance there was…

She sat up straight, her heart hammering.

This…this was his home. His ancestral home.

She'd researched this place in her greed to find out everything about him. She'd read sonnets about it, written by Moorish poets, sonnets about the princes who inhabited it, and defended and ruled the countryside at its feet. Back when she'd thought she'd meant something to him, she'd ached for the time he'd take her there, as he'd promised.

Now she knew she meant nothing to him, and he hadn't promised anything, and yet he'd just taken her there.

Life was truly incomprehensible.

Photos had conveyed a complex of buildings overlooking a tranquil sea with gorgeous surrounding nature. But its reality was way more. Layer upon layer of natural and man-made wonders stretched as far as her vision did, drenched in the Mediterranean sun and canopied by its brilliant skies.

The centerpiece of the vista was a citadel complex that crouched high on a rocky if verdant hill like something out of a fantasy. At its foothills spread a countryside so lush and a town so untouched by modernity, she felt as if they were traveling through time as they approached.

The complex sprawled on multiple levels over the rugged site, the land around it teeming with wildflowers, orange trees and elms. As they approached, Vincenzo folded back the roof so she could hear the resident mockingbirds filling the afternoon with songs. He told her they were welcoming her.

Then they were crossing an honest-to-goodness moat, and she did feel she'd crossed into a different era.

Driving through huge wooden gates, Vincenzo drove around a mosaic-and-marble fountain in a truly expansive cobblestone courtyard, parking before the central tower. He hopped out without opening his door and ran around to scoop her into his arms without opening hers.

Giggling at his boyish playfulness, she glanced around embarrassedly at the dozens of people coming and going, no doubt the caretakers of his castle, all with their gazes and grins glued on her and Vincenzo.

He climbed the ancient stone steps with her protesting that she was too heavy all the way. By the time they arrived at a stone terrace at the top, he'd proved she wasn't, for him. He was barely breathing faster. He'd always been fit. But he must have upped his exercise regimen. She couldn't wait to test his boosted stamina....

The moment he put her down on her feet, she rushed across the terrace and came up against the three-foot-high balustrade looking over the incredible vista that sprawled to the horizon. Well-being surged through her in crashing waves, making her stand on tiptoe, arch her back and open her arms wide as if to encompass the beauty around her.

Vincenzo came up behind her, stopping less than a whisper away, creating a field of screaming sensuality between them, his lips blazing a path of destruction from her temple to the swell of her breasts. By the time he took the same path back up, she was ready to beg for his touch.

She didn't have to. He finally pulled her against him, arms crisscrossing beneath breasts that felt swollen and heavy. His murmur thrummed inside her in a path that connected her heart and core, melting both. "*Dea divina mia,* my divine goddess, now I know what this place lacked in my eyes. Your beauty gracing it. I won't be able to think of this place again except as a backdrop to showcase and worship you."

That was…extravagant. When had he learned to talk like that? With the women who flowed in and out of his bed?

A fist squeezed her heart dry of beats.

Steady. She had no right to feel despondent or disillusioned. Vincenzo wasn't hers. He never had been.

But the thought still didn't sit right. Those women had always seemed as if they'd been there to serve his purpose. She couldn't see him serenading them. So where did the poetry come from? Why was he so free with it? She'd already promised him the pretense *and* the passion.

So was he only going all-out to make her feel better about both?

Yeah. That had to be it.

But he'd said his passion had always been real. Whatever his reasons for his past cruelty, it didn't matter. For now, she could have heaven.

"If you think I add to the scenery that much, I'll pose for a photo shoot if you ever need to put the place up for sale. I can see the ad with the title 'Property in Paradise.'" She turned in his arms. "But seriously, now I've seen it up close, I'm wondering how you don't live here most of the time."

"Maybe now I will." His tone remained that tempting burr. But she felt it. An earnestness. A query. One he couldn't be asking. This was a fake marriage, with a nonexistent future. He wouldn't be considering her or soliciting her endorsement before he made plans for his own future.

Ignoring a pang of regret, she pretended she didn't hear the subtext in his comment. There was probably none, anyway.

"So, what now?"

"We start preparing for next week."

"What's next week?

He pressed her against the balustrade and spanned her rib cage with his large hands, the translucence of his eyes bottomless reflections of the vivid sky. Then he said, "Our wedding."

Seven

"Our wedding?"

Vincenzo's heart dipped in his chest at the frown on Glory's face as she echoed his words.

Was she angry again? After the magical flight here, when she'd gradually relaxed, seeming to accept their situation and then enjoy being with him, he'd almost forgotten how resistant she'd been. But what if her acquiescence had been a lull, and now she'd come to her senses and would start antagonizing him again? He couldn't stomach a return to friction, would give anything for their newly forged harmony to continue. Even if it meant letting her make the decisions from now on.

She threw her hands in the air. "God, I was determined to stop repeating your words like an incredulous parrot. Then you go and say something that forces me into being one!"

She *had* sounded and looked deliciously startled frequently in the past couple of days. Was that all? She was annoyed at herself for parroting his declarations?

He watched her intently, considering his response so he wouldn't trigger a relapse into hostilities. "Why is what I just said worthy of incredulous parroting?"

"When you talk you don't hear yourself? Or was it one of the other Vincenzos who said our wedding is next week?"

Her smirk blanked out his mind with the memory of having those sassy lips beneath his, soft and pliant, burning with urgency, spilling moans of pleasure. He needed to devour them again. But he had to settle this first.

He backed her up against the balustrade, his gaze sweeping her from her piled-up hair to her turquoise stilettos, hunger an ever-expanding tide inside him. "That was the one and only Vincenzo talking. So is a week too long? I can make it sooner. I probably should. We probably wouldn't survive a week."

She picked up her dropping jaw and replaced it with a more bedeviling smirk. "It's okay, this happens with a newly installed sense of humor. Sometimes you can't turn it off. Or you're such a new user, you don't know how to. Let's hope you get the hang of it soon."

This wasn't the first time she'd made comments to that effect. Had he been that much of a humorless boor before?

He guessed so. He'd been too focused on what he'd thought paramount he'd forgotten to lighten up.

But back then he'd thought his behavior suited her, the driven, dead-serious woman he'd thought her to be. Serious about work and passion. A delightful, challenging wit hadn't been among the things he'd thought she possessed, what he'd told himself he'd have to live without, with so many qualities to make up for the deficiency. Now he realized being a sourpuss had made her turn her humor off, making him miss knowing this side of her.

How much more had he missed? Was it possible other things he'd believed about her would turn out to be as totally wrong? How, when he'd had proof of them?

No. He was leaving this alone. This bomb had already detonated once and destroyed his world around him. He wasn't lighting its fuse again.

What mattered now was that she seemed to relish his new lightheartedness. He'd never dreamed they could have anything like the time they'd spent on the flight, filled with not only mounting hunger, but escalating fun, too.

He wanted more.

He went after it.

"You're right. It's a joke thinking I can wait a few days. We'll have the wedding today."

It was exhilarating. Teasing her, soaking up her reactions, opening himself wide for her retaliations, every barb targeting his humor triggers.

She obliged him with another bull's-eye. "This is worse than anything I feared. That humor program had a virus that scrambled you up. We'll have to uninstall everything in your brain and reformat you."

He pulled her into him, groaning at the electric thrill that arced between their bodies. "I like me all scrambled up like that. So shall I rush the delivery of the catering, minister and guests? I can have everything ready by eight tonight."

She arched to look up, pressing her lushness closer to him. He'd never remained that hard, that long. And he loved it.

"So he first hits his opponents with a ludicrous offer, then, as they gasp in disbelief, he follows up with an insane one, making them grab for the ludicrous lesser evil."

"You're not an opponent."

At her raised eyebrow, though it was mocking and not cynical, he felt that nip of regret again. One that made him wish he could erase the past, both distant and recent. What he'd give to restart everything from this point, with them who they were today, with no yesterdays to muddy their enjoyment of each other, and no tomorrows to cast shadows over it.

He caressed that elegant, dense eyebrow. "Put that down before someone gets hurt. Namely me. At least more than I'm already hurting." He ground his beyond-pain hardness into her, showing her she should have mercy on him. The eyes that rivaled Castaldini's skies darkened, her body yielding, shaping itself to his seeking. Her response, as always, heightened his distress, his delight. He groaned with them both. "So you want to postpone the wedding till next week."

A choppy laugh shook those globes of perfection against his chest. How he didn't have them free of their restraints and in his hands and mouth already, he had no idea. "And *then* he makes it all sound like his opponent's decision."

"'He' has no opponents here. He's just negotiating."

"I can sniff out the faintest scent of negotiating a mile away. I can't even detect a trace now."

"It must be because I learned the undetectable negotiation method at the hands of a mistress of the art."

"Seems I didn't teach you but transferred it to you. That skill has been nowhere to be found when I most needed it."

He tugged a loose glossy lock from the satin hair that shone in his homeland's sun like burnished copper. "But 'your' decision to postpone is well-advised. Next week's forecast says it will be a perfect day for a wedding."

She curled that dewy, edible lip. "Every day is a perfect day on Castaldini. But…" Something like panic spurted in her eyes. "You're serious, aren't you?" At his nod, she grabbed his lapels. "And what do you mean *wedding?*"

It was his eyebrows' turn to shoot up. "The word has more meanings than the one agreed on since the dawn of humanity?"

She shook her head, something frantic creeping into her eyes. "I thought we were just going to get a ring, sign a marriage certificate and report to the king so he can officially send you to your UN post."

It pained him that she expected only a cold ritual to befit the barren deal he'd proposed forty-eight hours ago.

Sorrow filled him for what should have been with this woman his heart and body had chosen, but wasn't and wouldn't be.

Suddenly, all levity drained from him, loosening his embrace.

Unable to remain in such intimate contact with her anymore, he stepped away. And saw it. A quiver of insecurity. A crack in the veneer of confidence and cheek.

He should have felt that was the least she deserved. To suffer some uncertainty and trepidation. But he didn't. It hurt him to see her looking so...bereft. He hated to see vulnerability in those indomitable eyes.

He forced himself to smile at her, to reach a soothing hand to her cheek. "If you didn't think I was talking about a wedding with all the trimmings, why were you surprised at all when I said next week? Or today? The ceremony you describe could have been concluded in a couple of hours."

"Forgive me if I'm boggled by the idea of *any* brand of ceremony. I was never married before, you know, for real or for pretense, and a date, let alone one so soon, makes me feel this is actually happening."

He watched her lips shaking, attempting a smile of bravado and failing, and could no longer deny it.

His gut was having a fit, sanctioning no evidence but what it sensed. It insisted she wasn't the hardened manipulator he'd once thought her. That person would have grabbed his deal, would now be working his evident eagerness to milk more from him. But she wasn't. She was really shaken.

And for the first time, he put himself in her place. Taken away from everything she knew to a strange land, her choice stripped away, her family not only unable to come to her aid, but the reason for her predicament. Her only company and precarious support was the man behind it all. And he kept blowing hot and cold, to boot. She must be feeling lost, helpless. And to a woman who'd been mistress of her own fate for so long, that must be the scariest thing she'd ever experienced.

His gut finally communicated with his brain, reaching a decision.

If he took out the terrible blot of her betrayal from their lives, he could connect the woman he'd once loved with this woman he laughed so easily with, the woman he now wanted more than he'd known he was capable of wanting. And he didn't want that woman to be under any form of compulsion.

Taking another step back, severing any intimacy, he exhaled. "It doesn't have to happen."

More uncertainty flooded her eyes. "What do you mean?"

"I mean you don't have to marry me."

Glory wondered if the sun had overheated her brain.

That would explain feeling and hearing things that couldn't be real. When Vincenzo had stepped away, she'd felt as if she was teetering on a cliff without his support. Then, because of the distance that had come over him, she'd felt she'd fallen into the abyss of the past, discarded all over again.

That remoteness couldn't have been real. Not after all his pursuit and passion. And he couldn't have just said...

"I don't have to marry you?" There she went, parroting him again. She swallowed the knot of anxiety that rose in her throat. "Just a minute ago you wanted me to marry you in seven hours or seven days, and now... Just what are you playing at?"

He stuffed his hands into his pockets. "Nothing. No more games, Glory. But don't worry. I'll still help your family. Of course, they can never again as much as forge a note to your nephew's kindergarten or take a cent from a tip dish."

Her heart slowed, as if fearing every beat would make

this real. "Y-you mean that?" His slow nod, his solemn gaze cleaved into her. "Wh-what will you do about King Ferruccio's decree?"

"I don't know. I'm thinking on the fly here. Maybe I'll ask someone else."

Her heart boomed now, each beat almost tearing it apart. She couldn't bear thinking he'd marry someone else, even in pretense. "Why?"

His shrug was heavy; his spectacular face gripped in the brooding she hadn't seen there since she'd met him again. "It just suddenly hit me, how wrong this whole thing is."

It suddenly hit her, too. That he wasn't only confounding. He was nerve-racking. Heartbreaking. And he probably did suffer from a severe bipolar disorder. What else explained the violent pendulum of his mood swings?

He forced out an exhalation. "You can go back as soon as you wish. If you want me to escort you, I will. If not, the royal jet is at your disposal."

Feeling as if her whole world was being swept from under her, she leaned back on the balustrade before she collapsed.

He meant it. He was setting her free.

But she didn't want to be free.

She no longer knew what to do with her freedom.

Before he'd reinvaded her life, she'd spent years nurturing the illusion of steadiness. His hurricane had uprooted her simulated peace and exposed the truth of her chaos, the bleakness of her isolation.

But she'd already succumbed and had woven a tapestry of expectations around this time she would have had with him. She'd anticipated its rejuvenation, thought it would see her through the rest of her life. In her worst estimations she'd never thought it would all end before it began.

But it had. He'd suddenly cut her loose, letting her plummet back into her endless spiral of nothingness.

She pushed away from the balustrade as if from a preci-
pice and past the monolith who stood brooding down at her.

She looked around her stunning surroundings, every nerve
burning with despondency.

In a different life, Vincenzo would have brought her here
because he wanted to share his home with her. If not permanently, then at least sincerely, passionately, for as long the
fates let them be together.

In this life, he'd brought her here for all the wrong reasons,
only to send her away before she got more than a tantalizing
taste of the place that had forged him into the man she loved.

Yes, in spite of the insanity and self-destructiveness of it
all, she still loved him.

Now she'd only gotten enough of a glimpse of him in his
element to live with their memory gnawing at her, to mourn
what hadn't and could never have been.

Needing to get it over with, she turned and found him still
standing where he had been, his back to her, looking up at
the sky. Thunder filled her ears as her gaze ached over the
sight of his majestic figure…then she realized.

The din didn't come from her stampeding heart. It was
coming from above.

It took a moment to realize its direction then see its origin. A helicopter.

"The Castaldinian Air Force One, rotorcraft edition." Vincenzo gazed at her over his shoulder, his eyes grave. "Seems
Ferruccio couldn't wait to meet my future bride."

Hot needles sprouted behind her eyes. She didn't want to
meet anyone. She wasn't even a counterfeit bride now.

He turned, expression wiped clean. "Please say nothing
while he's here. I'll resolve things with him later."

She only nodded numbly, making no reaction when he took
her hand and led her from the terrace and down the stairs he'd
carried her up what felt like a lifetime ago.

By the time they exited the castle, the helicopter was landing in the courtyard, the revolving blades spraying the fountain water at them. Glory shuddered at the touch of the warm mist, cold spreading in her bones.

As the rotors slowed down, a man stepped down from the pilot's side. She recognized him on sight. So the king flew himself here. And without guards or fanfare. It said so much about him and his status in Castaldini.

But all photos and footage hadn't done him justice. He'd looked exceptional in those. But the man was way more than that. He was on par with Vincenzo in looks and physique. He could even pass for his brother.

King Ferruccio rushed in strides laden with urgency and power to the passenger side as it opened. In moments, his arms went around the waist of a golden vision of a woman, lifting her down as if he was handling his own heart.

"And the king has brought his queen," she heard Vincenzo mutter over the rotor's dying whirs. "Or maybe it's the other way around. She must be thrilled to see me entering the gilded cage at last."

Glory's heart contracted on what felt like thorns on hearing his words, and more as she watched the regal couple advance hand in hand, their bond blatant in their every nuance.

What attention they didn't have focused on each other, they had trained on her. She looked from one to the other, feeling like a specimen under a microscope.

Queen Clarissa was what Glory had always imagined fairy queens to look like. In a sleeveless floor-length lilac dress and high-heeled matching sandals, she stood maybe an inch or two taller than Glory, with the body of a woman who'd been ripened by the satisfaction and pampering of a powerful man's constant passion, by bearing his children. From the top of her golden head to her toes, she glowed in the afternoon sun as if she was made of its radiance. Glory could easily believe she had angels in her lineage.

King Ferruccio was as tall as Vincenzo, another overpoweringly handsome D'Agostino. There was no doubt the same blood ran in their veins. They had almost identical coloring, too. But that was where the similarities ended.

While Vincenzo was imposing, Ferruccio was intimidating. If his wife was the benevolent breed of angel, he was the avenging variety. And it had nothing to do with the way he looked. It was in his eyes. His vibe. This was a man who'd seen and done unspeakable things…and had those things done to him. Which made sense. He'd grown up an illegitimate boy on the streets, one who'd dragged himself from the dirt to the very top. She could only imagine what he'd been through, what had shaped him into the man who was now undisputedly the best king in Castaldini's history. She felt no one could know the scope of his depths, and those of his sufferings and complexities.

No one but his wife, that was.

They seemed to share a soul.

It hurt to see them together, to feel the love arcing between them in a closed circuit of harmony. What she'd once thought she'd had with Vincenzo.

Vincenzo, who was still holding her hand as they stopped two feet away from the couple, making her feel as if he couldn't let go of it. When he was letting her go completely.

Hand still entwined with hers Vincenzo bowed before his king and queen, his other hand flat palmed over his heart, in the Castaldinian royal salute.

What was she supposed to do? Bow, too? Curtsy?

Before her muscles unlocked, Vincenzo straightened, his face softening on a smile that she'd only seen before when he'd been talking about Clarissa.

With an arm going around her waist, he gave Queen Clarissa a tender hug with his other arm, kissing her gently on her cheek, before raising one eyebrow at King Ferruccio. "I see you've brought your husband with you."

So he was on teasing terms with his king. Figured. It was clear that though he observed the king's status officially, he was on the same level personally.

Clarissa chuckled, her thick, long hair blowing around her face in the breeze like strands of sunlight. "You know me, I can't say no to him."

Vincenzo's lips twisted. "I can train you."

Her chuckle turned to a snicker. "Like *you* can say no to him."

Vincenzo teased. "I'm not the woman who has the power to make a yo-yo out of His Majesty. It's your duty as his queen to save his subjects from his implacability, and as his wife to counteract the toxic level of yeses in his blood."

Clarissa gave her husband a look full of all they had between them. "I like him intoxicated." She turned teasing eyes on Vincenzo. "Now shush, Cenzo, and let me meet your much better half."

Then she turned those eyes on Glory. They were so unbelievable, Glory involuntarily stepped closer to find out if they were contacts. They weren't. She'd seen so-called violet eyes before, always blue with a violet tinge. But Clarissa's were pure, luminescent amethysts. Eyes to stare into for hours. Ferruccio evidently wanted to do nothing else for life.

Glory's lips trembled on a smile in response to Clarissa's exquisite one as she clasped her in a warm, fragrant embrace.

Already on the brink of tears, Clarissa's words almost made them escape. "Welcome to Castaldini and to the family, Glory. I'm thrilled to have another friend my age, especially since I hear we have so much in common, our professional training—" she pulled back, her smile becoming mischievous "—and being married to one of our impossible yet irresistible D'Agostino men."

In spite of her upheaval, her lips moved of their own accord. "Your Majesty…"

Clarissa held out a warning finger. "Stop right there! No YMs and not the *Q* word, either. Away from all the court stuff, I'm just Rissa—my husband claims exclusivity on Clarissa—" another melting look at her husband "—and I'm just part of a brigade around here, with the other members being Gabrielle, my brother Durante's wife; Phoebe, my cousin Leandro's; and Jade, my cousin Eduardo's. We used to call ourselves the Fabulous Four. Now we'll be the Fabulous Five."

Glory swallowed, at a loss on how to answer. Seemed Vincenzo's advice about saying nothing was the best one to follow in this mess. She smiled weakly at Clarissa, wishing the earth actually opened and swallowed people.

"You're real."

The deep, dark burr had goose bumps storming across her body. King Ferruccio.

Without coming closer, he made her feel his presence had enveloped her, immobilizing her for analysis as he cocked his head in contemplation. "I thought Vincenzo was pulling one over on me until I was forced to send him off to his new post, only to discover too late that you were a figment of his very creative mind."

Her bones tightened under his scrutiny. He felt something wasn't right. His eyes said he *knew* it. Shrewd man. That must be how he'd raised himself from destitute illegitimacy to become not only one of the world's most hard-hitting magnates, but the king who'd brought Castaldini back from the brink of ruin and into unprecedented prosperity in under four years. The intelligence she felt radiating from him was almost frightening, and he must possess all the additional qualities that made others follow him.

Under his probing, words formed on her lips. "I am real, I assure you, Your Majesty. Forgive me if I won't call you Ruccio, if that's your name in informal setting, according to the abbreviations I observed your names undergo."

A ghost of a smile played on Ferruccio's uncompromising lips. "Come to think of it, that contraction should have been my name's fate. Seems no one was bold enough to attempt it. But you can call me Ferruccio like everyone is free to, since my wife has her own exclusive names for me. But Your Majesty is certainly not something you're allowed to use."

Her smile attempted a semblance of steadiness. "It might be impossible to call you by your name just like that."

Ferruccio's gaze leveled on her. "In her incurable kindness, Clarissa has made it a request, but I have no such qualms. Away from the court I order you to call me Ferruccio. As your future king, that's a royal decree."

"See what I have to put up with?"

That was Vincenzo, his tone light and teasing, but his eyes made her feel he was following her breaths.

Ignoring him, Ferruccio maintained his focus on her. "But you're not only real, you're nothing like I expected. As soon as I had a name to his alleged fiancée, I investigated you." At Clarissa's silent reprimand, he caressed the hand that discreetly poked at him, his eyes on Glory. "And now I'm left with an unsolvable question. How was he able to get a woman of your caliber not only to take him seriously, but to agree, and so fast, to take on the onerous task of marrying him?"

Vincenzo snorted a laugh. "And that's what you say when you're trying your best to marry me off? What would you have said if you wanted to send her running away screaming?"

Clarissa tugged on her husband arm, her color high with embarrassment. "He must have done exactly what you did to make me undertake the same task with you." Her eyes turned apologetically on Glory. "Now you see the *impossible* part I was talking about."

Suddenly deciding to throw herself into the part Vincenzo expected her to play until his king and queen left, Glory quirked her lips at Clarissa. "And now that I do, I actually feel better about Vincenzo's exasperating tendencies. I now have proof they're genetic and therefore beyond his control."

Clarissa whooped with laughter. "I *knew* it! I liked you on sight, but now I know I'll *love* you! You're exactly the addition we need to our brigade!"

Ferruccio cast an indulgent look at his wife, then raised an eyebrow at Glory, clearly approving the comeback that bundled him and Vincenzo and put them firmly in their places.

Vincenzo's arm tightened. "How about we call it quits, Ferruccio, before we're cut down to an even tinier size?"

Ferruccio gave a tiny bow of his regal head. "By all means. Not that I'll quit being flabbergasted at your phenomenal luck anytime soon."

Vincenzo sighed. "Your flattery knows no bounds. Now before you have Glory rethinking her hasty and ill-advised decision to marry me, how about you go do some kingly stuff and leave me to resume what I was about to do before your… surprise inspection? I was about to take Glory to explore the place before dinner." He turned his eyes to Clarissa. "You, of course, are more than welcome to join us."

Clarissa looked up into her husband's eyes, exchanging what Glory had once thought she'd shared with Vincenzo. Such allegiance. Such understanding. Such adoration.

Clarissa pinched her husband's hard cheek. "See what you've done? Now make nice so you can stay for the tour and dinner, too."

Catching her hand to bury his lips in its palm, Ferruccio looked over at Vincenzo challengingly. "Why make nice when I can order him to invite me? Or better still, invite myself?"

Vincenzo raised him a pitying glance. "Seems you haven't lived on Castaldini long enough to realize how provincial it remains, don't realize what power I wield in my ancestral region. Here, I rule supreme. King or no, Ferruccio, one more word and I sic my whole province on you."

Ferruccio's eyes gleamed with devilry. "Let's not start a civil war over the dinner you've been cornered into feeding me. Now lead the way, Vincenzo. And try to do your 'ancestral home' justice as you act as the guide."

Grumbling something about getting Ferruccio later when he wasn't under Clarissa's protection, Vincenzo did lead the way.

And how he did. He detailed everything with the thoroughness of someone who took the utmost pride in the place that had been in his family for generations. As he should. This place was phenomenal.

And it would be the first and last time she was here. Why not just enjoy the experience while it lasted?

"The architecture of all the buildings is a symbiosis of every culture that makes up Castaldini—Roman, Andalusian, Moorish and some North African influences," Vincenzo said, his explanations all for her. "Geometric patterns rule, with accessory-heavy decoration, from mosaic to plaster carving to worked metal. The main castle is circular but the other annexed buildings and towers are quadrangular, with all rooms opening onto inner courts."

It was all right out of a fairy tale. Far grander and better preserved that any of the architectural wonders she'd visited all over the world.

She asked, "How long has this place been in your family?"

"Over five hundred years."

Wow. That really put into perspective the difference between them. Her family tree was known only three or four generations back on both sides. And there hadn't been a "family home" in her life, let alone an ancestral one.

Vincenzo underlined the unbridgeable gap between them. "My umpteenth great-grandfather was Castaldini's founder, King Antonio D'Agostino."

"*Our* umpteenth great-grandfather," Ferruccio put in.

Vincenzo countered, "*My* line is that of one of his grandsons, who started building this place, but it reached its present size by gradual additions of more quadrangles over two centuries. Leandro, a slightly less obnoxious cousin, inherited a similar place, which King Antonio himself had built. When we were young, we always liked to brag about which is bigger and better."

Glory's blood tumbled as her imagination flew on a tangent, to other bigger and better…things.

"You still do," Ferruccio said, his tone condescending. "I always leave you boys to squabble over size and quality. Mine is the undisputed best of all."

"But the royal palace isn't yours, my liege," Vincenzo calmly retorted. "As per Castaldini's laws, you're just the resident caretaker. You really should start building or acquiring a place to pass on to your children."

Ferruccio suddenly threw his head back and guffawed. "See that, Vincenzo? That's the take-no-prisoners attitude I want you to have when you're representing Castaldini."

Clarissa's eyes rounded. "You mean you've been poking him to get him to bare his fangs?"

Ferruccio grinned down at her. "He's been getting soft of late. Now that he has Glory, I was afraid he'd turn to putty and be no good to me in the war zone I'm sending him to. I had to do something to remind him how to use his fangs."

Vincenzo huffed. "Have I told you lately how much I love you, Ferruccio?"

"You're welcome to renew your oath of allegiance any-time, Vincenzo."

Clarissa spluttered as she smacked her husband and cousin playfully, and Glory had to join in the laughter.

After that the day flowed, filled with many unprecedented experiences with the most exciting people she'd ever met.

It was past midnight when she and Vincenzo stood in the courtyard, watching the regal couple vanish into the night.

Her heart twisted at the symbolism. This place and Vincenzo would soon disappear from her life as if they'd never been.

The moment she turned to Vincenzo, he turned to her, too, taking a leashed step closer, practically vibrating with intensity.

And she realized. That he was sending her away because he no longer wanted to coerce her. But he still wanted her. And she'd already decided that this passion was worth any risk.

Closing the gap between them, taking both his hands in hers, she took the plunge into the path to eventual heartache.

And she whispered, "I'll marry you for the year you need, Vincenzo. My choice this time."

<u>Eight</u>

"What did you say?"

As the exclamation rang in her ear, Glory sighed. "You heard right, Mom. I'm getting married. To Vincenzo."

Silence expanded on the other end of the line.

Which was to be expected. She herself still couldn't believe any of this was really happening.

After she'd told Vincenzo last night that she'd marry him of her own free will, she hadn't known what to expect.

Or she had. She'd expected him to be elated, or relieved, or best scenario of all, to resume his mind-melting seduction.

He'd done none of that. He'd just taken her hands to his lips, murmured a cell-scrambling *"Grazie mille, gloriosa mia"* then he'd silently led her to her guest quarters and bid her good-night.

After a night of tossing and turning and pacing her quarters, which looked like something out of a fairy tale, he'd come knocking with a breakfast tray. He didn't stay, said he had too many things to prepare. He asked her to invite everyone she wanted and to make lists of what she needed for the wedding. It *would* be in a week's time.

The first person she'd thought of had been her mother.

And here she was, pretending this was real to the person she was closest to in the world. But there was nothing to be gained by telling her mother the truth. Her mother had suffered too much, and God only knew how long her remission would last this time—or if it would. She would do and say anything to make her mother as happy as possible for as long as she could.

Glenda Monaghan's silence thickened until it weighed down on her. "Mom, you still there?"

A ragged exhalation. "Yes, darling. I'm just…surprised."

Her mother had been apprehensive about her first liaison with Vincenzo. She had feared Glory would end up plummeting into the huge gap in power and status between them. But on meeting Vincenzo, Glenda had thought him magnificent and later waxed poetic about the purity and clarity of his emotions for Glory. She suspected her mother had entertained dreams that her daughter would become a princess and had looked devastated when Glory had informed her that the relationship was over.

Glenda must be stunned her dream was coming true after all these years, and so suddenly. When they'd talked four days ago, none of this had been on the horizon.

Glory gave her mother a pretty little story about how she and Vincenzo had met again, rediscovering how they'd once felt about each other and resolving the issues that had separated them. This time, he'd popped the question and wanted to get married right away so he could start his new post with them as husband and wife.

By the time she'd told all those lies, Glory was almost panting, but she forced herself to go on. "Vincenzo will send his private jet for you. If you can come right away, I'd love it! If not, come a couple of days before the wedding if possible, to help me with all the last-minute things. All you need to do is buy something pretty to wear and pack a bag for two weeks or so. You should enjoy Castaldini at least that long."

When she finished, silence stretched again.

Then her mother whispered, "Is it only me you're inviting?"

Glory had known that question would come yet still wasn't ready to answer it.

From the time Glory was a little girl, her mother had tried all she could to defuse her dissatisfaction with her father and brother. Then, in the past few years, she'd fought to reinstate the relationship that Glory had escaped, always ready with an excuse for their latest damaging decisions or exasperating actions. Now the situation was reversed and it was Glory who had to hide the true extent of her father's and brother's transgressions from her mother. And she wasn't sure she could do that if she saw them again now.

But her established disapproval wasn't grave enough to warrant not inviting them to her wedding. If she didn't invite them, she'd have to give her mother an explanation why. She couldn't tell the truth. And she'd already told her enough lies.

But then, why not just have them here? She doubted she'd have enough mental or emotional energy to register their presence. And Vincenzo had stressed she could invite anyone. By "anyone" she believed he sanctioned her father's and brother's presence. And she did want to please her mom.

She forced lightness in her voice. "You're the one I can't wait to have here, but of course Dad and Daniel are invited." That didn't sound as welcoming as she'd tried to make it. Well, her father and brother would just have to make do with that level of enthusiasm.

"Don't you want your father to give you away, darling? I

know it's been a long while since you thought he was the best dad in the world, but he does try."

Yeah, he tried so hard his efforts could send him to prison for life. "I'm almost thirty, Mom. I'm perfectly capable of walking down that aisle on my own."

"I know you can do anything on your own, darling, but your father has dreamed of this day for so long, and—" her mother broke off, as if swallowing tears "—it'll break his heart."

Glory gritted her teeth on the surge of familiar guilt she suffered every time she felt she'd been too hard on her father. But once the sentimental reaction subsided she always realized that she hadn't been. If only she'd been harder, had known the truth earlier, she could have stopped him and Daniel from spiraling that far that they risked their freedom. There was one way out of this for now.

"Listen, Mom, I'm marrying a prince from a kingdom steeped in history and tradition and giving me away might not be part of the ritual here. If it is, I'll let Dad give me away."

Another fraught silence greeted her prevaricating promise. For an otherwise shrewd woman, her mother had a rationalizing disease where her husband and son were concerned. Glory barely suppressed her need to tell her mother to open her eyes and see her husband and son for the lost causes they were.

The one thing that had always held her back was knowing how much they loved her mother. Glory had no doubt they'd die for her mother in a heartbeat.

What an inextricable mess everyone was tangled up in.

Sighing, she soothed her mother. "Just pack your men up and bring them here, Mom. It'll all work out."

After that, she diverted her mom into talking about the guest list and wedding plans.

By the time Glory ended the call, she felt she'd run a mile.

Now on to the marathon of the next week.

* * *

After sunset, just as she was getting restless having nothing to do, Vincenzo came into her suite. He introduced the tall, graceful and extremely chic man with him as his valet and right-hand man, Alonzo Barbieri. After greeting her in utmost delight and kissing her hand as if she was his long-lost princess, Alonzo ushered in four other people, two men and two women, each carrying a heavy, ornate antique chest. They opened them on the coffee table then promptly left, leaving her gaping at the contents.

The freaking royal jewels of Castaldini.

She'd thought they would be— No, she couldn't have thought anything that could come close to—to…*that.*

Each piece on its own would have been jaw-dropping, but having them piled together—from hefty necklaces, bracelets and tiaras to intricate earrings, brooches and rings—the treasure was literally dazzling. There were even some scepters and goblets and ornamental pieces not for wearing. And were those…those…

"The royal crowns! What are those doing here?"

As she turned stunned eyes between the two men, it was Alonzo who supplied an explanation. "I applaud your knowledge of our history, *Principessa!*" Before she could wince at the title, he went on, "Those are indeed the crowns that had been worn by kings and queens of Castaldini until King Benedetto and his wife—Queen Clarissa's father and mother. But since their lives were marked by tragedy, King Ferruccio had new crowns made, with personalized changes, so the past wouldn't throw the least shadow on his and Queen Clarissa's lives."

More proof of how total Ferruccio's love for Clarissa was.

With that strange reticence that had come over him still subduing his eyes, Vincenzo said, "As my princess you're entitled to any piece you'd like. After last night, Ferruccio and Clarissa insist you should have as *many* as you'd like."

Alonzo chuckled. "They're ready to offer the whole treasure to you as the one who'll save *Principe* Vincenzo from unremitting bachelorhood. I am also offering whatever your heart desires for that Herculean achievement."

So Vincenzo hadn't even taken his closest person into his confidence. Alonzo clearly believed this was a grand love story with a happily ever after.

"Ferruccio is also putting the royal palace and everyone inside it at your service," Vincenzo said.

"He wants us to have the wedding there?"

Vincenzo nodded. "Being the control freak that he is, he insists I take my vows under his supervision."

"Can't we…" She stopped, swallowed. "Can't we have the wedding here?"

A flare of surprise then intentness incinerated the deadness in Vincenzo's eyes. "Is this what you want?"

Feeling suddenly shy and awkward, wanting to smack herself for behaving as if she was a real bride, she murmured, "It's just this place is magnificent, and it's your family home…"

Vincenzo spoke over her, his tone urgent. "If it's what you want, then we certainly will have the wedding here."

Alonzo looked scandalized. "But what about King Ferruccio's decree? And all this talk about being a knight in his round table and doing anything he commands?"

Vincenzo had said that about Ferruccio? Watching those two together, you'd never have guessed he felt that way about him.

Vincenzo twisted his lips at Alonzo. "That's until my bride says different. Then it's her desires that I follow, nobody else's, no matter who they are."

Alonzo whooped. "*That's* what I waited two decades to

hear. *Principessa,* you're a miracle worker. A miracle, period."

Feeling tears too near the surface, she wanted to get this over with. "Will you please do the honors, Vincenzo? I'm almost afraid to look at those pieces, I'm not about to go rummaging through them and chip or crack something."

Vincenzo's expression hovered on the smile she'd been missing, had even gotten dependent on basking in it. "Rummage away. Those pieces have weathered the test of hundreds of years. Choose whatever you want."

"I want you—" her voice trembled, holding back *only you* "—to choose the ring for me."

A moment of probing stillness. "Are you sure?" A tinge of teasing said *after all the fuss?* Then his lips spread. "I do have one ring, one collection in mind. I always felt it was made as a tribute to the beauty of your eyes."

He gave Alonzo a nod, and as if Alonzo knew exactly which pieces Vincenzo was talking about, Alonzo started sorting through the treasure. In minutes, without letting her see what he'd selected, Alonzo placed the pieces in a rectangular box he'd had under his armpit all along then handed it to Vincenzo.

Coming to stand above where she sat feeling as though she'd fall apart any moment, Vincenzo suddenly dropped down on one knee in front of her.

Holding her stunned gaze with eyes roiling like thunderclouds, he opened the navy blue velvet box. She relinquished his gaze to its contents…and the gasp that had caught in her chest when he'd knelt before her escaped.

A seven-piece set—necklace, bracelet, ring, earrings, tiara, armlet and anklet—lay on the dark velvet like a brilliant constellation of stars set against a night sky. They were all made from the most delicate filigree yellow gold she'd ever seen, and studded with magnificent white and blue diamonds in ingenious patterns. But it was the ring that her eyes couldn't leave. A flawless, vivid blue diamond of at least ten carats, the color of her eyes at night, with emerald-cut white diamonds on both the sides.

Vincenzo singled it out, turned his hand up, asking for hers. She placed it there without volition or hesitation.

The moment he slipped the ring on her finger, she knew what a huge mistake she was committing. She wouldn't survive losing him this time.

His watchfulness intensified as he singed her hand in a kiss, then with a long groan, he stabbed his other hand into the depths of her hair and hauled her against him, kissing her so deeply, so hungrily, she felt he might finish her.

Surrendering to his passion, her need, her panic subsided as she accepted that if she wasn't careful, he *would* finish her.

"We have only one hour left to go."

Glory turned her head at Alonzo's declaration. The man was the most outstanding organizer she'd ever seen. He'd marshaled everyone's efforts to get the most efficient operation going. And in just one week, he'd managed to plan a wedding more incredible than any in storybooks.

Alonzo took exception to her saying that. The wedding hadn't happened yet, and would she stop jinxing it?

If only he knew a jinx wasn't needed to spoil anything. Everything would self-destruct in a year.

But a year was a long time.

The week had passed faster than she could catch her breath. Now the wedding was an hour away.

Her mother had arrived only yesterday with her father and brother, and Alonzo had promptly swept them off their feet and into the rush of preparations, for which Glory was grateful. No one had time to think of any relationship issues. Amelia, who'd arrived the day after Glory had invited her, had been running interference for her whenever any awkward moment arose.

Clarissa and Gabrielle—Clarissa's sister-in-law—were now flitting about doing Alonzo's last-minute bidding. He'd already sent Phoebe and Jade, the other two in the Fabulous Five brigade, on errands. Though they were his queen and princesses, in those wedding preparations, he ruled supreme.

Everything around the castle and the town below now echoed the themes of Glory's dress and accessories. Everything was swathed in glorious white, gold and a whole range of vivid blues. Vincenzo had already told her that *she* was made of Castaldini's hues, her hair of its soil, her skin of its sunlight, and her eyes of its skies.

"You do look like a princess, darling."

Glory looked at her mother in the Andalusian-style full-length mirror before shifting her gaze to stare at her reflection. She had to admit her mother was right.

So clothes did make the woman. This dress made her feel like a different person. The person a dozen designers had turned her into as she'd stood for endless hours for them to mold this creation on her.

During the stages of its creation, she hadn't imagined how it would look finished. She'd last seen it when it had yet to be embroidered. The end product was astounding.

In sweeping gradations of brilliant blues on a base of crisp white, it looked like something made in another realm, from materials and colors that defied the laws of nature. Its fitted, off-the-shoulder bodice with a heart-shaped plunging neckline accentuated her curves and swells to beyond perfection, nipping her waist to a size she hadn't believed achievable—and without a breath-stealing corset.

Her one request had been that the dress not have a mushrooming skirt. But it was only when Clarissa had backed up her request that the designers had backed down. On hearing that they hadn't taken her request as a command, Vincenzo had fired them and gotten new ones who'd been doing everything she said before she finished saying it.

Now the dress had a skirt that molded to her hips before flaring gently in layers of chiffon, tulle and lace overlaying a base of silk. The whole dress was adorned in thousands of sequins and diamonds that echoed the colors of her jewelry, in patterns that swept around her body and down the dress and formed the crest of Vincenzo's province, where he was the lord.

Alonzo finished adjusting the layered veil from the back of her high chignon, then the tiara just behind her coiffed bangs, while Amelia hooked her twenty-foot train.

As they all pulled back to exclaim over her perfection, her mother neared, tears running down her thin cheeks. "Oh, darling, I can't tell you how happy…how happy…"

A surge of poignancy threatened to fill Glory's eyes, too, as her mother choked. She blinked it back. The last thing she wanted was to go to Vincenzo with swollen eyes and reddened nose. But there was something in her mother's eyes that gripped her heart in anxiety. Something dark and regretful.

Gathering herself, her mother continued, "I'm so happy I lived to see this day, to see you with the man who loves you and who will protect you for the rest of your life."

Alarm detonated in Glory's chest. Had her mother had a relapse and not told her? She'd always said the worst thing about having cancer was how it pained Glory and disrupted her life as she'd dropped everything and rushed to her side.

Before she could blurt out her worries, a burst of music shook the chamber.

"Ferruccio has brought out the whole royal brass orchestra to your door, Glory." Clarissa chuckled at her astonishment. "It's a royal tradition in all huge occasions, playing the anthem to herald the beginning of ceremonies. And Vincenzo getting married is certainly huge."

Another wave of anxiety drenched her. This was really happening. She had to walk out now and marry Vincenzo in a legendary ceremony in front of thousands of people.

She turned away from everyone, inhaling a steadying breath as she faced herself in the mirror one last time. She wondered if everyone saw what she saw. A woman lost in love but resigned that love would remain lost to her forever?

No, they didn't. Everyone behaved as if they had no doubt this was a match made in heaven, and made forever.

Alonzo touched her shoulder gently. "Are you ready for your groom?"

She wasn't ready. For anything. Yet she was ready for nothing else, ready for everything. She nodded.

Alonzo rushed to the table where he'd arranged the blown-glass bottles filled with the aromatic oils he'd rubbed on her pulse points as Castaldinian custom dictated. He picked up one of the oils and also took the crystal pitcher filled with the rose water he'd given her earlier to drink as another part of the ritual before rushing to open the door.

Her heart clanged, expecting to see Vincenzo. The father giving the bride away wasn't done in Vincenzo's province, thankfully. Instead, the groom came to take his bride from among her family and friends, to claim her as his, and take her from her old life to the new one with him.

Everything inside her stilled as she stared at the empty doorway. Vincenzo wasn't there, and Alonzo was pouring water in his hand and sprinkling it across her doorstep carefully, once, twice, three times.

"That's to ward away evil spirits that might try to enter with your groom and conspire to come between you later," Gabrielle explained, a red-haired beauty whom the matron-of-honor dress suited best, with her eyes reflecting its sapphire and cerulean colors. She grinned sheepishly at Glory's wide-eyed stare. "I've been investigating the myriad provincial traditions around here. I'm thinking of writing a book."

"You should," Clarissa exclaimed. "You'd be even more of a national treasure if you do!"

Amelia, who was having the time of her life rubbing shoulders with a posse of princesses, chuckled. "Make it a royal decree that she must, Clarissa. With all the fascinating stuff Alonzo introduced us to during the preparations, I can't wait to read that book. I want to adopt all of those traditions in my own wedding!"

Glory barely heard their banter, all her senses focused on the threshold as Alonzo stood to one side, pumping his chest in deference and pride and called out, *"Avanti, Principe."*

And Vincenzo appeared.

His gaze slammed into hers, compacting the dozens of feet between them, making her feel him against her, his breath hovering a gasp away from her inflamed flesh.

Air vanished from the world. Fire flooded her limbs.

And that was before she really looked at him.

Her heart emptied its beats in a mad rush.

This was Vincenzo as he was born to be. As she'd never seen him before. The prince whose blood ran thick with nobility and entitlement. The man who inhabited a realm she should have never seen, let alone entered. But she had entered it once, tangentially. Now she was stumbling all the way in, even if for only a year.

Her ravenous gaze devoured his every detail. His lavish costume complemented her dress, magnifying his height, breadth and bulk, worshipping his coloring and lines. A mid-thigh jacket in royal-blue silk, embroidered with Castaldinian designs, opened over a crisp white satin shirt and golden sash. His black fitted pants disappeared into knee-high shining black leather boots. A gold cape embroidered in blues and white flowed at his back down to his calf and completed the image of an otherworldly prince.

She'd always thought no description did him justice. Seemed there were always new heights to the injustice. Of his beauty. Of his escalating effect on her.

And he was hers. Tonight. And for a whole year.

Alonzo gave him the same water he'd given her to drink, and Gabrielle whispered that now the evil spirits couldn't come between them from the inside.

Vincenzo strode in, a predator who had his prey standing before him. His eyes swept her before returning to her face with a promise that turned her into a mass of tremors.

And that was before he stopped before her and said, "I'll kick these helpful ladies out and take the edge off so I can survive the torturous festivities ahead."

The wild gleam in his eyes told her he wasn't joking. He wanted to take her now, hard and fast.

Her lungs emptied on a ragged gasp. "Vincenzo…"

"Don't stand there devouring your bride with looks and intentions." That was Clarissa, her voice merry. She must have guessed what Vincenzo was saying. "The sooner you're done with the ceremony, the sooner you can devour her for real."

Unable to blush any deeper, she watched Vincenzo turn to his queen with a glare, felt him vibrating with control as he offered her his arm.

She clung to it as if to a raft in a stormy sea, felt his power moving her legs and his support holding her up as they exited the chamber after another water-sprinkling ritual.

It felt as if she was outside her body watching the whole spectacle unfold as they passed through the castle's torch-lit corridors to the courtyard where the ceremony would be held. Her dazed gaze swept the magical setting that had become even more so with extensive decorations and ingenious lighting. Alonzo had turned the main building, its satellites and the grounds into a setting for a dream.

They passed through hundreds, maybe thousands, of smiling faces, only a few registering a spark of recognition in her stalled mind. Princes Durante and Eduardo, Gio, Alonzo's partner, and other relatives of Vincenzo's whom she'd met in the past week. Her gaze hiccupped and lingered only once, on her father and brother. They looked so dashing in their fineries, so moved, looking at her so lovingly. Her resentment crumbled and her heart trembled with that affection that had and would always defy logic.

Then Vincenzo swept her away and to the stage that now blocked the doors of the central tower, facing the courtyard where guests milled in concentric semicircles of tables.

As soon as they took the last step up the royal-blue satin-covered stairs, where a sumptuously dressed minister awaited them between King Ferruccio and Crown Prince Leandro, who would be their witnesses, the live medley of regal music stopped. Silence and sea breeze lamented in her ears as Vincenzo handed her down so she could kneel on the velvet cushion before the minister, then he followed her, keeping her molded to his side.

The minister of the province's main church—a jovial man who'd told her how delighted he was to be finally marrying the confirmed bachelor lord of his province—gave a little speech then recited the marriage vows, in Italian then in English, for the bride's guests' benefit. As per Vincenzo's province and family traditions, bride and groom didn't repeat those vows or exchange ones of their own.

She welcomed that. She had nothing to say to Vincenzo. Nothing but the truth of her feelings. And those should not and would never leave her heart to pass through her lips.

Ferruccio came forward with their rings, blessing them

and their union as their king, accepting their bows with that still-pondering smile. This guy was just too astute.

His assessing eyes spiked her agitation so much it made her keep missing Vincenzo's finger as she tried to slip his wedding band on. Vincenzo took hold of her hands and branded them with a kiss that rendered them useless before guiding them through the achingly symbolic ritual. The imaginary pins holding up her smile started to pierce into her flesh.

Then it was Leandro's turn as the second witness to perform the last ritual, coming forward with a crystal goblet. Vincenzo clasped her to his side as he leaned down, plastering his cheek against hers as Leandro held the goblet to their lips for them to simultaneously sip the bloodred liquid that tasted and smelled of an elusive amalgam of spices, fruits and flowers. He recited the words that would "bind their blood" so that they'd never be complete without the other.

Then Vincenzo turned her to face the crowd, who were now on their feet in a standing ovation, holding up their similarly filled glasses and toasting the couple in unison.

This was really happening. She was standing with the man she'd thought she'd lost forever, before his family, friends and followers, before the world, as his bride and princess.

Acting as his bride and princess. *Never forget that, and you might yet survive this.*

Just when she thought the worst was over, Vincenzo made everything infinitely worse.

His magnificent voice rose, carrying on the deepening night's breeze. "My people, my family and friends, everyone blessed to call Castaldini home. I give you your new princess. The glory of my life. Gloria D'Agostino."

If he hadn't had her firmly tucked into his side, she would have folded to the ground.

The canopy of moonlit sky at his back blurred as he looked down at her with an intensity that flayed her already inflamed senses. He brought her back into her body, crushing it to his, and swooped down to claim her lips, reclaiming her wasteland of a soul, feeling like bliss, tasting like life.

The crowd roared its approval accompanied with a storm of clinking glasses as the orchestra played a joyful tune this time, with the majority of the crowd joining in, a song celebrating the newlyweds' future happiness.

As the festivities escalated into the night, she lost herself in the creativity of Alonzo's efforts and the enthusiasm of everyone present. The fantasy of it all deepened until she felt she'd never resurface, until her ordinary, solitary life blipped out from her memory.

Everything became replaced by the wonder of Vincenzo's nearness, by that of his world, and all the wonderful people who populated his life.

And her resolve was resurrected.

Nothing mattered but having this time with Vincenzo. And she would drain every single second of it dry.

Nine

"The ordeal is finally over."

Tremors drenched Glory at Vincenzo's deep purr.

It came from the darkness that enveloped the doorway of her hideaway.

At midnight, as per tradition, Vincenzo's friends had held him back while she'd been "spirited" away by hers. It was supposed to whet the groom's appetites even further, searching for his bride in the castle, until he caught her and carried her back to their marital quarters.

The ladies had deserted her somewhere she'd never been in the castle what felt like an hour ago.

She'd felt like someone in a movie who'd been suddenly left behind somewhere mysterious and otherworldly, filled with whispers of temptation beckoning to an unknown fate.

She'd felt his approach long before she'd heard his voice. She now felt his eyes on her as she stood in the dancing light of a flame-lit brass lantern. Her heart no longer had distinct beats, buzzing like a hummingbird's wings, failing to pump blood to her vitals. The world started to blotch crimson....

His voice brought her jackknifing back to focus. "While being forced to share you with every single person I've known in my life, I've been pretending sanity and civilization for the crowd and the cameras. Now the wait is over."

He appeared as if separating from the darkness, a piece of its endlessness taking the form of the epitome of manhood. The need radiating from him violently strummed her, the reverberations deepening her paralysis.

She could only hurl herself at him, climb him, tear him out of his clothes and devour him in her mind.

Then he was there, against her, pressing her into the wall. Her cry echoed in the almost empty chamber as he ground himself against her. Moans and groans filled her head, high and deep, the sounds of suffering. He was in agony, too. His flesh burned her with his torment.

"Ti voglio tanto...tanto, Gloriosa mia."

Her nod was frantic. "I want you too much, too.... Take me to our room...." She didn't know where that was. Another tradition of the nobility around here. The groom picked the quarters for his bride and prepared them for pampering and pleasuring her. Just imagining it made her plead, *"Please,* Vincenzo...*now."*

He roared as she sank her teeth in his neck to stress her plea. He snatched her off her feet, hurtled with her through the now-deserted winding corridors of his fairy-tale domain.

Doors opened into a place set up like an erotic dream. The vast chamber opened onto a semicircular balcony with wide-open ten-foot doors. The balmy sea breeze wafted in with the scent of jasmine and sandalwood incense, making sheer white curtains dance like gossamer spirits. The flames of a hundred candles undulated like fiery beings. A bed bigger than any she'd thought possible occupied the far end of the room. It was spread in satin the color of her eyes and covered in white and gold rose petals.

But instead of taking her there and putting an end to the torment, he only put her down on her feet.

She stood swaying with the loss of his support and watched him move to stand framed against the moonlit balcony door, her Roman god come to life.

Before she could ask why he'd walked away, his voice cascaded over her, intertwining with the music of the night. "Though I'm dying to end our suffering, there's one thing I want to do first. A wedding night ritual that used to be done here before modernism took over and people started taking too many shortcuts, even in passion. Something I never thought I'd have the chance to do, but always wished I could."

She groaned, louder inwardly. Not another thing to prolong her waiting! "What's that ritual?"

"A striptease. Of sorts."

Okay. Sounded good. Exactly what she wanted to do. Though she wasn't sure her system could withstand watching him strip at this point.

"It has rules, though."

Not so good. He expected her to follow rules, or do anything that required coherence now?

"Would you hurry up and say what those rules are before I liquefy completely?"

His chuckle was pure male pride. "We play a game. The winner gets to dictate the intimacies we share, until the other wins a next one."

"And the rules of the game, dammit?"

His laughter deepened. He loved watching her come apart. "Each says the most audacious thing that has ever crossed their mind about the other, confessing every uninhibited fantasy. According to the enormity of each confession, we shed one or more pieces of clothing."

Now, that wasn't good *at all*. She wasn't ready to expose her most private yearnings.

Which was stupid, when she was begging him to expose *her* to every intimacy he could think of.

But it was one thing for him to do it, for her to revel in having it done to her, another to put her needs into words. She'd been hoping he'd give her what she needed with nothing but surrender on her part, as he'd always done.

But that was exactly what this was about. Making her own her needs heard. Taking pride in them and responsibility for them. An opportunity to be on equal footing with him, at least in this.

And that wasn't bad. Also, she could see he believed he'd win without breaking a sweat, that he would have her writhing in submission before he was through.

He probably would. Didn't mean she'd make it easy for him, or that she would go down without a fight. Dictating intimacies was a hefty prize. Just the idea of having him doing her sensual bidding was worth any risk.

She took the first one. "The first time I saw you, before you ushered me into your office for my interview, you were in your meeting room among all those stuffy suits. All I could think as I shook your hand was whether you tasted as incredible as you smelled. I wanted to know if you looked even more heart-stopping in the throes of pleasure. I wanted to tell the others to get out so I could find out, right there and then. My fantasy went even further, that if they didn't leave, I wouldn't stop, even if it meant giving them a show."

His eyes had darkened with her every word, becoming obsidian pools. His lips belied his eyes' ferocity, spreading wider with approval as he clapped, lazily, sensuously. "I thought you'd balk. Well done."

He took off his sash and slid his cape off his shoulders in an arc, aborting its momentum with a tug that spooled it around his forearm before he let it pool to the ground.

"Taking off pieces of clothing should be simultaneous."

She jerked from her mesmerized gawking, fumbling with her train, almost tearing it off in her haste.

Then it was his turn. "The moment you walked into the room that first day and looked at me with those incredible eyes, I wanted to push you back on my desk, whether anyone remained in my office or not, spread your silky legs and devour you to a screaming orgasm before I even knew who you were."

The fire in her loins was spreading, consuming her, flowing down her thighs. And all he'd done was expose her to his visual and verbal desire and make her confess hers.

He prowled toward her, giving her a hormone-roaring show of contained power and inbred poise as he slipped off his jacket. By the time it thudded to the ground in his wake, she'd torn off her veil, tumbling her chignon in disarray.

"When you showed up on my doorstep that night," she panted, "I thought it would be the first and last time I had you alone. I fantasized about seizing the opportunity, dragging you in, tearing you out of your clothes and losing my mind all over you, even if you fired me for it."

He unbuttoned his shirt, exposing his Herculean torso and abdomen, shrugged the shirt off then yanked off his boots and socks. "All those licentious thoughts when you were a virgin, too."

As she bent to take off her stilettos, a warning finger stopped her. She straightened, swaying in place. "Being a virgin made my fantasies even more licentious. I had no expectations or experience to water them down."

His zipper slid down with a smooth hiss that made her start to shake in earnest.

He let his pants fall then kicked them aside. "Whatever happened to the fantasies after you experienced me?"

Her zipper was undone in a far less assured fashion. Her dress peeled off her swollen breasts under its own weight, sighing in a rustling mass around her ankles. She struggled not to stumble as she stepped out of it.

She stood facing him, in her white lace thong, jewelry and four-inch stilettos, her gaze glued to the erection stretching his boxers.

"They ended." At his frown, she elaborated, "I realized they were actually modest, almost pathetic. You surpassed any fantasy I was creative enough to have."

A shock wave of lust blasted off of him.

Her lips trembled in triumph. "Do I win?"

His chest was heaving now. "All those years, I fantasized about going back for you, dragging you away wherever I found you, taking you somewhere where there was only us, only ever us. I would be in my lab, or in a board meeting or at a summit and I'd sit and plan everything I'd do to you touch by touch. I planned whole nights of arousing you and taking you to the edge again and again until you were begging me to take you over it, to do anything and everything to you, with you. I mapped out the number of orgasms I'd give you, their variations and method before I had mercy on you, took you, rode you until I drained your magnificent body of every spark of sensation it was capable of. Then I planned how to keep you in my power, how to have you beg to be my pleasure slave, and a slave to my pleasure."

"Vincenzo, *pietà*...have mercy now...you win." She stumbled the last steps between them, crushed her breasts against his hard chest, assuaging the pain, accumulating more. "Now dictate. Any intimacy. And just *do* it."

He grabbed her head in both hands. "I always started our intimacies as the hunter, the seeker. Even when you did anything to me, it was at my request, my prodding. But I always fantasized that you'd take the initiative, do anything you want to me. This is what I dictate. That you show me *your* desire, *Gloria mia*." His hands stabbed into her hair, pulling her away by its tether, demand vehement in his eyes. "Do it."

Vincenzo watched Glory as she pulled away. Her eyes were eclipsed with hunger as she started demonstrating her fantasies.

She touched him all over, explored and owned and worshipped him, in strokes and caresses, in suckles and kisses, in nips and kneads—his chest and abdomen, his arms and hands, his neck and face—telling him how she'd always wanted to do that, every second of every day, how she'd thought nothing, real or imagined, touched him in beauty, in wonder.

He reveled in feeling his mind unravel with her every touch and confession, in feeling her craving cocooning him, claiming him. Then, without warning, she dropped before him, wrapping her arms around his thighs, burrowing her face into his erection.

His eyes glazed over at the sight of her as she knelt before him. The ripe swell of her buttocks, the graceful curve of her back, the gleaming luxury of her hair, her unbridled expression as she drew deep of his feel and scent, as she pulled his boxers down. His engorgement rebounded against his belly, throbbing, straining.

Then she was showing him in glorious sight and sound and touch. And words. Feverish, explicit, uncensored words, confessing all. Exposing the true extent of her desire.

His body hovered on the edge of detonation with every touch, yet plateaued in the most agonizing arousal he'd ever experienced. He felt his life depended on, and was threatened by, prolonging this. His groans merged as her hands owned and explored him, her breath on his flesh a furnace blast, her tongue as it swirled and lapped the flow of his desire a sweep of insanity. Then she engulfed all she could of him, poured delight and delirium all over him. And his mind snapped.

"Enough."

Then she was hauled over his shoulders, gasping and moaning as he hurtled across the room. Her teeth sank into his shoulder blade, unleashing a roar from his depths as he swung her over and down on the bed. He stood back for one more fractured heartbeat, looking down at her, a goddess of abandon and decadence lying open and maddened with need among the petals, her satiny firmness sparkling in his kingdom's treasures, trembling arms outstretched, bidding him come lose his mind. He first rid her of jewels, leaving only the ring, then he lost the last shred of the civilized man and let the beast claw its way out of his skin.

He came down on top of her, yanked her thighs apart and crushed her beneath him. She surged back into him, grinding herself against him, her legs spreading wider, her fingers and nails digging into him, her litany of "don't wait, don't wait, fill me, fill me" completing his descent into oblivion.

Incoherent, he gripped her buttocks, tilted her, bore down on her, then, in one forceful stroke, he plunged inside her, invading her to her recesses. She engulfed him back on a piercing scream, consuming him in her vise of pure molten pleasure.

His bellow rocked him, and her beneath him. *"Glory... at last."*

Her head thrashed, tossing her hair among the petals, her back a steep arch, her voice a pulse of fever. "Yes, Vincenzo, yes…take me, take me back, take all of me…"

But before he did, he rested his forehead on hers, overcome by the enormity of being inside her again. She arched beneath him, taking him all the way to her womb, her eyes streaming, making him feel she'd taken him all the way to her heart like he'd once believed she had.

On a fervent prayer that it was true, he withdrew all the way out of her then thrust back, fierce and full.

Then he rode her. And rode her. To the escalating rhythm of her satin screams, his frenzied rumbles echoing them. It could have been a minute or an hour as the pleasure, the intimacy, rose and deepened. Then, with relief and regret, both of them extreme, he felt his body hurtling to completion. Needing her pleasure first, he held back until her almost unbearable tightness clamped down on his length, pouring a surplus of red-hot welcome over his flesh as she convulsed beneath him, her orgasm tearing through her, wrenching her core around him.

Seeing her lost to the pleasure he'd given her hurled him after her into the abyss of ecstasy. His buttocks convulsed into her cradle as he poured himself inside her, surge after surge of blinding, scorching pleasure. Her convulsions spiked with every splash of his seed, her cries were stifled against his shoulder as she mashed herself into him. He felt her heart boom out of control along with his as the paroxysm of release wiped out existence around them....

"Dio, siete incredibile."

Glory thought this had to be the most wonderful sound in existence. Vincenzo cooing to her. That he was telling her she was incredible didn't hurt, either.

She hadn't slept, not for a second. The first time had also been like that, leaving her with the experience still expanding inside her, awake but in the stasis of stunned satisfaction.

She tried to open her eyes, but they wouldn't cooperate. They were swollen. Just like every inch of her, inside and out. From Vincenzo's ferocious possession, and her fierce response. A numb hand flew to her head, surprised it was still there. He'd almost blown it off with pleasure, discharging the accumulated frustrations and cravings of six years in one annihilating detonation.

And he'd only managed to whet her appetite sharper. She wanted him again, even more than before. Her addiction was fully resurrected and would keep intensifying. Until it ended again.

But now it was just starting. She wanted every second of it before she had to relinquish it all again.

Succeeding in opening her eyes at last, she found him propped over his elbow, draped half over her, his eyes smoldering down at her. "*Dio,* what have you done to yourself? How could you be even more beautiful than before? How could you give me even more pleasure?"

"Look who's talking." She dragged his head down to her, twisting beneath him, bringing him fully on top of her.

He started to kiss her, caress her, but she was too inflamed. She clamped her legs around his waist, thrusting herself against his intact arousal.

He eased her down, unlocked her legs and rose between her splayed thighs, probing her with a finger, then two. Her flesh clamped around their delicious invasion, but it was him she needed inside her. She was flowing for him. He attempted to soothe her frenzy, clearly wanting to take it slower this time. She wouldn't survive slower. Her heartbeats felt as if they'd race each other to a standstill.

"Just take me, Vincenzo," she cried, undulating beneath him, her breasts turgid and aching, her core on fire. "I've needed you inside me for so long…so long…and having you once only made me want more…."

"After six endless years without this, without you, you'll have more, as much as you can survive." He bore her down into the mattress, driving air from her lungs. "Now I take my fill of you. And you take your fill of me. Take it all, *Gloria mia*."

And he plunged inside her.

Her scream was stifled with that first craved invasion, that elemental feeling of his potency filling her, like a burning dawn, scorching everything away as it spread. He kept plunging deeper, feeling as if he'd never bottom out. Then he did, nudging against what felt like the center of her being. He relented at her scream, resting against the opening of her womb and stilling inside her, overfilling her, inundating her with sensations both agonizing and sublime.

Then the need for him to conquer her rose. Her legs clamped around his back; her heels dug into his buttocks, urging him on; her fractured moans begged for everything, insane for the assuagement of his full power and possession. And he answered, drowning her in a mouth-mating as he drove her beyond ecstasy, beyond her limits, winding that coil of need inside her tighter and tighter with each thrust.

Then he groaned for her to come for him and all the tension spiked and splintered, lashing out through her system in shock waves of excruciating gratification. His tongue filled her, absorbing her cries of pleasure as he filled her with his own, jet after jet of fuel over her fire.

He kissed her all through the descent, rumbling her name again and again, throbbing inside her until the tide receded and cell-deep bliss dragged her into its still, silent realm.

Glory had been awake for a while now.

She kept her eyes closed, regulating her breathing even as her heart stumbled.

From the flickering dimness illuminating her closed lids, she knew it was night again. Twenty-four hours or more had passed since Vincenzo had carried her into this chamber of pleasures. He had said he wasn't coming up for air for at least that long. And he'd kept his promise. How he'd kept it.

After the first two times he'd made love to her, he'd carried her to the adjoining bathroom, an amalgam of old Castaldinian design and cutting-edge luxury. By the time he'd carried her back to bed, he'd melted her into too many orgasms to count. Then they'd spent hours reviving every sensual bond they'd formed years ago. He claimed they'd never loosened their hold over him.

Then he'd let her have him at *her* mercy as she fulfilled her fantasy of losing her mind all over him. Riding him to the most explosive release in her life was the last thing she remembered before waking up minutes ago.

There was a problem, though. She'd woken up so many times, too many, from abandoned nights to feel him wrapped around her like that. Then she'd opened her eyes and he'd dissolved into the emptiness of reality. She was afraid if she opened her eyes now, he might disappear again.

"Gloria mia?"

She'd heard him crooning her name in her waking dreams before. Logically speaking, everything that had culminated in their wedding night had to be some lovelorn hallucination....

Every nerve in her body fired in unison as the hand cupping her breast started caressing it to the fullness of need again.

Okay. None of her tormenting phantasms had felt that real. That good. That meant that even if it made no sense whatsoever, Vincenzo *was* really wrapped around her after a night of magic beyond her wildest fantasies.

Then his silk-covered leg drove between hers, pressing just where she needed. He must have sensed she was awake. Or her heart must have been shaking the whole bed.

No use pretending to be asleep now.

She opened her eyes. The best sight in existence filled her

vision. Vincenzo. His every line thrown into relief by stark shadows and the illumination of the gibbous moon pouring from the open window. But it was his expression that had her on the verge of crushing herself against him and weeping.

She must be seeing what she longed to see. Or she was superimposing what *she* felt on him. He couldn't be looking at her as if he couldn't believe she was in his arms again. As if he was afraid to blink and miss one nuance of her, one second with her. As if he loved her. As if he'd always loved her.

As if responding to her need to escape the impossible yearnings, his expression shifted to another kind of passion as he weighed and kneaded her breast. "I think I will fulfill my fantasy, after all. I'll keep you here as my pleasure slave." She moaned, arched, pressed her breast harder into his big palm. Something elemental rumbled in his gut. "The way you respond to my every word and touch is pure magic. What you do to me by just existing is beyond even that."

Her hips moved to yield to the erection that she was still stunned she could accommodate. Her moan grew louder as he expanded and hardened even more. "It's only fair that I turn you inside out like you do me."

Indulgence smoldered in his eyes. "So we're even."

"*Not* unless we play musical slaves."

"After what you did to me last night, I might cheat and let you sit on the chair every time. I'll let you sit anywhere you want, as many times and as long as you want."

"Oh, I want. I *want,* Vincenzo."

Unable to bear the emptiness inside her that only he could fill, she tried to drag him over and inside her. He resisted her, slid down her body, looking up as she twisted in his hold.

"I have a six-year hunger that I need to appease, *gloriosa mia.* Surrender to me, let me take my fill."

And she collapsed, could do nothing but submit to his will and let him take everything he wanted, let him drive her to madness, over and over until he'd drained her dry of reason. Of worries. Of anything that wasn't him.

When next she woke, it was night again, and she was alone.

Before dismay could register, the door creaked open and in Vincenzo walked with a huge, piled tray in his hands. In a molded gray shirt and pants, he looked like a god come down to earth to mess with mortals' wills and jeopardize their souls.

His smile was indulgence itself as he put the tray aside to pull her up to a sitting position. The sheet fell off, exposing her breasts. As if he couldn't help it, he bent and saluted each nipple with soft pulls, soothing the soreness she'd literally pummeled him to inflict on her.

He pulled back reluctantly. "No more temptation, princess." He chuckled at her pout. "I'd do nothing but service and pleasure Your Royal Voluptuousness nonstop, but I have to refuel you so you can withstand the week ahead."

She sighed her pleasure as she sifted her fingers through the thick, silky depths of his hair. "I've been holding up pretty well for the past two days. What's so different about the week ahead?"

"First, for the past two days you haven't even left this room. You have been mostly flat on your back—or belly—and apart from a couple of memorable instances, I've been doing all the work." She smacked him playfully, giggling, her body priming itself again at the memory of all the "work" he'd done. "But I'm going to demand more of your participation over the next week, as it's all the time I have for our honeymoon. My post back in New York starts next week."

Her heart plummeted. That soon?

She must have looked as crestfallen as she felt. He smoothed her tousled bangs out of her eyes, his tone urgent. "I'll only work by day. The nights, I'm all yours."

She smiled, hating that she'd made him feel bad for having to work. "It's okay. I need to get back to work myself."

His eyes flared with possessiveness as he slid the sheet totally off her. "During the days only, *Gloriosa mia*. The nights are mine."

She nodded dreamily as she squeezed her breasts and thighs together to mitigate their aching throb. "Yes."

His eyes glazed over as he pushed her thighs apart, sliding two fingers between her soaked folds. "And afternoons and lunch breaks and whenever I can squeeze you in."

Her legs fell apart, inviting his fingers inside; her breasts jutted for him to squeeze away. "Oh, yes."

Her response tore away any intentions to prioritize food as he fell on her breasts again, suckling, his fingers plunging inside her, pumping. She poured fuel on his fervor, kneading his erection, sinking her teeth into his shoulders.

"*Dio, Gloria mia,* you make me insane...."

His growl was driven as he descended over her, pushed her flat on her back, impacting her with his full weight and rising between her spread legs only enough to free himself.

Then, without preliminaries, he drove into her, tearing a shriek from her depths. He rammed inside her in a furious rhythm, plunging deeper with every thrust, growling like a beast. The expansion inside her around his girth and length, the feeling of being totally dominated and mastered, had her sobbing, pleasure twisting tighter inside her until she feared she'd unravel once it snapped.

He rose on outstretched arms. "Look at us, *Gloria mia,* look what I'm doing to you, look how you're taking me...."

She looked, and the sight of the daunting column of flesh disappearing inside her, spreading her, joining them, made her thrash at the carnality of it, the beauty.

Then the tightness was quickening inside her, the familiar crescendo, her flesh fluttering around his girth.

He felt it, fell on her breasts, suckling hard, biting, triggering her. "Come for me, *gloriosa,* come all over me. Finish me with your pleasure as I finish you."

Everything snapped inside her like a high-voltage cable, writhing and lashing out and wreaking devastation. He drove the deepest he'd ever been inside her, roaring as he rested against her womb and razed her in the ecstasy of his release.

But feeling his seed splashing her intimate walls, filling her, branding her, spread regret along with the pleasure. Regret that his seed wouldn't take root. She'd made sure it wouldn't.

He collapsed on top of her, his breathing as harsh as hers. She wrapped herself tighter around him, relishing his weight. Without him covering her like this, anchoring her in the aftermath of devastation, she felt she might dissipate....

He drew up, supporting his weight on one elbow, fusing them in the evidence of their mutual satisfaction, his other hand securing her head for a deep, luxurious kiss.

The moment he felt her quickening beneath him again, he rumbled a self-deprecating laugh, then groaned as he separated their bodies. "Have mercy, *bellissima.* Now it's I who needs to refuel. I'm not a spry teenager anymore."

Her gaze clung to his undiminished manhood. "Are you kidding me? I've been wondering if you've hooked yourself to your inexhaustible energy source."

"I am hooked, all right, on a perpetually renewable source of passionate madness whose name is but a description of her." Before she could lunge at him, he jumped up, stuffing himself with difficulty into his pants. "*We're* refueling. Then I'm taking you sailing. We'll continue this session on board. Ever made love rocking to the undulations of a tranquil sea?"

Before she said no, since he hadn't taken her sailing before, jealousy sank into her gut.

He grinned. "Neither have I. Another fantasy I'll fulfill.

I wrote a list of one hundred and ten items while you slept. I intend to make serious headway into all of them during the next week."

Her tension deflated. He hadn't done it before. He hadn't done so many things, but he wanted to do them all with her. Because she was the only one who made him want them. Just like he was the only one who made her want everything and anything.

She arched sensuously, smoothing her hands down her breasts, her tummy, delighting in the soreness inside and out. "I thought we were going to take turns playing out fantasies."

He tugged her up by the hand, this time making sure not to come too close and be snared back. "*Incantatrice mia,* I just played one of yours now. Taking you with no foreplay, just rough domination and explosive satisfaction."

So he could read her like a hundred-foot billboard.

He brought back the tray, placed it across her thighs and bent for one last kiss before he withdrew quickly, making her bite him in her effort to cling.

He laved her bite with a wince of enjoyment. "Eat something else for now, *amore mio.* I have to go prepare the rest of the day, then the week. I promise your fantasies are going to be heavily featured and meticulously taken care of."

With one last wink, he turned and strode out.

She watched him go, everything on pause.

Had he said *amore mio?*

My love?

Ten

Amore mio.

The words rang in a loop inside Glory's head as she stood staring around her condo. *Amore mio, amore mio*—crooned in Vincenzo's voice, soaked in his passion.

He'd been calling her that constantly, among all the other endearments he kept lavishing on her. At least he had for the first six weeks after their wedding. It had been over a week now that he hadn't been around to call her much of anything.

They'd been back to New York after their honeymoon ended. Vincenzo had extended their time away to two weeks at a hefty cost to all the people who'd arranged their schedules counting on his presence a week earlier.

A wave of oppression descended over her as images from those two weeks in paradise bombarded her. At their end, she'd thought that if she died then, she would have certainly died the most fulfilled, pleasured and pampered woman on earth.

Then they'd gone back to New York. He'd started his position and she'd gone back to work, and instead of everything slowing and cooling down, it had gotten better, hotter. He'd kept his promises and more, making time for her, for them, always, but even better, making a place for her in his working life, and asking for and taking a place in hers.

He'd taken her with him to every function, showing her off as if she was his most vital asset. He'd come to her like he used to with his work issues, taking her opinion and following her advice. He'd thrown his full weight into making difficulties in her work disappear and making far-fetched hopes achievable, without her even asking.

And through it all he'd been saying *amore mio*. My love.

He'd called her that in the past. She'd believed he'd meant it. Then everything had happened, and she'd known the name had just been an empty endearment. Now, she no longer knew what to believe. After he'd confessed he'd lied about his reasons for leaving her. After the past weeks in his arms, in his life.

So what had it meant to him then? What did it mean now?

The need to ask, to understand everything that had happened in the past, mushroomed daily. She'd tried more than once to broach the subject, but he'd always diverted her, unwilling to talk about it, as if he hated to bring up the past, fearing it would taint the present.

She could understand that. He appeared to have decided to live in the moment, without consideration for the past or the future. And she tried to do that, too, succeeding most of the time. At least, when he was with her. The moment she was out of his orbit, obsessions attacked her, and questions that had never been answered preyed on her. And it was all because she'd done an unforgivable thing.

She'd let herself hope. That this wouldn't be temporary, that it couldn't be, not when it was so incredible.

At least it had been incredible until last week when he'd suddenly started becoming unavailable. Even though he'd apologized, blamed work problems, swore it would only be temporary, his absence had plunged her into a nightmarish déjà vu. Though he still came home, still made love to her—not like before when he'd cut her off suddenly—it still made her feel this was the beginning of the end. She tried to tell herself that the "honeymoon" was over, that it happened with everyone, that there was no way he could have sustained that level of intensity. It didn't mean anything was wrong.

Tell that to her glued-back-together heart.

But all her upheaval had one origin. The missing piece that could explain how the noble man she was now certain Vincenzo was could have been so cruel to her.

Her eyes fell on the prenup he'd left on her entrance cabinet what felt like ages ago, and something turned in her head, clicked.

Her eyes jerked up, slamming into their reflection in the mirror above as that missing piece crashed into place.

Her family.

God, how hadn't it occurred to her before? This had to be the explanation. He'd said her father and Daniel had been perpetrating crimes for a long time. What if it had been as far back as six years, and he'd discovered it when he'd been investigating them during his espionage crisis?

Then another idea whacked her like an uppercut.

Even if he'd found it out of the question to be involved with someone with a family of criminals, there had been no reason to be vicious with her over her family's crimes. That meant one thing. He'd thought she'd been involved in those crimes. Or worse, he'd thought she'd embezzle or defraud him, too, and had thought to preempt her, cut her off before she had the chance.

Gasping as suspicions solidified into conviction, she staggered to the nearest horizontal surface, sitting heavily.

Then another realization pushed aside the debris of shame and anguish.

He'd believed her an accomplice to her family, a danger to him, and he'd simply walked away. He'd turned vicious only when she'd cornered him. That meant one thing—he *had* felt something for her. Something strong enough that it stopped him from prosecuting her even when he'd thought she deserved it.

Following that same rationalization, the way he was with her now, even with his new evidence of her family's crimes, meant that he believed she couldn't be party to those. As for what she'd been seeing in his eyes, the way he said *amore mio,* this could mean…

In the next moment her trembling hope was shot down like a bird before it could spread its wings.

Even if he didn't think she was involved in illegal activities now, he would never think her worth more than a fleeting place in his life. And who could blame him?

She couldn't.

Her aching eyes panned around her condo. She'd come here to empty it, to end its lease. Vincenzo had asked her to do so a couple of weeks ago. She'd felt alarmed at what that implied and had groped for a reason to dismiss his request, arguing she needed a place to entertain family and friends away from their own private quarters. But he'd already thought of that, producing a lease to another condo, far more lavish, and a minute's walk from his building. It looked as if he was thinking of her all the time, going out of his way to provide her with anything that would make her life easier, fuller.

But she couldn't count on anything from him, or with him. She wouldn't do this to herself again. She had to live with the expectation that this would end, and after last week, it appeared that the end would be sooner rather than later. She had to be ready to fade back into her own life once he pulled away completely. But to do that, she had to make sure she had a life to fade back to.

She rose, headed back to the suitcases she'd packed, opened them and started putting everything back in its place.

An hour later, on her way out, she stopped by the entrance cabinet. After a long moment of staring at the prenup, she picked it up.

Vincenzo whistled an upbeat tune as he exited the shower.

He caught his eyes in the steamed-up mirror and grinned widely at himself. He felt like whistling all the time now. Or singing. He'd been struggling not to do either in all those stuffy meetings and negotiations he'd been attending. He'd had the most important one so far today, what he'd been working toward since he'd gone back to New York with Glory after their honeymoon six weeks ago.

The memory of their honeymoon cascaded through him again. He'd extended it for a week and had representatives of a dozen countries scrambling to readjust their schedules. When they'd complained, he'd told them they instead had to thank his bride for putting their agendas ahead of her rights and consenting to cut short her honeymoon for them. He'd seen to it that each and every one *had* thanked her, in all the functions to which she'd accompanied him.

A thrill of pride spread through him. She'd been beyond magnificent. A consort of a caliber he couldn't have dreamed of. Though she'd gone back to her own hectic schedule, she always made time for him. She aided, guided and supported him with her counsel, honored, soothed and delighted him with her company. Every moment with her, in and out of bed, had been better than anything he'd dared plan or hope for.

He'd never known happiness like this existed.

Just as he thought that, a frown invaded his elation.

He hadn't been able to have her with him for over two weeks now. With back-to-back meetings and unending follow-up work, he'd had to leave her behind, cancel dates and generally have no time for her. He hadn't even come home for the past three days.

He was paying the price for taking too much time with her during the first weeks of their marriage. Work had accumulated until it had become unmanageable, and resolving the mess had been like digging in the sea, with new chores only pouring over the unfinished ones. He'd needed to clean out his agenda then start fresh using the system Glory had set up for him.

So, for the past two weeks, he'd worked flat out to get this phase, the groundwork his whole mission was built on, out of the way once and for all.

Though it had been agonizing being without her, at least he'd succeeded in fixing the problem he'd caused by being too greedy for her. He was now out of the bottleneck and the first phase of his mission here had been concluded.

And before he entered the next phase, he had a prolonged vacation with Glory planned. A second honeymoon. He intended to have another one every month.

Grinning to himself again, luxuriating in the anticipation, he entered the office he hadn't used for weeks.

He saw it the moment he stepped inside and recognized it for what it was at once.

The prenup agreement.

Was his mind playing tricks on him? He'd left it in Glory's condo over two months ago.

A surge of trepidation came over him as he neared it, approaching it as if it was a live grenade. A quick, compulsive check ended any doubt. That *was* the copy he'd given her.

Why was it on his desk, as if Glory was loath to hand it

to him face-to-face? If she was, why put it there at all? After all this time? All this intimacy?

What was she trying to tell him?

Was she reinforcing his original conditions, telling him this was still how she viewed their marriage? As a temporary hostile takeover? But that had stopped being true almost from the start. He'd told her he'd changed his mind after *hours* of being with her again. She hadn't changed her mind after weeks of being with him? But she'd agreed to marry him of her free will, then proceeded to blow his mind with passion and pleasure ever since. He'd thought she'd been showing him that she'd forgotten how this had started, that she'd been demonstrating with actions how she now viewed their relationship, that she wanted it to continue. He sat down, staring at the offensive volume as if it was his worst mistake come back to haunt him. Which it was.

And it was his fault it was haunting him. He'd avoided a confrontation about the past, with her, with himself. He'd just been so scared it might spoil the perfection they had now.

But here was what avoidance had led to.

He now had to admit to himself what he'd been thinking and feeling all along.

He'd at first thought she'd changed her ways. But when he couldn't find a trace of subterfuge in her—something that couldn't be wiped so totally from someone's character—he'd been able to sanction only one thing. That she'd always been what he'd believed her to be from the start, the upstanding human being and the incredible woman he'd fallen in love with. And this had led him to one conclusion. That she'd been forced into her past betrayal.

There was only one scenario that made sense. As soon as he'd employed her, those who always looked for chinks in his armor got to her family, and through them, to her. Younger, vulnerable to her family's needs, she'd been forced to do their bidding, probably under fear of losing them to imprisonment through their crippling debts. That *had* been the first thing that had occurred to her when *he'd* threatened to imprison them.

But she must have hated doing it and soon realized there'd been no excuse for what they'd forced her to do. She *had* struck out as far away from them as possible, becoming the magnificent force for good she was now.

But after observing her with her family, with her mother especially, he was now certain Glory had no idea that he'd discovered her betrayal, or she would have understood why he'd kicked her out of his life. Her mother clearly hadn't told her of the climactic confrontations with him. Probably out of shame that she'd exposed her daughter to buy the rest of her family's salvation.

Or he might be all wrong and there might be another explanation. But whatever it was, he was certain she hadn't set him up in cold blood, or pretended emotions she hadn't felt. Everything in him just *knew* that her involvement with him had been real, and predated whatever she'd been forced to do. And that was the one thing that mattered to him.

Where he was concerned, from the moment he'd told her she was free not to marry him, that past had been wiped out from his mind and heart. Nothing remained in him now but that he wanted her, *loved* her, far more than he ever had.

But it was clear she had no idea this was how he felt. This must be why she was offering him the prenup. Showing him that he was free to keep his original pact if he wanted.

It was time to make a full admission, to leave her in no doubt what he wanted. Her. As his wife, for real and forever.

He heaved up to his feet, excitement frothing inside him, and swiped the prenup off the desk.

He'd take that piece of paranoid crap he'd regretted ever since it had passed from his hands to hers and tear it to pieces. He'd throw it at her feet along with his heart and his life. He'd...

His phone rang.

Gritting his teeth at the interruption, he answered the call. A moment later, he wished he hadn't.

A deep, somber voice poured into his ear, and everything inside him tightened, as if to ward off a blow.

Now what?

"Thanks for seeing me on such short notice, Prince Vincenzo."

Vincenzo's unease rose. Brandon Steele never asked to see him unless there was some catastrophe brewing.

"We're alone now so drop the titles, please, Brandon."

The man inclined his head silently, looking, as always, like a strange cross between a suave celebrity and a linebacker. He had a quietly menacing aura hanging over him like a cloak.

Vincenzo had hired him seven years ago to protect his research and businesses against sabotage and intellectual property theft. The agency Brandon owned and ran, Steele Security, had come highly recommended by Vincenzo's cousin Eduardo as the most effective undercover agency to handle financial fraud and industrial espionage.

Brandon held a spotless track record, had uncovered dozens of masterful infiltrations and conspiracies, saved Vincenzo and his cousins untold millions and smoothed the course of their rise to the top of their respective fields.

But it was one particular achievement that always made Vincenzo loath to see him, more now than ever.

He'd been the one who'd gotten proof of Glory's espionage six years ago.

Getting to the point as always, Brandon exhaled. "I don't know how to say this, Vincenzo, but what were you thinking? You married the woman who once spied on you?"

Was that it? Brandon was here to scold him?

"Things aren't as simple as they look to you, Brandon."

Brandon cocked one disbelieving eyebrow. "Aren't they?"

Vincenzo had no time for skepticism. If not for Brandon's untimely call, he could have been with Glory right now, resolving everything with her.

Vincenzo exhaled. "Did you detect another leak in my operations? And you jumped to the conclusion that the only new thing in my life is Glory, again, so she must be involved somehow?"

Brandon stared at him as if he'd grown a third eye. "I see you're not concerned about the prospect of a leak."

It was strange, but he wasn't. Or if he was, it was only mentally, for all logical reasons and considerations. But there was no trace of the all-out agitation and anger he'd once experienced, when his work had been the central thing in his life. His priorities *had* changed irrevocably. They all revolved around Glory now.

He sighed. "I thought your security system was now impenetrable."

Brandon gave a curt nod. "It is. And there is no leak."

"So you just want to reprimand me for marrying Glory? You don't know much about who she is now if you're even worried."

Brandon gave him a long-suffering look. "It's my business to know everything about everyone. I know exactly who she is and what she does. The body of work she's amassed over the past five years is nothing short of phenomenal."

He exhaled. "Just spit out the 'but' you're here to say."

"*But* I think this might be a far more elaborate facade than the one she had six years ago."

He waved the man's words away. "I don't care about the past anymore, Brandon."

"I'm not talking about the past."

Everything inside Vincenzo hit pause. "You just said there's been no leak."

"Not in *your* operations, no. But you are deep in negotiations with multinational interests on behalf of Castaldini. I caught leaks of vital info that only you could know, that could end up costing Castaldini the projects and investments you're on the verge of securing on its behalf."

Vincenzo's temperature started to rise, his muscles turning to stone. "The sides I'm negotiating with are privy to the same info, and the leak could be on their side."

"It isn't."

At the curt final statement, he found himself on his feet, agitation no longer in check. "Why on earth are you suspecting Glory when she had no part in any of this?"

"You mean she isn't privy to the details of your dealings and the innermost workings of your mind this time around?"

He shook his head, felt his brain clanging against his skull. "No—I mean, I *do* consult with her—you know there's no one better than her when it comes to negotiations—and she has been advising me, and I've used every shred of advice she gave me to my advantage, but that doesn't mean she—"

Brandon interrupted his ramblings. "*Do* you observe all the security measures I devised in your shared space?"

Vincenzo hadn't even given security a thought around her. But… "*No.* Stop right there. This isn't Glory's doing. I'm certain. Whatever happened in the past, it must have been against her will. She's worked so hard ever since to make good, to turn her life around. With only the power of her benevolence and perseverance she's done more for more people than I've done with all my power and money. I'm never suspecting her again."

Brandon gave him the look of a disapproving parent. "May I remind you it wasn't 'suspicion' last time? I gave you proof, proof you yourself verified, from her closest people."

Vincenzo's voice rose, no longer under his control. "I *told* you the past has nothing to do with the present. And then it turned out she actually saved me from making the worst mistake of my life."

"So you should forgive someone because she didn't succeed in killing you, but inadvertently made you jump and save yourself from falling into a pit? How far are you willing to stretch to make excuses for her, Vincenzo?"

"As far as I need to. When all is said and done, I'm in a much better place now and it is because of what happened."

"Even if it turns out for the best, a failed attempt at a crime still deserves punishment."

"And I *did* punish her," he bellowed. "I passed sentence on her without a trial, without even giving her the chance to defend herself. And what did all that righteousness get me? Six years of hell, without her. Now I have her back, and I'm never losing her again."

Brandon gaped at him for a long, long moment.

Then he grimaced. "God, this is worse than I thought. You're totally under her spell."

"I *love* her."

"And she betrayed you again. What a mess."

Vincenzo barely held back from punching him. "Stop saying that and look elsewhere, Brandon. You're not infallible, remember? You made a mistake with Eduardo's wife."

"It wasn't a mistake. Jade *was* hacking into his system."

"Under duress," he gritted out. "And she was doing that in order to fortify it, so no one could infiltrate it again. As I said, everything isn't always as it seems. You were right, but you were also wrong. You're wrong again now. I don't only love Glory, I *know* her."

Brandon pinned him with a conflicted gaze before he finally squared his shoulders and held out the dossier he had with him. It had the Steele Security insignia on it. Vincenzo knew from experience those were only used for final reports and verified evidence.

Trepidation overwhelmed Vincenzo as he looked at it. He snatched his gaze back to Brandon's, as if to escape an image that would sear his retinas if he gazed at it a second more.

Brandon looked at him like someone would look at a patient before amputating a limb. "I can't tell you how sorry I am, Vincenzo, but this is a compilation of all emails and text messages leaking the info. The originating addresses were expertly hidden, just not expertly enough to hide them from me. Everything was traced back to Glory's phone and computer."

Eleven

Vincenzo had no idea what he'd said to Brandon or when the man had left.

He found himself sitting in the bedroom he had only ever used with Glory. He'd bought this place six years ago when she'd consented to be his. He'd left it when he sent her away, but hadn't been able to sell it off. He'd only come back when he'd decided to have her back in his life.

The life that was falling apart all over again.

This couldn't be happening. Not again.

And he refused to believe it was. There had to be some explanation other than the obvious, other than what Brandon sanctioned. But Vincenzo couldn't think what it was. So he wouldn't even try to think. He'd stop everything, his very heartbeat if need be, until she told him what to think.

He sat there for what might have been hours until he heard her coming into the penthouse. The sense of déjà vu almost overwhelmed him, of that day more than six years ago when he'd waited for her in this room, listening to her advance and feeling that every step was inching toward the end of everything worth living for.

Then she entered the room. For the moment she didn't notice him as he sat to her far right on the couch by the floor-to-ceiling windows, her expression was subdued, pensive. Suddenly she started, her head jerking around, as if his presence electrified her.

Her uncensored reaction the split second she saw him was a smile that felt like a flare of light and warmth in the cold darkness that was spreading inside him.

Her rush toward him felt as if life itself was rushing back into his veins. Her eagerness flooded him, submerged him as she straddled him on the couch.

He let her deluge him in her sweetness, drink him dry in the desperation of her need.

Her kisses grew wrenching, her gasps labored. "I missed you…missed you, darling…Vincenzo…"

And how he'd missed her. Three days and nights without losing himself in the depths of her and drinking deep of her pleasures had him raving mad with starvation.

Her hands fumbled with his clothes, and he knew. The moment she touched his flesh he'd go up in flames, and he owed it to her to settle this before he let her drag him into their realm of delirium. His hands covered hers, stopping her.

She stiffened. Then slowly, as if afraid something would shatter if she moved too fast, she took her lips away from his neck. After a harsh intake of breath, she turned her head away and her rigidity increased as her gaze fixed on a spot on the couch. The security report file lay close to him. He knew she'd recognize it for what it was. But her gaze was fixed farther away, on the prenup.

She spilled off him, staggering up only to take two steps before slumping down on the opposite armchair. She looked at him as if waiting for a blow.

He had to hear her reasons from her own lips. "Why did you put this on my desk today, Glory?"

"Today?" Her eyes rounded. "I—I put it there over a week ago. I thought you'd long seen it, and when you didn't mention it I thought..."

"What did you think?"

A spasm seized her face. "I didn't know what to think."

"What did you want me to think when I saw it? What were you telling me?"

The pained look deepened; her voice sounded strangled. "I was offering you my answer to what I thought you were telling me, when you... When you..."

"When I what?"

"When you stopped taking me to your functions and started canceling our dates."

"What did you think I was telling you?"

"What you said when you didn't come ho...here the past three nights. What you just said very clearly. That this time around it took much less than six months for you to get tired of me."

Her lips, her chin, shook on the last words. The tethers of his heart shook, almost tearing themselves out.

"But then I expected that from the beginning," she choked out. "And now that I realize what you think happened in the past, I'm even wondering why you wanted me again at all. This is why I brought you the prenup, since I thought you must have been regretting not taking it, must be worried about repercussions with no provisions in place when you ended it with me again. But it's a good thing I didn't let my condo go as you told me to. I'll move back there tonight."

"Glory…"

She spoke over his plea, as if hearing his voice hurt her. "I will pretend we're still together so no one will know anything before you're ready to announce our split when the year is over. Until then, whenever you need me to make appearances with you, y-you have my number. If I'm not traveling, I'll play the part I agreed to."

And he was on his feet, then at hers, his hands going around her beloved head, making her raise her wounded gaze to his. "Every single thing you thought has no basis in fact. I didn't get tired of you. I would sooner get tired of breathing."

Redness surged in her eyes, her whole face shaking. "D-don't say that…don't say what you don't mean. Not again."

"The only time I said what I didn't mean to you was that day I kicked you out of my life. I did… I *do* love you, I never loved anyone but you, never had anyone since you."

Her eyes seemed to melt, her cheeks flooding with tears. "Oh, God, Vincenzo…I can't… I don't…"

"You have to believe me." He aborted her headshake, pulling her into a fierce kiss, before drawing away to probe her stunned face. "But you said you now realized what I thought in the past. You mean you now know why I left you?"

Her nod was difficult. "You knew about my family's crimes—thought me their accomplice?"

"It was much worse than that."

Her eyes flew wider. "What *could* be worse?"

And he finally confessed. Everything. Everything but the latest blow Brandon had dealt him.

By the time he'd fallen silent, she was frozen. Even her tears had stopped midway down her cheeks. She wasn't breathing.

It felt like an hour later when she finally choked out, "Your research *was* stolen and my…*mother* told you…told you…"

The rest backlashed in her throat, seeming to go down as if it was broken glass. Anguish so fierce gripped her every feature, radiated from her, buffeting him.

"I now believe that they must have forced you…or something…I just know it wasn't your fault. Just like I believe this latest security breach can't be your doing."

Her wounded eyes widened. "What latest security breach?"

Feeling as if he was spitting razors, he said, "Top secret data in my current negotiations have been leaked. According to this security report I got today, the leak came from your phone and computer."

She jerked as if he'd shot her.

He grabbed her shoulders, begging. "I can't think anymore, Glory, and I won't. I want you to tell me what to think. Trust me, please, tell me everything and I will solve it all. I'm on your side this time, and only on your side, and will always be, no matter what…."

She started shaking her head, her hands gripping it as if to keep it from bursting.

"*Amore, per favore,* please, believe me, let me help…."

Her incoherent cry cut him off as she exploded to her feet. Before another nerve fired, she'd hurtled out of the bedroom and slammed out of the penthouse.

By the time he ran after her, she was gone.

Glory stared at the woman she thought loved her beyond life itself. The woman whose betrayal had wrecked her life.

Her mother's silent tears poured down her cheeks, her eyes pleading.

For what? Glory's understanding? Her forgiveness? How could she give either when there was nothing left inside her? Everything had been destroyed. Nothing was left but shock and disillusionment. They expanded from her gut, threatening to burst her arteries, her heart. They crashed through her in torrents of decimating agony.

"You have to know the rest, darling," her mother choked out.

There was more? She couldn't hear any more. She had to get out of here, hide, disappear.

She escaped her mother's imploring hands as she ran again. She never wanted to stop running.

She spilled out into the street, ran and ran.

But there was no outrunning the realizations.

Everything was far worse than her worst projections. But one thing was worse than anything else. One realization.

Vincenzo's cruelty to her perceived betrayal hadn't been cruel at all. Cruel would have been to have her arrested. Even that would have only been his right, what he should have done. But he hadn't. That meant one thing.

He *had* loved her.

He'd loved her so much that even getting incontrovertible proof of her betrayal hadn't made him retaliate. He'd only tried to protect himself, cutting her off. Then, when she wouldn't let him, he'd pushed her away in a way he'd thought wouldn't harm her, since he'd believed she'd felt nothing for him, had been manipulating him from day one.

And she'd always thought getting answers would resolve the misery that had consumed six years of her life. In truth, it had dealt her a fatal blow.

Despair and exertion hacked through her lungs as more details and realizations sank their shards into her heart...

"*Glory.*"

Vincenzo. His booming desperation shattered everything inside her into shrapnel of grief, of panic. It all burst out into a surge of manic speed.

She couldn't stop. Couldn't let him catch her.

Not now that she knew he'd always loved her. Now that she knew it could never be.

* * *

Vincenzo arrived at the Monaghans' house just as Glory exited it. It was clear the confrontation with her mother had devastated her.

A man in his right mind would have caught up with her without alerting her. But the mass of desperation that he'd turned into had just bellowed her name the moment he'd seen her, sending her zooming faster, screeching for a cab.

But he could have overtaken a speeding car right now. A woman running in high heels looked stationary compared to his speed. He intercepted her as she opened the cab's door.

His arms went around her, filling them with his every reason for living. "Glory, *amore,* please, let's talk."

She pushed weakly at him. "There's nothing more to talk about, Vincenzo. Just forget I ever existed. In fact, when your situation allows, just prosecute me and my family."

Before he could utter another word, she surprised him by ducking out of the circle of his arms and into the cab.

His first instinct was to haul her out, carry her back to their home and tell her he'd never let her go again.

The one thing that stopped him was knowing it would be pointless without performing another imperative step first. Another confrontation with her mother. He had to break whatever hold she had on Glory, once and for all.

After Glory's cab disappeared, with his every cell rioting, he turned and walked back to the Monaghans' house.

The woman who opened the door exhibited Glory's same devastation. He wanted to blast her off the face of the earth for what she'd cost him and Glory, but he couldn't. She looked so fragile, so desolate, so much like an older version of Glory, that he couldn't hate her. He even felt a tug of unreasoning affection.

She grabbed at him with weak, shaking hands. "Glory wouldn't listen to me, but please, Vincenzo, you have to."

Suddenly, looking into those eyes that could be Glory's, everything fell into place.

It had never been Glory. It had always been Glenda.

He staggered under the blow of realization. How had he never considered this?

"It was you. In the past, and again now."

The woman's tears ran thicker, her whole face working. "I—I did it to save Dermot and Daniel!"

Her sob tore through him, with its agony, its authenticity. So he'd been right, just about the wrong person. Glenda Monaghan had been the one who'd been forced to spy on him.

She was now weeping so hard he feared she might tear something vital inside her.

His arm went around her as she swayed, helping her to the nearest couch. He sat beside her, rubbing her shaking hands soothingly. "Mrs. Monaghan, please, calm down. I'm not angry this time, and I promise, I won't hurt you or them. Just tell me why you did it, let me help."

"No one can help," she wailed.

He forced a tight smile. "You clearly don't realize what kind of power your son-in-law has. I would turn the whole world upside down for Glory, and by extension for her family."

"You're a scientist and a prince. You can't possibly know how to handle those…those monsters."

"Who do you mean?"

"The mob!"

And he'd thought nothing could ever surprise him again.

He raised his hands as if to brace against more blows. "Just tell me everything from the beginning."

She nodded, causing her tears to splash on his hands. It made him hug her tighter, trying to absorb her upheaval.

Then haltingly, tearfully, she began. "Fifteen years ago, I was diagnosed with lymphoma. Dermot panicked because our insurance would pay only for a tiny percentage of my treatments, and we were already in debt. At the time, Dermot and I worked in a huge multinational corporation, him in accounting, me in IT. Our financial troubles were soon common knowledge and a guy from work approached Dermot with a way to make easy, serious money."

She paused to draw a long, shaky breath.

"Dermot told me and I refused. But I was soon in no condition to work and with only one income and the bills piling up, it was soon untenable. Dermot began to gamble then fix books and was soon so deep in debts and trouble that when the recruiter approached him again, he agreed.

"For a while, I was so tired and drained, I was just relieved we weren't scrabbling anymore. I bought his stories that he'd entered a partnership in a thriving import/export operation. Then things started getting uglier with his mob bosses asking terrible things of him. And the worst part was they'd also dragged Daniel, who was only nineteen, into their dirty business.

"Unable to go on, Dermot had us pack everything and move across the country. We kept hopping from one place to another in his efforts to escape the mob. During remissions, I worked from home, but my relapses kept draining us. Dermot and Daniel kept trying everything to keep us afloat. But at least the mob was off our back. After seven years, I thought we were home free.

"Then six years ago, I got a call. The man said that they'd always wanted *me*, the real expert in the family, and that they had some jobs for me, if I valued my husband's and son's lives. They owned us. Not only with the debts but with what they had on them. They'd send them to prison if I didn't cooperate." Shame twisted in his gut, that he'd once employed the same method with Glory. "But it wouldn't end with prison if I said no. Accidents happened on the inside, even easier than on the outside. The job was you. They'd found out about your relationship with Glory and thought it put me in a perfect position to spy on you."

He stared at her, six years worth of agony being rewritten, the realization of the needless loss of his life with Glory choking him up.

Glenda sobbed harder now. "As a taste of what they'd do if I refused, they beat Daniel up—we told Glory it was a bar fight—and he was hospitalized for a month. I was ready to do anything after that. And I did. I used Glory's total trust in me, and your total trust in her, to hack her computer, and yours. Then you discovered everything.

"I was so scared Dermot and Daniel would be the ones who'd be dragged into this when everything they'd done came to light during the investigation. I found only one way out. To tell you it was Glory."

And he groaned with six years of heartache. "*Per Dio,* why? Didn't you think what you'd be doing to her, to me? Didn't you realize how much I loved her?"

"It was because I knew exactly how much you loved her that I did this. I knew you loved her so much you might forgive her, or at least wouldn't be able to bring yourself to punish her, would let her get away with it—let us—let *me*—get away with it. And I was right. You did."

He shook his head in disbelief. "You don't consider breaking her heart a punishment?"

"It was her heart or my husband's and son's lives."

Silence crushed down as he gazed into the woman's drowned eyes, the pieces falling into place like hammers.

Then he said, "Then it happened again."

Her tears ran continuously now. "They gave me the new assignment as soon as your wedding was announced. I begged them to let me go, tried to tell them that there was no way you wouldn't be prepared this time, that you wouldn't find out. They only said that with Glory as your wife now, it would be impossible to guard yourself, and that even if you found out, you wouldn't be able to expose her—or rather me. They didn't care what happened as long as they got their info. I owed them for giving them what had turned out to be useless info before. And they still owned my men. So I did it again. But I was only waiting until you caught me at it."

"But you still left tracks leading to Glory, to take refuge in my love for her again."

Her face crumbled. "And I was right again. Even when you thought she'd betrayed you twice, you wouldn't have ever hurt her."

His groan was agonized. "I already hurt her beyond what you can imagine. I'm only now beginning to realize the magnitude of the pain and damage I caused her."

She clung to his arm, her feeble grip barely registering. "I beg you, don't blame yourself. It was all my doing."

He covered her hand with his. "I do and will blame myself. I loved her, should have given her the benefit of the doubt. I didn't. And I hurt her so much she no longer wants to have anything to do with me."

"No, Vincenzo. You're her heart. She must only be running away to lick her wounds. She's shocked and anguished at what I did. Don't give up on her, I beg you."

He hugged her gently, defusing her panic. "I would give up on life before I gave up on Glory." He withdrew to wipe the tears of the woman he now hoped would live to see his and Glory's children and be their grandmother for long years to come.

"Now give me names. I'll get those people who've turned your lives into a living hell off your backs once and for all."

Keeping his promise to Glenda had taken far longer than he could stand. Two full, unending days.

But at least it was over. He'd terminated the hold those mob bosses had over the Monaghans' lives.

Contrary to Glenda's belief, he wasn't so refined that he couldn't handle criminal scum. He'd negotiated a perfect deal with them. He'd paid more than handsomely for the lost revenue ensuing from losing some of their efficient operatives. And he'd let them know how much they'd lose, in every way, if they came after his and Glory's family, or his work, ever again.

Now one thing remained. The only thing that mattered to him anymore in the world. Glory.

"We'll get to her in time, *Principe.*"

Vincenzo gritted his teeth at Alonzo's assurance. He didn't know if they would. The flight taking her away to Darfur was in less than an hour. She must already be at the gate. Not that he'd let that stop him. Even if she flew away, he'd follow her. To the ends of the earth.

In minutes that passed like torturous hours, Alonzo pulled up at the airport's departure zone. He lowered the window as Vincenzo exploded from the car, yelling after him, "Just ring when you get your princess back, *Principe.* I'll be waiting to drive you back home."

Vincenzo ran, Alonzo's last words skewering his heart.

If he didn't get her back, he'd never go home. He had no home to go to without her.

But then, not getting her back wasn't an option.

He tore across the airport, only stopping to ask about Glory's flight. It was boarding in twenty minutes.

He bought a ticket, produced his diplomatic passport and begged for security checks to be rushed so he could catch up with his runaway bride. Then he was streaking across the airport, bumping into people left and right. He'd run out of sorrys by the time he'd reached her gate.

She was standing in line, holding her boarding pass and

one of those nondescript handbags of hers, looking terrible. And the most wonderful sight he'd ever seen. The only one he wanted to live his life seeing.

His heart kicked his ribs so hard it had him stumbling into another run, pushing through the line to reach her. She was so deep in her misery she only noticed the commotion he'd caused when someone bumped into her. Her eyes, his own pieces of heaven, looked up at him with a world of pain and desperation.

The drain of anxiety and the surge of relief shook his arms as he enfolded her and his voice as he groaned against her cheek, her neck, her lips, "Come home with me, *amore,* I beg you."

She only went inert in his embrace.

Deadness crept up Glory's body like fast-growing vines.

She welcomed its suffocation, its stability, which allowed her to stand in the circle of his arms, feeling his beloved body seeking her and enfolding her, without collapsing in a mass of misery.

It also gave her the strength to push away, even though she felt she pushed away from her life source.

She staggered a step, barely aware of the hundreds of people around, watching them. She had eyes and senses only for Vincenzo, for noticing how his hair and face were captured by the atrocious lighting of the airport, enhancing every gleam, emphasizing every jut and hollow.

A blaze of love and longing shriveled her heart. She'd been too optimistic thinking there had been a chance she'd survive this. There wasn't.

He reached for her again, hands urgent, coaxing, moving over her back, her arms, her face, leaving each feeling forever scarred with the memory of what she'd never have again.

"Come with me, *amore,*" he urged again.

"I can't." Her voice sounded as dead as she felt.

"You can't do anything else, *amore*. You belong with me. To me. You're the only one for me."

"That's not true, never was, never will be."

His arms fell away, and he looked at her as if she'd just emptied a gun in his gut.

"You—you don't…" His bit his lower lip then his voice plunged to a hoarse rasp that sounded like pain and dread made audible. "You don't love me?"

She should say she didn't. He'd stop blaming himself for his role in her devastation, stop trying to make amends. This was what he was here doing, after all. And she no longer blamed him for anything. She only wanted to set him free.

She still couldn't bring herself to lie. Not about this.

She escaped answering. "I am not the one for you, Vincenzo. *Anyone* else would be better for you. Anyone who doesn't have a family with a criminal history."

His devastated expression fell apart with the snap of tension, morphed into the very sight of relief. "This is what you meant? What you're thinking?"

"It's not what I'm thinking. It's the truth."

"According to whom?"

"To the world."

"Does it look like I care what the world does or doesn't think?"

He spread his arms, encompassing the scene around them. Everyone was staring openly at them, the buzz of recognition, curiosity and amusement rising. Some were even taking photos and recording videos.

Embarrassment crept up her face. "You do care or you wouldn't have married me as a social facade. And when the truth comes out…"

"It never will."

"…it will cost you and Castaldini too much. That's why

it's a fact that any woman who doesn't have a family with a criminal history and connections would be better for you."

"No one is better for me. No one is better, period." She started to shake her head, her heart ricocheting inside her rib cage at his intensity and the unwilling rise of hope. He caught her face, his hands gentleness and persuasion itself. "And pretending to care about that social facade was just so I could have you without admitting the truth. All those years I've been looking for a way to have you again. Because I haven't been truly alive since I walked away from you. And now I can't live without you. I only cared about your family's crimes when I thought you'd been involved in them, but lately, not even then. And now none of that is an issue. I've managed to wipe your family's slate clean."

"Y-you did…? How?"

He told her, quickly, urgently, as if needing to get this out of the way, to move on to what he considered relevant.

And she felt her world disintegrating around her again.

"I never suspected… I always thought… God!" Tears gushed, then burned down her cheeks. "The years I spent being angry at Dad and Daniel, thinking they were irresponsible, criminal, when they…they…"

He dragged her to him, protecting her from her anguish, all the missing parts of her fitting back. "You can now have your family back, forgive them for everything that has been beyond them and be happy loving them again."

She raised her eyes to his, unable to grasp the enormity of it all. "How can you be so…so forgiving, so generous, after all they've done to you?"

"Conceiving you is an achievement that would make up for any past or future crime. And then they were under threat. A threat I ended, so they can now go on with their lives without the shadow of fear."

She started to protest and he scooped her up in his arms,

clamping his lips over hers. As the power of his kiss dragged her down into a well of craving, she thought she heard hoots of approval and clapping.

He pulled away, groaning, "*Gloria mia, ti voglio, ti amo*— I'm going crazy wanting you, loving you."

She felt he was letting her look deep into his soul, letting her see what she'd always thought would remain an impossible fantasy. Vincenzo didn't only love her, his love was as fierce and total as hers.

But this was why she'd had to walk away. So she wouldn't disrupt his life and destiny.

She had to protect him, especially since he clearly wasn't willing to protect himself. "You can't only consider your heart...you have duties, a status, and I'm..."

He clamped his lips on hers again, aborting her panting protest. "My first duty is to you. My status depends on honoring you first."

She shook her head. "My family...if the truth comes out... God, Vincenzo, you can't have them for your in-laws...."

His expression was resoluteness itself. "I already have them as my in-laws, and they'll always be my in-laws, and I will be proud to have them as the family of our children."

"Our ch-childr..." With those two magical words, a fierce yearning sheared through her, draining every spark of tension holding her together. She swooned in his hold.

His arms tightened until she felt he was trying to merge them. "Yes, our children, as many and as soon as you want."

The magnitude of what he was offering, the future he was painting, stunned her into silence as her mind's eye tremblingly tried to imagine it all. A future, a whole life, filled with love and alliance and trust, with him. Children with him. Even her family back, because of him.

Vincenzo took advantage of her silence and strode away with her still in his arms, talking to many people, then on the phone. She watched everything from the security of his embrace, as if from the depths of a dream. Somewhere it registered that he was arranging their exit after they'd been checked in as far as the boarding gate and arranging for her luggage to be sent back.

Then a sound penetrated the fog of her bliss. A horn.

Her dazed gaze panned around, found Vincenzo's car with Alonzo at the wheel, waving to them urgently as he stopped in an unloading-only zone.

In seconds, Vincenzo had her inside the cool, dim seclusion of the limo. As Alonzo maneuvered smoothly into the traffic, Vincenzo bundled her onto his lap.

After a kiss that left her breathless, he drew away, his faced gripped in the passion she couldn't wait to have him expend all over her.

"I have to get this out of the way once and forever, *gloriosa mia,* then we'll never speak or think of it again. You had nothing to do with your family's mistakes. You are the one woman I could ever love, the soul mate I would be forever proud to call mine, and to call myself yours. I truly care nothing about what the world will bring me as long as you're mine forever."

Her head rolled over his shoulder, her lids and insides heavy with need. Every nerve alight with delight at his declarations, she caressed the wonder of his hard cheek. "As long as you understand it will probably take the rest of my life to get used to all those unbelievable facts."

He pressed another urgent, devouring kiss on her lips as if compelled to do it. "I don't think there is any such thing as 'getting used' to this—" he hugged her tighter "—what we share. Just to always marvel at it, be humbled by it and thankful for it."

Then his smile suddenly dissolved, leaving his face a mask of gravity. Her heart quivered with a tremor of uncertainty.

Then, with all the solemnity of a pledge, he said, "Will you marry me again, Glory? This time with our love declared, because we are each other's destiny?"

Joy exploded inside her, making her erupt in his arms and rain tears and kisses all over his beloved face and hands. "Yes, Vincenzo. Yes, yes, *yes,* to everything, forever."

Smiling elatedly, as choked with emotion as she, his own eyes filling with tears, Vincenzo took her lips, drowning her in the miracle of his love.

Deep from the security of his love and embrace she heard Alonzo exclaiming, "*Eccellente.* I not only get my princess back, I get to arrange another wedding. But now with true love declared and the catastrophe of separation averted, this calls for a much more elaborate ceremony."

Glory gaped up at Vincenzo. "There could be anything more elaborate?"

Vincenzo poured indulgence over her, pinching her buttock playfully. "Have you even met Alonzo?"

Carefree giggles burst out of her for the first time in... She didn't even remember when she'd laughed so freely.

But she still had to make a stand. "While I loved the first ceremony, Alonzo, I really would rather we used all the expenses in something...uh..."

Alonzo smirked at her in the rearview mirror. "Is *worthwhile* the word you're looking for?" At her apologetic nod, he sighed. "I can see it's not going to be as much fun as I thought having a philanthropist for a princess."

At her chuckling sigh, Vincenzo smoothed the hair he'd mussed off her face lovingly. "How about we have everything? The figure you name for your worthwhile endeavors, the all-out-expenses wedding—" He turned to meet Alonzo's eyes in the mirror. "Preferably a double wedding this time."

She looked between both men then exclaimed, "Gio proposed?"

A smile of pure happiness spread Alonzo's lips, even as his green eyes misted. "Ah, *si*…and how he did."

She waited until he stopped at a traffic light, then exploded from Vincenzo's arms and jumped on Alonzo, hugging him and soundly kissing him on his widely smiling cheek.

After she milked him for details and whooped and exclaimed with excitement over being his matron of honor, he resumed driving.

She returned to the place she never wanted to leave, burrowed deep in Vincenzo's embrace, letting the last of her tension escape in a long sigh.

Stroking her hair gently, Vincenzo echoed her sigh, the sound of contentment. "Take us home, Alonzo."

Many, many hours later, a delightfully sore and thoroughly sated Glory turned luxuriantly in her lover, prince and husband's arms, filling her eyes with his beauty. "Is it possible? Could everything be so perfect?"

He shifted to accommodate her closer, sweeping caresses down her back and buttocks, as if imprinting his love into her, coating her with satisfaction. "If you need some imperfections to settle your mind, I have plenty for you. Like having to start my negotiations from scratch and roping you in as my top consultant. Like trying to create a method so I can get hands-on, steady involvements in your missions."

Her eyes widened with each word. "God, Vincenzo…you mean it?" At his smiling nod, she tackled him on his back and attacked him with kisses and tickles. He was guffawing by the time she pulled back, frowning. "But wait—that's only more perfection." She threw herself beside him on her back, covered her eyes and cried out, "Argh, I can't stand it."

He rose above her, letting her fill her soul with his unbridled love. Then he suddenly cupped her breast, lazily flicked